MW00624102

Advanced praise for *Haunt Your Heart Out*

"Featuring wonderfully developed characters and fluid, well-paced writing, Roberts's latest is highly recommended for fans of small-town and supernatural romances."

— ★ *Library Journal,* starred review

"Filled with cozy small-town vibes, a sweet and lovely romance, and some delightfully spooky ghost stories that will make believers out of us all, *Haunt Your Heart Out* will warm the hearts of everyone this holiday season."

—Jenna Levine, *USA Today* bestselling author
of *My Roommate is a Vampire*

"With fake ghost hunting shenanigans and small-town fall vibes, *Haunt Your Heart Out* is the perfect romance for curling up next to the fire in a warm, cozy blanket with a hot cup of tea while watching the leaves change outside."

—Jo Segura, *USA Today* bestselling author
of *Raiders of the Lost Heart*

"Cozy, healing, and brimming with fantastic ghost stories, *Haunt Your Heart Out* is sure to be your favorite fall escape! This book begs to be savored while snuggled-up with your favorite beverage."

—Courtney Kae, author of *In the Event of Love*

"Roberts has penned a romance that is the perfect combo of spooky, sweet, and spicy! Not only is *Haunt Your Heart Out* a heartwarming love story, it also offers a realistic portrayal of the journey of self-acceptance. This is a must read!"

—Falon Ballard, author of *Just My Type*

"Full of Vermont ghostlore and friendly apparitions, *Haunt Your Heart Out* is as cozy and charming as the Stowe bookshop Lex loves. This warm and gentle romance is perfect for the holiday season."

—**Alexandra Kiley, author of *Kilt Trip***

"Opposites attract in this spirited, small town romance between a homebody bookseller and an adventurous filmmaker . . . A perfect autumnal read, Roberts's cozy romance is a ghoulishly good time."

—**Lindsay Hameroff, author of *Till There Was You***

"Layered characters and a tension-filled plot make *Haunt Your Heart Out* a joyful, romantic escape for anyone who thinks spooky season should last through December."

—**Ivy Fairbanks, author of *Morbidly Yours***

"*Haunt Your Heart Out* is the cozy, warm, mischievous and spooky romance you've been craving! Roberts's sexy, steamy romance will have you rooting for Lex and James's haunted ever after."

—**Maggie North, author of *Rules for Second Chances***

"The perfect book to curl up with for a cozy, romantic, and spooky read. This book will make readers swoon and have their ghost hunting equipment—and hearts—registering all kinds of romantic paranormal activity!"

—**Mallory Marlowe, author of *Love and Other Conspiracies***

Also available by Amber Roberts
Text Appeal

HAUNT YOUR HEART OUT

A Novel

AMBER ROBERTS

alcove
press

Published in the United States by Alcove Press, an imprint of The Quick Brown Fox & Company LLC.

Alcove Press and its logo are trademarks of The Quick Brown Fox & Company LLC.

Library of Congress Catalog-in-Publication data available upon request.

ISBN (hardcover): 978-1-63910-948-7
ISBN (ebook): 978-1-63910-949-4

Cover design by Ana Hard

Printed in the United States.

www.alcovepress.com

Alcove Press
34 West 27th St., 10th Floor
New York, NY 10001

First Edition: October 2024

10 9 8 7 6 5 4 3 2 1

For Christie.
Lulu's book has always been *your* book.

CONTENT WARNING

Haunt Your Heart Out is a feel-good romance that centers love, hope, healing, and happily ever after. It also includes subjects that some readers may find difficult, including past death of a grandparent (off-page), family tensions, and descriptions of anxiety and depression. Ghost stories appear throughout, and while these tales are mostly told in a comedic or lighthearted way, one ghost is briefly mentioned to have died by hanging, which recounts existing Stowe, Vermont lore.

If these elements are sensitive for you, please take care.

CHAPTER ONE

Three feet of snow. Three feet of snow, and a broken shovel. Three feet of snow, a broken shovel, and ten minutes until I was supposed to clock into work.

No, it wasn't some deranged Christmas carol. Just my life. On a Tuesday. In December.

I stomped out into the center of the driveway and shook my fist at the leftover flakes drifting from the post-snowstorm clouds hanging in the air. Damn blizzard. Damn shovel. Damn it.

Swearing, flailing, and a half-assed attempt at shoveling didn't get my car out of its spot, so I went for the next-best thing: flagging down the next car to pass by and begging the driver for a ride to the bookstore. It was only a few miles down the road, no big deal. A local would know me and be thrilled to help; a tourist would think it quaint and brag for a lifetime about getting the cold little country girl to work on time so she could sell books to the needy readers of Stowe, Vermont. Sure, I could call my best friend Natalie to pick me up, but with last night's snowfall, she was likely already at work. This way would be a lot quicker.

I snatched my bag from the passenger seat and climbed my way up and over the built-up snowbank, waving my buffalo plaid earflap hat like a flag. Not frantic enough to scream *emergency!*, but intentional enough so the next driver wouldn't mistake it for clumsiness.

My efforts were rewarded within moments when a shiny blue sedan with New York plates slowed, then came to a complete stop in front of me. The tinted windows rolled down to reveal a broad-shouldered man who appeared about my age—thirty-three—or maybe a little older. He greeted me with an amused smirk. He had a Yankees cap pulled low on his forehead, but there was a little crinkle in the corner of his eyes that sent a tingle through my ribcage. "Need a lift?"

While a set of green Vermont plates would have felt more welcoming, there was no time to be picky. I had a store to open, on time, and this was the car to get me there.

"Sure do," I said. "Thanks."

He leaned across the passenger seat and popped the door open from the inside. "Where to?"

I climbed in, sneaking another totally respectful appraising glance at the guy's perfect features. "Just down the road to Main Street, only as far as the bookstore. I swear, these snowbanks pop up overnight."

"I hear the Abominable Snowman is quite active in this area. Maybe he's to blame?"

"Fairly sure you're thinking of the Snow Miser, but yeah, they're all in cahoots." I clicked my seatbelt into place and smiled toward the driver, who carefully pulled away from my snowbank-crowded driveway for the winding trek down the dirt road.

He pushed limits, speed-wise, topping 27 in a 25MPH zone. The rebel. Ski- and snowboard-topped SUVs passed us, heading back up the hillside. Tourists taking advantage of the good powder, leaving us working stiffs hard-packed trails and whatever's leftover at the bar.

Not that I was a skier. Or snowboarder. Or participated in any form of winter sport, really. Outside, cold. Inside, cozy.

Jordan, my perfect sister, and her husband, Lucas, were skiers. Mom and Dad preferred the act of bragging at the lodge about their doctor daughter and her handsome husband to the actual act of skiing, which kept their bones (and reputations) intact. Win/win.

"Here to ski?" I asked the driver.

"Haven't thought that far ahead," he said, rolling to a stop at the sign at the bottom of the hill. "But maybe I'll work it into the schedule."

I pointed to the left, directing him toward the center of Stowe—where the magic happens, especially after the first big snowfall of the year. Giant, fluffy snowflakes continued to drift from the sky, which was giving way from cloudy grey to almost blue with wisps of yellow that hinted at sun to come.

"If you haven't already staked out the food situation, here are some inside tips." I gestured at each restaurant as we passed, pointing out my favorite spots to grab a bite. "You're not going to want to miss the seafood at Sal's. Have the scampi, and don't bother waiting for a table—you get better service at the bar and Sal himself loves to tell stories about his life in Italy. For pizza, always Nonni's. Baja's is prime Tex-Mex for the area, but I'm sure what you're used to is far superior. The Barn is *the* place for breakfast, but watch out, I hear it's haunted."

"I can handle a few spirits," the driver said, his gloved hands flexing on the steering wheel. His chin tightened a bit as he smiled, and holy crap I could have cut a mango with that jawline.

I returned the smile, thinking back to the vlog I hosted back in high school. YouTube was still this shiny new thing, and my parents thought that handing me a video camera was a good idea; something to keep me occupied while they traveled for business and to visit my sister, who'd been newly enrolled in college across the country. Obviously, with Alkaline Trio and AFI on my iPod on repeat, I made it my mission to make things weird: I maintained a vlog sharing spooky tales about Stowe's "haunted" happenings. While the ghostlore was mostly fabricated by yours truly—with some local legends mixed in—my semi-regular videos had earned a semi-regular following. And lots of believers.

"This one?" the driver asked, flicking on his signal and slipping into my usual parking spot in front of the store.

I nodded. "Thanks for the ride," I said, leaping from the car without so much as asking his name. New York plates. Not worth the effort. He'd be gone as soon as the powder was packed, just like the rest of them. I didn't even watch as he pulled out of his parking spot and back out onto the road.

A truck with a giant V-shaped plow rounded the corner then, flinging snow and grit everywhere, and splashing through a salt-and-slush puddle before coming to a stop in the spot my chauffeur had just vacated.

Though her official title was "best friend," Natalie filled the role of family better than my closest relatives. She and her trusty rusted plow truck cleared snowy driveways in the winter—when she wasn't rolling up her sleeves to help her parents run their multiple Hallmark-esque hospitality-focused ventures. She cranked down her window—halfway, since its ability to open fully had disappeared somewhere in the early 2000s—and grinned through the gap.

"Getting rides from strangers, Lex? Looks like your morning started off pretty great."

"I had a little snow situation." I mimed measuring the height of a snowbank, putting the peak at an exaggerated chest level.

"I told you to get a new shovel before the weather rolled in," Natalie said. "Someday, you'll listen to me."

"Someday, you'll show up with a shovel for me, and I'll be off the hook."

Natalie thrust a thumb over her shoulder. My eyes followed the gesture to the bed of her truck where a shiny new shovel waited.

I grinned. "Have I told you lately that I love you?"

"Only every day." She leaped from the vehicle, a silent plea for coffee on her lips.

"I'll let you in to make your own while I get the store opened." I jiggled the key in the lock, double-kicked the base of the door to loosen the stick caused by years of shifts in humidity and moisture, and shoulder-shoved my way into the building. "Charles's opening-hour call should be coming at any—"

The phone rang. I tossed my head back, groaned, and rolled my eyes before I turned on my helpful voice, snagged the handset, and greeted the bookstore's owner.

"Good morning, Dog-Eared Books and More, where select used paperbacks are three for two, this is Lex, how can I help you?"

Charles cleared his throat but said nothing.

"And home of the Coffee of the Month Club," I amended. "Charles, I'm going to have an asthma attack if I have to keep saying all of that, every time."

"Our customers may not know our specials if they're from out of town. They count on you to make sure they're getting the best deal."

Out-of-towners were probably the wrong audience for a club that required monthly visits for the full benefit. But Charles wanted what he wanted.

I could almost hear the rays of sun bouncing off the Florida coastline through the phone. I shuddered at the mental image of Charles lounging beachside, daring the sun to take its best shot. His skin was practically leather, showing off a texture that had taken years of exposure to build up. Since hitting retirement age, he'd spent summers in Vermont and winters in Florida. I was "in charge" during his absences—air quotes required, because his micromanaging never took a vacation.

Natalie fired up the milk steamer and I slapped my palm over the phone's receiver too late.

"Is someone using the espresso machine?" Charles asked.

"Of course not, just me, prepping. I'm about to unlock the door, looks like there's someone waiting, talk to you tomorrow."

I dropped the phone back into the cradle, raised my eyebrows at Natalie, and sighed.

"When is that guy just going to chill?" she said.

"Never. He's a demon put here to make my life miserable. Dreams, so close, but yet . . . Charles."

"Maybe he'll meet someone down there, and he'll be so desperate to offload the store, you'll get to scoop the place up nice and cheap."

"Fantastic, and I can buy it with my loads and loads of cold, hard cash."

"Or you can ask your parents for a loan," Natalie said.

I snorted. "That'll go over well. 'Hey, parents dearest, I know my house is a bit, uh, shabby, but I wish to purchase a failing bookstore and turn it into something fabulous. May I borrow a couple-ten thousand bucks and pay you back once I'm actually turning a profit?' Yeah, right."

"Bank loans, then. Equity is your friend. There are avenues." She punctuated her admonishment with a final burst of steam from the espresso machine.

"Give me a door, I'll create a barrier, Nat. It's my best talent."

She topped her macchiato with an overwhelming spritz of whipped cream, drizzled a bit of maple syrup over the top, then sprinkled on some maple sugar for good measure.

"You're gonna spill that in the truck, so consider this your warning that it's hot, will burn you, and will make that retro interior sticky as all hell. No lawsuits."

"It's the first big storm of the season, doll. Caffeinate or die. I can't skimp." She capped her travel mug, waggled her fingers, and headed toward the door. "I'll get your driveway plowed at the end of my run, but I'm not clearing off the car. That's all you."

"You got it." I offered a mock salute. "Call if you're driving by, I'll arrange a curbside coffee delivery."

"You know I will." She breezed out the door. A flurry of flakes dashed through the crack as she pulled the door shut, and the little bell above the door jingled in her wake. I steadied a precarious sci-fi stack—lots of Asimov, very few books published post-*Snow Crash*—and slipped behind the giant wooden desk that stood in as a checkout counter.

Dog-Eared wasn't large, nor did it stock any of the latest bestsellers. The standard answer was "we can order that in for you, if you'd like," which didn't do much good for weekend skiers. But it did have mismatched rugs made for sprawling, the comforting smell of old paper, and that good floor creak that promised the perfect unexpected read just around the corner. This wasn't a store for the flashiest covers or new twists on favorite tropes. This building housed paperbacks with worn-soft edges, travel mementos and old receipts tucked inside as bookmarks. Some contained hidden inscriptions, long forgotten and left behind for the next reader to discover. Searching inside covers for heartfelt notes gave me life, and I'd gathered the best of the best to add to my own personal collection. The volumes lined the walls in my reading nook at home, my own little sanctuary.

The bookstore's convenient location, right beside the public bike path and adjacent to some of the top tourist traps in the state—none of which included public restrooms—meant Dog-Eared got a hefty load of traffic, all meant for the bathroom. Rarely were purchases made to go along with the toilet-and-hand-washing visits. Occasionally, a ragged paperback would catch the eye of a passerby. Business was far from booming; it was the coffee sales that kept the doors open.

Which left plenty of time for me to sit and contemplate the world. And I would never run out of anything to read, even if the most recently published book on our shelves had come out around the same time as my final vlog upload—fifteen years ago. As the offloading space for estate sales and library discard bins, Dog-Eared lived up to its name.

I plucked my latest read from the shelf behind the desk, angled myself just-so to catch the light coming through the dirty window, and lost myself in a bit of Isabel Allende. Few customers meant plenty of free time to come up with marketing plans to boost patronage. The things I'd do if Charles allowed me even a smidge of freedom to bring the store into the twenty-first century . . . But there wasn't an idea Charles hadn't shut down with a grunt and quick subject change.

I left college partway through my second year. I hadn't even gone far from home: the University of Vermont was less than an hour away. But from the very first week, the course load was intense and I'd struggled to make it to my therapy appointments. The stress of rushing to my therapist's office between classes only added to my already crushing anxiety—I couldn't help feeling that I should be able to make it all work, just like everyone else was. An "it's not them, it's me" dilemma. My roommate transferred midyear, leaving me with a highly coveted single for the second semester. But the "spacious" room felt more like a cavern—and with the silence came an antsy sort of loneliness I couldn't shake, one that vibrated somewhere deep inside my ribcage. I craved the comfort of home. School smarts were all my sister's territory, anyway.

I'd been at Dog-Eared ever since—about thirteen years. No matter the marketing scheme or business proposal I pitched, Charles deemed it unnecessary. He was of the mind that the customer preferred the bookstore of yore, which left little room for improvement. After a few years of trying my best to turn the place around, I'd accepted my role as the reliable shopkeeper who didn't rock the boat.

But I held on to hope that someday I'd be a lotto ticket closer to my big fortune, and the opportunity to buy the store. He'd sell, for the right price. I bought one scratch ticket per week—my own small act of rebellion because Dad hated that I bought them at all—won minuscule amounts occasionally, and never counted on anything. Everyone talks about how they'd quit their job the second a fortune fell into their lap. I'd buy my workplace so I never had to leave.

After a grand total of seven transactions and thirteen "can I use your bathroom" pit stops, I closed up shop and skated my way home on the salt-slush sidewalk.

I prepped myself to perform a half-assed driveway- and car-clearing when I got home, but Natalie had already plowed all of the snowbanks into submission and swiped the car spotless. Wipers pointed skyward, warding off ice gremlins that would contribute to future stuck-wiper drama. I snapped a selfie with the car, added a heart eyes emoji and "thank you" to the photo, and sent it off to Natalie.

* * *

Nat and I made a point to have dinner together at least once a week, and usually more often if our schedules aligned. I knew, without a doubt, that she would come through my door every Tuesday night with a bottle of wine and dessert. She was the most reliable person on the face of the planet; our friendship knew no bounds.

Living so near each other our whole lives had given us the opportunity to forge a bond so close it rivaled siblinghood. I used to go to her house for dinner almost nightly. My parents weren't exactly warm and fuzzy, and meals at home were more like a med school interview than a family occasion—if my parents were even home for dinner in the first place.

My sister's favorite-child status was solidified early when she'd earned the "Future Woman Leader" award in first grade. I was still in diapers at the time, so how was I going to compete with that? For me, dinner at Natalie's was an escape. A chance to gather around the table, laugh, and talk about the day without a lecture.

For Natalie, dinner with her family was akin to talons gripping her until she died a suffocating, horrible death. Our different outlooks performed a constant balancing act. I'd never convinced her that her parents weren't trying to destroy her life by holding her near, expecting her to help them with the family businesses. She'd never convinced me that my parents weren't choosing their more successful daughter over the failure when, during my freshman year at UVM, my parents picked up everything and moved to California to be closer to Jordan and her family. Nat couldn't believe I wasn't thrilled at the freedom. My parents, abandoning me to live my life in the state I'd vowed never to leave.

After losing my grandfather the next year, I left school—and the parents never forgave me for it. They wanted me to "live up to my potential," which they reminded me via multiple emails with the subject "Re: Your Education." Nat's parents had helped me pack up the dorm and moved me back into the house my grandfather had left me.

Natalie tapped the front door's rattly windowpane, then slipped inside when I shouted "It's open!" She snagged two wine glasses from the cabinet, popped the cork from the bottle of red she'd brought, and poured a hearty serving for each of us.

We ate, swapped stories about the day, then finished the bottle of wine by the fireplace. Things were light and easy, until the edge of a picture frame caught my eye. The silver frame had been a gift from my ex, some mini-milestone gift, and I'd slipped a goofy selfie of our trip to the zoo into it the day he gave me the frame—but now it rested face-down, because I couldn't bear having the photo stare at me each day, even if I wasn't ready to part with it.

"I wonder how Kyle's celebrating our one-year breakup anniversary," I murmured. "He's probably gotten everything he set out to do with his life."

"Stop, and back it right the hell up. 'What if I went with him anyway?' No. We're not doing the what-ifs. You had perfectly valid reasons to want to stay in your comfort zone, and he wasn't willing to discuss an alternate plan. He's the asshole. Forget him." Natalie pointed at me with the same hand that held her glass of wine.

She'd been there from the first fight to the big break-up, and I knew she'd have had my back no matter what. I'd been willing to overlook Kyle's bad habits and terrible table manners, but I wouldn't budge when he wanted me to move away to Nashville. I belonged in the house my grandfather had left me. Sure, it was a bit outdated, and I could have wallpapered the entire first floor in the repair bills I'd been collecting like Pokémon cards, but I wasn't going to leave. Not for a partner. Not for anything. Walking the worn stone path beneath the towering maple trees my grandfather planted and tended felt as much like love as one of Natalie's mom's hugs—and I couldn't get either if I moved away. I wasn't like my sister, who could make a friend at the drive-through window. I didn't *do* lonely. I needed this house and this town—with its weird ghost stories and secret spooky spots—more than they needed me, but I wasn't too proud to admit it.

"Any dating prospects?" Natalie asked.

I shook my head.

"Would you even admit to me if anyone caught your eye?"

"So." I slapped my palms on my thighs, an attempt to startle her out of the impending dating pep talk. "How are your parents?"

She made a lip-zipping gesture and accepted my plea for a subject change. "Dad's trees are selling like wild, Mom's been completely swamped at the inn. Corporate parties, mostly. City people trying to impress clients with rustic locations and lift passes. The usual. Bring on spring."

I held up my glass in a toast. "Bring it on."

Haunted Happenings transcript

Date: November 16, 2006

Location: Emily's Bridge

> Luna: We've waited until sunset, and so far it's been quiet, but we all know how that goes. Waiting it out. As long as it takes. It's just a game of . . . oh wait, wait a minute. What was that? I saw a little shimmer—maybe a glint of frost in the air? Or something more sinister?

[Camera cuts momentarily.]

> Luna: Okay so it was a false alarm. Just a car driving over the bridge. For those of you who don't know, we're at Emily's Bridge, a location that's well known for hauntings. Here with me is my camera person, Natalie—say hi, Natalie!
>
> Natalie: Hi!
>
> Luna: Now, we've come here alone, so we don't disturb our intended spirit. Last night's visit to the Whitfield Inn didn't turn up any ghosts but tonight we're—
>
> Natalie: Shhh, shh, see that?
>
> Luna: Hold the camera still, Natalie. You're going to miss it!
>
> Natalie: Oh my god, Luna, what *is* that?
>
> Luna: I see a figure. Definitely a figure. She's in the center of the bridge, walking back toward the entrance nearest us. Are you getting this, Natalie? It's a ghostly outline, a woman in a white gown, like a tattered wedding dress. She's moving, shuffling side to side on the bridge over there. I think . . . I

think I'm going to go try to talk to her. Natalie, can you get closer? Can you get this on film?

Natalie: My camera seems to have some interference, it's . . . the light settings keep shifting. I don't think I can get closer. Go ahead, I'll film from here.

Luna: I'll get closer. Emily? Is that you? I have a gift for you. It's a button, with an embossed forget-me-not design—whoa!

Natalie: Luna, what happened? Are you okay?

Luna: Cold. *So* cold. I think . . . maybe she hugged me? Emily, is that what happened? I feel . . . I'm still cold. But I feel . . . something. It was a lot like loneliness at first, and now I'm . . . Okay, there's a car coming through. Emily, I'm sorry, I have to leave. Thank you for being here with me today.

Natalie: I'll cut after this car comes through.

Luna: No, no they're going too fast. She's not going to like that. Wait, are they *stopping*? Oh, amateurs.

[Squealing tires and screams coming from inside the car.]

Luna: Did you see that? The sides of the car? It was like someone had clawed it. Did you get it? Please tell me it's on film.

Natalie: Of course I got it. You think I'm new at this?

[Microphone crackles and camera is obscured by a hand as it is adjusted.]

Luna: That was . . . intense. I've never seen anything like it. Emily was not pleased with them intruding like that. I'm feeling pretty closed off right now, like she's asking for some privacy, but I think we've made some progress with her tonight. We'll be back, Emily. We'll come again. Don't let them bother you. Stand up for yourself. You're worth everything.

[Microphone crackles, camera cuts.]

CHAPTER TWO

Some nights, I kept the bookstore open a bit later, just for kicks. It rarely drew customers, but it was an excuse for me to put off laundry. I'd pitched author signings and open mic nights to Charles, who'd insisted there wasn't a market for "that sort of thing." The Montpelier night scene begged to differ, but what did I know?

The après-ski crowds swarmed the streets; LED holiday wreaths, menorahs, and kinaras attached to the phone poles bathed them in an eerie, festive glow. Just another reminder that people stopped into our town only briefly, just to rush home and pick up their lives where they'd left off. Nobody stuck around. They were in and out in a week, with nothing but vacation photos languishing on social media posts and in automatically backed-up cloud storage to prove they'd enjoyed themselves. They barhopped until they dropped, but I always held out hope that someone would slip into the store and be relieved to escape the hustle and bustle.

I'd set a goal to finish *The Return of the King* in a single day, so I downed a bit of espresso and settled back in. I scraped a fingernail along the cracked spine of the book as I relived the tale, fueled by caffeine and nostalgia. The goal was lofty, though, and my eyelids were heavy by eight-thirty, so I abandoned ship and prepped a hot chocolate for the trip home instead.

The front door swung open, and a man swept in as I drizzled chocolate syrup over my drink.

"We're closing, sorry," I said, without sparing a glance.

"I'll just be a minute," he said, glancing around and rubbing his hands together. "I was hoping I could use your restroom."

I stole a peek when I heard a newly familiar voice: the stranger who'd given me a lift to work just yesterday. He wore a long black wool coat, a knitted scarf, pressed-enough pants, and the notable Yankees cap to top it off. The cap's brim shadowed most of his face, as it had in his car.

"You've gotta make a purchase, customers only." The tone was meant to be joking—friendly, even. But the last few years of pointing to the dark back corner and handing off a key had influenced me more than I'd realized.

He pressed his lips together, more challenge than smile. "I don't see any signs."

I grabbed the chalkboard marker and scrawled "Bathroom for Customers Only" on the menu board. My brain always shut down when pretty people were involved, so it was probably an attempt at flirting gone terribly wrong.

His eyes flashed amusement and a subtle dimple appeared in the middle of his chin. "My mistake. I'll have a latte, double shot. Soy, no foam."

"Not from around here, then?" I asked, cringing inwardly that I'd created more clean-up for myself through the failed flirting attempt.

"Why would you assume that?" he asked.

I tilted my head and raised an eyebrow.

"There's nothing strange about a soy-no-foam order."

"It's not the order," I said, snagging a to-go cup from the counter and pointing it at his head. "It's the hat." And the out of state plates on his peppy sedan.

He brushed his fingertips along the hat's brim. "I've been found out."

"I'm surprised you haven't been assaulted. Brave of you to wear that around here. This is Red Sox land."

"Thank you for your concern, but I think I can take 'em." He tossed a playful wink in my direction.

I interrupted his peacocking by grinding fresh beans—an unnecessary move, ingredients-wise, but absolutely required to drown him out before my idiot heart took over. Confident, fast talker, and not sticking around. Exactly the type I'd fall for.

I tugged the key from its hook and slid it across the counter to the man. "Down that way, take a left at Nietzsche."

He disappeared between stacks of books. I tended to his coffee order, peering down the aisle after him, hoping to catch another glimpse.

A few minutes later, the floorboards creaked under the weight of his footfalls. When he reached the counter, I slid the capped to-go cup across the counter and crossed my arms.

"What do I owe you?" he asked.

I pointed to the cash register, the amount lighting the room with its digital green glow. "Unless you want to sign up for the Coffee of the Month Club. Ten percent off your cuppa, every time, if you get the featured beverage. A free coffee every ten purchases."

"I'll pass," he said. He patted his back pockets, then his coat, then dug into the front pockets of his pants. He pulled his hand free and slid a few quarters from his palm onto the countertop, counting under his breath as the metallic ring echoed through the bookstore.

"Misplaced wallet?" I asked. "It's cool, I'll just take this one for the road."

"Must be in the car back at the inn." He sighed and fiddled with his coat's pocket flap. "Sorry to have wasted your time. Excuse me, I'm expected at the cemetery in a few minutes."

I clenched my hands into guilty little fists beneath the counter. I'd mocked the guy for his preferred sports team, heckled him about his coffee order, and been all grumpy because he was an out-of-towner— and he was here because someone had *died*. Way to go, Lex. Stellar performance.

"You know, I may have forgotten to mention that new coffee club members get a free beverage. Just need your cell number, right here." I nudged a membership slip toward him and lifted my shoulders apologetically.

He shoved his hands into his pockets and shifted his weight from one foot to the other. "Is that so?" he asked, eyes scanning the floorboards.

"Oh, and we promise never to sell or give away your information or spam you. Or anything."

He accepted the pen and tapped the tip to the sign-up slip. I braved a glance at his profile as he bent to jot down his information. Rough hair grew at his chin, like he'd skipped a couple days shaving. Travel and grief do that to you. His jawline tightened as he started to write, so I averted my eyes in case I was making him uncomfortable. He finished, and passed the slip to me. "Seems like a punch card would be a less sketchy option, don't you think."

"I don't make the rules . . . James," I said, reading his name off the slip of paper. "I just do what the boss tells me. Thank you for joining the Dog-Eared Coffee Club. Just give us your number next time you're in and we'll track your purchases in our system." If he ever came back, which was unlikely given his here-for-a-funeral status and out-of-state area code. Not sticking around.

"Thanks, uhh . . .?" He pointed at me with his free hand.

"Have a good one," I said. Don't give him your name, check. Suggest he enjoy a trip to the cemetery, also check.

"Absolutely." He took a sip of coffee as he backed toward the door. "Thanks again. I owe you one."

"We're even," I said. "Consider it payment for yesterday's wonderful taxi service."

Falling snow danced around him as he crossed the road and half-jogged toward the park. I fiddled with the slider top of my travel mug, staring after him until he disappeared beyond the streetlight's glow.

* * *

James didn't show up the next day. Not that I expected an appearance—it was just a simple observation and reading into things was a dangerous game. The store was slow, as usual. Only a handful of customers, a rush on drip coffee when a caravan of skiers dropped in on their way toward the resort, and an antique book collector who stopped by looking for a copy of some obscure book—and to criticize Dog-Eared's cataloging methods.

I flipped the sign to "closed" and started counting out the register when I heard a tiny tap at the window. I finished tallying my handful of pennies, not willing to get tripped up somewhere in the thirties only to have to start counting the register all over again. If it was important, they'd stick around until the change-counting was complete.

When I had the chance to squint through the smudged windows, I spotted a familiar silhouette. Long jacket, ball cap, and a hand holding up a driftwood key chain in the window.

I scurried to the door, flipped the lock, and beckoned for the bathroom key. After realizing the key was gone this morning, I'd picked the bathroom deadbolt and left it unlocked all day. Not having to hand it off to customers had actually been a real time-saver.

"Missing something?" James asked, dangling the key slightly out of reach.

"What, did you steal it just to have a reason to come back?"

"Of course not. I tucked it in my pocket while I was washing my hands last night and forgot to return it because you tricked me into signing up for your secret club. No foul intentions. No harm."

I hopped to grab the key from his hand and snatched it from his grip before he could tease me with it any more. He grinned and stepped around me, then headed toward the coffee counter.

"Your timing is terrible." I wrinkled my nose as if it could convey an apology I wasn't sure I was prepared to give. "We're closed. Again."

"Just checking out the décor," he said, meandering. His hands were shoved deep in his coat pockets and his feet crossed with each step. The movement turned his walk into a swagger. "Cozy little place you have here. Smells like a library."

"Might be the books," I said.

He pressed his weight onto one foot, testing a creaky floorboard. "Noisy."

"Creaky floorboards add ambience," I said. "Now that you've returned the contraband, can I finish closing up?"

"Go right ahead." He took two strides across the floor and settled into the ragged armchair by the window.

"Door has to be locked if I'm counting cash. Owner's rules." I waved him toward the door.

He got up, walked toward the door, and flipped the lock. "Better?"

I snorted a laugh. "Close enough." My heart wasn't going to survive.

James crossed toward the desk, swept his hat off his head, and leaned onto the desk with both hands in fists. He gripped his hat, and his eye contact sent a shiver through my spine.

"I wanted to properly thank you for the coffee last night."

"Oh, that." I shrugged, not at all coolly. "No big deal, benefits of the club."

"Absolutely. That's right, the club. Well, thank you for bringing it to my attention." He smirked, and his dimple appeared. Without the brim of his cap in the way, his eyes glittered from the overhead lights. Was he trying to torture me?

"I'm trying to close up here. For real." I hit the button to close out the register and nodded toward the door.

"Right." He pointed with both hands at the door. "I'll just go then. But, hey, I hope to see you around."

He pressed himself away from the desk and walked to the door, not a second glance spared. He flipped the lock and tugged it open.

"I'm sorry, by the way," I said, fully aware that it was shitty to apologize to a guy I didn't know for the death of a person I'd probably never met.

He glanced back at me with a grin. "No worries, I'll make a note of your business hours so I'm more likely to be served next time."

Next time. Like he wouldn't be skipping town in a couple of days. He jogged off in the direction of the park again, offering a low wave to the driver who let him cross the road. My eyes remained glued on his disappearing silhouette until there was no discerning his shadow from December's pitch black.

With the register counted, money tucked away in the safe, and lights switched off, I walked back to the desk to turn off the banker's lamp. And there was James's hat, exactly where he'd been leaning minutes before.

I'd never figure out where he was staying, not with twenty-five inns and a handful of B&Bs within spitting distance of the store. Even if I did know, I wasn't going to fall for it. He'd probably left it on purpose. He wasn't going to come in here, all scruffy beard and charm, and get me to chase him down. Not in *my* town.

I hung the hat from a hook on the wall using the adjustable back strap, then made my escape.

CHAPTER THREE

No fresh snowfall meant Natalie and I could meet up for our standing Saturday morning date, since there were no driveways to plow, paths to shovel, or sidewalks to salt. When we were teenagers we would have spent the day tucked away in Nat's bedroom scaring up schemes to perpetuate local legends. We'd been all about haunting-related hijinks, from harassing tourists to sleepovers in the cemetery just to prove we could.

Many assumed there had to have been something to the dozens of ghost stories and eerie sightings for the tales to keep circulating, even all these years later, but it was less *spirits* and more Nat and me who haunted the town. Unsupervised, we turned corn fields, empty buildings, and covered bridges into the *Twilight Zone*, and each of the low-budget "hauntings" was catalogued on my vlog. Existing local legends inspired us—we'd grown up hearing ghostly stories about Emily's Bridge and the Green Mountain Inn—but after a while, our imaginations took over. The film work was closer to *Blair Witch Project* than *Slender Man*. We had fans, regardless.

Adulthood had forced us to quit the bogus ghost gig, but now our Saturdays were better than sacred. By this time each week, I was more than ready to turn the bookshop over to Darla, the college student who worked weekends. She completed school assignments while business was slow and churned out coffee when customers appeared.

That Saturday was cold enough that breath could freeze before passing lips, and tiny ice crystals formed beneath noses with each exhale. A bone-deep chill, and not enough moisture in the air for snow to fall. Ice on the sidewalks crunched and squeaked beneath frigid feet, and the sky's vivid blue warned locals to stay tucked indoors.

Nat and I couldn't let nature push us around, though, not on our designated day. So, we shuffled along the sidewalk and dashed through the door at The Barn. The renovated outbuilding served up omelets, waffles, and pancakes, all with a side of hash. The fancy exterior disguised the fact that it was nothing but greasy spoon fare inside. We waved at the host as we slipped through the waiting crowd and grabbed our usual spot at the counter.

Our weekend hangouts rarely deviated from breakfast at The Barn—stuffed French toast drowned in local maple syrup—followed by whatever felt right. Snowy weekends prevented the breakfast-and-wandering portion of the day, but on those days I'd climb into the cab of Nat's truck to ride along while she plowed driveways. Coffee and conversation weren't limited to dining establishments and couches.

"So, I deleted that dating app from my phone," I said, blowing the steam off the top of my scalding coffee. Frank's heating element setting must have said "molten lava," the way it both tasted metallic and could melt rocks, but loyalty to the locals who'd practically raised me kept me coming back anyway.

"No, Lex! Come on," Natalie said, then gripped my bicep and jiggled me side-to-side.

"The last few matches were only looking for a hookup, but I need long-term."

"Don't you dare use bad matches on a subpar dating app as an excuse to stop dating. For every good date, you have to suffer through a few bad ones. Those are the rules."

"I'm not putting myself in the position to get my heart broken again. The second I fall for someone, they'll take off."

"That's dramatic. Not everyone leaves," Natalie said. "Hey, Frank, tell Lex that not everyone leaves."

Frank, the owner, looked up from the bacon he was frying and shrugged. "I'd leave if I could."

"Very nice, how inspiring. Thanks, Frank."

He saluted us with his spatula. "Glad to help."

I downed the last of my coffee and picked at the crumbs on my plate. "Kyle left me for a music career."

"To be fair, he thought you'd go with him."

I grimaced. I could have happily settled down with him if it hadn't required a multistate move and a crash course in folk music. Kyle had offered a long-distance relationship, but I knew it wouldn't fill the part of my heart that craved companionship and nearness. The desire for sharing space—making up for the empty house I went home to as a teen, perhaps. "Carley? They took off for that job in Washington."

"Sure, but even you thought that relationship was on its way out." Nat raised an eyebrow.

"Amanda left too. No excuse for it."

"She finished her degree. What did she have to stick around for? You started the relationship knowing she'd go. You can't judge the rest of the world by your exes."

"Can we judge it by yours, then? When was your last date again?"

"Last week, but that's irrelevant. Our romantic goals are totally different. I'm fine going with the flow, but you need to know someone will be around for the long haul. My point is that people leave, Lex, but not *all* people leave. Besides, I've got nowhere else to be, so I'm sticking around whether you like it or not."

"I like it." I gave her a toothy, greedy grin. "If you leave, all I'll have left is the memory of you and a montage of our ghostly greatest hits. And trust me, I'd rather not have the thought of you dangling from a tree to hang glowing orbs on repeat in my brain because it was terrifying to watch. You're the last thing I've got around here."

"And you're impossible." Nat pushed her empty plate across the counter and tucked some cash beneath it.

We took Natalie's truck up the road to the tree farm to say hi to her dad and brother. Even in the chilly weather, business was going strong. A line of cars streamed out of the parking lot, loaded with trees and wreaths and all manner of Christmas cheer.

I scanned the line, watching for familiar faces, when Natalie jumped into the fray to help tie a giant tree to the top of a not-so-big sedan.

It was better to let the experts handle it. My only experience with tree-tying was the one year in high school when I decided to help out to earn a bit of cash. Jordan was away for her first year of college. Instead of her coming back to celebrate with us, my parents dropped every Christmas tradition we had to go spend three weeks with her. They'd offered me a ticket, too—but between wrapping up an unwieldy term paper and cramming for exams, it was all I could do to remember breakfast in the mornings. There was too much going on for me to consider a holiday trip so I told them to just go without me. Grampa offered to hang back with me—and triple-checked that I'd be fine on my own—but I didn't want him to stay home just to watch me do homework, eat cold pizza, and plot the next few episodes of *Haunted Happenings*. So he went to California with the rest of the family and I was left to hang out at the inn with Natalie's family, sharing her room. It was a cold snap kind of stretch, too bitter for galivanting to stage hauntings, so I offered to lend a hand. I wasn't suited for tree cutting, netting, or loading. Instead, I huddled in the semi-heated hut, accepted tree payments, and watched soaps on the tiny tabletop TV until school was back in session.

When the tree was successfully secured, we said our goodbyes and speed-walked back to the truck. I'd promised popcorn and movies by the fireplace, and Nat wasn't going to let me forget it. But I caught a glimpse of a familiar face peering at the branches on trees, inspecting for fullness and prickliness and whatever else one could desire in an evergreen.

"James!" I grasped Natalie's arm and pulled her in front of me to block the view, peeking around her shoulder to make sure he hadn't seen me. I tugged her toward the passenger side door so I could keep using her as a shield, then released her when I was safely tucked inside. She scurried around the truck and climbed in beside me.

"I don't blame you for hitching a ride with him the other day. He's gorgeous," Natalie said, her eyes locked on him as he moseyed around the precut tree area.

I groaned, then filled her in on the latest bits she'd missed, from the coffee and funeral to the stolen key and forgotten hat.

"Sounds like someone *liiiiikes* you." The tone could have been mistaken for a middle schooler's taunting.

"It doesn't matter if he likes me; he's here because someone died, Nat. What am I going to do, offer to comfort him while he's here, then just send him on his way? Besides, he has a New York license plate, see? Further proof that it's a terrible idea."

"Hey, just because he's from out of town doesn't mean you can't get to know him a little while he's here. Besides, it looks like he's getting a tree. Maybe he's sticking around for a few weeks. You might find that you enjoy conversation with someone, even if it's not leading anywhere. You can't hold his place of residence against him, and you especially can't hold his hat hostage just because he's a tourist."

Deep down, I knew that being irritated by this guy, without knowing a thing about him, was silly. I could admit it. But letting him pretend he'd forgotten his hat, just to make me fall for him, would mean he'd won. I could play that game, too.

While Natalie's brother carried James's chosen tree to the line for netting, James rushed back to the car, climbed inside, and blew warmth into his hands. I watched him, considering whether he'd be the type to press chilled fingers against the small of my back for the squeal it would produce. He probably would. Then he'd grab me by the belt loops and pull me into him, an apology to chase away the shiver. I bit my lip and tried to push the idea away. It wouldn't budge.

"Maybe I should go tell him his hat is at the store."

"That's more like it." Natalie patted my shoulder. "Get over there and let him know when he can come get it." She winked.

I rolled my eyes. "This isn't a move. It's my duty, as an employee, to ensure any items lost at Dog-Eared are returned to owner. Don't read into it."

I shoved open the truck's heavy steel door, tugged my hat down to cover more of my face, and pressed my hands deep into my jacket pockets. Walking between Nat's truck and James's car took both hours and seconds, all at once. There was no sense in getting worked up about it, but I knew the moment I tapped on his window he'd turn on that smile, his eyes would twinkle, and I'd forget the most important detail: that he wasn't from around here, he'd be leaving, and there was no sense in getting to know him.

He rolled down his window without looking and held a couple of folded bills through the gap.

"I know my soy-no-foam is good, but damn, what a tip."

His head snapped up and he smirked. "You work here, too, huh?"

"No, I saw you from across the lot—" I closed my eyes and took a breath. He was mocking me, and I'd played right into it. "Your head looked cold. You forgot your hat at the store the other night. I wanted to let you know where it was in case you were looking for it."

"How thoughtful. I was, actually." The playful gleam in his eye matched his megawatt grin. "A special woman bought it for me."

So, that was the game he wanted to play. Bringing up other women to get a rise out of me. I wasn't going to give him the satisfaction. He thought he could flash a grin and get what he wanted, but I knew better than to fall for a pretty face and smooth lines.

"Yes, I'm sure you treasure each and every article of clothing your mom gives you."

The barest of hesitation crossed his face, a darkening behind his eyes and a pull in one corner of his mouth. His grin dropped a few degrees, but he pressed his lips back into a fond smile to replace it. "She had great taste."

Had. Past tense, had. What was it with me dredging up death every time I talked to this guy?

I leaned my head into my hands and groaned. "I'm so sorry. I didn't mean to—"

"I'm sorry, too. Her gifts suck lately. You should see the stuff she sends now. She got remarried, her new guy is a Cubs fan. The Cubs, can you imagine?"

"So she's not dead?" Heat rushed to my cheeks.

"Not unless you know something I don't. She's an ER nurse in Colorado."

"You're cruel."

He grinned. "And you're holding my hat hostage."

"It's at the store. Come by Monday, and you can have it back. Completely intact, I promise."

"I'll see if I can squeeze in a stop." He brushed his fingertip along the dashboard, then examined the dust that stuck to it. What an arrogant move.

Yet, somehow, I couldn't help but trace his jawline with my eyes. A straight shot, right down to that dimpled chin. If he smiled again, I'd be a goner.

Natalie's brother appeared beside me, a tree slung over one shoulder. "Hey, Alex," he said.

"Alex, huh?" James asked. Another grin lit his face. "Let me guess, short for Alexis?"

Now he was toying with me. "No."

"Alexandria?"

"It's not short for anything. It's just Alex."

"Well, 'Just Alex,' I'll swing by the store on Monday to claim my property."

"You do that." I spun and marched across the lot toward Natalie's truck. I climbed into the passenger side and narrowed my eyes at her.

"Wow," she said. She opened her hands, flinging her fingers outward. "Wow! You two are *fireworks*. The sparks, god, I could feel the heat from here."

"Are you kidding me? That's what you call sparks? He spent the whole conversation mocking me."

She sparked fingers in the air again. "Fireworks."

"Ugh, can we please drop this? Not interested. I can't feel my toes. Take me home."

She laughed, shook her head, and put the truck in gear.

CHAPTER FOUR

Sorting bookstore donations was my favorite task. Dog-Eared drop-offs were often old Dog-Eared purchases, so pricing was easy enough—especially if the old tags were still attached. The inventory system was more a game of memory than an actual method, but Darla and I were well loved for our quick retrieval of requested tomes. We'd created a sense of order that Charles had never quite managed. Now, books were arranged by subject, then author name, as opposed to Charles's original plan of "fill shelves to bursting, we'll figure out the rest later." And by "we" he meant "anyone but him."

The first year I was on staff, I spent the winter organizing and labeling the shelves, only for Charles to lecture me about how the store lost its charm when the shelves looked like every other bookstore's shelves. Organization: what a travesty. But when sales rose because people were able to find what they wanted rather than play a literary version of roulette, he let me have my organizational methods.

I spent most of the day tugging and tagging books, pulling stacks of paperbacks from within boxes, paper bags, and plastic bins, and wishing people had better places to pawn off their copies of *The Secret* and *Twilight*. Anything Dog-Eared couldn't put on the shelf was reboxed and saved for the town-wide book sale, a library fundraiser that shut down Main Street every summer.

I examined, priced, and shelved dozens of books—but only after checking the inside cover of each, mining for handwritten treasures. Among the day's finds were a copy of *The Da Vinci Code*, inscribed "Really makes you think, doesn't it?" and a book of daily affirmations that included the note "Give yourself permission to make space for yourself. You are loved. You are powerful. Yours."

Natalie rushed through the door at noon, a takeout bag from our favorite sushi place tucked beneath her arm, and a box of donuts in her other hand. We ate lunch over stacks of books, and Natalie begged me for the latest gossip.

"Gossip about what?" I practically snorted. "Same old sleepy bookstore, same old town. Anything I know, you know."

She leaned back in the desk chair and swiveled back and forth. "Yeah, nothing changes around here. Doc Cecil probably started the morning telling everyone in the coffee shop about the time he saw an apparition stuck in a witch window on Mountain Road." Stowe had a rich history of being haunted, with a ghost story for each historic building and shadowed pathway—which meant that Natalie and I had had plenty to work with while staging our hauntings. We started with the enduring local tales before weaving my own fictional accounts into the mix. Doc Cecil—not actually a doctor—couldn't explain what he saw in that window, and neither could Nat or I. We hadn't been involved in that sighting, simply because we weren't born yet. "How can this place be such a draw for you?" she said. "I'd be a couple thousand miles away if my parents wouldn't murder me for it. What's keeping you here?"

"It's home." I shrugged. "It feels right."

"Even with your family gone? Couldn't anywhere feel like home, if you gave it a chance?"

"It was home long before my parents left. It was home before Jordan left. Grampa left me the place; it's where I belong."

She gave me a look. "Even if you're draining your savings to keep it standing?"

This was far from the first time we'd had the "what if things were different" conversation, and it was making me anxious, as it always did. What if I'd moved when my parents did, instead of staying here for some college boyfriend who was just going to break up with me when I dropped out of school? What if I'd sold the house, taken the money, and started fresh? What if Mom and Dad had stuck around instead of dropping everything to move when Jordan made their dreams come true with perfect baby twins? What if I'd taken the chance and found a new corner of the country to call mine? It would eventually come around to me wondering what would have happened if I'd followed Kyle to Nashville, and whether I'd be happy. I wasn't in the mood to discuss hypotheticals, so I excused myself from the conversation before it had a chance to really get going.

I made coffee instead, then yanked a couple of dollars from the tip jar to pay for it.

Natalie spun in the desk chair, then leaned back as far as she could go without tipping over. She sat up, gasped, and clapped her hands over her mouth. "Is that *the* hat?"

I glared at the Yankees cap hanging from the peg. "Oh yeah, that's the one."

"Look at the little shrine you've made. You've got it bad."

"I wanted it out of the way."

Natalie jumped from her chair and swiped the hat from its hanging place.

"Would you leave it alone, please? It's just there until he comes back to get it."

She let her hair down and crammed the hat onto her head, shaking her wavy black hair into place around her shoulders.

"Oh my god, Nat, put it back." I rushed toward the desk with our coffee mugs, foam nearly sloshing over the top in my hurry. "Just take it off, please."

"Okay, okay. You worry too much. Taking it off now."

She plucked it from her head and put it on mine instead. With hands still full of coffee, I had no choice but to let it happen. A faint mint and cedar scent curled through my nostrils. Of course it would still smell like him. I shoved Nat's coffee into her hand, grumbled "Careful, it's hot," then flopped into my own chair.

"Looks good on you," Natalie said with a sly grin.

"You're the devil," I said. A text came through, so I pulled my phone from my pocket.

Mother: *Hello Alex. Your father and I have business in the area and will arrive tomorrow for a short stay. Apologies for the late notice, but we only just found out ourselves. Would you meet us for dinner when we arrive? We'll be renting a car at the airport, so we can meet anywhere you please. Within reason. Don't recommend Al's French Frys again, you know we can't eat like college students anymore. Please confirm a time and location, and let us know when you've made reservations.*

I closed my eyes tight, gritted my teeth, and whined. No way was I replying yet. I needed to rehearse saying "no" first. I waved my phone in Natalie's direction. She took it, scanned the message, and patted my shoulder.

"You'll survive this visit, just like every other," she reminded me. "They'll complain, you'll pretend to listen, they'll offer stern warnings, and they'll fly out a day or two later."

"Want to crash dinner with us?" I asked, hopeful. "They're buying."

"Thanks for the offer, but I'm not sure being a buffer sounds like such a good time."

"Your loss," I said. She'd been cleaning up the post-parents mess for more than fifteen years, and she was probably due a break at this point. "Maybe I should just accidentally drop my phone in front of your plow— you know, just so I have an excuse for not answering their message."

"That sounds like logical thinking, there's no way that could go wrong."

"Best case, she figures it out and emails."

"What's the worst case?"

I flicked the empty takeout container and startled as cold condensation splashed back. "They show up here, drag me into the street, and publicly humiliate me."

"Sounds about right." She nodded. "Need anything? Ben & Jerry's? Gummy bears? Both?"

"I'll be fine, really. Maybe they'll decide to fly home early to remind their favorite daughter how special she is."

"You can tell them we already had plans. Dinner at my parents' place. They'll set an extra place for you."

"They'd tell me I could 'simply reschedule,' because I should drop everything when they drop in without notice." Kyle would have cleared his schedule to see them. Out of the two of us, he'd definitely been their favorite. He set a terrible precedent.

"Tell them you have a date." She grinned at me. "Get them off your back about being single *and* get out of dinner."

I shook my head. "They'd probably demand to meet the person and assess their worthiness."

"Then I guess you'd better have a backup plan." Natalie laughed, and I raised my eyebrows. She plastered a serious look on her face.

"I'll call them later to grovel. 'Oh, goodness me I misplaced my phone and missed your message. How could I be so daft, please forgive your lowly daughter.' Then I'll agree to dinner after they strongarm me into it. It'll be fine."

"Suit yourself. You're always welcome, you know that."

Natalie tugged the door open, then sidestepped as a couple approached the entrance, gesturing to let them slip inside before she ducked out the door and jumped into her truck.

The couple approached the desk. One pulled a list from his pocket. "I heard you may be able to track these down," he said.

I accepted his list and scanned the titles, all from a mystery series that had been out of print for at least a decade. "I'm pretty sure I have some of these around here, but others might be difficult to find. Let's see what we can do."

As I rounded the corner of the desk, the bell above the door jingled. I glanced up to greet the customer, and my blood froze. I clasped my hand to the Yankees cap that still sat on my head, averted my eyes, and tugged the cap off. It fell onto the desk, and I let it rest where it landed. James meandered toward the front desk with that same calculated swagger as the day we'd met. His long wool coat draped perfectly along his frame, the hem swaying slightly with each step. The twinkle in his eye told me he knew exactly what he'd seen.

"I'll be right back, I need to help these customers." Crap. Of all the used bookstores in all the state, he had to stroll into mine.

James nodded, flashed a smile, then drew a thumb along the corner of a weathered Steinbeck, letting the pages run along his fingertip like shuffled cards. I closed my eyes tight and wished that he'd just grab his hat and go so I could avoid the awkward chat that would be coming. Resist, Lex. Resist.

I scoured the shelves for the customers' books, peering at James over the edge of the list. He'd settled in my favorite chair in the most peaceful corner of the store. It had the best natural light and was closest to the warmest creaky iron radiator. He was flipping through one of the books from my stack—my pile of inscribed books meant for me, and me alone—examining *The Da Vinci Code* like it was news to him.

I rang up the books I'd managed to find, miskeying the prices multiple times out of distraction. James had crossed one leg, resting his calf against the opposite knee. He jiggled his foot as he flipped page after page, teasing me.

I ushered the customers out the door, took a long, meditative breath, then marched toward James.

"Your hat's on the desk," I said. I could have told him that to begin with, but those eyes . . . that jawline . . . that chin.

He pressed a finger to his lips, looked me in the eye, and *shushed* me. "I'm reading. This is fascinating."

"You've never read Dan Brown before?"

"Oh, no, I have. But this gives it a whole new meaning." He flipped to the note written inside the cover. "I didn't peg you as the conspiracy theory type, Just Alex."

I pressed my fingers to the bridge of my nose and inhaled again. Breathe in, breathe out, don't yell at the guy here for a funeral. "Alex," I corrected him. "Just Alex. I mean, Alex, no 'just.'"

"Oops, yes sorry. Just *Alex*, of course. That makes sense." He flashed a toothy grin in my direction, unapologetic no matter the spoken apology. "So, you a Dan Brown fan?"

"I don't see how that's any of your business."

A bemused smile flashed across his face before he put on a mock-serious expression. "I'm getting the feeling you don't like me very much."

I drew my eyebrows together and fixed him with my best glare. "It's not just you. I'm starting to think I don't like anybody." The words fell from my mouth before I'd thought them through. The truth in the statement hit me like the burst of cold water when my shower runs for more than five minutes, but something about him pulled the honesty from me. A quiet intrepidity.

"You don't even know me," he said with placating hands, palms up.

"I know your type." I walked to the desk, grabbed his hat from where it had landed earlier, and strolled back to him with what I hoped was a confident gait. "You come here, ski for a week or two, then take off. You tip the inn's staff well enough that they're falling over you for more than just your looks. You stay briefly, you leave without a second thought. Now, if you don't mind, I have books to shelve and a store to close."

I flipped his hat toward him, and he accepted it with his free hand, keeping the thumb of his other hand between the pages where he'd stopped flipping through the book. "You're spunky, Just Alex. I like it."

"You can't just sit there and read—this isn't a library," I sputtered. Anything to avoid a stunned silence. *Protect your heart, Lex.* I couldn't get hurt if I didn't let myself like him. "If you want to keep coming in here, you have to buy something. And not coffee, because I don't want to clean up the mess."

He tapped a finger to his full and pouty lips. "Make a recommendation, then. I prefer fiction, but you're the expert."

I stared him down. Was he serious?

He didn't flinch.

I marched through the aisles, tugged *Slaughterhouse-Five* from the classics section, then spun to head back to the chair where I'd left him.

James was close enough behind me that I smacked him in the chest with the book.

He took my wrist in his fingers, turned my hand over, and examined the cover. He pulled his lower lip between his teeth—sexy and pensive, which was likely the intent given the show he'd been putting on. He flipped *The Da Vinci Code* closed and handed it to me, then tapped the cover of the Vonnegut. "I'll give it a shot."

"It's worth more than a shot. Lose yourself in it. Trust me."

"Okay, I'll lose myself in it. But only because you told me to. What do I owe you?" He plucked a ten from his wallet and handed it to me.

"I'll get your change."

"Keep it," he said.

"The book is like, two-fifty. Just hang on a second."

"For the coffee the other night. It kept me warm and awake while I was at the cemetery, and I owe you."

I sighed. "Fine, you win. But only because I feel bad that I gave you shit when you were on the way to a funeral."

His laugh echoed through the store; not even the area rugs were enough to dampen the sound. "I guess if a funeral gets me special treatment, it's worth it."

"I'm sorry for your loss?" I said, a question hanging at the end due to his baffling laughter.

He nodded solemnly and pulled the door open, then turned back to me. "Go out with me."

I hadn't *not* noticed how attractive he was, but I was a magnet for people with one foot out the door. Which, I suppose, made him exactly my type on two counts. I wrinkled my nose, considering whether his offer was earnest. "What? Are you serious?"

"As death." He quirked an eyebrow.

I almost accepted. Worst case scenario, I'd get a free dinner in exchange for an hour of lousy conversation. Best case, we'd hit it off, and I'd actually enjoy myself.

Until he went back to New York, and I got left behind. Again.

I didn't meet his eyes. "Thanks for the offer," I said sincerely, all my previous bite gone from my tone now, "but I'm not really looking to start anything new right now." *Especially with someone who's going to disappear.*

"Suit yourself," he said gently. He offered a thumbs up, then tapped the cover of his new book and tucked it inside a coat pocket hidden in the lining. He slipped his hands into the outer coat pockets. "I'll see you around, Just Alex."

He was maddening. So self-assured and cocky. He knew exactly how frustratingly handsome he was—and that made it worse.

And yet, while I watched him stroll out the door, as easy as a day at the park, I imagined my name on his lips again, only this time with his body pressed against mine as he swept me into a deep kiss. If his affection was half as purposeful as his strut, there wouldn't be a chance in hell for my heart.

* * *

I resolved to call my parents to break the news that I wouldn't be subjecting myself to dinner with them this time. Gripping the concrete-heavy receiver, I hoped for voicemail, and swallowed back my frustration when my mother answered.

"We've already made donations to multiple charities. We're not interested in supporting your cause at this time."

"Mom, it's me."

"Me? Me, who?"

"God, Mom, it's Lex."

"Oh, of course. Alex." The line buzzed slightly in the silence after her greeting. Talking on the phone with my parents was always an awkward experience; I never knew when to speak or when it was okay to simply end the conversation.

"Hi, how are you, how's the sister? Did her kids graduate from college yet?"

"Everyone's fine. I won't dignify your snide comment about the children with an answer because I know you're simply trying to get a rise out of me. We made a reservation for 7 P.M. tomorrow evening when we didn't hear from you. Better safe than sorry, and all. I'll email you the details. We'd appreciate it if you'd show up on time, especially since you canceled your Thanksgiving visit."

I pinched the bridge of my nose to stave off the headache I knew was coming. "I told you, I had car repairs and had to work Black Friday, so I couldn't make it happen this time."

"I can't believe you're still at that fire hazard masquerading as a bookstore."

"Oh, don't worry, we hosed it down with liquid asbestos, so we're good to go." She didn't even grunt in reply. "I'm kidding. Seriously, wow."

"If you lived on the West Coast, plane travel wouldn't be necessary for us to see one another. Selling that little house has so many benefits. Even if he was stubborn and sentimental, your grandfather never meant for you to stick it out there forever."

I balled my free hand in a fist and shoved it deep inside my sweatshirt pocket. There it was again: the tightness in my chest as my brain hounded me with the hypotheticals. Each time the topic came up, my ribcage became a hive full of bees—the more my parents insisted selling was the right choice, the angrier the bees became. It wasn't just selling; it was picking up and moving. Leaving everything I knew. Even if I didn't swap coasts, I'd still be out of place wherever I ended up. Somewhere with unfamiliar intersections and roads, faces I didn't recognize, comforting routines obliterated. There would be restaurants with menus I hadn't memorized—I'd have to make a choice even though it's impossible to see the words through the dark edges that creep into my line of sight when I'm on the spot. Literally everything would be more difficult.

I clutched the phone to my ear and dragged my fingernail along the textured edge of the case to regain a bit of focus. "I love that little house, and I've put a lot of effort into it. I've almost paid off the window replacements, and next spring they're evaluating the septic."

"It was meant to be a stepping stone, Alex, not your final resting place. Honestly, the way you hold on to these tiny nonsense things, as if it would be the end of the world to move. There's nothing worth-while keeping you there. Nothing but my father's willfulness, which you seem to have inherited right along with that house."

She could insult me all she wanted, but coming for my house was another story. I'd already explained my feelings, multiple times. She'd never get it, but that was the choreography that defined our relationship.

I took a breath. "The thing is, I can't make it out to dinner this time. I've got . . . a date." I had no idea why I'd just said that. She'd probably find a reason to drop by the house anyway just to make sure I wasn't lying about my prior engagement—at the very least, video call to catch me in my lie—but it was too late now. I could take Nat out for the night—she'd been my cover story before, and I knew she would again. "Maybe next time you're in town." If they made the trip specifically to visit, rather than cramming me in like an afterthought on a business trip.

"Oh?" Her voice pitched up slightly. "A date? Anyone I know?"

"No, Mom. Nobody you know. Just . . . someone I've been . . . uh . . . seeing often . . . recently." My heart rate increased the longer we were on the phone, and with each second she was closer to her asking for my date's name, date of birth, education history, and current career prospects. "I'm sorry, have a safe rest of your trip. I'll talk to you soon, okay? Say hi to Jordan for me. She hasn't replied to my last three voicemail messages, so I may need to resort to skywriting to stay in touch with her."

I hung up, certain I'd get an earful for it later.

CHAPTER FIVE

A fresh dusting of snow fell overnight, enough to turn the early December landscape into a scene straight off a Christmas card. I parked my car in front of Dog-Eared, skated my way to the door, and dashed inside in time to catch Charles's daily call on the third ring. I inhaled in preparation for my monologue.

"Good morning, Dog-Eared Books and More, where select used paperbacks are three for two and home of the Coffee of the Month Club, this is Lex, how can I help you?"

He didn't respond right away, likely proof that I'd caught him off-guard by rattling off the mile-long greeting. He cleared his throat, a sputtering *ah-he-hem*, stalling for time as he searched for the morning's criticism. "Darla tells me you've rearranged the nonfiction section."

"Only slightly, Charles. Customers were tired of searching for the history books alphabetically. So I sorted by era, then by author within each era. Like other bookstores would."

"I suppose that's a sensible choice. I'll let it slide. Future reorganization, however, must go through the proper channels. Next order of business, are we meeting our Coffee Club quota?"

I reached for the latest sign-up slips—only three of them in the last week, because all of the regulars had already jumped on board. It wasn't like Charles used the email addresses for anything logical—say, a newsletter or promotional messages. Talk about missing the point of data collection. "We're gearing up for some big movement in that program, don't you worry, Charles. Our busiest weeks are coming up. Perhaps if we swapped to a punch card program instead of an opt-in format, you'd get more bites. Tourists aren't willing to share their personal info, but they may fill a punch card in a weekend."

"No, no. I've already paid for the sign-up slips. We've got a thousand of them in the office. We'll see this through."

I spun the slips on the desk, suppressing a yawn. The slip on top caught my eye. James Coen, with the out-of-town 315 number. James. With the crooked, playful grin and deep brown eyes. His jagged, purposeful letters, scrawled with enough pressure that the pen left minor indents at the start of each letter. James.

I smoothed my hands along the paper, pressing the wrinkles out and examining his careful handwriting. The determination of the pen strokes suited what I knew of his personality: devious, but in an appealing way. Approachable, yet self-assured.

"We'll amp up the program, Charles. Customers are waiting for drinks. I'll talk with you tomorrow."

I hung up the phone and fiddled with the paper some more, worrying at the corner with a thumbnail until the edge turned fuzzy. Natalie couldn't get away for a night out like I'd hoped—the inn was short-staffed, so she was helping out her parents for the evening.

I wracked my brain for someone else to ask to be my alibi, but—and this surely said more about my introverted nature than anything—the only person who came to mind was James. He had seemed nice enough. I could be social; it didn't have to *mean* anything. Even if he had been on my mind the last few days. What harm would it do, really?

I grabbed the phone and punched in James's number.

It rang a handful of times before his voicemail picked up. I inhaled, then forced a slow-and-steady stream of air though my lips.

The only thing worse than leaving voicemail messages would be having the person pick up and having to speak to a human.

"You've reached James. I'm not here so leave a message. Bonus points for knock knock jokes." *Beep.*

"Hey, James. It's me. Lex. Umm, Alex. Alex. Anyway. I'm sorry for calling you like this, it's just that I was wondering if you'd be interested in hanging out sometime. Tonight, maybe. I know you already asked me this, and I said no, but . . . I was thinking, and maybe I'd like to, well, I don't know. Make more suggestions for where to get meals or something. Sometime. I mean tonight. Okay. Oh, and knock, knock . . . Nobel . . . Nobel, that's why I knocked. Wow, telling a joke in a recorded message is impossible, don't judge me based on—"

The voicemail beeped again and cut me off, midramble. I took a deep breath and held it while I struggled to decide whether the message saved before it cut me off, or if something had glitched and sent my nonsense to the void. One would hope the latter, but I was rarely so lucky. I'd already made a first impression. And a second. I dialed the number again and waited for the voicemail to beep, then left another, more succinct message.

"Hey James, it's Lex. From the bookstore. I'd like to take you up on your offer. If you'd still like to get together, ignore my previous message and give me a call at Dog-Eared."

I settled the phone back in its cradle, and buried my face in my hands.

* * *

I'd only just kicked my feet up for a book and lunch break—Tolstoy and takeout, a match made in heaven—when the bell above the front door let out a muted jingle. Shuffling feet wandered serpentine through the aisles, so I continued my routine. A few pages later, the footsteps picked up pace, coming toward the desk. I tucked the closest piece of paper into my book and brushed crumbs from my fingertips as the customer approached.

"Good afternoon, is there anything I can help you find?" I asked a moment before they rounded the corner.

"I've been receiving harassing phone calls from this establishment." James sidled up to the desk, leaned a hip into the corner, and crossed one ankle over the other. His cap cast a shadow over his face, but his teasing smile couldn't be missed.

Every blood cell rushed to my cheeks. Determined to play it cool, unlike every other time I'd spoken with a dreamboat who was a thousand times cooler than me, I forced a nonchalant shrug.

"Sorry, sir. You should have read the fine print. You opted in to rambling phone messages from the store's only full-time employee. Guess you'll check out those contracts a little closer next time."

He sucked air through his teeth and shrugged back. "See, here's the thing. The woman said her name was Lex, and I have it on good authority that your name is, well, just Alex."

"You're never going to let that die, are you?" I narrowed my eyes, but the furious blush had begun to subside, for which I was grateful.

"Consider it dead. Murdered, even. They'll never find the body—I know a guy with a pig farm."

A laugh slipped out. His satisfaction at my amusement was plastered across his face in a grin that set his eyes sparkling. "So, *Lex*, I got your messages–"

I winced. "Oof, both of them?"

"Yes, both of them. Seemed urgent, what's up?"

I smoothed my jeans and turned the swivel chair a bit to avoid eye contact. "I'm a terrible person."

He tilted his head to the side. "Let me judge."

I caught the mildest whiff of his cologne and savored it a moment—handsome, good taste, *and* he smelled divine, the world was cruel—before snapping back to attention. "My parents are in town."

"Wow, you move fast." He pressed himself away from the desk, straightened, and brushed his hands together. "Alright, I'll meet your parents."

"Oh, god no. No, trust me." I was shaking my head wildly. "That's not an option. They want me to go to dinner with them, and I may have hinted that I've been seeing someone—you know, just . . . around—and that I have a date tonight, so I can't meet them for dinner. And while it sounds like I'm only asking out of desperation, please know that I am sure you'd make adequate company, even without my parents involved."

James lifted an eyebrow. "Really now?"

"You're insufferable." And far too easy to fall into comfortable banter with.

"And you're using me to get out of dinner with your parents, who I assume are wonderful people," he teased, the skin at the corners of his eyes crinkling.

"Hardly. As if being the disappointing child my whole life wasn't enough, now, my lack of ambition and multiple failed relationships have them worried I'll never amount to anything."

He nodded. "Tonight, then?"

"That's it? I drop that on you, and you're in, just like that?"

"Absolutely. Besides, if you recall, I happen to have asked you to dinner first, and was shot down. If spending time together, strictly hanging out—definitely not on a date—is what it takes, I'm in. When should I pick you up?"

"The store closes at five, want to meet me back here at six?"

"Six it is. Oh, and dress warm. Layers."

"Imagine you telling a Vermont girl, through and through, how to dress." I crossed my arms and plastered a smug, crooked smile on my face.

"Trust me," he said. He tugged the Vonnegut paperback from his jacket pocket and set it on the counter. "This was an excellent recommendation. What else do you have?"

I tapped a fingertip to my lips and made a show of considering the options, but I didn't need time. I crossed in front of James and wandered the creaky floors toward my favorite corner of the store to tug a book from the shelf.

"Philip K. Dick?" He flipped the paperback over to skim the back.

"Androids. Mayhem. Morals. Report back."

"How many pages should my essay be?"

"At least a hundred, single-spaced. And don't mess with font sizes. Bumping it to thirteen won't get you ahead."

He winked and counted a few dollar bills onto the counter, then raised a hand to his cap's brim and dipped his head. "Tonight."

"At six." I nodded.

He left, the doorbell jingling behind him.

Operation: Avoid My Parents by Conning a Total Stranger Into Spending Time with Me was a go.

CHAPTER SIX

My closet was devoid of anything considered both "warm" and "stylish." Booties, a mini, and a black top with sheer black sleeves had been my go-to going-out outfit while I was with Kyle. Flashy enough to call "fancy," subtle enough to keep from drawing attention. Seasonality was beyond my fashion abilities, and that standard kept me from stressing out while getting ready.

This time, the standard wouldn't do, unless I wanted to freeze my ass off doing whatever James had planned. Based on his fashion sense alone, it would likely be a party at a ski lodge—his wool coat and ball cap combo screamed "Let's hit the slopes, but gently because I've got a conference call first thing in the morning." Professional, with a love of letting loose, so long as it's not too loose. He was probably a lawyer, or an insurance salesman. Something that allowed for squeezing in a funeral and a weekend lift pass.

I grasped for hangers and slid sections of clothes along the creaky wooden rod in my closet. Too short, too flashy, too floral, too showy.

At a loss, I invited Natalie to a video chat.

"I don't know what to wear," I said before she'd even gotten out a "hello."

"Where are you going?"

"No clue; he said to dress warm. Are jeans and a sweatshirt too meh?"

"As someone who never wears anything but jeans and a sweatshirt, I can assure you, it's too meh. Show me what you've got."

I turned the camera to my closet and slid piece after piece into view, slowing each time Natalie let out a considering *hmm*.

"No, no, not that. Absolutely not. Why do you even *have* a sweater with cats in pumpkins? No, nope. That, there! That's it."

I tugged the hanger from the closet and eyed the outfit. "This is my Marty McFly costume from Halloween."

"Yup. Wear the vest over your chunky white sweater, and those black pants you wore to my brother's birthday party. Winter boots. Done and done."

"I'll look ridiculous."

"You'll look warm."

I dropped my head and groaned as my clock flipped to 5:48 P.M. "Shit, I'm going to be late. Gotta go, thank you."

I tugged the outfit on, jammed my feet into my clunkiest winter boots, grabbed my puffy, nineties-chic winter coat, and tore out the door. No mascara refresh, no lip gloss. I tugged on my coat and jumped in the car.

I got to my usual parking spot with thirty seconds to spare, but James was already sitting on the bench in front of the building. He stood and pet the wavy-eared black Spaniel sitting by his feet, wearing a dog jacket that bore an uncanny resemblance to the vest I was hiding beneath my coat.

James picked up two travel mugs from the bench and handed one to me. I inhaled the coffee aroma before taking a cautious sip. Still steaming hot, and exactly the right amount of cream. Good guess on his part.

"We can stop for a hot chocolate or decaf instead, if you'd prefer. I always forget that some people like to limit their caffeine intake—I'd take it in IV form if I could."

"I can drink a triple-shot at midnight and still fall asleep immediately, so this is great. Thanks." I dropped to one knee, turned away from the dog, and glanced toward the ground to let her approach me.

"I hope it's okay that I brought my dog," James said. "She's been cooped up all day and her schedule's been a mess the last few days."

All the more reason to leave your dog home while you're off mourning your dead. But I couldn't keep a plant alive, so who was I to judge?

"That's fine, I like dogs. I wasn't ever allowed to have one, so I get the snuggles in where I can to make up for it." She sniffed a shoe, then along my leg, before nuzzling at my jacket pocket.

"Nothing in there for you, pup," I said, tugging the pocket open slightly to prove it. The nylon shell rustled as she nosed at the gap.

"This is Lucy in the Sky with Diamonds." James smiled.

I smiled too. "That's . . . a mouthful."

"Sure is."

"Do you ever call her just Lucy?"

He raised an eyebrow and pressed his mouth into an amused half-grin.

"Yeah, yeah. You know what I mean."

"No, actually. Sometimes I shorten it to Lulu, but usually it's 'Hey, knock it off, that's my shoe.' She answers to anything, though."

I gave him a wide smile, challenging his statement.

He nodded toward the dog. "Go for it, call her anything."

"Hey, Lucy!"

She looked at me and wagged her tail a few swipes before plunking into a perfect little sit.

"Good girl." I turned back to James, stroking my chin and squinting to make a show of considering the next name. "Hey there, candlewick!"

Another wag—this time her full body was engaged.

"Oh, who's a good lightbulb?"

More wags, and a bark. Lulu wiggled closer to me, straining against her leash to place both snowy paws on my thighs. I flailed my arms as I nearly tumbled backward, but James caught my shoulder before I fell. He steadied me and offered a hand. I clasped it, my bare palm against his gloved one.

"I thought I said to dress warm," he said.

"This is warm. I'll be taking my coat off when we get wherever. I overheat easily, anyway."

"Suit yourself," James said. He let out a short whistle and Lulu snapped to attention, the tail-wagging amped up to near-weapon status. "Let's go, Lulu, we've got a fun night ahead of us."

We took off on foot, and picked our way along the sidewalk, doing our best to avoid icy buildup and footprint ravines.

"How far are we walking?" I asked after stumbling for the third time.

"We're almost there," James said, waving a hand toward the cemetery gate.

"I don't understand." I knit my eyebrows. Cemeteries didn't exactly scream "first date." I eyed the street, calculating which direction I'd run if this turned into a serial killer scenario, or worse, a "let me show you my granny's grave" thing.

"We're a bit early, but Julian and the crew will be here soon."

"The . . . crew? Julian?" Maybe I'd misread the situation entirely. James was looking for a group hang, not a date. Slightly embarrassing, but in my defense, he'd been flirting since we'd met.

"Film crew. Julian and I are documentary filmmakers."

Okay, or he was looking for a local expert for their film. "What? Why didn't you just say that?"

"And miss seeing this look on your face? No way." He winked, clearly pleased with his surprise. "We're taking a deep dive into Stowe's haunted happenings."

I swallowed—hard—at the way he'd dropped *haunted happenings* into the conversation. It was probably a coincidence, because alliteration is king—and even I could admit it wasn't a very original title. But what were the chances? A group of ghost hunters, exploring the same cemetery where I'd set up a tripod more times than I could count to film my own ghost stories?

"We got into town just a few days before you and I met," James continued. "We've covered a few locations already. Tonight, the plan is to get some graveyard footage while he narrates a ghost tour. Sorry, you're not easily creeped out, are you?"

"No way," I said.

I wasn't. Not when it came to Stowe's eerie phenomena—Natalie and I hadn't spent all that time researching and recreating legends only for me to be freaked out as an adult with a fully developed amygdala. Most of the stories we'd made up, anyway. The ones we hadn't had obvious explanations—one too many maple bourbon shots at the bar resulting in apparitions, like the guy who'd thought a cow was the devil's messenger sent to set him on the right path. He'd been cheating on his wife with the bartender at Slopeside and after the cow incident he vowed to change his ways. He divorced his wife and tried to get the bartender to run away with him, but the joke was on him because the wife and bartender became best friends.

I had to give James—and Julian—credit, though. Monetizing the very same hobby Natalie and I had established simply to pass the time was a pretty solid move.

James jiggled Lulu's leash, and she quit sniffing at the snowy hedge and trotted back to his side. "Good, because things get pret–ty wild around here when he's got the cameras out. Tour groups are usually about a dozen people. Tourists, usually." He nudged me with an elbow, throwing my assumptions back at me. "Whoever he can scrounge up in town that day. He wanders around the ski lodge and stops into stores to invite people out on whichever ghost hunt we've planned for the night. I'm off-duty tonight, so we just have to act surprised when he says he senses something. Cameras might pan the crowd, don't look directly at the lens. Just be, that's all."

"Quick question." I'd started to shiver a bit, so I took another sip of my coffee to warm me from the inside out. "If we're acting, is it still a documentary?"

James tapped a finger to his nose, smirked, and strolled through the cemetery gates with Lulu padding behind him. He wandered casually along the plowed path and took occasional detours toward gravestones, avoiding the deeper snow in favor of already flattened footpaths. We didn't speak. He walked, paused, looked, and sipped his coffee. No hurry, no reason to rush.

I wrapped my arms around my middle, chasing away the shivers that threatened to give me away. Another layer would have been the logical choice in twenty-degree weather, but it was too late now. I wasn't going to admit that I was cold. Not a chance. I'd have been perfectly dressed for the ski lodge party or heated outdoor patio dinner I'd expected. The things that made my town a *destination*. Of all the surprises he'd sprung on me so far, this one was the most interesting—and the one that brought up the most questions.

"Know anyone here?" I asked.

"I've befriended a few ghosts in my visits, sure." He waved toward a headstone. "That's Nicolas—he died in a tragic wagon accident. You see, he was distracted by a gleaming orb in the sky. His dying words were about otherworldly beings coming to claim Earth for their own."

I eyed the headstone he had indicated. "That's Mr. Henning's grave, he died in his sleep three years ago. The guy was a hundred and two, and the most exciting stories he ever told were about drinking from the garden hose and his days fishing in the creek before the state required you to pay for the privilege."

James leaned closer. "I'm talking about the ghost in front of the headstone, obviously." He raised his eyebrows and sipped his coffee.

"Obviously." I returned a half-smile, trying to decide if he was serious.

The LED glare of headlamps popped into view as a camera crew and small crowd of people shuffled into the cemetery.

James leaned in toward me to whisper. "They started the tour down at the inn, so they're filming already. We'll just sneak into the shot when he stops at the maple over there. Don't draw attention; act like we've been here the whole time."

We waited until the cameras panned the cemetery, then slipped into the gaggle of ghost hunters. Not a local in sight, which was probably for the best—they'd likely assume I was starting the vlog again and there would be mixed feelings on the matter. Besides, Julian would get a better response out of people who hadn't grow up hearing this town's slew of creepy stories packaged as cautionary tales. They parted easily to let us into the crowd, and we were settled—alert and ready to act—by the time the camera hit the group again. Lulu peeked from person to person, likely deciding which may bear treats. When nobody reached for a pocket, she snorted, shook, and fell into step beside us as if she'd done this dozens of times before.

We followed Julian, a man with thick hair, warm olive skin, and a close-cropped beard, whose casual saunter and friendly storytelling cadence took up all the space, making him seem taller than his five-foot-eight (give or take) frame. He chatted easily about the depth of history and meaning within the cemetery, and how *grave* tales accompanied each headstone (I narrowly avoided sighing at his pun). He pointed out the oldest stones in the cemetery, rattling off a mix of well-researched facts—which were confirmed by inscriptions carved in granite and worn away by the seasons—and completely fabricated stories.

James wasn't here for a funeral after all. No wonder he'd looked baffled whenever I brought it up. He'd been scoping out the cemetery for filming.

Julian pointed to a gravestone and claimed the "spirit resident" here was not the person whose name was on the stone but rather a doctor who'd been brutally murdered, the body hidden so well it still hadn't been found to this day. The ghost haunted empty graves like this one—where, Julian claimed, grave robbers had dug up the original resident in the 1880s—and was forced to remain a spirit until his body was found and properly buried. I admired his ability to spin half-truths into something spooky. If only I'd had half the ambition; though I'd tried to include facts as research allowed, my stories were usually the tallest of tales—beanstalk required.

I leaned in toward James, and he met my lean part-way. My cheek brushed the shoulder of his wool coat, his cool, clean scent wrapping me like a blanket. I spoke in a hushed tone, trying not to draw attention to myself.

"The grave *is* empty, but only because the man's will demanded he be taken back to New York City for burial. They'd already dug the grave and etched the headstone so they just left it. As for the ghost squatting in the empty grave, I assume he's talking about Dr. Thompson, who disappeared when I was a kid, and *she* was later found, alive, in Vegas. Married to a drag king Elvis impersonator. Not dead." I rolled my eyes. "There aren't many modern graves here—the town stopped selling plots in the nineties or something. Most of these graves are from Revolutionary War soldiers, actually. Soldiers who came home, lived long lives, and died quite untragically. Sorry."

James chuckled but didn't reply.

Grave after grave, Julian chatted about romance gone wrong and woeful accidents, stories too wild to be true and ghosts "too ghastly to speak of." Grave after grave, I whispered footnotes and flat-out denials where necessary. James raised his eyebrows at each correction I made, but never contradicted me.

"And here we have poor old Frederick, dead of an accident in 1908. His carriage overturned right over there, exactly on the cemetery line, and his spirit still haunts this space today." Heads turned as Julian gestured to the alleged site of the accident.

I inhaled, ready to correct the story in another whispered exchange, when James gasped.

"I see something!" he said loud enough for the folks around us to hear. "It's like. . . . a fog. I see it, right there." He pointed a shaky finger toward the headstone. Sharp inhalations sounded around us and the tour-goers chattered about the fog. Most confirmed that they, too, could see a mist rising from the grave, while deniers squinted and tried to spot something that wasn't there.

My eyes were drawn to the spot as well, against my wishes. I wasn't going to fall for a story like that. All of this was clearly staged, so searching for a ghost was embarrassing to say the least, but still, I scanned the cemetery, searching anyway. I pulled my arms around myself and shook away a shiver, freezing but still unwilling to admit it.

James grasped my wrist—a new shiver ran through my spine at the gentle contact—and tipped his head toward the exit. "Ready to go? My work here is done."

We shuffled through the crunchy top layer of snow, boots kicking up chunks of melted-then-frozen-then-melted precipitation. As we trudged toward the exit, I chewed the inside of my cheek, trying to avoid starting a Q&A session.

"I'd pay money for *your* tour, forget about Julian," James said. "The narration is much more believable." He scanned my profile, and I pretended not to notice. "The company's a million times better, too."

When our eyes met, his mouth curved upward, and his lips parted in a smile so bursting with sincerity that my breath caught.

I cleared my throat and broke eye contact. "So, you're a filmmaker on the move, huh? How fancy," I said, paying more attention to crossing the empty parking lot than was necessary. *Get attached, get your heart broken when he leaves.* It was lesson I'd learned a dozen times over.

He shrugged. "Julian and I are making a documentary about Stowe's haunted history for an indie docu-film festival contest. I can't take much credit, though. The film is mostly Julian's doing; I kind of fell into this business. It used to be that if he couldn't find the bodies to fill scenes, I'd jump in when needed. Riding along and crashing with the crew was a cheap way to travel. I've always explored wherever he and the crew landed, but this time, I've got the 'codirector' title."

"Sounds like a story a fugitive would tell. Admit it, you're on the run." I narrowed my eyes. "What is it, bank robber? Murderer? You can tell me. I won't tell a soul."

"It's not really what I'm running from, I guess. More what I'm running *to*. I figure, if I tag along long enough, maybe I'll find my calling. There are dozens of states and hundreds of countries to explore. One of 'em has to be right for me, right?"

And there it was. A man on a mission, searching the world for "just right."

"Cold?" he asked.

I nodded.

He wrapped an arm around my shoulders, tucking me into the warm nest of his body. I pressed into his side, letting him envelop me in his radiating heat. I exhaled, forcing the tension from my shoulders and neck, making myself chill and accept the closeness. He was just keeping me from freezing. Nothing more. The plan was still the same: hang out and move on.

But the more I leaned into him, the warmer he felt. I wanted to collapse into him and soak it all up.

"How the hell are you so hot?" I asked.

He grinned and waggled his eyebrows. "Hot?"

"You know, your body temperature is above average." My cheeks burned, despite the frigid outdoor temp.

"I have about twenty hand warmers tucked into my inner pockets. I thought a Vermont girl like you would have learned that trick by now."

Lulu shook, the echo of her dog tags ringing through the frigid winter air. She pranced, weaving back and forth, tugging her leash against the back of my knee as she danced between us, her paws barely keeping contact with the ground for more than a second with each hop.

"You're not the only one who's chilly, I guess. I should probably get her home."

"Oh," I said, glancing at the dog. He'd fulfilled his required duties. I'd been occupied long enough to get out of dinner, so he was off the hook. But a mild flutter had begun in the pit of my stomach—hesitation to say goodbye, a wish for just a little more time before parting.

"I'm about a thirty second walk, that way." James pointed across the road, toward the spookiest inn in town.

"You're staying at the Green Mountain Inn?" I hiked an eyebrow sky-high and crossed my arms.

"No," he said. "I cut through the tree line to get to the lodge we've rented for the season."

The air *wooshed* out of me, starting low where my reluctance to part had been and barreling through my chest. The season. Until spring?

"And here I thought you were a vacationer."

His arm tightened around my shoulders slightly as we stepped off the curb to cross the road. "What? Why'd you think that?"

"Yankees cap, New York plates, out of state area code, a strut like you've got somewhere better to be . . ." I ticked items off down the list of signs.

He *tsked* and shook his head. "Sounds like someone's been paying some close attention."

I reached a hand across my chest and flicked his arm lightly. When we reached the opposite side of the road, we stepped up onto the sidewalk in sync. "I just like to know everything I can about the people who come into my store to harass me."

He released his hold and the chill snuck back in where his body had been pressed against mine. He took a step toward the inn's parking area, then stopped so abruptly I bumped into his shoulder.

"Well, I'll just head back to my car, then." I pointed, limply, in the direction of Dog-Eared. A long, cold walk in the dark.

"Do you . . ." He shoved his hands into his pockets. Lulu barked and pulled slightly against the leash, in the direction of the lodge.

My breath hitched as I waited for him to continue his thought. Not an inn, not a brief stay. It wasn't forever, but it was longer than only a few days. My determination to avoid getting close was waning.

"Look." He brushed the back of a gloved hand across his forehead and shuffled his feet in the crunchy rock salt strewn across the sidewalk. "I know I'm just some kind of parent-deterrent, but I'd like to get to know you better, Lex. Would you like to have dinner with me?"

Yes. Dinner, or drinks, or another forty-five minutes spent wandering a cemetery alone or with a dozen other people, just for the chance to watch his eyes light up when I reacted to his teasing.

"Sure, when are you available?" I fumbled for my phone to make a show of looking at my calendar to set a date. He didn't have to know that my only solid plans were opening and closing the store daily until I died. I had to look like I had a life.

"How about now?" He offered his hand.

My mind went blank. I reached out and twined my fingers within his. He squeezed my hand gently and tipped his head toward the hedges at the back of the inn's parking lot. "Let's get Lulu inside, and I'll warm up my car."

I ducked between icy cedar branches and brushed away the twigs that tugged and snagged in my hair. Lulu bounced and barked, then rushed toward the door, tugging James along behind her. His body jolted away from mine as Lulu dragged him toward the front steps. He released his grip on my hand just in time to keep me from tumbling to the ground from the pull.

But my resolve was crumbling, and I was about two well-chosen words away from falling anyway.

Haunted Happenings transcript

Date: December 9, 2006

Location: Gazebo, Stowe Free Library

> **Luna:** Hello and a haunted evening to you all. It's a snowy night here in Stowe. We got a tip about some activity here at the gazebo in town and thought we'd come to investigate. The word around town is that people are hearing whispering while they sit inside the gazebo, usually right in the center. So, we're going to spend a little time listening in to see what's going on. I'll just [Luna grunts] sit here [grunts again] and see what I hear.

[Silent timelapse video spanning 10 seconds.]

> **Luna:** I have been here about twenty minutes and, so far, it's been quiet. I'm wondering if it's these string lights keeping any spirits from stopping by. They're pretty bright so what if we—

[Lights all shut off suddenly. Luna and Natalie gasp.]

> **Natalie:** Luna. Luna, I didn't do that. Did you?
> **Luna:** I didn't move a muscle.
> **Natalie:** Me either. I'll . . . Hang on, adjust the settings on the camera, don't let the spirits go anywhere.
> **Luna:** [Sarcastic] Sure, okay . . .

[Slight rustling noises while camera view cycles to a night vision coloring.]

> **Luna:** All good? Okay, I'm getting the thumbs up from Natalie that the camera is good to go. Seeing anything strange on your end, Nat?
> **Natalie:** You've definitely got company. I'm seeing a halo on the viewfinder here. Can you get them to communicate?
> **Luna:** I didn't bring anything. I didn't expect any visitors. Uh, hi, spirit? Are you there?

[A pause. The string lights flick on and off; Luna and Natalie inhale audibly.]

> **Luna:** Oh, okay. Well. Hi, hi there. I'm Luna. This is Natalie. I'm not sure how to figure out your name. Too bad we can't get a hint.

[A beat of silence before the lights begin to turn on and off.]

> **Natalie:** That's my cue, I think it's time to get out of—
> **Luna:** No, wait, Natalie. Is that Morse code? [Luna squints at the lights and whispers, inaudible.] Carol . . . Caroline?

[Lights flick off, then back to solid.]

> **Natalie:** Okay that's it. [Boots crunching on snow, filming continues shakily as Natalie walks around the back of the gazebo.] Who's out here? Come on, stop messing around. [Camera pans the area but there's nobody to be found.]

CHAPTER SEVEN

James chose the pizza place slash bar mostly frequented by the après ski crowd. I held my fingers to the car vent to chase away the tingling cold as he navigated dark, snow-swept streets. James fumbled in the compartment between our seats and tugged a pair of gloves from inside it, handing them to me. They were black leather and worn to perfection, the tiny bumps on the palm and fingertips ghostly reminders of a grip no longer providing fully fledged traction. I slipped my hands inside, grateful for the extra layer against the cold, and mentally kicked myself for forgetting my own gloves in the first place.

There was a line when we arrived, but he slipped past the waiting crowd and led me to the bar. The local nightlife and I weren't well acquainted. Natalie and I had our fair share of girls' nights out, but they tended to end before nine, and I never had more than two drinks since I could get a hangover by *looking* at a bottle of vodka. But I listed drink names in my head while I hopped onto a stool and waited for James to do the same.

Instead, the bartender pointed at James, then jabbed a thumb over his shoulder toward a booth in the back of the restaurant. James offered his hand again—though I was getting used to the warmth of his smooth palm against mine, something swelled inside my chest each time we made contact. He led me to the empty table, grabbing two menus on his way past the end of the bar. He waved them over his head. I turned to look at the bartender, who offered a two-finger wave in response.

"What service," I said.

"I tip really well. It comes in handy when I want a last-minute table. I also interviewed the restaurant owner about the alleged ghost that haunts the kitchen, and they're all really excited about maybe making it into the documentary."

I'd done a whole segment about a kitchen ghost in this exact location—a chef with Julia Child-esque energy who'd fought her way to the top of the male-dominated field and refused to give up the space she'd carved out for herself, even in death. It had to have been a coincidence. I forced the thought from my mind as James took off his coat and unwound his scarf from around his neck, then held out a hand to accept my coat.

"Oh, thanks." I unzipped my puffy monstrosity, cringing at the nylon rustle that came with retro skiwear. If we'd ended up at a themed party at a rented chalet, I'd have fit in. I slipped into the booth, folded my hands on top of the table, and eyed the other patrons. It was jam-packed with people fresh off the mountain, goggle marks still pressed deep into their windburn-flushed cheeks. They mingled at the bar, gathered around the pool tables, and carried half-full pint glasses throughout the restaurant as they chatted. These were not the themed party type; here one minute, gone the next, heading home to the city to start another week at the office.

"What's with this documentary? Do you do any actual research, or just plunk yourselves in any cemetery and make up stories?"

James ran a hand through the hair at the back of his head. "I keep telling the guy he's going to have to get better at research or some local is going to call him out. He's always been a good storyteller. He's got a film crew following him around because he's convinced them this is their big break. Hell, he convinced me to join this one by letting me pick the location. But what he's got in creative drive, he lacks in forethought."

I supposed I couldn't judge them for running around my town, telling ghost stories without any qualifications. I'd made up dozens of ghost stories with even fewer qualifications—and much older, crappier film equipment to boot.

"How'd you get into film making? Hollywood born and raised?" I asked.

"I'm originally from Syracuse, but I've moved around a bit over the last few years. Trying to find where I belong, you know? My father made it clear that I hadn't lived up to his standards, and I was ready to be anywhere-but-there, so here we are."

I pressed my lips together and nodded. Strained parental relationship. Yeah, I knew a bit about that. Maybe he *also* had a sibling who never answered the phone when he called and left his texts on "read" more often than not.

"What about you?" he asked.

"Me? I'm a lifer. I was born here, I'll die here. Nothing can tear me away."

"You've never thought about moving?"

"No, no way. This is where I belong. I'm not a wanderer. I like to have roots."

"Roots are good. Do you have family nearby, then?"

I shook my head and scanned the restaurant again, avoiding eye contact—and having to give answers.

The restaurant's owner stopped by the table, apologizing for the interruption and asking James to come back to the kitchen so he could show him a newspaper clipping he'd found related to the restaurant's ghost story. The timing was perfect. James hadn't done anything to deserve the torture of the whole, lonely story anyway.

"Go ahead. I won't disappear, I promise. I'll order the pizza while you're gone. Any preference?"

James shrugged. "All pizza is good pizza."

He dashed off to the kitchen with the owner, and after tapping an order into the touchscreen, I busied myself picking at my cuticles waiting for him to come back. When he emerged from the kitchen again, he was laughing with a server. The corners of his eyes crinkled, and he threw his head back to let his laugh ring throughout the building. He patted the server on the shoulder as they parted, then took his seat across from me.

"You seem to have settled in nicely in the short amount of time you've been here."

"I don't want to live my life wandering between work and home. If I'm going to be somewhere, I'm going to connect with that place. We've made stops in Phoenix, stayed in Montana for a bit. Oh, and there was a communal farm in Connecticut—*that* was an experience. But with those projects I was just along for the ride. This time I get to drive a bit. The best part of joining the crew is that I get to talk to everyone. Learn the stories. Even if we're talking about ghosts, each of these people puts so much of *them* into the interview. It's not about a ghost anymore. It becomes about how the ghost exists in relation to the person telling the story. Where the story and storyteller merge is where it all comes together. Part of the story is the place, and the place is the people."

"That's exactly why I'm not planning to leave." I sucked air through my nose and held it in my lungs for a moment before exhaling. I turned my eyes to the table. So much for sparing him my woe. "My grandparents worked themselves to the bone to get here, to this town. They built the house I live in with their bare hands. They're gone now, but I can't help but think they'd be thrilled that I'm still enjoying the life they built here. Even *if* I'm the only one who stuck around. This place is the memories and stories I know so well."

A server swept in with a giant supreme pizza balanced on one hand, and two plates in the other. We thanked him, and James offered me the spatula to take the first slice.

He didn't pry, and he didn't give me the sad look. The one that said "Wow, you're all alone, you poor lost soul. Why don't you go make a life somewhere else?"

Instead, he loaded his plate with two slices, lifted one from the plate and raised it in a foodie-style toast, then ate. After a few bites, he struck up the conversation again. "That's part of the reason I love the bookstore so much."

"Other than the prime literature at incredibly reduced rates?"

He nodded. "I contacted Charles, the store's owner, to request that we film a segment for the documentary there. There's a tale we would like to investigate, involving a bookstore ghost and the ladder that killed her. It's one of those tales that just *screams* cult following, if we can hit the right notes."

I swallowed. That one was way too specific to have been a coincidence. My complete infatuation with Belle exploring Beast's library had made its way into *Haunted Happenings* in an early episode, complete with a tragic ending that would have made Disney quit animation altogether. Unlike the rest of the episodes we filmed, this one had nothing to do with historical events or strong, independent feminists. I wove my jealousy of Belle's books and rolling ladders and animated awe into a ghost story so obviously fake the episode hadn't even gotten a fraction of the views as the rest of them, more than fifteen years later.

"Did he, uh, give you an interview?"

James laughed. "No. He sounded really freaked out, actually. Didn't seem like a fan of spooky stories, in general. Especially not ones that take place in a building he owns."

"Where'd you hear that one?" I asked, plucking at my napkin.

He pointed at me while he finished chewing his latest bite. "There's this great vlog online, from the YouTube glory days—before everything was 'like, this; subscribe, that.'"

"*Haunted Happenings*?" I asked cautiously.

"Yes, that's the one! You know it? I shouldn't be surprised, I guess. Small town, tight community."

I pressed my lips together to suppress a nervous laugh, then began my own monologue. "Welcome to haunted Stowe, Vermont, where a population of restless spirits and wandering sprites roam fearlessly in the afterlife. This highly active town boasts ghosts innumerable, with hundreds of separate sightings each year. Born to a duo of ghost-hunters, I'm your host, Luna Noctem."

James dipped his chin and raised his eyebrows, then offered a tiny golf clap at my performance. It would be silly to keep it from him now. I had to come clean.

"It might be difficult to recognize me without the masquerade mask, purple hair, and Hot Topic dress. Allow me to reintroduce myself." I stretched a hand in his direction. "Luna Noctem, nice to meet you."

The corners of his mouth rose in a tentative smile as his eyes tracked my face, likely trying to detect my younger self in the features. He grasped my hand in a firm handshake, then cleared his throat. "How long were you going to let me run around your town talking about ghost stories before sharing this information?"

I smirked. "It's good to stay a step ahead of the competition. In this case, a whole season ahead, since the twenty-two episodes I filmed basically count as a season of network TV." I drummed my fingertips on the table. "It all started with this book I found at a library book sale, actually. It's full of Vermont ghost stories, and the inscription inside included an AOL Instant Messenger screen name. I messaged the guy like the nosy creeper I am, and learned more than I ever wished to know about ghosts. Turns out, he'd met a man in a Northeastern USA ghost sighting forum, sent him the book as a gift, and they eventually started a relationship. When they split, this book didn't make the cut. Curiosity got me and I became a regular on the forum—mostly it was something to fill the time since my parents were never around. Then my best friend and I launched the vlog, and it started gaining traction. Before we knew it, we had people messaging us on AIM and emailing, asking us to help them prove their ghost sightings to skeptics . . ."

James leaned forward, an elbow propped against the table, hands casually draped. "How do I know you're not just saying this to woo me?"

"Oh, trust me." I cocked my head. "I've already had great success at that. Anyway. We ended the vlog when I went off to college. There were"—I swallowed, trying to decide when was too early to casually drop my anxiety, depression, and attachment disorder details on the guy—"too many all-nighters to squeeze in ghost hunting. Sorry I didn't say anything earlier. I wasn't trying to, like, keep it a secret or anything. It's just one of those silly things I used to do to pass the time."

"No problem," James said. "I wasn't exactly forthcoming about my mission, either. Besides, I might have been a bit starstruck had I known the truth about your identity. After all, you're—I mean, Luna is—a big part of what we're doing here."

I raised an eyebrow, but didn't interrupt. The conversation was about to get extra weird, or really flattering—and I wasn't against sticking around to figure out which.

He cleared his throat. "I found the vlog during my senior year. My parents were divorcing and everything felt, uh, unbalanced. I wanted to be anywhere but there, doing anything but listening to them argue over who would keep the boat, and who would fork over the tuition for my first year at college. *Haunted Happenings* gave me an escape, I guess. It was my gateway to ghost lore, but it was also a way to help me disappear."

"Ironic," I said, folding my hands on the table in front of me. "I'd started recording because my parents were never around, and I felt forgotten. I was looking for something to ground me and something to help me leave a mark."

"It seems we both got what we were looking for, then," James said. He shook red pepper flakes onto the slice of pizza that remained on his plate, then ate.

We fell into an easy silence, nothing but bar chatter cutting through. After I finished my third slice, I leaned back in the booth and watched as he wiped grease from his fingertips. His movements were slow and steady, nothing hurried or urgent about it.

It was a relief to simply exist in each other's worlds without the expectations or pressures that often came with first dates. My getting-ready jitters had been for nothing, it seemed. I could open up about it, let him know what was on my mind. But would making myself that vulnerable ruin the good thing we had going? There was only one way to find out.

"I like how quiet is easy with you around," I said. "There's no need to fill the silence."

He leaned forward, placed both elbows on the table, and clasped his hands one on top of the other. "I like you." He tipped his head and gave me that lopsided grin that promised mischief. His bright eyes were a bullet train on a direct route to my soul. Last stop, coming right up—get off now or you're going along for the ride.

"I think I like you, too." The admission was torn from me. I'd lost control of my mind and mouth. It was something about the dim lighting in the restaurant and the way his eyes didn't leave mine for a second while he was making his confession. The sincerity and the suddenness collided, catching me off-guard, and I was entirely unable to contain the truth.

"I'm going to kiss you now," he said. He rose from his side of the table, took the two tiny steps required to get to my end, then slipped into the booth beside me. Supporting himself with a hand on the bench between us, he brought his free hand to my cheek. My hair rustled beneath his palm, so he brushed it out of the way and tucked it behind my ear, looking at me and through me and into me all at once. His eyes—usually dark under the shadow of his infamous ball cap—glinted deep brown and gold in the overhead lamp. We sat that way, eyes locked, for breath after breath, or maybe just a single exhale.

"So do it then." I raised my chin and lifted my eyebrows. *Come and get it.*

"Okay," he whispered. He drew his thumb along my jawline, then swiped a fingertip across my lips, which pressed together involuntarily the moment the contact disappeared. My mind went from level-headed to romance-cover-level dramatics in a second. My heart crashed inside my chest like waves on the rocky shore, his eyes the nearest thing to a lighthouse beacon, drawing me in with a siren's song rather than warning me away. The only thing that *was* was him and me, and the mere inches of space between us.

He closed the distance. Smooth lips pressed against mine and a Fourth of July grand finale lit up behind my eyelids at the subtle scrape of his stubbled chin and evergreen snowmelt scent.

William Goldman had ranked the best kisses through history in terms of passion. Ten-year-old me heard that line and resolved to base every romantic interaction I'd ever have on Buttercup and Westley. A worthy scale, yes. But this kiss was more than passion alone. His lips were wanting and giving, all in one. My lips curled into a smile against his mouth.

So much for resisting.

CHAPTER EIGHT

After one kiss from James, Vermont's most attractive and surprisingly sensitive out-of-towner had gone from convenient excuse to the only thing on my mind. I couldn't pinpoint the moment that had done it. It could have been the way his dog wagged her tail whenever he spoke or the fact that we were already connected through the ghost stories we used to navigate the world. Or that he'd been willing to hang out with the weird woman who worked at the bookstore simply because she wanted to avoid her parents. He added his phone number to my contacts, helpfully listed under the name "Ghost Guy," as if I'd forget, before we said goodbye that night.

I arrived at the bookstore the next morning to find a pair of gloves, a snack-sized zipper-top baggie with dog treats, and a note classily duct-taped to the door.

Will you do me the honor of joining Lucy in the Sky with Diamonds and me on a walk tonight? I'll provide the gloves this time so you don't freeze again. Meet you here?—James

I yanked the gloves and treats off the door's glass, rushed inside to catch my daily Charles check-in, then stabbed the dial button on my phone so hard I nearly dropped it.

It rang. And rang. And rang. I was left, yet again, leaving a horrendous voicemail message.

"Hey there, Lulu. Tell James that I'm absolutely interested in a walk. Exercise is important. Oh, and a horse walked into a bar. The bartender said, 'Why the long face?' If you're not laughing, you're not cool."

Five minutes later, my phone dinged to alert me to a message. Short and sweet:

Ghost Guy: *Looking forward to it.*

After that, the day crawled. No customers in sight, and I'd already completed inventory. No used books to sort, no new personalized copies to add to my own bookshelf. Silent as the grave.

Had my name been listed beside the "Owner" designation on the business cards, there'd be a knitting club that met on Sundays—regardless of book purchases made—and a Thursday night puzzle club. Maybe a weekly true crime podcast listening meeting—with themed coffee specials and a dessert case full of Homicide Halvah and Murderous Macaroons. Wednesday afternoon Lunch and Learns, where local experts popped in to discuss their specialties. Summer book clubs to encourage kids to keep reading. I'd be the Dolly Parton of Stowe, literacy education for all.

Charles insisted money wasn't made by providing free services. But what would I know about building a community? Obviously the guy soaking up sun somewhere along the Florida coastline was better equipped to embrace "local." I was sure he aimed to keep his fingers clutched around the building's deed 'til death.

Which is why the next phone call I received made my jaw literally drop.

I'd already had my daily Charles check-in, so I assumed the call was someone checking if I had a book in stock. When his voice came through, a bit quieter than usual, a little unsure, my heart jumped into my throat. I feared the worst: family emergency or some other bad news.

"Lex, are you aware that Dog-Eared may be haunted?" he asked.

"Is it?" I asked, trying to decide if this news was a pro or con for him. Was it finally the time to pitch my Creepy Caroling idea, where everyone dresses up like a favorite gothic literary icon and sings holiday songs after dark?

His serious tone told me that, no, this was not that event's moment to shine. "I had a very disturbing call from a crew of ghost-hunting experts earlier this week, and I've been trying to decide if I should tell you or not. They want to stake out the store and try to film the ghost for their documentary. They sound very legitimate."

Oh, Charles. His reaction wasn't entirely out of character, given the speed at which he'd once removed a Ouija board from the store after pulling it from the bottom of a dropped off box. I suppressed a laugh.

"I'm happy to give them a tour," I offered. "I can let them in on all of the extra creepy spots, like in the corner by the old map books where there's always a chill in the air. Or the spot where the ladder sticks, and you can almost hear someone screaming as you try to guide it into place."

"Lex, please, stop. I never knew about those things!" He sounded off now—I couldn't quite place the emotion in his voice. Not spooked, but not quite *Charles*, either. "Why didn't you tell me?"

"Well, Charles, it's just ghost stories, right? No big deal."

"Nobody's going to want a haunted building," he said. "Now what am I going to do? All this time, I thought I had an investment property on my hands, and its value is gone, just like that."

"I'm sure someone will still value the store, ghosts or no. It might even be a big draw for customers." I chewed my bottom lip, hoping he'd be soothed. Just what I needed: Charles selling the store because something I'd made up ages ago scared him off.

"I just can't take that risk. I've been considering selling for a while. The back and forth is beginning to wear on me, and now with this . . . it might be time to let go and settle down here."

Shit.

The property would probably get snapped up by a big chain or some city businessperson hellbent on franchising and divvying up Dog-Eared's charm across their hundred other locations, making it *part* of something instead of something all on its own.

All I wanted out of the world was to be able to be surrounded by the words penned by hundreds—thousands!—of brilliant, thoughtful people. I'd done my best to build my own little library, but space was limited and the floors in my house would have buckled by the time I was satisfied. I didn't have the space—or funds—to expand my collection much more. Dog-Eared was my own little haven, bursting with the books I couldn't cram onto my own shelves.

My chest was hollow. If he sold the store, I could find another job. Employment wasn't a concern—there were plenty of local shops looking for a hand and, with ski season in full swing, an abundance of temporary tourism options. But I didn't want those options. I wanted the one I already had.

The truth was, I wasn't ready to let the store go. It had started as a safety net but had become something akin to a fuzzy blanket on a blustery evening. It was part of me—and I'd infused the space with pieces of myself. But I couldn't expect to change his mind, either. He'd established the store, and it was his to do with as he wished. If he chose to offload it, I didn't have much choice but to accept Dog-Eared's fate.

Unless . . .

"I want to buy Dog-Eared, Charles."

The words tumbled out before I even knew what I was saying. But that didn't make them any less true. The phone crackled as Charles remained silent.

"Charles."

He *hmm*ed, like he'd zoned out and was just coming back to the conversation.

"I want to buy the store. I've worked here since high school. You couldn't wait to hire me again when I came back after college. I know this place. I know the customers, and I know the business. I'd fight to keep it the same . . . well, mostly the same. Everyone wonders why I don't move. But Charles, *this* is my move."

"Lex, I'll need to think—"

"You don't have to think. This is the perfect solution. Trust me. This is Dog-Eared's next phase. I can run this store, I can manage a business. Give me one good reason why this isn't the right option."

The line buzzed and crackled slightly as I waited for his answer. He stayed silent.

"I'll pay whatever you want, I won't even haggle. I need this store, Charles. It's the best thing I have going right now."

The line was silent for a long stretch. So long that I'd have assumed the call had dropped, if it weren't for Charles's rhythmic breathing coming through the receiver.

"Legally, I don't have to disclose paranormal activity while selling, but I suppose I've already let that secret slip." He inhaled into the receiver, and it rattled through to my end of the line. "Okay, Lex. Yes. I'm happy to pursue this sale with you. You won't find a better deal. I already spoke to a business real estate agent: Forty thousand dollars takes it all. Inventory, retail space, the business."

"Charles." I nearly choked. "Are you serious? Forty thousand? I don't know if I can pay that." Not because it was an unreasonable amount—in truth, it was a steal—but because his main reason to unload the business was based entirely on a lie. He said he'd been considering selling, but how much of that was honest consideration, and how much was based on the ghost story I'd invented—and James had shared?

"I know the building needs work. But it's got good bones, and there's value in the inventory itself. It's a good investment, especially for someone unconcerned with ghosts."

"Charles, that's not the prob—"

"I know you won't have the savings to cover it," he interrupted. "I'm willing to hold this offer for a short while, so you can arrange financing. But as I said, I've been mulling letting the store go for a while now, and now that the decision's been made, I'd like to get on with it. If you're not going to take it, I will have to list it for sale. What do you say? Are you interested?"

I'd figure out the logistics later. I could pull together my savings, look into business loans, find grants or other assistance to make it happen. My alternative was possibly losing the store to someone who didn't understand it, and that was no real alternative at all. "Absolutely," I said. "I'll need some time, but I am definitely interested. Please, please don't let it go to anyone else until I've exhausted my options."

"Of course not. Does one month sound fair? With the option for extension if you have leads on funding."

"More than fair, thank you so much, Charles. I'll start looking right away."

"If you could, please, keep this between us for now. I'll let you decide what to tell the ghost hunters about the interview—as long as they allow us to strike it from the final cut if for some reason your funding doesn't come through, and I have to sell by other means. We don't want rumors of a haunting holding up a sale."

"Definitely not. You know how ghost stories spread." Slowly, often popping up years later at inopportune times. Or, potentially the most opportunistic of times . . .

We hung up, and I flopped backward in my chair to absorb the news.

He was offering my wildest dreams at a too-reasonable—if currently out of reach—price. The stipulation that I not share the news was smart. There were plenty of people in town who would try to outbid me, and I didn't want to find out if there was a sense of loyalty at play that would keep him from taking the highest offer. Plus, he didn't want the sale to drag, and a bidding war would cause it to. How quickly would he change his mind about that, though, if he found out the store wasn't actually haunted? There wasn't a second to waste. If I missed this chance, I'd never forgive myself.

I stuck the "Back in 5 minutes" sign up on the door and walked across the street to the very same bank my grandfather had used from the moment he settled in Stowe. Half an hour later, paperwork started and a list of required documentation in hand, I slipped back into the store and sank into my favorite comfy leather chair to admire what was potentially going to become my very own bookstore.

If Charles didn't find out the truth about the ghosts.

CHAPTER NINE

By closing time, snowflakes had started to drift lazily from the low-hanging clouds. There was moisture mingling with the flakes, so the chilly twenty-eight degrees wasn't as brutal as it would have been on a dry day. I shuffled papers into manageable stacks, reset the café for morning, slipped on my jacket, and tucked James's gloves into a pocket. The bell chimed a sweet goodbye as I tugged the door shut and jiggled the key in the lock. A separate jingle came, muffled through the falling snow and evening dark. Cheerful and rhythmic, a perfect match to the dog's pleasant little trot.

"Hey there, Lulu," I said, squatting to greet the dog first. I pulled a treat from the baggie in my pocket and wiggled it in front of her snow-covered snout. "I've got something for you, you know. I've been waiting all day to see you."

James sniffed a laugh and crossed his arms, which tugged the leash slightly and made the tags jingle again. "*Lulu* has likewise been looking forward to our walk."

My chest warmed at the sound of his voice. Deep and rich, and cutting straight through any sense I had left. I turned to glance at him, a satisfied smirk plastered across my face. My heart was screaming at me to go in for the kill, but my brain held my limbs hostage.

In the end, my heart's stubbornness won out. "I've got something for you, too, you know." I stood and gripped the lapel of his jacket. The fuzzy wool nipped at my fingertips, loops of fiber snagging against my dry skin. Before I could change my mind, I tugged him closer and closed the distance between us.

"Lucky me," he said. His breath dashed across my face, chasing away the chill that had begun to settle at the tip of my nose and cheeks.

"Hello, you." I leaned in for a kiss, and he slid an arm behind me as our lips connected, tugging me closer. His icy chin and nose were contrasted by his mouth, hot and wanting. The pressure of his soft lips let up ever so slightly, and I cracked my eyes to peek. He was peeking back, the street lamps sparkling in his eyes like fireworks reflecting against the still surface of a lake.

Blood rushed to my cheeks, the warm flush warring with below-freezing temperatures. After a delicious moment, we broke free. My fingertips tingled so I wiggled them to regain feeling—and control—then took a shaky breath.

"You've become a regular." I tugged the gloves from my pocket and pulled them on.

James grinned. "Lulu likes you, what can I say? She's been asking when we'll hang out again, and I just hate to disappoint her."

"Of course, anything for Lulu. So, what's on the agenda, then?"

"Well, since you're the area expert, I was wondering if you wanted to let me in on those local legends you were whispering about in the cemetery."

"I see." I crossed my arms. "You're just using me for documentary research. Free consultant."

"Far from free. I had to woo you with pizza and become the biggest-spending patron at your fine book-and-coffee establishment."

"You've got the patronizing down."

He pressed a hand to his chest and bowed his head. "Thank you, from the bottom of my heart, for the book recommendations and caffeine. Without either, I'd be lost."

"Okay, but are you serious about this tour guide business? Because the ghosts around here and I go way back. We're basically best buds. So, if you're interested, I've got things to show you."

James swept a hand through the air and took half a step backward. "After you."

I dragged him all over town, from the little row of must-be-haunted houses along Maple Street to the inns that gave me a goosebumpy feeling every time I caught a glimpse of a shadow in a window. I zig-zagged my way through town without stopping for breath, and Lulu and James kept up admirably.

We wandered until traffic slowed to a trickle and tourists disappeared to snuggle inside their hotel rooms and rented chalets for the night, resting up and icing muscles stressed from their runs down the slopes. But our trio kept wandering. Shin-high snow and weather-obstructed views couldn't keep us indoors. Not on a night as gloriously blustery as this.

Something about gliding my way down my icy hometown sidewalk hit different with company, especially when they were seeing it with new eyes. Seeing what I saw in it, reveling in the history and tales whispered from person to person. With bits and pieces of my vlog stories woven in, I painted the town as a significantly eerie locale—not that there weren't enough stories to have earned it the title already. All my vlog had done was add to the already long list of rumored hauntings.

"You like this place a little, huh?" James leaned against a lamppost and kicked one heel up, toes tipped into the building snowpack.

"Just a little." I beamed, eyeing the immense red building across the road from us. The white trim was obscured by falling flakes, but the walls stood out like a beacon against the snow. I nodded my head toward the building. "Do you know about that one?"

James examined the building, one eyebrow hitched as he considered. "Isn't that the one with the piano-playing ghost?"

"Ohh, he shoots, he misses. Tap-dancing ghost, actually. He dances on the roof when it snows. I thought you said you were a ghost hunter. This seems like super important supernatural expert knowledge."

"I'm new to the area. There's a learning curve. He hasn't revealed himself to me yet. Pick the excuse that most resonates with you." He raised a brow. "Is this really the kind of thing locals would chat about randomly?"

"Oh, we all talk about Boots."

"Boots?"

"The ghost. Boots. He's kind of a big deal."

"Then I am grateful for the tip. Maybe we'll talk them into granting us an exclusive interview. Thanks for the free advice."

I kicked a clump of snow in his direction. It splattered against his dark jeans, leaving a white dandelion-puff-shaped silhouette on the denim. "Next time, don't expect me to give this info for so cheap. I expect compensation in exchange for the tour guide treatment."

James tilted backward, crossed his arms, and grinned. "Oh yeah? What kind of compensation?"

"Make me an offer I can't refuse." I leaned in and wrinkled my nose teasingly, then brushed a snowflake from the front of his coat. He reached up and wrapped his hand around my wrist, covering my hand with his and looking into my eyes.

Lulu dashed behind me, pulling her leash like a tripwire against my legs, and I lurched forward from the force. James swept both arms around me and pulled me in close. Not ignoring the opportunity so perfectly presented, I pressed him against the lamppost. Lulu barked and stepped, foot to foot, beside me.

"Proud of yourself?" I asked, narrowing my eyes playfully at the dog.

"Good girl." James nodded at Lulu, pulled his arms tighter around my waist to draw me into a cold-and-snow scented embrace, then dipped down for a kiss. His lips pressed into mine, and for a glorious moment, my heart stopped beating. When he pulled my lower lip between his teeth, it took every ounce of willpower to keep my knees from buckling. We swayed together, silhouetted in the glow of a streetlight.

Lulu let out a sharp bark and tugged at her leash, aiming homeward and shuffling her feet in the snow to get her point across.

James broke away from the kiss and pulled his Yankees cap off his head. He swiped his dark hair back into place, tugged the cap over it again, and adjusted it, pulling the brim low enough to shadow his eyes. I'd daydreamed about this very sight for days. As my heart thudded against my ribcage, he stepped away. A vacuum of cold and ice replaced the warmth he was putting off, and I shivered, missing the proximity immediately. Not just for the outer warmth, but for the way it made my head spin when he was close.

"She's cold, isn't she?" I asked.

"We've been out here for hours. You sure know how to pack it all in. I should get her back." His eyes held mine as he drew a thumb along my cheek. "Come home with me?"

My legs quivered, from cold or excitement or a bit of both at once.

My phone rang. I intended to hit *ignore*, but I groaned when I caught the name on the screen. I turned it toward James. "My mother. I should answer this. I've been ignoring her to prevent being the disappointing daughter—again—but there's only so much avoiding I can do."

James squeezed my hand and leaned in to press a final, quick kiss to my forehead. His lips were icy against my skin, but the contact still managed to warm me from the inside out. He held Lulu's leash with one hand and offered a low goodbye wave with the other. Nothing but the crunch of his footsteps broke the winter silence.

I filled my lungs with icy air, closed my eyes, and answered the phone.

"Hi, Mom, what's up?" My squeaking footsteps echoed in the opposite direction as James's as I trudged along the sidewalk back to my car.

"'What's up' is that your father and I want to talk with you."

"Is this one of those meetings that could be an email?" My car's lights flicked on when I hit the unlock button and the interior light sparkled off the frosted windshield. A million snow crystals danced in my vision. I started the engine, poked at the defrost settings, and shook off a shiver. My toes were solid ice and moisture crept up my pant legs, but nothing could freeze out the warm throb in my chest that seemed to pick up pace as I pictured James strolling away.

"It can wait until Christmas. I just wanted to confirm when your flight is."

"Not booked, because I had to use my trip money to fix the furnace last month."

"You're never going to get a plane ticket this close to Christmas," she scolded. "You should have gotten your flight settled weeks ago."

"I'm not coming, Mom."

"Of course you are. It's the one time per year you visit us, and we were all counting on you being here."

Probably so they could all unite against me in the California versus Vermont debate.

"I can't produce a full bank account just because the calendar says it's December." I pinched the bridge of my nose. "You said we needed to talk. Is it a Christmas-visit-only discussion, or it something we can just talk about now?" Over the phone, not in person where my facial expressions would give me away.

"If you insist." Mom sighed. "Your father and I have a plan for that house of yours. It is obviously a money pit, and we would like to cover the cost of listing the house for sale, including paying the closing fees."

"How is selling my home going to make *any* of this better?" I smacked a fist off the edge of the steering wheel, then shook away the tingle it left behind. "It's where I live, Mom. It's where you grew up."

"You're perfectly capable of relocating. Rent an apartment. There are plenty of lovely places available here."

"You've got to be joking."

"Please, try to understand our position here. You've just canceled Christmas because of another home repair. We couldn't help but notice the peeling exterior paint during our last visit. If you can't catch up, you'll be bleeding equity. Had you followed through with college,

80

maybe you'd have a career to support your scrambling to patch windows and walls as quickly as they crumbled."

Had I continued with college, I'd have started missing classes because I was inching toward never being able to leave the dorm. I'd have failed out instead of deciding to leave for my own mental health. Familiarity meant safety; routine brought relief. Coming home—pressing reset—let me feel something like whole again. That and regular sessions with my therapist. But it wasn't convenient for them to accept or understand my choices.

"My job supports me just fine." I drummed my fingertips on the gear shift.

"We want to know that you're planning for your future. You're thirty-three—it's time you acted like it. Make a career move, get a real job, and stop playing small-town bookseller like your life is a Christmas movie."

My heart was caving in. *They'd* chosen to leave; *they'd* found a city to call theirs and decided to create a new life there without me. They'd known I'd never follow, not that they'd given me the chance. Picking up and taking off because their favorite daughter was more fun to brag about to all their friends was shitty enough without also forcing me to change to suit them.

"I like my job, and I like my house. Grampa built that house—specifically so his grandkids would have somewhere to go home to. I *like* being here. I like my home. For once, I'd like you to consider my feelings and how hard I'm trying to build the life that's right for me."

I could almost hear her eye-roll over the phone line. "Alex, you're so dramatic. Please at least consider the idea, and what doors it may open for you. And we're not finished discussing your Christmas visit."

The line went silent without a goodbye. The idea of selling *my* house—just giving it to some new person like they'd have any claim to it—left a dark pit deep inside my ribs. My family never believed my choices were valid. Not in a million years would they consider where I was coming from. I didn't fit their mold for perfect, and my refusal to bend to their will kept me planted in the "bad daughter" zone.

Maybe Jordan had an opinion on the house situation. She'd grown up there, too. We'd shared a room for years, until she begged her way into taking over Mom's office because it was too embarrassing to share a room with her little sister. Even if she didn't have the same attachment to the physical location, maybe she'd stick up for me. Having her in my corner might be enough to get our parents to back off.

The phone rang a few times before her energetic voice came through the line—on her voicemail recording. I hung up without leaving a message. I couldn't remember the last time she'd returned my call, or even answered without letting me go to voicemail. It was pointless to keep trying when all it did was set me up for disappointment.

I tossed my phone into the passenger seat less gently than intended, and it bounced and skidded between the seat and door. I leaned forward and rested my head on the still-chilled steering wheel until I gathered myself enough to drive home.

CHAPTER TEN

Julian and James treated me to lunch at the top pizza place in town. While both gregarious, their affable natures presented differently. James's immediate conversation was his priority—and his attentiveness was unmatched. Julian, however, put out a welcoming air that could pull an entire room into any discussion. Magnetic. They complemented each other perfectly, and it was clear why James got along with him so well. I'd only just met Julian and was already counting him among friends.

After we ate, we wandered a couple of shops, and dropped into The Barn for some coffee—no cameras and "minimal ghost chat." The fact that I'd been duped didn't occur to me until we were crammed together along the counter at The Barn, on our third round of subpar drip coffee, and Julian popped the big question.

"So Alex, I hear you're something of an expert in the paranormal?"

I leveled a glare at James. "You know, giving up your sources is frowned upon."

James held up his hands and shook his head. "I said ease into it, dude. This is not easing into it."

There were worse things than to be hailed as the town's ghost expert—but I hadn't been on the scene in years. Besides, the kind of hauntings I was an expert in probably weren't quite right—or real enough—for a couple of real-life ghosthunters.

"I know a bit about the spooky history of the town, yes. I can get you in touch with people who know more."

"Would you, say, give an interview?"

"What, for the show?"

"Documentary," Julian said.

"Tomato, to-mah-to," James replied with a smirk.

I paused. "I think I need a little more information before agreeing to anything." Because what would happen if they disproved the bookstore ghost—would Charles take back the offer? If James and Julian realized none of *Haunted Happenings* was true, would they reveal it all as a farce, or be upset with me for deceiving them? "Are you ghost-hunting, ghost-busting, or ghost-making-up?"

Julian tapped his chin as he considered. "Ghost-investigating, I'd say."

"I'm listening." I turned toward him and crossed my legs.

"Okay, so you have three kinds of ghost people. Believers, skeptics, and undecided." He counted on his fingers.

"Are you trying to convince the skeptics, or contradict the believers?" Persuading skeptics, I could do. Assisting as they tried to debunk *my* stories would be a hard pass.

"I'd say neither. Even if there's no such thing as ghosts—as in spirits that haunt from beyond—just a discussion about whether we have supernatural visitors leaves an impression on a person, no matter where they land on the belief scale."

"Sounds like a psychology experiment to me." I raised my eyebrows as I sipped the last of my coffee.

Julian cracked a wide smile. "Part of our goal is to examine how the suggestion of spirits affects people while *documenting*"—he raised his eyebrows at James—"local legends and exploring how ghost stories are created and spread. But yes, we're also trying to get footage of actual ghosts and hauntings as we do it. A double-whammy."

"And since Luna seems to have contributed to the popularity and longevity of several local legends, we thought you'd be an ideal interviewee," James suggested.

"Are you just trying to ride whatever's left of my lingering YouTube fame?" I raised an eyebrow.

"The number one rule in show biz is to use your connections," Julian said. "No qualms here."

"Nor here," James said.

"Entirely qualmless, myself," I said. If anything, keeping an eye on their filming progress could nudge them toward the supposed bookstore ghost a bit, just to ensure Charles kept thinking the store was haunted. It probably wasn't the most moral decision I'd made, but they seemed more interested in telling a great story than verifying the presence of ghosts. Authenticity seemed to be the last thing on their minds—there was no way Julian thought his cemetery tales were factual. They'd recruited tourists from inns and resorts rather than locals who could contradict them.

But they both seemed to land somewhere between believer and undecided—maybe even excited at the prospect of *proving* the stories? There was no benefit in revealing that *Haunted Happenings* was fake. Their creative spark seemed to come from their curiosity, and I wasn't going to ruin it by telling them ghosts *weren't* real. We could all benefit: they'd weave a riveting story, Charles would get to fully retire, and I could buy the store. No harm, no foul.

If they wanted to play with ghosts, I could make that happen. I gestured to James and Julian to hold please, grabbed my phone, and dialed Natalie's number. She answered on the third ring—the huffing and puffing coming through the line meant she was either shoveling, cutting trees, or some combination of the two.

"Hey Nat, sorry. I'll call back?"

"No, no, we're good. What's up?"

"I was wondering if we could hook up the boys for a little fun." After being spoiled by rides whenever I wanted, I'd come to believe a horse-drawn sleigh was the only way to travel—especially when ghost hunting was involved. "Free at all this week?"

I savored the cautiously excited look that crossed between Julian and James, let a tiny smirk slip, then forced my face back to neutral.

"Dad's closing the tree farm early on Thursday to catch up on some workshop stuff. Where to?"

"I thought we'd give James—that guy from the other night—and his friends a real welcome and introduce them to Emily."

James's head swiveled at the mention of Emily. I'd covered her on *Haunted Happenings* so he definitely knew the story.

"Is Luna making a comeback?" Nat asked. "*Haunted Happenings*, the reboot?"

"Don't get ahead of yourself," I cautioned.

"Fine, fine. Just saying, you've got fans out there who would love more episodes."

"Two are sitting right here." I nudged James's knee with mine, and he bumped me in return. "They're filming a documentary about Stowe's ghosts and wanted a little insider information."

"Ah, so you're keeping your eye on the competition," she joked.

"Not quite. They're looking for proof that the town's ghost stories are true and thought we could help." I eyed James and Julian, who both leaned in to listen as I explained the situation to Nat, trying to get her on board—without giving away the vlog's secret. Given that she'd been suggesting I revive the vlog for years, it didn't take much convincing.

"Going all out, or is this strictly a research mission? I can recruit the guys."

Nat's older brother Derick and his friends always provided the best special effects. They were pros when it came to capturing flickering lights, levitating orbs, and eerie sound effects on film.

"Leave them out of it for now, but depending on how the trip goes tonight, we may need them later."

Natalie teased me about trying to impress the tourists—"usually you're chasing them away, not inviting them for a night out"—and we hung up.

"It's settled," I told Julian and James. "Thursday. Come prepared to be scared. And, umm. Dress warm." I plucked at the collar of James's wool coat and wiggled my eyebrows at him.

*　*　*

Thursday evening, James and Julian bundled up, as recommended, and met me at my place. I pressed thermoses filled to the brim with hot cocoa into their hands, handed off baggies of marshmallows, and tipped my head toward the back door. "This way."

They exchanged curious glances but followed me through the kitchen and out the back. James had a small camera bag slung over his shoulder. Just as I tugged the door shut behind me, wobbling lights and tall shadows climbed across the snow-covered back yard and a gentle jingle rang through the flake-filled air. Natalie's sleigh came into view through the falling snow, complete with two giant horses who tossed their manes. She circled the backyard in a dramatic arc before pulling to a stop at the porch steps.

"This is Natalie and the team." I ruffled each horse's mane as I introduced them. James lit up, following me down the steps and shuffling booted feet through the snow to get to the horses. Julian was more hesitant, but he followed James. "Holly and Jolly. Hey boys, how's it going?" I pulled a carrot from my pocket, snapped it in half, and offered a chunk to each horse. They left behind slime when they lipped the carrots out of my palms, so I scrubbed my hands off on my jacket and pointed the way for Julian and James. They climbed into the sleigh one after the other—Julian gripping the back of the seat as he shuffled in, as if the horses would take off without warning, and James practically bouncing with delight—and slid over to make space for me. I wiggled in, then tugged the festive plaid wool blanket up over our legs.

I handed Natalie her thermos. "We're ready to roll."

Natalie and I had gotten together for a haunting pregame planning session at my house earlier in the day. We'd toned it down considerably from the days of yore, when we'd covered a whiteboard in enough dashes, dots, and arrows to rival a football playbook. All the camera angles we'd need to get the spookiest orbs and reflections. Storytelling bullet points for me to memorize after I found out that "on the fly" wasn't a mode that worked for me. Staging for when we pulled Natalie's brother and his friends in for the more involved vlog episodes. This time, I'd filled her in on the bookstore news, and we focused on how to sell a haunting without being in control—and ambience was our method of choice. I'd forgotten just how alive I felt while plotting and staging tales of the undead—how strangely wonderful it was to plant pieces of myself throughout this town, even if the method was unconventional.

She tapped the reins and jiggled the switch, and the horses pulled away in total sync, like an equine ballet. Julian grasped the blanket's edge as we pulled away, the lurch of the sleigh traveling through his whole body until he regained balance. James *whooped*, then chuckled as the sound rang through the dark forest. They both gripped their thermoses of hot chocolate as we slid through the snow. Lights hung from the sleigh, illuminating only a sliver of the path ahead, darkness swallowing up the world behind us as we pressed on. The soft swish of horse tails, subtle click of hooves, and occasional scraping of sleigh runners against stone or log were all that dared break the quiet of the night.

"You're allowed to talk," I told James. "Honest."

"It's just so peaceful." He reached beneath the blanket and squeezed my gloved hand in his. I couldn't feel his skin or even the heat of him through the layers of winter gear, but my chest warmed at the contact.

"This is my preferred mode of transportation," Natalie called over her shoulder. "Usually, the horses are busy pleasing tourists by hauling trees from stand to car during our Old-Fashioned Christmas week, running sleigh tours for guests, Valentine's couples' rides through town, or hauling wagons filled with sap barrels during sugaring season.

Nighttime sleigh rides are the only chance I get to really enjoy it, so thanks for the opportunity."

"You just do this for fun?" James asked.

"Not as much lately," I answered, "but yeah. We used to tack them up and take the wagon to the store in secret, until we got the wagon stuck in the mud on a back road one day. We had to ride the horses home. After Natalie's dad dug out the wagon, he decided it was better to teach us to do it the right way rather than risk something worse."

"You had to clean stalls for a week to keep him from telling your parents about it," Nat said.

"Yup. They were the cleanest stalls I've ever seen. Spotless. Five-star accommodations."

"He didn't tell?" Julian asked.

"No, but they found out anyway. They were in Chicago at the time. Or maybe Washington. Who knows. Not here, as usual. Anyway, someone called to berate them for letting their daughter run around like a feral child. I was grounded, which didn't do much good because I was staying with Natalie for the month and her parents don't believe in grounding to teach lessons."

"Nope." Natalie laughed, and the sound bounced off snow-covered logs and returned to us muffled. "They believe in physical labor. Was that the summer we had to scrape and paint the shed?"

"No, the shed was because you stole your brother's car and hid it down by the brook. The wagon was when he made us weed the garden, and you pulled up the radishes instead of the weeds."

"Eww, radishes." Natalie stuck her tongue out in an exaggerated grimace that rivaled Mr. Yuck stickers. "I maintain that I had no idea what I was doing, it wasn't premeditated, and I never would have had I known my parents intended to serve radish salad at the inn all summer."

"I gather you two have known each other for a while?" Julian asked.

"Only since birth. Her brother and my *perfect* sister are the same age, and we were born within weeks of each other. I'm like Nat's family's second daughter, though. I spent more time there than at my own home, even when my parents were around. It's probably why their picking up and leaving didn't sting as much as it should have. I still had family here, even if it wasn't by blood."

"Aww, Lex," Natalie said. She looked back at me and reached one hand behind her. She flailed her hand, trying to make contact, so I reached up and accepted a squeeze. "Lucky for Lex, I'll be stuck here forever. So she'll have company in her stubborn desire to remain in Stowe until she croaks."

We took the bumpy path down the side of the hill—more of a grass-and-rock ramp than travel-worthy roadway—and cut onto the dark dirt road that bisected the woods. The whisper-quiet swish of sleigh runners turned sharp and metallic on the icy lane. Julian and James jostled and gripped the blanket at their knees as we took the sharp corner.

"Amateurs." I sniffed a laugh and James widened his eyes in mock surprise at the insult.

We slid along the road briefly, and Nat slowed the horses to stop at our destination.

"Oh, I'm definitely sensing something here," Natalie said. She pressed fingertips to her temples, closed her eyes, and swung her head back and forth as if relying on echolocation to spot a spirit.

I snorted. "Don't mock the poor guy, Natalie. He makes a living doing this."

"Here to help, not ridicule. Got it." She looped the reins in one hand and hopped out of the sleigh. She rubbed Jolly on the back and gave him a scratch beneath the harness. "I'll hang with the boys if you want to do your thing. If it seems quiet, I'll tie them and join you."

James and Julian jumped from the sleigh and started toward the bridge.

"Wait," I said. I reached into my pocket and tugged a few quarters from inside. "She likes it when we bring gifts."

I tucked the quarters into their palms, then swept a hand through the snowy darkness. The sleigh's lanterns cast a wizardly shadow across the snowbanks built up along the edge of the road. From the pull-off, the road narrowed. The sweep of dirt and gravel gave way to a wood-floored covered bridge; its weathered siding stood shadow-dark surrounded by trees. Lantern glow flickered through the windows to sparkle off the snow crystals drifting within the bridge. Squat shadows were cast by the roof peak into the woods beyond, the silhouette dancing against icy branches and evergreen boughs.

"This"—I turned to face the men and walked backward, arms spread to welcome them to my domain—"is Emily's Bridge. Tragic story. Or stories. You'll never hear the same one twice, but they're all equally distressing. She either hanged herself, fell from a horse to her death, was brutally murdered, or some combination of those."

Julian shoved his hands into his jacket pockets and took slow strides. He turned his eyes toward the treetops, scanned the bridge roof to ground, and turned a full circle to examine the forest surrounding us.

"I can't believe you haven't filmed at this place yet. It's a local legend." I slowed enough for James to catch up. He took in the sight with as much awe as Julian, a grin splitting his face. Wonder and fascination lit up his features, which warmed the little hollow in my chest where my heart thudded away.

"We'd thought about it but were focusing on some of the lesser-known stories. Besides, we weren't sure we could top the activity you caught on film." James scanned the dark sky, turning on his heels for a full three-sixty. "It's even more amazing in person. Your episode left out how stunning the view is."

"This might be the coolest place we've checked out so far. Thanks for making sure we didn't skip it." Julian pointed toward the camera bag James carried and offered a beckoning gesture. James passed off the bag, and Julian busied himself turning on and adjusting settings on the little handheld camera. "Lex, you looking for a consulting position? I know of a soon-to-be-famous ghost-hunting operation that could use your expertise. The travel budget may be small, but the experiences are enormous."

Natalie's laughter rang behind us. "Yeah, right," she called out. "Like you could drag Lex away from here. Her roots are deeper than a pine tree's."

"Oh, come on. Maybe you'd consider it for the right price?" Julian asked, panning the camera to capture the view.

"Probably not," I said. And there it was. Further proof that everyone's goal was "get out of Stowe or bust."

"Or for the right guy?" He teetered his eyebrows and bobbled his head toward James, who pressed his hair away from his face with the back of a gloved hand, then glanced at the ground.

"Finding where you belong is an important discovery. Maybe quit hassling people who are lucky enough to know where their place is," James said. Jeez, could he get any more attractive? He tucked his hand into his pocket and jutted an elbow out to create a crook. Yup. Yes, he could.

I slipped an arm through the gap he'd left and tugged him closer. He tipped downward and kissed me on the top of the head and more heat bloomed through my chest at the intimacy of the moment. "Would you protect me if Emily showed up?" I asked.

His answering chuckle was more discomfort than a confirmation. Like maybe I'd dipped into territory I didn't have any right to be in, yet. Chemistry did not equal a vow to protect someone against the paranormal. "I mean, you're not obligated, or anything. Just, like, would your instinct be to run away and save yourself, or would a sense of morals require you to stick around and fight her off?"

"I think the more important question is would *you* protect *me*? From what I know of this area, people aren't exactly pleased with outsiders. It probably goes for the ghostly residents, as well."

I kicked a chunk of snow out of our path and laughed. "It's a rough crowd. Most of them have been here their whole lives. It's an unofficial rule that you've got to have three generations in the state to count yourself as a true Vermonter. I'm still a Vermonter by default, even though my parents moved away. But it's a strike against me, to be sure."

"So, do we go *in* the bridge?" Julian asked, bouncing on the balls of his feet.

"Go ahead."

The three of us strolled into the gaping mouth of the covered bridge. I placed my quarter on the inner truss, and James and Julian followed suit. They eyed the interior and strolled without hurry. Though slow, Julian's stride was confident. He peered into the rafters and tapped his knuckles against the wall. A satisfied *hmm* escaped him as the rapping echoed through the bridge.

James lagged behind with hesitant, shuffling steps.

We'd only taken a couple steps into the bridge before a deep, menacing laugh ricocheted off old wooden siding and bounded away into the darkness.

"*What the—*" Julian yelped.

James's grip tightened on my arm.

I threw a glare over my shoulder.

Natalie tipped out of the shadows beside the bridge and poked her head into the opening. "Gotcha," she said. Her voice was joy and mischief dancing through the chill air.

Julian's nervous laugh turned to a chuckle, and he gestured for Natalie to join him. James didn't loosen his grip.

I smirked. "You're not scared, are you?"

He wrinkled his nose and shook his head.

"Oh my god, James, are you *scared* of ghosts? You're part of a traveling ghost-hunting documentary!"

"Just chilly. Are you chilly?" He shook in an exaggerated shiver as if to prove the point.

Just as I was about to remind him that Vermont girls know how to dress warm, he slipped his arm free from my grasp, gripped my elbow, and pulled me into a hug. My limbs went loose as he enveloped me.

"Hey," I whispered. I smiled as I stared into his eyes. The lantern light flickered behind him, casting his shadow across my face. "You're dreamy."

James broke into laughter. The sound bounced off the inner walls, then rushed its way toward the icy road and woods beyond. "You gonna do something about it?"

I rose onto tiptoes and leaned in close enough that I could feel the warmth off his face. "Maybe." I placed a gentle kiss on his lower lip, then pulled it into my mouth less gently. He leaned into the kiss and wrapped his arms around me to pull me even closer.

"This place is cool and all, but I prefer your company to ghosts."

"The ghosts are much better conversationalists, I assure you."

He pulled back and turned away, his hand dropping from my waist to grasp for my hand. We twined fingertips and he turned his eyes upward to examine the rafters inside the bridge's roof. "Do you remember that day?" he asked, his usual confidence masked with a bit of caution.

"Sure do." I followed his gaze upward. "It's been made immortal on the internet so I can rewatch any time the details feel fuzzy."

He shoulder-bumped me. "You know what I mean."

I exhaled slowly as I considered my response. My hot breath mingled with the cold air, sending misty clouds swirling. Apologizing to business owners for scaring customers away with ghost stories was something I'd gotten used to—but taking the magic away from someone who wanted to believe wasn't a step I was willing to take. Aside from the fact that my chance to buy the bookstore depended on the ghost stories persisting, I'd breathed life into those stories because the distraction had made my complicated teenage years easier. James seemed like he was searching for something to believe in now, just like I was then. I couldn't ruin it for him.

"I remember it." I swallowed. "We'd filmed a few earlier videos, but something about that specific encounter was different. I'd had a difficult week, and I needed to feel a connection. Emily gave me that. Sharing the story of someone so strong and sure and, frankly, out for revenge gave me something like hope." Whether an actual ghost had been involved didn't matter—the power of storytelling meant Emily lived on, which was a comfort when I dreaded being left behind.

"Did you ever experience anything like that again?" He laced my gloved fingers with his, and my stomach took a quick loop-de-loop.

"Almost every time we filmed. Not always on the same level, but yes." While not quite an answer to the question as he'd intended it, it was the truth: each vlog helped me feel more connected to this town, my neighbors, and my very wonderful friend who froze her ass off behind the camera at all hours of the night just for the chance at adventure. And mischief.

"The hauntings around here are the real deal, then?"

I shrugged. "Some people think so."

"What do you think?"

"I think that when people can't explain something, they make up a story to explain it for them. A weird prickle of goosebumps or eerie sound might be ghostly, or it might be your brain trying to make up for not understanding."

He cocked his head and lifted a brow. "That's a very scholarly answer."

"I spend ninety percent of my time reading. What did you expect? What about you—do you feel a presence? Tell me the truth, are you scared?"

"I'm totally freaked out." He brought both hands up to cover his eyes. "All this ghost-hunting stuff scares the crap out of me, but I didn't figure that out until we were already in too deep. Should have known, though. I slept with a night-light until I was twelve. These days, I can't even watch trailers for scary movies. I'd prefer not to poke around where I don't belong. Just in case. At least while I was watching *Haunted Happenings*, there was a screen to separate me from the stuff you were encountering. I know, the irony. It's overpowering. I just really need to win this documentary competition, even if it means facing fears I'd rather not."

"Don't worry, your secret's safe with me. Wouldn't want to ruin your cred."

Natalie's laugh echoed through the bridge, and Julian's danced through the air alongside it. I pointed in their direction. "Looks like they're hitting it off."

"Not surprised. Everyone gravitates to him. It's why he's able to travel the country gathering stories in towns where he's only just landed. People feel like opening up to him about anything. His films haven't gotten the attention they deserve yet, but he's made a hundred friends in every state. He's pretty suave."

"Look who's talking." I dragged one boot-clad toe through the built-up snow and dirt that was strewn across the wood plank floor and leaned into James's side. "You're pretty suave yourself."

"Okay, here's what we're thinking," Julian called to us. He had one hand in a pocket, and he pointed with the other as he worked out the details in his head. "I've got plenty of anchor locations in here—we can set up the cameras, and the crew can control them remotely. We'll have to give it a couple of test runs and make sure the weather cooperates. If it's too cold out, it'll be nothing but a foggy mess if anyone so much as exhales in front of the lens. But I've worked with worse. Fix it in editing, no big deal. My new friend Natalie here has promised me some ghostly apparitions if I can round up the crowd."

"Time to dust off the goodies from our haunting days." Natalie grinned.

James turned his eyes toward me, so many questions plastered across his face.

"She means the vlog, of course," I covered. Now was not the time for him to figure out that everything was fake—not when I had an offer on the table from Charles.

"Absolutely, yeah, for the vlog . . ." Natalie flashed an apologetic grimace in my direction after almost breaking the first rule of haunting club. "Remember that one episode we did, where the guy forgot his car? Just ran on down Hollow Road shouting apologies for bothering the spirit."

"If we could re-create that," Julian said. He popped his hands into dual fireworks. "Someone would absolutely pick it up."

James shook his head and turned his whole body in a lazy half-circle to face the horses. "Remember me when you're famous," he said.

"You'll be standing on that stage with me when I accept that Oscar. We do it all together, man."

Everything Julian does, James does. Everywhere Julian goes, James goes. Joined at the hip, those two. It was beginning to sound like the only thing permanent in their lives was the likelihood that they'd find some new adventure across some distant horizon. Leave behind the new for the newer, over and over again until they ran out of novel experiences—or died.

James knocked a chunk of ice around the wooden floor using the toe of his boot, suddenly less talkative than I'd ever seen him. The guy always had a joke to crack or a verbal jab to sling.

"Hey." I gripped the sleeve of his jacket. Even if my gloves blocked the feel of the wool, the motion had become my best reminder of how good I had it. If I focused on the wonderful *now*, I didn't have to worry about what happened when he moved on to the next stop on his filmmaker road trip. I'd never been good at optimism, but James's carefree manner made me want to give it a try. As long as I didn't ignore the likely outcome, I deserved to enjoy the time we did have.

"Hey yourself." His face flipped from pensive to cheerful, and his shadow stood tall in the lantern light.

"Want to let them plan? Get out of here before any apparitions drop in? The walk back home is short, and I brought a flashlight." I tugged it from my pocket and clicked it on.

"Hey, you're ruining the vibe," Natalie hissed.

"Yeah, what she said!" Julian added.

"We're headed back—it's freezing and you're both out of your minds. Enjoy the ghost hunting."

"Suit yourself!" Natalie turned back to Julian, who had already resumed plotting his camera angles and lighting set-up.

"Don't forget the car's at Lex's place—make sure you're decent when Natalie drops me off," Julian said with a smirk.

"You can't rush perfection." James spread his hands and bent at the waist into a dramatic bow.

I snorted in faux disgust, then pulled him into a kiss. "Save the showing off for later."

"Later?" James offered the crook of his elbow again, like an old-timey gentleman. It was endearing. I left him hanging, and instead took a few slow steps ahead of him, throwing a little extra swing into my hips and ass.

"You know the best way to warm up is to get naked and climb into bed together, right?" I said. "Don't waste energy on verbal sparring—you'll need it when we get back to my place." I looked over my shoulder at him, swung the flashlight toward the road ahead, bit my lip, and winked to make doubly sure James caught my drift.

"Oh." He took a long stride toward me and swept me into an eager embrace. His icy nose and lips sent a shiver from head to toe, but the warmth of his tongue slipping between my lips chased it away. He growled against my mouth, low and self-assured, like he knew exactly what he was doing to my knees.

"Get a room," Natalie called through cupped hands. Julian whooped, then chucked a snowball in our direction. It skidded across the plowed and sanded surface and broke into a hundred tiny pieces.

"Oh, I intend to." I grabbed James by the hand and tugged him down the road.

We made it onto the sleigh-wide path that cut from the road to my backyard before he stopped short and pulled me back to him. He scooped me into his arms, and we fell into each other. His breath came heavy and quick, but it wasn't only from trudging up the snow-covered dip. He swept his fingers up through the hair at the base of my neck and paused, his palm cupping the back of my head.

The flashlight glinted off snowbanks. The tree-lined trail opened to the vast canvas of sky that consisted of nothing but velvet night and crystal stars twinkling like beacons. Even with a thousand stars winking above me, my eyes remained fixed on his. Nothing was more spectacular in that moment than the way he gazed at me. A shiver ran through me when he inhaled, then pulled me in for yet another knees-to-jelly kiss. He snickered against my mouth.

"What?" I pulled back a bit to narrow my eyes at him.

"I bet this is where you brought all your gentleman callers in high school."

"Bold of you to assume I'd limit myself to only *gentlemen*," I said. "I'm pan. For the record."

James nodded. "I'm bi. For the record. But the question still stands: is this the Lex version of Lookout Point?"

I laughed and it echoed back at me, mockingly. "Never."

"What, not even once?"

"Not even once." I brushed a few snowflakes from his shoulder. "I wasn't what you'd call, umm, popular. There's a nook under the bridge where couples were often busted for getting *friendly*, but not me."

He crossed his arms and scanned the tree line. "There."

He grasped my hand and tugged me through a mound of snow and just into the woods. The flashlight dropped into the built-up snow when his pull jolted it from my grip. He spun me around and leaned me against a tree, surprising a squeak out of me. He ignored the sound and pressed kisses along my jawline, down my neck, and across my collar bone. He interlaced our fingertips and raised my hands above my head to push them into the tree trunk.

The textured bark nipped through my jacket and pressed against my spine. He leaned into me, pushing me tight against the tree while he kissed and played against my throat. His stubble scraped the delicate flesh, and I rolled my head back farther to give him better access to the spot. Instead, he drew his tongue across the bump of my collarbone before moving to the side of my neck. The frigid air danced across the area where his tongue had been a moment before, turning the trail to ice. I tipped my mouth toward his ear as the smallest moan escaped me.

He slid a knee between my thighs to put pressure where the heat was building, so I rocked against it to show him my interest—a little encouragement to keep things moving in my favor.

"Hmm." He pressed the knee upward again, less gently this time. "Is this okay?"

"Hell yes," I whispered. "This is the most okay I've been in a long time."

With a glint in his eye, he brought his hand to his mouth, tugged the glove from it with his teeth, and let the glove fall into the snow without a care. With deft fingers, he reached beneath my jacket and plucked my jeans button free.

My breath came in shallow huffs as he slid his chilled fingertips beneath my shirt to play against my stomach. Core warmth and icy extremities became my new favorite combination as he slipped his hand farther inside my shirt, then dragged one knuckle directly down the center of my stomach. My back arched involuntarily. He took the moment of surprise to slide his hand downward, into my unbuttoned jeans and beneath the band of my underwear.

He ground his knee into me from the outside, and his cool finger met the slickness of my clit on the inside, which solicited another moan that started in my stomach before climbing through my chest to sneak from my lips. Warmth built as he rubbed with one finger, then added a second.

When my limbs loosened and my arms went slack from the gloriousness, he slid his fingers inside me and pressed his chest against mine to hold me tighter against the tree trunk. His knee still provided a pleasurable pressure between my legs, but now his fingers were doing the work. I moved on him, encouraging him to continue and helping him reach the spots that would make me come. Hot breath gusted against my cold skin where his head leaned toward me, and I groaned as my pleasure turned to swells of something more, something hinting at release.

He slid his other hand along my arm, over my coat, and to my shoulder, where it remained while he leaned back and looked at me from beneath sensual, lowered eyelids. He was going to watch me as I came, and I was ready to give him the show he desired. My thighs quivered and my breath hitched as he pressed his knee upward once more, sending a flood of warmth to my core as my body trembled in an orgasm that left me breathless.

With his teeth pressed into his lower lip—his satisfaction at my pleasure made very well clear—he loosened the press of his knee without hurry and hooked his finger at the edge of my waistband. I let my head fall backward against the tree as giggles shook me.

James brushed my hair away from my face and kissed the space where my jaw and earlobe connected, then rested his forehead on the tree beside my head. We laughed together, bodies jiggling against each other and our voices flitting into the pitch-black woods.

When my breathing had slowed to something closer to normal, James retrieved his glove from the snow and I went searching in the powdery drift for the flashlight I'd dropped. The impact had either broken it or switched it off, so there was no glow to go by. Eventually, we gave up and started the dark trudge back.

We hadn't walked more than five minutes—stolen kisses and weaving into each other's paths reducing our forward progress—before the jingle of sleigh bells danced through the air.

We flagged down Natalie and Julian, but our laughter had given us away before they spotted us. Natalie pulled the sleigh to a stop and we climbed aboard.

"Wow, you couldn't even wait for the room, huh?" Mock surprise played in Natalie's voice.

We covered ourselves with the heavy blanket and didn't even bother to sputter excuses. We rode back to the house leaning into each other, arms twined and knees touching.

CHAPTER ELEVEN

James made twice-daily stops into Dog-Eared over the next couple of days. A coffee here, a new book to add to his growing collection there. Business had picked up as tourists stopped in on their way out of town to pick up gifts and trinkets from our tiny window display. Stocking stuffers to go along with the tiny bottles of maple syrup they'd gotten from the sugar shack down the road, evergreen-shaped keychains with "Vermont" etched across them, and local liquors sold in gimmicky bottles meant for the out-of-state crowd. Paperbacks were left behind, unwanted.

I sorted used books and tallied the store credit owed each customer. Charles had created a revolving "take a penny, leave a penny" situation rather than a money-making operation, except replace "penny" with "book." Which is why the coffee and trinkets were necessary. If he adjusted the payout—a flat fifty cents per book toward store credit—maybe he'd be making some money.

I'd pulled three books from the latest box and set them aside to add to my own collection. One, a copy of *Romeo and Juliet* with the note "To my Juliet, with love. Wishing to create our own love story as sweet as this," which proved the giver must never have studied

Shakespeare, or preferred tragedy to true love. Though, the fact that their Juliet had dropped off the book at a used book store was evidence that perhaps their love story had a similar, hopefully less tragic, ending. Either way, the book had made it into my stack, where the secret would remain hidden.

The door swung open and a disheveled James hurtled toward the desk, glancing around the store.

"Hey, I was just about to kick back with a lunch break book. Got time to join me?"

He shook his head, his eyes wide and worried. "Have you seen Lulu?"

"No. What's wrong?"

"She's missing. I got back home from a consult at the historical society and the door was wide open. I think I forgot to latch it, or Julian did. Either way, the door was open and Lulu was gone, and I've been calling her and asking around and nobody's seen her."

I grabbed my keys from the desk, yanked my coat from the coat hook, and grasped for his hand as I passed, tugging him toward the door. "How long has she been gone?"

I flipped the sign to "closed," pulled him outside, locked the door behind us, and scanned the sidewalks looking for the familiar curly-haired dog. There was no sign of her, no doggie footprints on the sidewalks.

"I don't know," James said. "I left around eight this morning and got home at eleven. I checked the yard, asked the neighbors, stopped into surrounding businesses, and nobody's seen her. It could have been any time this morning. She's never wandered off before. She's probably freezing. Sorry I didn't call before stopping at the store, I left my phone at the house. I didn't know where else to go."

"We'll find her." I directed him to my car and shoved him into the passenger seat, shutting the door gently behind him. I got into my seat, started the car, cranked the heat as high as it went, then turned to James. "Let's go over it again. Where have you looked?"

He listed the places he'd checked, then I handed him my phone. "Call the animal shelter, file a report. Police department, too. We'll find her."

"Don't you have to work?" James pointed at the store's door where two ski-jacket-clad men jiggled the doorknob, peered through the front window, and consulted the hours sign hanging in the window.

"It's fine, they'll come back if they desperately want a book. More likely they just want to use the bathroom. Call the shelter."

While he called, I backed out of my spot and began the slow crawl through town, eyes peeled for a cold canine on the lam.

"Text Natalie," I told him. "Let her know we're looking. She's probably out plowing parking lots today so she can watch while she plows and let us know if she sees anything."

"She's just all I've got right now. I've had her since she was a puppy. My parents . . . I mean, they're just . . . my family, my dad, isn't . . . warm. Lulu is warm. I'm so sorry. Sorry I'm rambling, and sorry to drag you away from work."

Apologetic and worried James was a complete turn-around from confident, witty James. He looked smaller, his shoulders collapsed and his head dipped. He held worry in the corners of his eyes and in his clamped-tight jaw. His brows pulled in as he scanned snowbanks and yards.

"Work doesn't matter, I promise you. Text Natalie. Tell her if she finds Lulu, she can drop her off inside my house. She has a key and can get Lulu inside."

While we searched, James's knee bounced enough that the car was jiggling along with it. I reached over and squeezed his leg. James scrubbed his hands across his face but stopped tapping his foot for a moment.

"Hey, it's going to be okay."

He nodded, lips pressed into a disbelieving line and eyes filled with concern.

We worked through the streets one by one, at a crawl, then back-tracked to make sure we hadn't crossed paths. As we turned onto the main drag for our third sweep of town, I caught a dark blur out of the corner of my eye. Lulu! I slammed on the brakes, threw my car into park, and flailed in her direction.

"There she is! Over there, running toward the parking lot!" The car was still running when I shoved my door open, jumped out, and ran toward Lulu.

"Lucy in the Sky with Diamonds!" James dove out of the car and overtook me as he ran toward his dog. "You're in so much trouble, what are you trying to do to me?"

He caught up with her, and she yipped at him, then jumped up to put both paws on his stomach. He knelt on the ground, wrapped her in a giant hug, and pressed his face into the fur at her neck.

At a glance, Lulu looked perfectly fine. Balls of snow had gathered in her fur, weighing down her wagging tail and the hair at her stomach. No limping or sign of soreness, just a furry, shivering ball of fluff enjoying the reunion as much as James was.

"Let's get her in the car, she looks like she could use a warm-up." I rested my fingertips on his shoulder as he cycled between telling Lulu how much he missed her, how worried he'd been, and how happy he was to see her. "Want to come back to my place? It's closer, and I have a fireplace. I just need to stop by the bookstore quickly to close out the register and drop off the bank deposit. It's been a slow day, so closing early won't be a big deal."

"You don't mind having a dirty, wet, *naughty* dog in the car?" He rested his forehead against hers and smooshed her furry cheeks between his palms.

I shook my head.

"Or in the house?"

"Not a problem. I can make lunch."

"Lunch sounds perfect." He stood, scooped Lulu up into his arms, and carried her back to the car.

* * *

Lulu enjoyed barreling through the house, bounding off furniture, and knocking my plants off windowsills and shelves. Her zoomies lasted for fifteen minutes—then she curled up beside the fireplace and dozed, snoring loudly.

James settled into a chair in the kitchen, perched on the edge like he was prepared to dash out the door to take Lulu to the vet at the first sign of distress. She snoozed on, unaware that she'd shaken us both to the core—and I didn't even know the beast beyond a handful of strolls through town.

"We have two options. Soup from a can in, oh, ninety seconds. Or soup from scratch using last night's leftover chicken and whatever veggies happen to be hiding in my produce drawer."

"I don't want to impose," James said. "Honestly, the fire is plenty. I can't ask you to do that."

"Oh, I'm not doing it alone. We are going to make this soup together. Pick your weapon and get chopping." I pointed to the knife block and winked at him.

He dragged a knife from the block and examined the edge a moment.

"Oh, it's dull. I might have knives like an adult, but hell if I know how to sharpen them."

I lifted my brows at him as he crossed the kitchen and started tugging open drawer after drawer until he found a sharpening block.

"I didn't even know I had that," I said.

"Dull is dangerous. Let me sharpen this, *then* I'll chop some veggies."

"Deal."

I tugged the carrots, potatoes, and onion from the drawer and piled them on the cluttered countertop, then grabbed the bamboo cutting board from the drainboard. He dragged the knife against the stone and a satisfying *swiick, swiiick, swiiick* echoed through the otherwise quiet kitchen with each tiny swipe. His eyes focused on the blade, and mine were drawn to the way his rolled-up Henley sleeves showed off the muscles in his forearms. They tensed with each drag. Only slightly, but it was enough to get my attention. The subtle tightening had my eyes trailing up his arms, to the sleeved biceps, then to his square shoulders. I stopped my appraisal at his jawline, where the concentration was most evident.

I settled into the chair beside his, chin rested in one palm, eyes fixed on his profile. He licked his lips, then gritted his teeth, and I swallowed a sigh to keep from giving myself away.

"It's really difficult to sharpen a knife while I'm being watched," he said, not taking his eyes from the blade.

"It's really difficult to focus on anything else with you flaunting your bare forearms like that. Honestly. Unfair advantage."

He let out a chuckle that matched his smile's power in wattage. If I'd have been standing, my knees would have been weak.

"How dare you come into my kitchen, sharpen my knives, *and* make me swoon. You are a true terror, James. An absolute nightmare."

"Wait until you see how I use this thing. I've worked in multiple kitchens, and they don't skimp when it comes to knife safety certifications." He ran a fingertip along the freshly ground blade, examined the edge, and rubbed his fingertips together, satisfied with his work. "Though, based on the texts you sent Natalie, I'm not sure I need to work so hard to impress you."

My stomach dropped straight through the Earth's crust and deep into the core. "Oh, god."

"Hey, now. You handed me your phone, after all."

"How many did you see?" I grasped for my pocket, but my phone wasn't there. James's eyes sparkled as he watched me pat my jeans searching for the device. "Can we just forget how incredibly ridiculous I am and pretend you didn't see any of them?"

"Oh, what, you'd ask me to forget about how the hair at the back of my neck is perfect for tugging? Or how my lower lip is begging to be sucked on?" He sucked his own bottom lip into his mouth experimentally, then let his teeth slide over it.

Heat crawled up my neck and my cheeks were on fire, but if I was already going down, why not own it? "So, did you see the one about your ass then?"

"Hmm, I absolutely did. One of my favorites, actually. Poetry. If you play your cards right, you might *get* to see what my ass looks like out of my jeans. You won't be disappointed."

"Your confidence is astounding."

"You like it."

I bit my lip and peered at him, challenging him to put the knife down and make his move.

He met my gaze and smirked, the dimple popping up in his chin to give his amusement away. "So, are we chopping some veggies here? Tell me what to do."

And just like that, we were cooking again. The glint in his eye told me he was enjoying toying with me. "Veggies are on the counter. Slice 'em, dice 'em. Whatever makes you happy. If you're good with that, I'll get the stock and chicken ready to go."

It took everything I had to keep from whimpering as he transitioned seamlessly from knife-sharpening to seduction to veg-prepping. He sliced completely uniform carrot rounds, diced perfectly shaped potatoes, and sliced the onion without shedding a tear—and I kept watch in my peripheral to make sure I didn't miss a moment of it.

When he wrapped up his precise prepping, I tossed the soup ingredients into the stockpot and brushed my hands together.

"And now, we've got about twenty minutes before it's ready. Any recommendations for how we spend our time?"

He crossed the kitchen in two long strides, a wicked grin replacing his usual playful smirk. With a hand at my elbow and another cupped behind my head, he dipped me into a kiss so smoothly my heart rate kicked up to double time. His tongue swept across my lips, then teased between them until I let him in. Our tongues mingled and blood rushed through my veins, swooshing in my ears and pulling away from my brain, leaving me lightheaded and euphoric. He let out a low growl.

"My lower lip is ready and waiting," he whispered, his lips still pressed against mine.

I dragged my teeth against it obediently and giggled when his lips tightened in a satisfied grin. He pressed his weight into me, hips against hips and chests heaving in unison, pushing me a half step at a time toward the living room. I shuffled backward, fully trusting that he'd keep me from colliding into furniture or tripping over discarded boots. I gathered the front of his shirt into my fists, willing inertia to take over, and we careened toward the couch.

My ass pressed into the cushion, and he knelt beside me, one knee throwing the balance off, so I tipped into him. He tilted his head and leaned in to taste my mouth, my jawline, my neck, my collarbone, trailing kisses and licks the entire way.

"Sorry about work," James said between kisses. "I shouldn't have pulled you away."

I pressed a hand to his chest, and he backed away instantly. The way he let me lead was so damn hot.

"It's not a big deal. So, people didn't get their afternoon dose of caffeine. It's not going to make or break the store, promise." Lulu trotted over and pressed her chin into my knee. I scrunched her ears in my hands, which roughed up her wiry fur, giving her a bit of doggy bedhead. "Besides, puppies come first."

"Really, thank you for helping. The way I move around, I don't have many connections. Just as I get to know people, I move on. Lulu's been with me everywhere I've landed, and I couldn't imagine not having her around. I shouldn't have bothered you with this, but I was scared, and I saw your car and realized that having you beside me would probably calm me enough for rational thinking. Everyone I know in the area was working, so . . ."

I shot him a fake judgmental scowl.

"I know, you were working too. Have I said I'm sorry? And thank you?"

Everything screamed at me to back up: his confessions about not having many friends, and the reminder that he moved around constantly, never settling or allowing roots. He'd be leaving here, moving on just like he'd moved on before. Maybe he'd seek out a beachy retreat, or a desert, or a lakeside cabin next. Find the next documentary subjects.

But, this time, all I wanted to consider was the moment.

"Make it up to me." I took his hand and pulled him onto the cushion beside me.

He settled into the seat, turned toward me, and kissed me slow and back-bendingly deep.

I dragged my fingertips up the back of his neck and received a full-body shiver in return that had nothing to do with our chilly hunt for Lulu. His lips parted against mine, and he traced the line of my upper lip with his tongue. My tongue met his and the two mingled, gently testing, seeking, wandering.

He'd smoothed on some minty lip balm at some point and the wintery tingle transferred to my mouth. I gripped the hair at the base of his neck—it was as marvelous as I'd imagined—and pulled him closer for another taste.

He slid a hand along my waistline and slipped his fingertips beneath the bottom edge of my sweater. A finger played at my waistband, hesitantly, giving me the option to say no.

He broke away from our kiss and leaned in to rest nose-to-nose. "I don't mean to be presumptuous, but . . ."

"By all means, presume, James." I tugged my jeans button free and arched my back, tipping my head away from his. He trailed kisses along my jawline, down the center of my throat, and along my sweater's neckline, sending a fresh wave of shivers straight through my core with each. He finished with a tiny nip at my collarbone, the scrape of his stubble leaving my limbs useless.

His fingertips slipped beneath my waistband, and I adjusted my weight to provide a bit of room for him to explore further. I warmed at his touch, and each kiss built upon the insistent wanting.

Until James rolled into town, it had been months since I'd kissed anyone, let alone had sex. Even when I'd still been with Kyle, sex was rare—he just wasn't into physical intimacy, and we'd found a balance that worked for both of us. There was only so much one could accomplish with a vibrator.

James gripped either side of my waist and pulled back to look at me with a full body sweep. My chest heaved as I worked to catch my breath, but it was impossible. One eyebrow hitched upward, his mouth quirked into an amused grin, he waited.

"If you're interested in continuing this discussion," I said, leaning in to kiss his crooked smile, "there are condoms in my nightstand drawer. Gentleman's choice."

James ran a tongue along his top teeth, winked, and leapt off the couch, bolting for my bedroom. I swiped my hands through my hair, dragged my forefinger and thumb along my lips to wipe away any smudged lipstick, and straightened up in my seat while I waited for him to come back.

He returned with the whole forty-pack box of condoms in his hand, his lips pulled to the side. "Is this all you have?"

"Ha ha, super funny. We're going to go through forty condoms." I tossed a throw pillow his way, and he knocked it aside with the giant condom supply.

"Okay, well don't get your hopes up there. All I meant was that these are expired."

"Oh shit. By how long?" I tallied all of the reasons not to use expired condoms and considered bringing up the FAQs page on the brand's website to see how serious they were about those expiration dates.

"About, oh, nine months."

I gritted my teeth. An entire box, nine months gone. Shelf life was what, four or five years to start? I'd probably bought the box before Kyle opened up about being ace-spec.

"It's, uh, been a while." There. I admitted it. Out loud. "You don't happen to have a secret stash in that coat of yours, do you?"

James crossed the room, shaking his head. "I'm good to wait, though." He tossed the box of useless latex onto the side table and sat beside me, lacing his fingers with mine. "Besides, you don't need condoms for this." He pulled me into his lap, and I straddled him. He reached for the back of my neck and pulled my head toward his for another round of kisses that wiped my mind blank.

CHAPTER TWELVE

I sat across from James at the kitchen table, enjoying the soup we'd made together. His lips and hands and the speedy rise and fall of his chest had distracted me from the clock, so I had let it simmer for slightly too long. But mushy carrots were a small price to pay for the thorough attention I'd received.

My stack of unshelved new additions marked the middle of the table. James ran his finger along the spine of the top book—a Celtic mythology collection—then dropped to the next spine, and the next, to repeat the exercise.

"You have eclectic taste," he said.

"You could say that."

"Myths, classics, guides to illustration. A *C++ for Dummies* book." He tapped each spine as he listed it off, then rested his hand on top of a weathered Western with a haggard cowboy on the cover. "I've been looking for this one."

"You lie." I tossed my napkin at him, and his eyes glittered as he laughed. Beyond his chin dimple and wit, it was my favorite feature.

"What's with the varied subject matter? Opening your own library?"

I pressed my lips together and scanned the stack, assessing whether it was worth sharing my secret with him.

"It's like your calling card, isn't it. You're a serial killer, and you steal a book from each person's house after you off them."

"You caught me." I pointed my spoon at him and wrinkled my nose. "That's why I've given you such fantastic recommendations. That way, I know there'll be something on your shelves that fits my aesthetic. This," I wiggled the copy of *C++ for Dummies*, "doesn't really match the curtains."

"Well, I'll have to make sure my shelves are fully stocked so you have plenty to choose from."

I leaned against the back of my chair and kicked a foot up onto the seat of the chair beside me. James slouched, then copied me, running his toe along the arch of my foot and sending a shiver down my spine.

Comfortable, simple. Playful. Safe.

"They're all inscribed," I confessed.

He waited for me to continue.

"My grandfather built this house, and my family moved in with him after my grandmother died. When my sister and parents moved away, I stayed in Vermont. They decided on change, and I chose roots. I went to college twenty minutes from here, came home every weekend and for random weeknight dinners, then my grandfather left the house to me when he died. My parents think it's a money pit and want me to sell it. It's got some quirks, is all, but I'm working on it. Little by little. I'm probably going to have to get a home equity loan to catch up on repairs. I don't care. I like it here."

James swept a glance through the kitchen, eyes settling on the giant window over the sink, then on the woodwork surrounding the doorway. "They did a wonderful job. It's a gorgeous home and there's so much potential. I can see why you stayed."

"My grandfather used to mail letters to my grandmother. They were apart for most of the time he was building this house. She was with her parents, in New York City. They visited when they could, but he was working on a farm to save money to bring her here, to their house. He sent her letters daily. But he also tucked love notes and memories in the wall frames like little time capsules. As he built, he hid his thoughts and feelings behind wallpaper, inside the walls, and under floorboards. I found the first one when I upgraded the bathroom. The tiny closet had a scrap of paper tucked inside the wall. It was the most romantic thing I'd seen. I found another when I stripped the old wallpaper from my room and found a pencil-scribbled note behind it, obscured by the wallpaper paste and torn backing, but still legible. And another note when the electrician was poking around, the paper was nestled inside the ceiling."

James dragged his toe along my foot again and smiled. "That's sweet."

"He was a sweet guy and everyone here loved him. He's been gone a long time, but people still call me 'Tommy's granddaughter.' I live in *his* town, and it's heaven. I want to tear every inch of wallpaper down just to see what messages he's left behind, but I also want to keep it intact so I don't spoil all of his secrets."

James's mouth parted into a knowing smile. "So you look for secret messages elsewhere."

"Exactly. People love to scrawl their thoughts inside book covers. Some of them are meant to make the person sound more intelligent, like the people who gift *For Dummies* books, or the long-winded notes left in the margins of Tolstoy. Others are sincere reminders that the giftee was on someone's mind, a little 'hey, I'm thinking of you.' I couldn't mine all of my grandfather's thoughts, so I went searching."

"So, what else do you have?"

"For books? I'm thrilled you asked." I brought my bowl to the sink and tipped my head, beckoning him to follow me. We passed Lulu, who had turned my fuzziest blanket into a perfect little dog nest.

"You coming?" I asked her. She lifted her head but didn't budge. "She just makes herself right at home, doesn't she?"

"She's moved around. A lot, actually. This is her seventh home. Well, seventh location, I guess. We had a couple of apartments in

Arizona. She's gotten used to the road, and change. It's not ideal, but it is what it is."

"How do you get used to that?" For each moment I forgot he wasn't here for the long haul, there were three new tips reminding me that he would eventually disappear. *Way to stick to your guns on not falling for the hot, temporary resident, Lex.*

I waved him up the narrow stairway to the upper, mostly unused level of the house. He went first, glancing back at me as he creaked ever upward.

"I didn't have a choice at first, but I learned to roll with it."

I lifted the rattly gate latch and tugged the door open to reveal my book nook. I stepped aside to let James pass.

He leaned in the doorway, hip cocked, arms crossed, and heel nonchalantly kicked up. If there was one stance James had perfected, it was the cool, carefree lean. "This is a well-stocked library."

His eyes scanned the floor-to-ceiling shelves crammed with books, and I savored watching him take in the scene. Scribbled-in clothbound books from the 1800s, a hardcover with a dedication jotted on the title page from a debut author to their favorite English teacher, others with various holiday greetings and birthday wishes, more still with scribbled notes about how the book brought a certain person to mind. Personal. Thoughtful.

And, for some reason, each book had been discarded.

"I sort the books at Dog-Eared before they go on the shelves. I grab any that catch my eye. Which is . . . a lot of them. So, this side is regular books, and this side is inscribed books. I've got more shelves in my office downstairs, but this is my happy place. It was my grandmother's sewing room when they lived here. I don't sew—I shouldn't be allowed near sharp objects, honestly—but I wanted to turn it into my own little retreat like she had. It gets chilly during the winter since the heat in this house *sucks*, but I still bundle up and come sit in her chair to read."

James pushed himself upright and strolled into the room, turning to examine the shelves. "May I?" He pointed to my grandmother's creaky old armchair. He sat when I nodded permission.

It was easy to have him hanging out in this room with me. From the first time I scooped up a book at a yard sale, my parents had considered my collection a "phase." I basked in the validation James was giving me now.

I plucked a book off the shelf and passed it to James. It was a beaten-up copy of *Great Expectations*, with the note "Granddad loves this one, and you will too. Happy first birthday, love Grammie G."

"I found this one a month after my grandfather died. I have no idea if he'd ever read *Great Expectations*, and I'm even less sure he would have liked it. He would devour his *Old Farmer's Almanac* when it arrived, and peek through the pages year-round, but I don't think I ever saw the man pick up an actual book in his lifetime. But it made me think of him. I found his first letter a few weeks later, and it felt like a sign." I shook my head. "Sorry, this is stupid. We don't have to—"

"It's sweet, and possibly the most whimsical type of collection I've ever heard of. Don't hold back, I can take a little weird. Trust me. I'm here to film a ghost documentary, in case you forgot. This is sensible in comparison." He returned to Dickens with a satisfied grin. "What will you do when you run out of space up here?"

I shrugged. "I don't know. My parents have been trying to talk me into selling the house for years since they think putting my hard-earned money into repairs is a bad investment in my future. But how do you put a price on the one constant in your life? I like working at the store—enough that I actually put in an offer to buy it from the owner since he's decided to retire."

James broke into a surprised grin. "Congrats!" He leaned in and rested his elbows against his knees, truly pleased at my news. "Did he accept?"

"He did! I'm looking for funding, but that's what makes my house repairs so tricky. If my parents knew, they'd insist I choose one or the other—and they'd push me toward letting the house go. I like living here. They can't stand anything that goes against their plan for my life. Pleasing them is, uh, what's harder than 'impossible'? Because it's that."

James picked at his thumbnail and jiggled a crossed foot. "I've had a little experience with imperious family members."

"Yeah?"

"I was supposed to be a lawyer," James said, as if that explained it.

I pressed a thumb to my chest and grimaced. "Doctor."

"Oh, very nice. Well, my mother set me up on a blind date with her friend's daughter, completely ambushed me, and then I was in trouble when there was no love at first sight. Top that."

"My parents think I'm a failure because I don't already have a PhD, a successful career, a spouse, two kids, and an organic vegetable farm."

"Well, Alex," James said wryly, "how can you expect to amount to anything without having the organic veggies locked down already?" He smiled in challenge. "My father bought me a Princeton sweatshirt, adult medium, on the day I was born. The day I received my rejection letter, he burnt it."

"You're lying."

"*You're* running out of steam."

"No way, never surrender. My father named me Alex because, and I quote, 'a man's name will take you places ambition can't.' The man ended up with two daughters, and only one lived up to his expectations."

"My father named me James because people are more likely to take you seriously with a one-syllable name."

I snorted.

"I'm serious."

"No, no. I believe you, I'm right there with you on the overbearing parent train. It's just. Lucy in the Sky with Diamonds, it makes so much sense now."

His eyes crinkled at the corners. "Julian calls her 'Ice.' As in, the slang for diamond."

"I wholeheartedly approve."

James fiddled with the corner of the book cover with a smile playing at his lips.

"So, we've eaten. Your dog is warm. We've played the world's worst version of 'I know you are but what am I?' and, um, gotten to know each other better. Shall I drive you home? We can discuss our unfortunate situations further on the way there, and you can take your leave without any lingering awkwardness."

He stood, replaced the book gingerly, and slid his way across the creaky, uneven hardwood floor until we stood parallel. Warmth shot through my middle as he took my hands in his, raised them to his mouth, and planted a kiss on my knuckles. "I'm not in any hurry to leave, but if this is a hint, I can take it."

"Not at all. I did have plans involving a giant bowl of popcorn and terrible television, and I refuse to alter them. But company might make the television a little better, and the popcorn seem less lonely."

And, as if we'd been sharing evenings together for months, we settled in on the couch with popcorn and TV, as promised, and a fuzzy dog between us to warm our feet. It was my house and had been for ages—but for the first time in a long time, it actually felt like home.

Haunted Happenings transcript

Date: December 14, 2006

Location: Stiller's Christmas Tree Farm, Stowe, Vermont

Luna: [whispering] We've been tipped off to a very special haunting. We're at a Christmas tree farm, and there have been multiple sightings here this week alone. Every night, just as the sun starts to set, something spooky appears. We've had twelve separate reports, one from a group where six out of seven saw the very same phenomenon.

[Boots crunching on snow, camera follows Luna.]

Luna: [whispering, but louder] This little saltbox-style building has been on this property for decades. It's a workshop and storage space now, but it used to be a house. And that window up there? That's where the action happens. There have been reports of a light flickering in the window on the left—exactly where the bedroom had been before the residents left.

My research shows that, after a stint in the US Army Signal Corps as a Hello Girl during World War One, Marion came back to her childhood home—with a fellow switchboard operator, Ethel. They were rumored to be a couple, completely in love, though there is no paper trail to confirm this . . . for obvious, yet completely discriminatory bullshit reasons. But, I digress. When Marion took a job as a switchboard operator in New York City in the early 1920s, Ethel stayed behind to start a millinery business and storefront. Though parted and likely never reunited, it is said that Ethel lit a candle in this window every night, and Marion promised to do the same in her city apartment.

[Luna walks past the camera; camera pans toward a group of people gathered in the snow.]

Luna: We've asked those who witnessed the lights to join our peek into the paranormal. Let's keep our eyes—and lenses—on the window to see if we're greeted by a glimmer of hope.

[A glow appears in the window. Crowd murmurs. Scattered exclamations.]

CHAPTER THIRTEEN

Nat and I hadn't lost our touch. From the perfect camera angles to the right lighting for the job, the plan to rig Emily's Bridge for filming came together quickly. The crew wanted to amp up the spooky atmosphere for their big night, so we tugged out the fog machine the inn used for Stowe's annual Hallows' Eve event and fired it up to test it in the cold. Spooky tendrils of smoke curled from the mouth of the machine and crept low against the snow and gravel like cats slinking on nimble feet. It played against the icy build-up and snowbanks before dissipating. Julian pressed his fists against his hips and nodded, scanning the scene.

"Will it work?" I asked.

"Absolutely, now that's what I call ambience. Here, check out the cameras." Julian pointed toward the bridge, where a camera was tucked in a corner so carefully even I couldn't pick it out. "A couple more like that, we've got all the angles we need. We'll have the single camera guy on the ground getting a bit of the action down here. It'll be perfect."

"So where do you stand on all of this ghost business?" Natalie asked. "Hauntings: Real or fake?" If I had been close enough to pinch her, I would have. She was treading way too close to "secrets" territory moments before we tried to pull off a hoax in front of haunting pros, and I was only days away from the loan decision from coming through.

Julian squinted as he thought. "I don't believe I am reason enough for any spirit to choose to appear."

Natalie tilted her head. "Solid answer."

"What next?" I asked, desperate to change the subject.

"Showtime." Julian waved jazz hands and grinned.

Showtime was nine, when it was dark enough that the stories we were spinning would feel more believable. After night swallowed up the woods, the paranormal seemed more, well, possibly normal. What looked like a broken tree branch in full daylight morphed into a hint of something creepy as the sun set—but by full dark, that same branch turned into nightmare fuel. Dancing lantern light added to the horror as it played against each bent branch or snowbank to turn it into something worth worrying about, again and again until the sun began to peek over the mountaintop.

The people who lived on the road often complained about the "ruckus" caused by people playing around at the bridge. "Ghost hunters" shouting and squealing their tires inside the bridge when something just the other side of ordinary tingled in spines, creating the sensation of someone tapping you on the shoulder or breathing down your neck.

Natalie and I—along with her brother Derick, and his friends—had taken it upon ourselves to scare off the adventure seekers by giving them something to be afraid of. Usually, it was Derick in the rafters, dangling buttons tied to fish line onto unsuspecting visitors to illicit shrieks of terror and clumsy scurries to car doors, or letting strands of ball chain drag across the tops of sedans for a nails-on-chalkboard sound that always earned terrified shouts.

Our new plan of action was more nuanced than in the early days, due to keeping it hush-hush so James and Julian didn't find out.

After dropping out of college, in an attempt at willing my depression away by busying myself with anything I could, I'd thought about reviving the vlog. But I'd lost the drive. Instead, I pored over a book on the psychology of human fear—and how fear can lie if the circumstances are correct. That's why the smaller touches usually had the biggest impact: the gasps, a flicker of light, a scraping rather than a banging. The only thing scarier than the fear of being alone was the fear of *not* being alone, and that was a mindfuck in the truest form.

Julian's method wasn't much different: He'd lull the tourists into a false sense of security with larger-than-life stories that were too unbelievable to be true—but creepy enough that they were difficult to shrug off as tall tales.

We drove back to the tree farm parking lot, which Natalie's dad had given us permission to use as a meet-up location for the ghost tour. James and Julian had rounded up plenty of people to get the best reactions for ideal film splicing. I knew nothing about the process, so I had to take his word for it.

As we pulled in, James squeezed my hand on top of my knee and took a shaky breath.

"You going to make it, there? The fun hasn't even begun," Julian said.

"This is a bit more involved than our usual haunted wander."

"You can wait here at the empty tree farm all by yourself if you want. Though I bet a tree farm ghost would be worse than Emily. Nobody comes to visit here, like they visit the bridge. Poor, sad, angry ghost," I said.

"Yeah, yeah. Hilarious." He wrinkled his nose and narrowed his eyes as he reprimanded us for mocking him. "Got your hand warmers?"

I gripped the sides and jiggled the jacket, then nodded. "I should buy you a heated coat for Christmas," I joked, then realized that its usefulness depended on a lot of things—namely his being in an area where a heated jacket made sense. If he moved to some other, warmer spooky locale for the next round of filming, a heated jacket would be overkill.

Julian, James, and I waited for the first tour group—as usual, tourists invited earlier in the day by Julian after he befriended them at the ski lodge and restaurants—who filtered in and shuffled around the parking lot until the show began. The lone camera guy gave the signal and Julian put on his showman face.

"Welcome to this haunted evening, I'm pleased you could join us as we uncover the secrets of this spooky location." He clapped his hands once, then rubbed them together. "How many of you are from Stowe?"

My hand was the only one that went up.

"Ah, a local, I see. So pleased you could join us. The rest of you, thank you for taking time out of your visit to explore the paranormal with me. Some ground rules, before we start." Julian listed the important information—stay with him to ensure no ghostly entanglement, no climbing, scaling, or otherwise misusing the location, and pretend the camera isn't there. "Oh, and if you think you've been possessed, please remember that while I'm a professional, my expertise is in film, not exorcism. You signed a waiver releasing me from any possession-related liability." The usual.

After the laughter—sincere with a hint of "what did I just sign up for"—Julian gave them all their last chance to back out. Nobody budged. The camera guy started filming, and Julian led the group along the stretch of dirt road toward the bridge.

"A little history lesson for you," he said. "Emily's Bridge was built in 1844. The supernatural record of this specific location begins after Emily's untimely death, on this site in 1849." He continued the tale, recounting Emily's despair when her paramour didn't arrive at the bridge for their elopement. He left out the part about the stories having originated sometime in the seventies.

"During the day, the area surrounding this bridge is generally calm. A serene, snowy scene with an occasional feeling of unease. After dark, however . . . well, if Emily is feeling restless tonight, you'll get to experience what hundreds of visitors do every year. Moaning. Crying. Rattling."

James grasped my hand as Julian continued to tick off the ghostly activity.

"Don't worry." I shoulder bumped him as we crunched our way toward the bridge. "I'll protect you."

James squeezed my hand in his. "Do not judge me if I yelp, gasp, or run away."

"No judging, I swear it. You ready for this?"

He gulped as we rounded the last bend toward the bridge. Fog rolled out of the opening, creeping low and slow across the snow-covered road. The sky was a deep black except where the crescent moon and glinting stars shone. A perfect night for a ghost hunt.

The group huddled near Julian while he crept around the site. For the first few moments, we explored outside the bridge. The wind blew, leaving bare trees creaking and evergreens rustling. The breeze was stiff enough to send the last of the most stubborn autumn leaves tumbling from the branches, skittering across the dirt-and-snow road toward the opening of the bridge. Caught up in a mini tornado, they whirled at the mouth of the bridge, daring the group to step closer.

"It appears we have been invited in," Julian said, taking advantage of serendipity and spreading his arms to encourage the group to follow him. All he had to do was warm them up. The haunting was inevitable. Natalie had seen to that, with her brother secretly tucked away in the trees, spying on the progress to remotely initiate scare tactics and build on the group's gasps.

Julian crossed into the bridge, dragging a fingertip along the truss slowly, dramatically. "Greetings, Emily, we don't wish to intrude. We want to say hello." He pulled his fingers away from the wooden support and looked upward, toward the ceiling—where the cameras, mics, and speakers were carefully camouflaged.

An echoing whisper sounded at the end of the bridge, earning gasps from the attendees. James gripped my hand with both of his, linking his arm into mine.

"Protecting *me*?" I asked.

"You said you wouldn't pick on me," he said.

"No," I whispered back. "I said I wouldn't judge you. Nothing about picking on you. But—"

A rattle sounded, and James and I both jumped. I tugged him closer. "I'm sorry I picked on you. Truce?"

"A little different on this side of things, huh?" he asked.

"What, holding fear rather than simply sharing it with an audience? Yeah, a little."

Julian continued recounting the various versions of Emily's story, punctuated by rattles, creaks, and thumps. Faster at times, which Julian attributed to angering her with false stories. Occasionally, melancholy whispers bounced around the interior, spreading from speaker to speaker unbeknownst to the visitors—or the tour guide. Those, Julian claimed, were Emily's relief that her story was being shared, and with such an understanding group. His eyebrows pulled closer with each unexpected noise.

"Some claim to feel extreme cold. Some, the sensation of a fiery hand pressed against their cheeks or the back of their neck. For the most part, Emily wishes only to remind visitors that she lived. That she *was* though she is no more. Others, however, aren't so lucky. The roof of a car scraped long and deep. Scratched flesh, damaged clothing, ghostly handprints left behind on jackets. The spirit, visible in the peripheral, stalking, creeping, following."

The rattle of chains against the wooden floor sent a shriek through the group, which turned to nervous laughter and whispers. James and Julian exchanged a startled glance—neither knew that some of Derick's friends had hidden themselves in strategic locations to help me pull this haunting off. A thrill shot through me at the collective gasps that cycled through the attendees. James and Julian wanted their guests to experience the rush of a haunting—and helping them catapulted me back in time. I'd missed this. Not enough to make it a career like they were, but the nostalgia felt like watching a favorite movie. Gleeful comfort.

A shriek from one of the tour-goers echoed through the woods, bouncing between the bridge and the snow-bent tree limbs. A wave of nervous chuckles swirled through the group, each person checking out their feelings internally, and collectively shaking off their fear. Part of me wondered how much of Emily's story was perpetuated by late-night teenage pranks just like this. We hadn't made her up, but we'd given her some staying power.

I pulled James even closer and squeezed our interlaced fingers. "I hope Julian understands that you're the best friend on the face of the planet," I said.

He shrugged. "The research part isn't all bad. I get to meet some interesting folklorists, at least. Some of them are pretty. Makes up for the"—another rattle, another round of shouts, another flinch from James, another wide-eyed glance toward Julian—"creepy stuff."

"Over there," Julian gasped, pointing toward the fog. He recovered from the shock quicker than I'd expected, and the film kept rolling. "It's time. Gather around, and I'll explain these highly specialized paranormal investigation tools before we use them."

He showed off his EMF reader and temperature gun, both of which were "sure" to prove the presence of a poltergeist. Nothing a little movie magic couldn't manage: The hidden cameras and speakers all sent the little LED lights dancing across the display, giving a double-duty performance that surprised, spooked, and satisfied the ghost tour group—and, likewise, the tour hosts. The same questioning glances continued to crop up between Julian and James. The camera guy even peeked around his equipment for a moment, mouthing something vaguely like "what the hell was that?" before tucking himself away again behind the viewfinder.

* * *

"That was spectacular." Julian's echo bounced off snow-covered trees and through the bridge. "A bit more footage like that and we're golden. Taking it all the way, the big screen!"

"Yay, hauntings," James said, punching an unenthusiastic fist toward the onyx sky. He'd done an admirable job of keeping his cool, but his eyebrows arched higher with worry at each ghostly groan and creepy creak. "You weren't kidding about this place being active."

"Ghost stories don't happen by accident, James," I said playfully. "I've spent time getting to know them all, and I'm glad Emily came out to play tonight."

"So, uh, are we good here?" James asked, fiddling with the flap on his coat pocket.

"Yeah, yeah, scaredy-cat. Let's break down here, and I'll grab some filler footage before we call it a night, just to make sure we're good to go. Anyone in?"

James avoided making eye contact with Julian. The chicken. Though I did feel a little sympathetic, especially considering my secret role in the night's events.

"As long as my name is in the credits beside some awesome job title, like Ghoulish Ghost Grabber, I'm completely at your service," Natalie offered.

"I'll have a word with the director about the credits. I've got a little sway and can make things happen," Julian said. "Drinks first? Then back here for stills and ghostly diegetic sound effects?"

Natalie agreed, then joined me where I was looping some wires out of sight until we broke down the equipment. She slipped up beside me, linking her arm in mine. I squeezed her forearm with my gloved hand.

"He says they have almost all their planned tours finished. They squeezed this one in because it was too good to pass up, and they've been waiting for approval to film in a couple other spots—Dog-Eared included. He says they're close, though."

I closed my eyes and sucked the cold air through my nose to fill my lungs. "Then what?"

"Then what, what?" James asked, appearing beside me.

"Just talking about your big filmmaking debut," Natalie covered smoothly, knowing I wasn't willing to get into a discussion about feelings and futures. Especially not in fifteen-degree weather after I'd numbed my fingers setting up for his future on the road. "And what comes next for the project."

"Ah, that. Well, we've got a bit of editing ahead of us still, but Julian's been knocking most of it out as he films each location. These things never move quickly. The contest deadline is March, and after that, he pitches it to film festivals. If someone picks it up, that's good news. If not, we beat on. Julian's always ready to film something else if it means he could become an internet sensation."

"And you?" I asked. "Are you looking for fame?"

"Nope."

"Not even a little?"

"Not at all. He's the one looking for praise and awards. I'm just trying to figure out what I want to do next week."

"Not one for planning ahead, then?"

He slid his hands into his jacket pockets and shoved a snowball around with the toe of his boot. "My plan is to figure out what makes me want to plan ahead. Might be cooking. Might be trucking. It's definitely not being a lawyer. The documentary isn't my thing, either— but he needed a codirector, and the prize money is something I can't pass up. Besides, I'm always wondering what's hiding in the shadows waiting to spirit me away. I don't understand wanting to be scared like that. Paying to have someone shout boo so you can scream to feel alive."

So the pitching . . . and leaving . . . weren't necessarily his next steps. Even if he and Julian did everything together. My heart lifted with the teensiest bit of hope.

"How far ahead do you plan?" I asked, equal parts joking and gentle prodding.

James laughed and slung an arm around my shoulders. "I am planning on taking someone home to warm up within the next five minutes."

"I accept." I grabbed him by the lapel and kissed him again, deeper, to hold on to the now and ignore the nagging at the back of my mind.

CHAPTER FOURTEEN

I'd only been to James's place a handful of times, mostly to pick him up in the driveway. Because he shared the space with Julian and their crew of four others, the space was never empty—and rarely quiet. But Natalie and Julian were keeping the crew busy, providing the ideal opportunity for a change in scenery.

James unlocked the door, and we were greeted by a bounding Lulu. Our ear scratches were repaid with play bows galore. She woofed her little Lulu bark and nuzzled my leg, then zoomed between James's legs to bounce at the leash that dangled from the coat rack beside the door.

I bent and ruffed up the long hair at her neck, and she woofed again, sat on my foot, and leaned her whole body into my leg so she could look upward at me, tongue lolling.

"You're ridiculously cute, but I'm not the person you need to ask." I pointed at James, who put his hands on his hips while staring her down.

"A quick walk, and then I'm off-duty," he told Lulu. Then, to me: "Get comfy, I'll be right back."

After he disappeared out the door with the furry date-snatcher, I checked out the décor around the apartment. I dragged a fingertip along the edge of the entertainment center and walked my fingers along the wall as I examined the space. A corkboard map of the world hung—slightly crooked—on the wall, with a rainbow of pins scattered across the entire display. Most of the markers landed throughout North America, but a not-insignificant number of pins were stuck on other continents as well. A print-out of Pinky and the Brain was taped to a bottom edge, with "1) Film Documentaries, 2) Take Over the World" added in funky bubble letters. Lofty goals.

A few pictures hung on the fridge: Julian and James sitting on a guard rail with a backdrop of cacti and sand; the entire crew on a couch with their cameras and sound gear in laps; Julian high-fiving someone who looked like a member of Fall Out Boy; a much smaller puppy Lulu stretched out on a couch with James sitting on the floor resting his chin on the cushion nearest her face, her tongue lolling.

I was pulled from my perusal when James opened the front door, and Lulu tore into the room, mini snowballs flying off her shaggy coat as she barreled through the space. He held a tall thermos in one hand.

"I see you made a little pit stop."

"Check out the dessert menu," James said, gesturing toward a cooler that sat on the counter. I peeked inside to find various grocery store clamshell packages and a bag of marshmallows. The more I pawed at the goodies, the more deliciousness I found: chocolate chips, strawberries, apple slices, and sponge cake.

"Open the bag." He tipped his head toward a reusable grocery bag beside the coffee table. I peeked inside, wondering how much more dessert the guy thought I could pack in.

"A . . . fondue pot?"

James nodded. "The forks are in the outer pocket. Candle and lighter, too." He smoothed a big wool blanket on the floor as I plucked the fondue pot and various accessories from the bag. James arranged them, and I added the ingredients, dessert, and thermos to the blanket.

"Okay, so I have it on good authority that these apples go perfectly with chocolate, but I have some caramel if you'd prefer. The cake might dip, but it might fall apart. We may finish dessert looking like we just learned to eat, but it will be worth it. Dig in."

Note to self: implement fondue nights at Dog-Eared immediately upon securing a business loan. "You've thought of everything," I said.

He smiled, lit the fondue pot, and dropped chocolate chips into the bowl on top, then turned his attention to the candles that were arranged on the coffee table beside us.

"Oh, so this is probably the wrong time to suggest we brainstorm the next stop?" I settled into my spot, leaning back to stretch my toes far enough to brush the arch of James's foot. James narrowed his eyes playfully as he poured something dark and steaming from the thermos, then passed me the mug.

"A rich hot cocoa, sourced directly from the bakery on Main Street."

"You mean the competition?" I smirked.

"We'll call it 'research.' We're sizing up the octogenarian baker who probably changed your diapers when you were a child."

Not untrue. Miss Beecher was honorary granny to anyone under the age of forty.

"She said this is the flavor you and Nat always ordered when you were filming the vlog." He grasped for the remote and the television screen flashed on, a Yule Log video crackling to life across the giant screen. "I actually *was* hoping the nostalgia of some peppermint hot cocoa might earn me a few extra spooky secrets."

"Well, the secret was that we tipped a few shots of whipped cream flavored vodka into the cups to really warm us up while we were out all hours of the night chasing ghosts."

The candlelight flickered in James's eyes, amplifying the amused sparkle that I'd grown so fond of. "How do you know you didn't hallucinate the spirits you were chasing, then?"

I grabbed his hand and pulled him in for a kiss—partly because I craved the taste of his lips, but also to stop the unintentional guilt-tripping. Joking about hallucinating the ghosts was a little too close to the truth—even if I'd known they weren't real, the act of creating them and sharing their stories had helped me feel less alone—and now it turned out that their continued existence was my key to business ownership. I needed those ghosts—always had. "It wasn't *that* much vodka. But I think I've got something for you."

I pulled out my phone and brought up a photo of Dog-Eared—before it was Dog-Eared. The building had been standing as some form of business since the mid-nineteenth century, and this particular photo featured a hardware store sign and a handful of Ford Model Ts. "So, it's not the oldest building in the town. It's not even the most haunted. But it *is* haunted. You saw the vlog: we've called her Mary, and the rumors of her existence started when books by authors named Mary started disappearing or ending up in mysterious places. And I want to tell you all about her." So what if it was fake? It supported James's project—and gave me the upper hand when it came to buying the store.

"Charles was hesitant to let us film at the store."

"Not a ghost guy. Doesn't even like to stock ghost stories. Someone donated a Magic 8 Ball once, and he hurled the thing like Pedro Martinez gunning for a career record."

James smiled. "Don't think you can derail me with a baseball reference—did you get the okay to film there?"

"Sort of. You can film an interview with me—with one exception. He reserves the right to have you cut it from the documentary at his request if my bookstore purchase falls through."

James ran a thumb along his jawline as he thought.

"But if I get the business loan, it'll stay in—no question." I swallowed, hard, and held in the guilt. It wasn't just my life I was messing with here—his documentary was at stake. But if I played my part well enough, we'd all win.

"I'll run it by the group, but chances are good they'll be on board."

I stabbed cake with my teeny fondue fork and dunked it into the melted chocolate, plucked it off the fork, then washed it down with a tiny sip of hot cocoa. The combination was damn near perfect and a tiny moan escaped.

"Just wait until I take your order for the next course."

"Oh, there's more, is there?"

"It's an off-menu item, for VIPs only. And if there's anything this establishment prides itself on, it's the fact that we aim to please. No matter the request."

"*Anything* I want?" I asked, tapping my fondue fork against my lower lip.

"You're the boss." He leaned back, supporting himself by resting on his hands behind him, one leg hitched over the other. Cool and casual.

I stabbed a strawberry, dunked it, and devoured the chocolatey treat.

"I'm thinking we should move this meeting to a more private venue. Bedroom?"

"And on that note." He blew out the fondue pot candle and quickly gathered the leftover desserts into their respective containers.

I dipped my finger into a gob of melted chocolate that had dripped onto the blanket, then swiped it across James's nose. Ignoring the direct assault, he closed the last container, wiped away the chocolate, and slipped a bit of an apple to Lulu, who took it politely between her teeth before sneaking off to her bed to nibble the treat, then wrapped his arms around my waist and hoisted me over his shoulder.

"Something about that absolutely did it for me, and I don't want to unpack it at this moment." I grasped at the back of his shirt, tugging it from where it was tucked into his perfectly fitted jeans and fisting the loose hem in my hands. "Right now, all I want is this shirt on the floor."

"Can do," he promised. When we were concealed in his bedroom, he flopped me onto the mattress and finished untucking his shirt, then moved to sit on the bed beside me. As he unfastened his buttons and shed his collared shirt—but kept on the white T-shirt beneath—I eyed the space to see what I could learn about the man getting naked beside me. Everything was in perfect order: The dresser top was spotless, his sheets were pulled up and tucked neatly, and he had a pair of bookshelves that stretched floor to ceiling—jam-packed with books, organized by size. He could have run his own used bookstore out of his bedroom.

I scooted to the opposite edge of his bed and leaned in to examine the titles. For a guy who made an effort to appear indifferent to literature, he'd amassed quite a collection. Everything from *Lord of the Rings* and *The Wheel of Time* to the top sellers from the Business section— name a title, it was here. He even had an eReader on one of the shelves, but a thin layer of dust showed it had been resting there a while. Analog fan, intriguing. I dragged my fingertip along the shelves and stopped at *The Chronicles of Narnia*, aligned in the current publication order.

"This won't do," I said, before plucking Narnia from its place and rearranging the books—no matter what the spines said, they should be displayed in the order they'd been released. No excuses. James grunted at my fiddling but didn't object. He knew to let a professional do their job.

I finished my reorganization, then scanned the spines to further catalog his preferences. Wide, leatherbound books and hardcovers and trade paperbacks, nonfiction and classics, poetry anthologies and biographies, some fantastic romance novels from recent years. They were in perfect order—if you count an arrangement by book height an acceptable sorting technique, which I did not. Everything fit in his strange sequence, except for a handful of books that appeared out of place. Why were those books important enough to mess up his clear and deliberate organization technique?

The stragglers at the end of the middle shelf, directly beside his desk, were paired two-by-two. The same titles, different covers, matched up. Closer investigation revealed names I knew well: George Orwell. Philip K. Dick. Jane Austen. Joseph Heller. Mary Shelley. Toni Morrison. My favorite authors, standing like columns against a slew of other books without pairs.

If I hadn't recognized the sticker on the spine of *Dracula*, I'd have assumed he was a serial classics collector. I stashed books with inscriptions from perfect strangers, so collecting multiple copies of the same books wasn't unheard of. But I knew the titles he had stashed away. All books that I'd recommended. And he had multiples.

James climbed farther onto the bed and crawled over to meet me where I sat. He moved my hair out of the way and kissed me at the curve of my neck.

"Has another bookstore employee been forcing good literature on you?"

"You're not the only collector," James said, resting his chin on my shoulder.

"How many of these have you read?"

James sucked his teeth, then tilted his head to look me in the eye. "All of them. Multiple times."

"No! Why did you pretend you hadn't?"

"Because it's sexy when you lecture me about literature."

I shot him a stern look.

"Okay. At first, I was trying to judge your taste in books. But then, you were so into giving me recommendations that I couldn't ruin it. I dual-majored in humanities and teaching, so most of those were required reading. The ones that weren't just spoke to me."

"My short-lived experience attempting a degree in Library Science and Media means everything has a chance to become a learning experience, so recommendations are part of the deal."

"Why short-lived?"

I shrugged. "Dropped out. I worked too hard, stressed myself out, went down an anxiety spiral, and didn't have a support system beyond Nat and her family—but didn't want to be a burden, so I hid the worst of it. The college health center wasn't equipped to help. Not that it was their fault, they just didn't have enough staff, and there wasn't enough support to go around."

"I'm sorry to hear that."

"It was a dream I had, but it didn't work out."

"Would you go back to school?"

I shrugged. "I think the time has passed. My anxiety and I have learned to coexist; biweekly appointments with my therapist are an incredible help. But I think I'm exactly where I need to be now. Besides, the thing I need least right now is school loans. I've only just paid mine off—with no degree to show for it—and I'd like to keep my debt to a minimum. How about you? How'd you end up filmmaking instead of teaching?"

"I got tired of providing free labor for Julian and the crew and demanded a cut." He rose his eyebrows and flopped backward onto the bed. "We'd been traveling together, and usually I'd stop in to apply for open positions at local businesses. I'd work wherever I could get hours, save what I could, pitch in for rent, help pay for gas for that soccer mom van that Julian and the crew rides around in. But there's also something about committing things to film that piqued my curiosity. It's like committing words to the pages of a book—I like creating something that will persist, whether on film or on paper, bringing ideas to life. It's the way the ideas grow and change with each person who encounters them that I love about film. Don't get me wrong: I'm not a filmmaker, and I don't see a future in this, but thanks to Julian's storytelling, these ideas all have a life of their own once they've left his curation." He shook his head. "Sorry, that sounds silly, I guess."

He may have thought it was silly, but it made perfect sense to me. I may have created my ghosts to surround myself with whatever comfort I could conjure, but they'd become something bigger than me. They left my immediate control and became something to other people. They became something to James and Julian, who crossed an entire country to research the phantoms I'd set free from my imagination.

"Anyway, you know that this specific documentary is a contest submission. The prize money is the real draw."

"You mean it's not the ghost hunting that you love?" I bumped him with my knee.

"If I could win the prize money without the ghosts, I would jump on that chance. They're, uh, more willing to come out and play than we expected, honestly. I was hoping we'd get away with debunking the stories."

"Debunking my ghosts, James, really? Rude." I leaned back to lounge beside him.

"They've made it clear that they'd prefer to remain . . . bunked . . . I thought I'd be teaching literature or history by now, not intentionally scaring myself so I can win a contest. But, turns I wasn't cut out for teaching after all—my weeks spent student teaching proved that I would have been terrible at it."

We sat in a moment of comfortable silence, his fingers flirting with the sensitive skin at my wrist and palm. The conversation had moved beyond reflection, and my thighs pressed together as I imagined his hands elsewhere on my body.

There was something I hadn't had the opportunity to try until exactly this point in my life, and I had an inkling that James would be a willing participant. I scanned the room until my eyes landed on the camera and tripod I knew he had. What better time to try out a longstanding fantasy than right now?

He'd waxed poetic about committing moments to film—which tracked for a guy who seemed to be on the road a lot. It might be too personal for him. But, maybe . . .

"Maybe there's a different subject you'd like to teach," I suggested. I dragged my fingertip along the curve of his collarbone. "I mean, it's been an awfully long time since I was on camera. Maybe you could give me a few tips. Isn't there some advice about picturing the audience naked to relieve nerves?"

James's eyes widened, and he licked his lips at the scandalous recommendation. "That's for public speaking, and actually significantly creepier than ghost hunting."

Good lord, he wasn't wrong. "Okay, shit, sorry. How about we're both actually naked, instead? We can do a test-run on film, then check the footage later to pinpoint my best angles."

He cleared his throat, leaned closer, and in a deepened tone said, "Are you . . . suggesting what I think you're suggesting?"

"I mean, only if you're open to it. Zero pressure. Sorry, I shouldn't have asked, it's totally—"

"For your eyes only?" he asked.

"Absolutely. My eyes only. We can even delete it right after. Immediately. If you're into it?" I chewed my lower lip, waiting to see where it landed on the weird-requests scale.

"I am completely into it."

"Yeah?"

He flipped himself over to pin me to the mattress and leaned in for a kiss. The growl he let slip had me melting into the mattress. Using both arms, he hefted himself back off the mattress and turned to retrieve the camera and tripod. The muscles in his whole arm tensed as he twisted the knob to raise the tripod, knocking my vision out of focus at how much I wanted to trace his bicep with my tongue.

"How much are we documenting?" He curled a finger in my direction to beckon me nearer, pointing at the viewfinder to indicate that I should take over. I joined him beside the camera, and he gently guided me with one hand at my hip to have me take control.

"Anything you're comfortable with. And we can stop at any time. Safe word is 'That's a wrap!'" I giggled, but cut the laughter short as he slid up behind me—his erection measurable through his pants.

He leaned in to press a button on the camera and the viewfinder flashed to life. "You're the director. Set the scene."

"I have to line up the shot first." I turned toward him and grasped his chin in one hand, then pressed a line of kisses along his jawline and down his neck. "Set's hot, we just need the star of the show." I used two fingers to press him away from me, toward the bed.

He lowered himself onto the mattress, hitting the eyeline perfectly before aiming his fervent gaze directly at the lens. Even through the viewfinder, it hit me like the heat pouring out of a woodstove. Warmth pooled low in my belly as I adjusted the camera to capture the whole bed—the pristine comforter wasn't going to be wrinkle-free for long. I pressed *record*.

"You're a mysterious scholar, visiting my library to quench your thirst for knowledge." Biting a thumbnail, I moved toward him until my thighs touched the mattress, then I slid one knee between his legs, savoring his sharp intake of breath. I slipped my hands beneath the bottom edge of his T-shirt and slid his shirt up and over his head to expose his broad chest and solid build. With a hand on each bare shoulder, I dragged the tip of my nose along the soft, exposed flesh of his neck and chased it with a playful nibble. Goosebumps cropped up along his biceps. The tiny bumps were glorious under my fingertips, multiplying my want by ten, ten thousand, ten million. I grasped his wrist with one hand, turning his palm up, then seized the opportunity to tease each curve and dip along his arm, whispering my fingertips from the dimple of his shoulder blade, down the smooth skin of his arm, and across the inner crook of his elbow before raising his hand to my mouth to kiss along his palm and wrist. I leaned back again and bit my lip while perusing his body, appreciating his stocky-but-tall frame—more subtle muscles from hefting camera gear and playing fetch with his dog, rather than lifting weights. I was torn between the desire to drink it all in and the thirst for more than simply looking.

"I like where this is going," James said, leaning forward and grasping my belt loops to tug me into his lap and shifting his weight until I straddled him. Deft fingertips undid the button-up front of my shirt. With an eyebrow rising toward the ceiling, he pulled the placket open and admired my curves before leaning in to kiss the skin my lacy bra didn't cover—following the slight curve of one cup, then the other—before slipping his hands underneath the back of my shirt and plucking the clasp open.

We hadn't even begun, and I was going to come undone if he kept his eyes on me like that much longer. I hopped off his lap and shed the shirt and bra but maneuvered his hand to let him free the button of my jeans. The intentionally slow unbuttoning and unzipping process had me shifting on my feet, counting the milliseconds until he stripped me bare and explored all the places that could make me shake. Eventually, thankfully, mercifully, the denim dropped to the ground, followed by my lace underwear, freeing me to lunge at him. Impatient, insistent tugging finally got me the result I craved: his crisp pressed pants were stripped off and discarded on the floor beside my own clothing.

The both of us finally unclothed, I hoisted my leg up onto the bed and corralled him, encouraging him to make his move. He crept his fingers up across knee and thigh until he found the groove only inches from where I wanted him. Firmly, he gripped the curve of my ass in his hand to pull me closer, fixed his eyes on mine, then leaned downward to tease the rise of my hip and crease of my thigh with his tongue while leisurely drawing the knuckle of a thumb over my clit.

My whimper was met with a low, rumbling growl. Want and need had nothing on the yearning building between my legs.

When he looked up, not at me, but past me—acknowledging the camera lens that was capturing the moment—I lost every bit of composure I'd tried to keep.

"Jesus, that's hot," I admitted from somewhere deep in my throat.

"Good performance is all about knowing where to look." He grasped my thigh and flipped me onto the mattress, pivoting to place the length of our bodies perfectly within frame before taking a long, appraising sweep of my entire naked body. "Didn't put down any spike tape, I hope I didn't ruin your shot."

"You're in it. No way could it be ruined." I captured his bottom lip between my teeth and pulled gently backward, encouraging him to move closer.

He kissed me, first experimentally, then deeply, slipping his tongue between my lips to tangle with my own. My skin crackled with built-up energy that needed to release. Every flirty exchange between us had stacked like a house of cards and the rough hair on his knees scraping between my thighs as he leaned into his kisses was a fuse too near a powder keg of desire. He moved downward, trailing a fingertip between my breasts and down the center line of my stomach before slipping his thumb between my legs. My thighs twitched and my back arched involuntarily, eliciting a tiny laugh that morphed into a moan halfway through.

"Did you bring any of those expired condoms?" he asked. I wrinkled my nose and narrowed my eyes at the joke but he didn't wait for an answer. He moved away from the bed, stopping only to caress the inside of my knee, before selecting a condom from the drawer beside his bed. He didn't turn away from me or the camera as he rolled the condom into place. My gaze landed on the way his eyebrows arched as he focused.

He dragged his fingers along my torso—fingertips down, then a gentle scratch of fingernails on his way back up—before leaning in and wrapping his mouth around my nipple. His hot tongue swept across the hardening surface and in a quick circle around my sensitive areola. He tip-toed the pads of his fingers down the center line of my stomach then circled my clit a few times with excruciating slowness, tightening the orbit each time before dipping a finger—then two—inside while adding pressure with his thumb where his fingers had recently teased.

My head lolled backward as I enjoyed the sensations—and of being the only thing he was focusing on, the thing keeping him in this space at this moment, willing to commit the desire and whim to film. He took a long, relaxed exhale as an opportunity to slide between my legs, shifting my thighs wider apart to settle in place. I peeked at the camera quickly, nothing demure about it, and nodded for him to continue.

Without hurry, he pressed into me until his hip bones and my thighs were sharing space. The smooth motion ended with a small hitch as he shuddered before coming to a rest. Though I'd had my fair share of sexual partners, I rarely let myself simply enjoy the pieces that got me to orgasm. In the past, I hadn't fully appreciated the concept of taking our time. I was never in a rush to finish but also never truly gave myself the time to delight in the build-up.

This time, I craved the moments in between. I wanted to relish the gentle whimpers and contented sighs, the relief, the indulgence, the pure adoration that passed between us. I wanted to luxuriate in it all—memorize the milliseconds and keep them in a special place in my mind, so I could revisit them later. With our bodies pressed together, nose to nose, he smoothed my hair away from my face, but the effort to tame my waves was wasted: I didn't intend to come out of this experience with anything but bedhead.

I grasped him with both hands wrapped around the back of his head to pull him in for another kiss, shifting my hips as I did to ensure I had every inch at my disposal. He grunted as I wrapped my ankles around his thighs and tugged him closer, deeper, before moving on him to fully appreciate the position.

I grasped for his pillow. "Can I use this?" I asked. He nodded, and I folded it into a crude wedge before sliding it beneath the arch of my back, raising my hips even more. The shift in position sent a shiver through my body, which he met with an insistent thrust. We'd exhausted the slow and steady portion of the encounter. All of James's fingers pressed into the flesh along the tops of my legs as he used both hands to gain purchase. Moving together, each exploring the other with wandering hands, we discovered the miniscule shifts and larger thrusts to bring the other to the edge. When his hand traveled between my legs again, I nudged it out of the way to take over. His touch was sublime, but playing with myself freed his hands to rove—and I needed him to cover as much ground as possible. His earnest observation and quivering breath were testament to how well the stimulation worked for him too. As muscles tensed and the hint of an orgasm began to creep in, James grasped the hair at the back of my head in one hand and braced himself on the mattress with the other arm. His eyes narrowed, then widened, as he watched me come undone beneath him.

A moan tore from my throat as I shook, lifting my head enough to feel the pull of his fingers at the roots of my hair and trembling even more for it. He sucked his lower lip as I fixed my gaze on our torsos and hips, his happy trail, and the way our chests heaved with pleasure.

I lifted a hand to his face and dragged the pad of my thumb across his lips. He kissed, then drew it into his mouth, teasing the curve of my thumb with his tongue before giving a quick, possessive nip. In answer, I flipped him onto his back and pinned his arms to the bed so I could sink onto his dick as deeply as possible.

The bedhead I had hoped for was more than accomplished, but to ensure it met my expectations, I skated my fingertips up my sides and across my breasts—taking a moment to roll my own nipples between my fingertips—then up my neck to tangle my mess of hair in my own grasp.

James drew in a breath, rising his torso off the bed as I arched my back and knotted my fingers in my loose strands. He palmed my ass and groaned, pulling me down onto him, then letting me rise so he could do it again and again—until he flung his arms outward to clasp the sheets as he shook beneath me. When the pulsing slowed, he flopped an arm across his forehead and exhaled long and deep. The sideways grin plastered across his face was ridiculously kissable—so I helped myself to a peck at the corner of his mouth before backing off him and strolling toward the camera to end the recording.

"Do you want to watch it?" he asked.

"Oh, god no!" I laughed. "You?"

He scrunched his nose and shook his head. "Delete it?"

I turned the screen toward him, and he clicked through the settings to bring up an "Are You Sure?" prompt. We pressed the SELECT button together, then triple checked to make sure our sex tape couldn't be recovered under any circumstances.

CHAPTER FIFTEEN

I'd assured Charles—in a dozen and a half different ways—that we'd (a) keep our paraphernalia to a minimum, and (b) ensure no ghosts were left behind after our prodding. To assuage him further, we left the creepier devices out of it. That meant no electronic voice phenomenon detector, but the IR thermometer was fair game.

I fed the mic wire up the back of my shirt and slid it through the buttons on the front, then James clipped it into place.

"Interview first," he said. "Then maybe a little tour?"

"If Mary's willing to visit, I'm happy to introduce you." Faking it was going to be more difficult while indoors, during daylight, and without the handful of clandestine helpers from the night of the bridge. But this was also the most important haunting to get right—I needed Charles to remain convinced the store was haunted. Natalie had stopped in early to hide a desktop AC unit inside one of the store's wall vent grills. With luck, I could keep the remote in my pocket secret, and the cooler air it pushed would be enough to trick an IR sensor.

"Nervous?" James asked.

I gave him a flirty smile. "After the practice session I had last night? No way, this camera isn't ready for me."

The tint that crept into James's cheeks was exhilarating. If I didn't have to put on a believable show, I'd tease him a bit about it—and how he hadn't been bashful the night before. But my head was too full trying to remember the tale I'd told on *Haunted Happenings* all those years ago.

"Julian's asking the questions." James cleared his throat. "He's better on camera, and I'm not sure I can handle being on camera with you again quite so soon."

"And I thought you were a professional," I joked.

"Shall we?" Julian asked, sliding between us and settling into his seat to the left of the camera. He smoothed his jacket, adjusted his mic, and directed minor adjustments of the lighting. When he was satisfied, we dove into the Q and A. After some getting to know you chat and a quick set-up from Julian regarding the purpose of the interview, we got down to the details.

"Dog-Eared Books and More is nestled inside a creaky old building," Julian prompted.

"Sure is. The creak is part of the draw."

"Tell me about the building's history," he said.

"Love to. The building was completed in 1871, and was first a hardware store—which included the area through the wall behind me, actually."

"How long has the bookstore been here?"

"The owner, Charles, opened the store in 1975. That's when the building was divided into two sections, the hardware store downsizing significantly, and Dog-Eared filling this portion. The hardware store has been owned by generations of the same family since it was opened, but the seventies wasn't a decade known for its booming economy. The owners chose to downsize during the recession—keeping the most popular items in stock, but moving to a by-order method for big-ticket items or products that took up a lot of space."

"When we asked the bookstore's owner for an interview, he seemed surprised about the location's paranormal activity."

"He's not comfortable around ghosts, so we hadn't made him aware."

"Not a fan of your vlog, then?"

I laughed. "He wouldn't enjoy a single second of it."

"Is the hardware store haunted, too?" Julian asked.

I hadn't considered that part of the interview. I couldn't fake a haunting over there. But if I were a ghost, I'd stick to the bookshop with impeccable vibes. "Nobody's mentioned a ghost, but that doesn't mean Mary doesn't swing in to check it out every now and then."

"Mary." Julian tented his fingers. "Sounds like she has a pretty sweet set-up. What's her story?"

"We believe she's Mary, the first owner of the hardware store. She was an active participant in the suffrage movement: She was also one of the state's first female public library trustees—a position that wasn't open to women in Vermont until 1900—and fought for women's right to vote. Based on town records, she lived long enough to see the 19th Amendment passed in 1920 but died in 1942. So, while she saw white women allowed to vote—and presumably voted herself—she didn't see legislation remove barriers like literacy tests, denial of citizenship, poll taxes, and other discriminatory practices that would allow *women of color* to vote."

"And what links this ghost to this specific, accomplished woman?" Julian asked, in a tone that allowed me to make the connection for the audience, rather than question it.

"We realized there was a ghost here when books by people named Mary started disappearing. Mary Shelley, Mary Higgins Clark, even Louise Meriwether—it seems this ghost isn't a stickler for spelling. To this day, books by Marys are as likely to disappear as they are to be purchased. She's assumed Mary until proven otherwise. Regardless, the mischief is minor compared to some of the other spirits that stalk this town. She's been nice to coexist with."

"Was a rolling ladder *truly* to blame for Mary's death?" Julian asked, leaning in with an elbow on his knee.

"Nobody knows for sure," I replied. "But I think she likes that there's a little mystery surrounding her demise."

I pointed out a section of the store where the temperature was often chillier than the rest of the building and clumsily led him to the cool spot as encouragement to examine it more closely. But the rest of my storytelling was more nuanced. Fifteen minutes of chatting got Julian enough backstory and anomaly anecdotes to support the ghost-spotting portion of the filming. "We'll keep chatting while we explore. Maybe we'll get a few flickers, maybe not. Some ghost stories are just stories after all—and this is a fitting location for a disproven tale."

Disproving Mary would mean Charles would pull the sale. I couldn't let that happen—not now. I hadn't gotten funding yet, but I still had time. "She's real, I'm sure of it," I grasped.

"If she's here, we'll find her," Julian said. He pulled a cylindrical REM pod from its case and placed it reverently in the center of the room. "This device picks up paranormal interference and includes a temperature sensor, so we can compare the data with our IR camera results. If there's energy in this space, we'll find it." He pressed a button on the REM pod and it flickered to life, cycling through its start-up phase before settling down. "The lights will activate if Mary, or any other ghosts, influence the field."

If luck was on my side, the AC remote would trigger the REM pod and solve a few problems with one quick click. I waited for Julian to retrieve and power-up his IR reader, which he swept back and forth to get a read on the space. The open space clocked in at an ambient sixty-eight degrees, with higher temperatures where heat poured from the old, clunky radiators along the walls. After some initial readings, Julian began narrating his actions.

"So far, no abnormal findings." He turned the IR screen toward James, who examined the screen and nodded. "The REM pod is quiet, too. Lex, do you want to do the honors of speaking to Mary? She knows you best, so she might be most willing to respond to you."

"Absolutely," I said. "Hey there, Mary. Are you around?"

Nothing. Of course I couldn't count on some unexpected interference popping in at just the right time. We waited a bit, but I had to move things along or risk Julian declaring the story false. Of all the stories, of course it would be this one that didn't make it through their investigation.

"I've brought something you might like to see," I said. I lifted a book off the desk beside me, *Pride and Prejudice*. "There's a sister in this book called Mary. A lot of people overlook her, but she and I? We see eye to eye. It might just be her declaration, 'I should infinitely prefer a book,' that I like best." I set the book back on the desk and slid it toward the edge with a fingertip—giving the cameras something to capture while I fidgeted near my pocket for the AC remote. "It's here if you want it," I said. With all eyes on the book on the corner of the desk, and my pocket hidden as best I could, I depressed the power button and waited.

The REM pod flickered to life, an unexpected—but welcome—side-effect of the remote's electromagnetic waves. The IR sensor displayed a quick burst of purple-blue, picking up the cold air coming from the vent, which was conveniently within range of the pod. A series of gasps came from the crew members, who all turned questioning gazes toward Julian.

"Jeez, Julian, you look like you've seen a ghost," I said, nudging him with an elbow.

"I, uh, it's . . . maybe?" He sputtered. "Are you all getting this?"

The cameras and mics were trained on the IR sensor's screen, which continued to show a cool stream through the room. I tapped the remote, to end the ghostly wisp. The REM pod flashed once more then went dark.

"Mary?" Julian asked. "Are you there?"

I let the silence hang for a moment, seeing how long I could stretch the suspense. Just like in the vlog days, leading unsuspecting classmates to scare themselves silly in the dark. The power was intoxicating, honestly.

"You try, James," Julian suggested.

James shoved his hands into his pockets and hunched a bit, clearly uncomfortable with the *presence*. "Mary?"

Silence.

James nodded toward me; I raised my eyebrows in response, then rested my hand on the remote in my pocket a second before whispering, "Mary?"

Again, I fired up the AC unit, and the flashing lights and infrared imaging "proved" Mary's presence. There was only so much I could get away with, though, and I didn't want to push my luck. If they were caught faking their footage, could they even qualify for the prize? I hadn't read the rules—and digging into the specifics too much could have given me away—but it was a distinct possibility.

"Thank you for coming to say hello, Mary. And thank you for fighting for a brighter future for women like me." I allowed the pod to flicker a bit longer, then gave the ghost an out. "We just wanted to say hello, and we appreciate your time. If you're busy, we understand." I clicked the AC unit off, and the cool burst and flickering lights cut away.

"Mary?" I asked.

While we waited for a response, James gripped the back of the chair nearest him, his fingernails scraping at the fabric in his discomfort. Poor guy. I owed him.

"Mary? Are you finished talking for today?"

I kept my hand clear of the remote, letting the ghost rest and hoping Julian had gotten enough out of the encounter.

He scanned the room, swiveling his head slowly from corner to corner. To my relief, he nodded at me, his palms pressed together thankfully at his center, before closing out the scene. "And there we have it: Vermont's very own suffragette ghost, who haunts a bookstore. No better place for her, from the sound of it."

He rattled off a quick monologue, then called cut.

"We're clear," James said, the color still not quite back in his cheeks.

"You okay?" I asked James, as the crew scurried about to wrap cords, pack sound equipment, and stow away ghost-spotting devices.

"I'll never get used to that," he said, tugging at his collar.

"Not used to the totally chill ghosts yet?"

"Even if I'd seen this happen a hundred times, I'd still prefer to run away than stick around and chat. Ironic, right? When the credits roll, I'll be in there as 'codirector,' and I spend most of my time white-knuckling it in the farthest corner from the action."

I laughed, then rubbed my hands up and down his arms to shake out some of the tension he was holding. "I better get a prime spot in the credits, too. If it weren't for me, Julian wouldn't even know about half the places you've crammed into this documentary."

James shook himself out with an exaggerated full-body shiver. "Source credit where it's due," he said. "Okay, okay. How about"— he raised his hands like Vanna White—"Location Manager: Alex McCall."

"Ugh, please, drop the A."

He smirked. "You got it, Just 'Lex.'"

I hurled a glare in his direction. He cringed, then flipped on his million-watt smile, flashing his perfectly straight teeth. His chin dimple begged for forgiveness, and I obliged.

"So, what's next then? Shall this location manager set up our next venue? Julian sounds sure this is the project that'll make him famous, so we don't want to skimp." I began tidying a few stacks of books that we'd set out as props.

"He's got his heart on one more venue, but he's basically finished. Just tying up loose ends. Then we submit to the contest and prep for whatever documentary film fests he can talk his way into. Notoriety doesn't come knocking—you've got to chase it with a sizzle reel in-hand."

"Ah." I plunked a stack of books onto the table and focused on looking anywhere but at James.

"And, I've said something horribly wrong." He leaned in to grasp my fidgeting hand.

I sighed, and braved eye contact. "Life on the road really means life, out there—on the road—doesn't it?"

"Got to keep it interesting. Why not try everything before deciding to settle?"

"Branching out is overrated. Why change a good thing?" My stomach dropped as I argued. The drifter and the homebody, what a combination. "Pick-up-and-leave isn't as easy for me as it is for, well, everyone else on the planet."

He shrugged. "I get that. Having the courage to try isn't always enough. But staying put can be just as exciting when you know where you belong."

"Exactly. I'm working so hard to turn Dog-Eared into something and keep my family home from falling apart. Leaving feels like betraying that effort. Like I'm laughing at past-me for trying."

"That's not betrayal. People change, move on, find new things to put effort into. Taking that chance for yourself is always okay. Don't let your grouchy internal monologue win. If you had the opportunity to make a change, what would it be? You say it, it happens. Like magic."

"I would convince Charles that the coffee club is a terrible idea because it invites all sorts of trouble."

"May I remind you that *you're* the one who called *me*." He raised his eyebrows playfully.

"Like I said. Trouble." I fixed him with a challenging stare.

He grasped me by the elbow to pull me into a hug and kiss the top of my head. "Like finds like, I suppose."

CHAPTER SIXTEEN

James stayed at my place that night, preferring a ghost-free space to the rental where Julian and the crew would be editing and rewatching the day's footage. We lounged in my bed until way-too-late at night and woke up wrapped in each other—likewise, way-too-late in the morning. Our peaceful sleeping-in ended with me sitting bolt upright, completely naked, gaping at the alarm clock that I'd forgotten to set.

I flipped the blankets open and felt goosebumps pop up across my arms and stomach as the chilly air hit my skin. James grasped for the corner of my comforter and nestled himself back under the covers with a groan, but I yanked the blankets away again.

"I'm going to be late." I buried the panic for a moment to bite my lip as I eyed the muscles that stretched across his shoulders and down his back. "You're gloriously, wonderfully naked and while I value that, I don't think it'll win any arguments when Charles asks why the store's still locked up."

James rolled out of bed and gathered his clothes, taking every opportunity to bend, reach, and stretch. The tease.

As the shower faucet spurted to life, the sound of my ancient coffee grinder came down the hallway. Before the shower had warmed to my preferred scalding temperature, the pipes thunked, leaving me with even worse pressure. Water dribbled from the shower head, separate streams turning to a central trickle. There wasn't enough water pressure to wake a housefly on the best of mornings, but this new low brought spurts interrupted by gasps of air. I scrubbed and rinsed the best I could, barely able to get the conditioner out of my hair.

After the unsatisfactory shower, I dashed into the kitchen where James stood, a travel mug and neatly folded breakfast burrito waiting for me to devour and dash. Manners took a backseat as I dove in to the burrito, desperate to replace the calories burnt the night before.

"Should I pack you a lunch, or would you eat it before you got to the store?" he asked. His lips pulled into an amused smirk.

"No food item would be safe. I'll order something in." I finished the last bite of the burrito, and James gathered the plate to rinse it before I'd finished chewing.

The faucet sputtered and spat, providing less water pressure than the shower.

"Well, that's not good," James said.

"The pressure here always sucks, but what can you do, huh? The plumber told me the cost to upgrade and I choked. Visibly choked. I'll get to it when I can afford it."

"I think we've got more going on here than bad water pressure." James turned off the spitting faucet. "Frozen or burst pipes, maybe." He fiddled with the faucet; the spitting continued.

I grimaced. "That sounds expensive."

"Can be." He popped the cabinet open and peeked under the sink, then strolled into the bathroom to inspect that faucet. I sipped my coffee, following but dreading his findings. "I'm going to check out the basement, just to be safe."

I gestured toward the door that led downstairs. I avoided the space whenever possible. It was dark and moist, with plenty of shadows to freak me out. He trotted down the stairs and yelped, which didn't help my fear of the lower level any.

Then, the sound of feet shuffling through water—water, in my basement!—lured me to the depths below. The floor was soaked halfway across the basement, pouring from the pipe along the exterior wall. James splashed toward the shut-off valve and turned it until the water slowed, then stopped.

"There's water in my house," I said, aware how obtuse it sounded. The basement had flooded, of course there was water in my house.

"Just a bit," James said.

As I stood a few steps from the basement floor, examining the latest damage to my beloved building, my lips started to tingle and a bit of numbness crept into my fingertips—usually the first clues that I was heading toward an anxiety attack. I clenched my fists, closed my eyes, and sucked air through my nose to fill my lungs, then exhaled through my mouth. Catching the signs early enough usually meant I could breathe my way back to the moment. When I opened my eyes again, James was examining the drenched space with his hands tucked into his back pockets.

"For fuck's sake, what the hell am I going to do now?" I'd already taken advantage of every small repair business in the town. I'd paid Katerina in cookies when she fixed my kitchen light fixture. Connor was waiting for the fifth and final payment for the window he'd replaced over the summer. I owed half the town my entire worth and then some. Another repair meant another step backward in my bookstore purchase plan.

James splashed back through the ankle-deep water, walked up the stairs in his soggy slippered feet, and wrapped his arms around my waist. "You," he kissed me, "are going to work. I'll figure this out."

Maybe there was someone left in town who didn't know my financial situation. Maybe James would talk them into getting everything fixed up, then I could weasel my way into a payment plan. It was the least sustainable home ownership method, but it had worked up until this point.

Three hours into my shift, I got a happy, if unexpected, call from James: He'd stopped the leak, fixed the broken section of the pipe, and was researching plumbers and water damage specialists in the area.

"How handy." Despite my joking tone, the news cleared some of the stress that had kept me wound tight all morning. "Do you have a toolbelt to go along with those skills?" I asked.

"I do, in fact. Canvas, tan."

"Very impressive, Mr. Fix-It. But here's the thing, I can't afford a plumber. Or anyone with the term 'specialist' included on their business card. I've got a business loan application pending for the bookstore purchase already, and I can barely afford the oil to heat that place as it is."

"You're going to be able to afford fixing a mold problem even less. Pipes aren't something to mess around with. I can do the basics, and I'm not against bucket-draining this basement for you—but anything else is beyond me. You need a professional. One who can tackle everything. I know you're into the whole rustic aesthetic, but you can't keep cobbling things together and expect the house to come out for the better."

"James, are you mocking my house?" I gasped loud enough for the dramatics to make it through the phone line intact.

"Just picking on *you*, of course. Never the house. But, really, Lex. Maybe a home equity loan would be a good option."

A loan. More money. I'd only just finished paying off my student loans for my brief college experience, and that took more than a decade. I didn't need to add more debt to the pile. Then again, since I'd paid off the student loans, I wouldn't necessarily *miss* the money. It would be the same-old broke instead of a new broke.

"Depending on if you're using the house as collateral, your business loan might be affected by this damage. Best to reach out and discuss your options, I think."

Of course he was right. After hanging up with James, I was on the phone with the local bank, scheduling an appraiser to get *another* loan process started.

* * *

Banks didn't waste time when large sums of money were involved. Carina, the loans officer, had an appraisal set up for the next morning. The appraiser showed up bright and early, a ladder and tablet in-hand.

While the appraiser ducked into closets, examined light fixtures, and grunted at the dated counter tops, I followed him through the house with my coffee mug hugged between my hands. I sipped each time he jotted down something on his clipboard. The action kept me from trying to peer at the paperwork.

"Been here long, then?" he asked from his place atop the ladder, his voice coming muffled from inside the attic crawl space above the stairs that led to my little library.

"You could say that." Basically since birth.

He strode from room to room, pressing his pen to his chin as he considered each corner of my home. The windowsills in the kitchen— a long scratch that had been painted over, without being properly filled first, from my Matchbox car phase. Everything was a race track to a five-year-old. When I got bigger, it was where I'd sat in the afternoons to watch for Natalie to show up on her bike. I'd picked and worried at the edge of the sill, anxious to escape the scrutiny of my parents for the welcoming embrace of hers. Mom always made me wait to go, because she said it was rude to show up at someone's house unannounced and uninvited. When I told that to Nat's parents, they said there was an open invitation, and I didn't even need to knock.

The appraiser used the edge of his clipboard to move the curtain out of the way to check the window in the living room, and my sun catcher jiggled on its hook. Natalie and I had made them to match: friendship sun catchers. It had been in that corner of the window since the summer before we started eighth grade.

He ran a thumb across one of the bricks on the outside of the fireplace, where I'd scratched a heart using a red thumbtack—I'd read in a magic spells book that it was a sure way to ignite a fire in my crush's heart. It never worked, but the evidence of my first love lived on in the masonry built into the thing I loved the very most of all.

He stepped on the one creaky floorboard just in front of the stairway, the one that I'd listen for every weekend, because when it creaked it meant my grandfather was coming to wake me up extra-early in the morning with cider donuts—because my parents detested sweets and sunrise was the best time for us to share a treat.

When we reached the stairs, his ladder clunked against the wall. I held my breath until I could glance to check for damage. There was a tiny scuff on the wall, marring the floral wallpaper my grandmother had let me pick out when I was four and had no eye for interior design. The swirling, vining florals and vertical stripes had a pearlized finish that shimmered slightly, even decades later—except for the one spot where I always trailed my finger along the textured wallpaper on my way up the stairs to my book nook.

He stomped up the rungs on his ladder and poked his head through the attic access. "Insulation is surprisingly good, for a house this age."

"I had it updated when I fixed the roof—there was a leak. Two years ago."

"Roof damage." The tip of the pen hovered just above his paper as he considered his next note.

"There *was* roof damage. It's been fixed now," I corrected. "No leaks. Good as new."

He amended his note, then tapped the door with two fingers. "What's back here? Closet?"

I popped the rattly iron gate latch and opened the door for him.

"Hmm." He made more notes on his paper, then pulled a measuring tape from his coat pocket. "The original tax appraisal says this is a three-bedroom, but you'll lose points here. Can't call this a bedroom—no fire escape, doesn't count. Any other inconsistencies?"

"Not that I know of."

He tutted, measured, and noted his findings while my chest caved in as my favorite place in the world was reduced to nothing more than shorthand on a form that was barely legible because it was a photocopy of a photocopy . . . of a photocopy.

"Well, it's not as bad as it could be, but don't hold your breath. There's damage that'll cost you, fixtures are outdated. Wallpaper's a huge mark against you. I'll work up the assessment and send you"—he flipped to the contact information on the first page—"oh, the bank— the official report in a few days."

As he stepped out the door onto the front porch, I reached out to shake his hand, but he pressed a business card into my palm instead.

"Thank you," I said. *Thanks for nothing.*

* * *

Bad news accompanied the bank's appraisal and home equity value report—terrible numbers on both counts. While there was enough equity in the home for a repair loan, they couldn't grant me both the home repair loan *and* the business loan. And because I'd applied for the business loan using my house as collateral, it hurt my chances of getting approved to buy the bookstore in the house's current condition.

Natalie offered sympathy and dinner. Gatherings at the Stiller house were always loud, entertaining, and filling. You never left without enough leftovers for a week, and a frown never lingered for more than two seconds after crossing the threshold.

With Christmas just over a week away, they were in a celebratory mood. While some people were drained by human interaction and needed an introvert-style recharge at this time of year, Natalie's family thrived on engaging with locals and meeting the visitors. The inn was always packed to bursting, the noisier the better, and it wasn't unheard of for people to show up at the tree farm for a six-foot pine only to stick around for an hour to gossip after the tree was loaded on top of their SUV.

Spending summers, vacations, and random holidays at Natalie's house had taught me their ways, and I could nearly fake their level of enthusiasm on any occasion.

This occasion was something different entirely.

I'd just willingly walked a man through my house so he could tell me how little it would be worth to anyone. "Be ready to take a loss" and "don't hold your breath" weren't polite ways to talk about a building that was as good as family.

"Lex, you've barely touched your broccoli," Natalie's mom said. "I roasted it the way you love it. Are you feeling okay?" Had we been sitting near enough to each other, she probably would have placed the back of her hand against my forehead to check for a fever.

"I'm fine, thanks, Mama Stiller. I had a big lunch, that's all."

Natalie pushed her potatoes around her plate and bunched her mouth to one side. Her nose wrinkled. I raised my eyebrows, urging her to keep quiet.

Her parents had never approved of the way my parents raised me—or didn't raise me. They disapproved of their lack of proximity, pushy nature, and harsh criticisms. They'd taken up their complaints with my parents directly when they left me to fend for myself as a college student—and my parents pushed back, insisting that I would ask for help if I couldn't handle it. As if my parents were approachable enough for that.

If Natalie's parents knew I was struggling, they'd fall over themselves to help. But I could manage on my own. I had to.

To prove how fine I was, I stabbed a piece of broccoli and nibbled at the edges, allowing an *mmm* between bites to really sell it.

"So, what's new with you?" Natalie's dad asked.

"Same old stuff, Papa Stiller. Books and more books. I have a vision, but all Charles sees is the present. At least I get to surround myself with paper and ink all day. I could be plucking splinters from my hands every night." I pointed at his bandaged finger—nothing unusual, since blades were unpredictable beasts and flesh was weak.

"You ready to take me up on the offer to revamp your bookcases? I could add more space in that nook of yours, all it would take is a weekend and your preferred stain color."

I swallowed a bite of broccoli and tried to force the hollow feeling in my chest away with it. The remaining vegetable mocked me from my fork. A delicious bite of my favorite side dish, but too heartsick to enjoy it.

"I don't think winter is the best time to be constructing bookshelves, Pops." Natalie stabbed a potato. "Let's talk about something other than Lex's house, okay?"

"I've been promising those shelves for years, and it seems like the perfect time to get it done. After the Christmas rush, just before sugaring season gets started. Could there be better timing than that?"

I sucked air into my lungs. Exhaled slowly. Loosened my jaw and focused on my breathing—my therapist would have been so proud of me in that moment. Mindfulness, just like she'd taught me. Too bad I still couldn't manage to put it to use with my own parents.

"Thanks, but really, let's wait a while. I might not be in that house forever, you know? Let's hold off until we know where I'm going to land."

Natalie's mom's hand lowered, her fork tapping against her plate. She leaned toward me. "Are you moving?"

"Ugh, I don't know. I just met with an appraiser today to assess, but the repairs are just so expensive. So, barring miracles, I might be moving. Don't ask when, or where, because I have no idea."

"That's terrible, Lex, honey. I'm sorry. And what timing. Couldn't your parents loan you the money?"

"I'd rather not ask them. It'll give them leverage in the 'it's time to sell' argument. It's fine, really. I've been angry about it, but I think it's time to move on. I'm just going to enjoy it while it lasts and look for new opportunities when things change. I've got my job, and my books. Since when have I needed any more than that?"

Natalie's mom pressed her lips into a thin line. Her dad scraped the leftover bits of food on his plate into one final bite. Natalie's eyes tracked between them, testing, waiting.

"I have a favor to ask," Natalie said, either to prevent more questions or to save me from the awkwardness. "Dad, I was hoping to borrow some tools. And the truck. And, maybe, Derick. This weekend."

"This weekend?" Papa Stiller put his fork down. "As in, the weekend before Christmas? As in, the busiest weekend at the inn and tree farm?"

She flashed her teeth in a pleading smile. "It's for a good cause?"

"Name the cause, and I'll name my price." Her dad leaned in and winked, in the craftiest, dad-est move I'd ever seen him pull.

"I met this guy." Natalie glanced between her parents, then continued when neither jumped in. "So, he films a ghost-hunting show. He wants to get some shots at the Stone Chapel, but I told him he can't make the hike through the icy woods alone. I need Derick, because he can get Todd and Sammy on board, and we—Julian and I—could use their expertise. And by expertise, I mean strength, because we need to haul a lot of equipment up there."

Her dad folded one hand over the other and leaned his chin on them, his elbows braced against the table.

"And I'll take two weekend shifts at the tree farm," I offered, hoping the promise of a full staff would get him on board.

He pressed his lips together, glanced toward her mother, then turned his gaze back to Natalie. "I can't get manual labor out of you anymore for these things, so if you get in trouble, you're in charge of bail."

"We won't get in trouble. He got permission from the owners, and we're getting guests to sign consent forms and stuff. He's a professional, Pops. We've got this."

"Aside from the tools and crew."

"Yes, aside from those things. Which, I have now. Thank you." She plucked a roll from the center of the table and slathered butter on the top. We finished dinner, devoured dessert, and sipped tea together, just like every meal we ever had there. My house would always be home, but this table would always mean family. I'd created a place to call home by filling it with things. Books and trinkets, photos and throw blankets. The atmosphere had become something warm and welcoming. Their house was welcoming simply because *they* were in it. My heart lifted, because Natalie had them—then fell, because Natalie felt stifled by them.

We could argue the facts day in and day out, but the truth was, I'd never understand why she felt smothered, and she'd never have to know how it felt to be left behind. They'd never do that, and they'd always welcome her back.

Meanwhile, I was getting the silent treatment because I'd replied to my mother's email—subject line "Re: Arrival time? Please confirm"—with a gentle reminder that I'd had to cancel the trip due to a bleeding bank account.

Nat didn't know how good she had it. Never had they told either of us we were wrong. We always had the chance to explain. But Natalie didn't want their explanations. She wanted her freedom—even though she'd never told them as much, out of a sense of obligation, guilt, and loyalty.

I considered her side as I wandered home, but by the time I made it to my front door, I understood something they probably couldn't. By holding on tight, they were probably contributing to her slipping away.

* * *

James had texted a handful of times. A photo of Lulu sporting a brand-new dog jacket, with her leash in her mouth and ready for a walk. A forwarded article about the annual Midwinter Fest with "Can we go?" and a heart-eyes emoji. And one that said to give him a call when I got home because he missed me.

I dialed his number with one hand and unlocked my door with the other. While it rang, I tilted my head to press the phone to my shoulder and tucked away my coat and boots.

"Hey, there." He picked up after the third ring, and the greeting was less than enthusiastic.

"What's up?"

"Just hanging out with Lulu. Julian's out. The rest of the crew is trying out night skiing, which sounds like a great way to break bones."

"Looking for company?" My tone was equally hopeful and chill; we can hang if you want, but no pressure.

"Not tonight," he said.

My heart sank at *his* tone, which was far less chill. I snapped to attention at the unusual lack of energy in his voice. "Is everything okay?"

His inhalation came clearly through the phone receiver. A sharp intake of breath, silence, then, "My dad is coming to visit this weekend. Just got the itinerary."

"My condolences."

"Yeah, skiing, then dinner. A hearty helping of 'why aren't you living up to your potential.' He's staying somewhere, I don't know, not with me at least."

"Hey, you know, I used you as an excuse to get out of dinner once before, so I can return the favor if you want. Tell him you have a very important date with the hottest girl in town. You absolutely can't cancel because she would be devastated."

"Devastated, you say? Well, we can't have that." The phone rustled as if he had shifted positions. "I can't cancel though—I have to prove, I don't know, my ability to function like an adult human being. But I fully intend to make it up to you. What'll it be? Dinner and a movie? A weekend getaway? An all-expenses paid shopping trip to every used bookstore within fifty miles so you can pick their shelves clean and finish building your library fortress?"

"Tempting," I said. A library fortress for a house I was going to lose within months. "I don't think it's prudent to add to the collection when the building is on the verge of collapse."

"I am such an ass, I'm sorry. I completely forgot about the appraisal. How did it go?"

I recapped the details—the value sucked, and the home equity loans were terrifying to navigate—and chewed the inside of my cheek waiting for his response.

"Please don't take this the wrong way. But, your grandfather, he wouldn't have wanted you struggling like this. Scraping for cash for temporary repairs. Trying so hard to make his dream work. Have you considered that selling might be your best option?"

"No, no way. Because then my parents will think they won, and they'll expect me to upend my life and move to California."

"So is it the house you're attached to, or the idea of sticking it to them one more time?"

"I . . ." I stumbled over my words—any words—to avoid pausing. If I paused, I'd sound unsure. I knew I wanted the house, not just the win. I was sure of it. Wasn't I? Yes. I knew what I wanted, and it was the life I had built. "I'm happy here. Right. Here."

"Will you be happy right there forever? Is it worth considering a change? I know you love it, and I know you love your store. And your friends. And your weird, quirky town with its ghost stories and creaky barns and narrow, icy as all hell streets. But would it be so terrible to consider a new life somewhere else?"

Why were we talking about this again? "I can't just take off, drop everything, and move on, like you. You and Julian, on the road, just living life as it comes. Like some modern-day version of Sal and Dean. Hopping from job to job, woman to woman, as it pleases your rebellious spirit?"

"Hmm, Kerouac?" he asked.

I blinked and adjusted the phone at my ear. "Yeah, Kerouac."

"Which one am I?" He'd slid quickly from quiet to teasing.

I let a tiny, shaky laugh slip, relieved that he'd diffused what could have been an unnecessary, stress-induced argument. "You're Sal, of course."

"I've always thought of myself as a Dean, actually." The conviction in his voice had me picturing him standing with fists on his hips, confident and determined.

"I'm not so sure that's something you want to admit to your girl— umm, to the person you're seeing."

"Yes, it would be horrible to admit to the girl that I'm seeing that I was a Dean. You win this round, I'm a Sal, and there's no denying it. Listen, I'm sorry. I know you're upset about the house, but it's not for sure yet. Maybe there's another option. There's still time to figure something out. Maybe I can help. I've got to hang up now, Lulu's asking to go out and I need my beauty sleep."

I closed my eyes and breathed deep. "Good night, beautiful," I said.

He snorted a laugh and hung up without acknowledging the whole "his girl" slip-up, which fueled my anxiety for the entire night. I wasn't sure if that, or the house-related stress was worse.

Haunted Happenings transcript

Date: December 22, 2006

Location: The Barn Diner in Stowe, Vermont

> **Luna:** Happy haunted holidays! I'm harassing, erm, hanging out with Frank—the owner and head pancake flipper at The Barn. Tell me about your latest haunted happenings, Frank.
>
> **Frank:** This is ridiculous, don't you have school or something?
>
> **Luna:** Christmas vacation, Frankie.
>
> **Frank:** Homework, then?
>
> **Luna:** Finished it. We heard there's a ghost in the kitchen. Really likes toast. Ring a bell?
>
> **Frank:** I have no idea what you're talking about.
>
> **Natalie:** [Leaning in-frame and staring into the lens.] A skeptic, ohh, intriguing.
>
> **Luna:** [to the camera] Everyone's entitled to their beliefs, Nat. Give him a break. [to Frank] Are you sure you haven't heard anything? The theory is that she's the woman who owned this building before you turned it into a diner. Did you know she used to bake bread to give away, until arthritis kept her from kneading all of the dough?
>
> **Frank:** Would you get that camera out of here? You're going to get me in trouble.
>
> **Luna:** For not disclosing the ghost to customers?
>
> **Frank:** For destruction of property when I throw the camera out the window. I'm trying to run a business here.

Luna: [shrugging] You win some, you lose some. [Grabs a wrapped muffin off the counter and raises it to Frank.] I guess if every haunting was true, we'd have our work cut out for us. Thanks for your time, Frank.

[Camera zooms in on Frank's face as he attempts to remain unamused. Obviously, he's finding the antics hilarious because Luna and Natalie are delightful.]

Frank: [Hiding face behind a spatula.] Where are your parents?
Luna: Free-range teen! Have a good one, Frank!

[Luna leaves through the front door, camera follows.]

Frank: [off-camera] Hey, that muffin costs three ninety-nine!

CHAPTER SEVENTEEN

The Christmas rush hadn't slowed since mid-December—it was turning into the year of the Dog-Eared Café stocking stuffer. Customer after customer ordered their caffeine to go and plucked up gift certificates in tiny to giant sums. Stowe souvenirs in the form of snowboarding cow magnets and Vermont-shaped bottle openers were snapped up as well, mostly by tourists, from the look of their puffy jackets with fur-lined hoods, weekend-only lift passes tacked into place on the zippers.

I pushed coffee club memberships on visitors—with minimal success—and watched as the paperback table stacks thinned as readers discovered the little gems hidden throughout. The climbing daily totals made me look good—which would work in my favor if I got the loan and ownership landed in my court.

When. *When* it landed in my court.

The bank had called to clarify a few details after Charles supplied a glowing business reference. They promised a decision before December 31 at the very latest, so Schrödinger's Business Loan would be decided soon. Not soon enough for my nerves, but in time for me to meet Charles's deadline at least.

I'd amp up the holiday cheer next year, when the store was mine. Secret Santa book grab bags, with five surprise paperbacks following a specific theme. Seasonal, reloadable gift cards to replace the handwritten certificates that were easy to lose—or forge. Peppermint mocha coffees, for the love of Rudolph.

Julian had invited Natalie to check out the footage from the bridge so they could fill in any gaps. She dropped everything to spend her morning with the guy. They were magnetic, the way they fell into step together. Even though Natalie had never worked in film beyond the role of my intrepid camera person, she seemed to have an instinct for what was necessary. While setting up at the bridge, his points and waves and gestures translated into something Natalie simply understood without effort, and she matched them sweep for excited sweep.

The fact that they got along so well was fantastic, but it also meant I was shelving new books without her texts or presence to keep me company.

The bell above the door jingled, which summoned me from my little back-of-the-store corner where I was shelving multiple copies of *A Brief History of Time*. A woman tugged her phone from her pocket and swiped open her notes app to show me a list. I'd seen her around town for the past few years, but the familiarity stopped there.

"I'm starting a book club in the area, and we are trying to track down a few copies of any of these." She flashed the screen in my direction to reveal a list of not-quite-new mystery titles.

"I've got at least one of each of these in stock. I think I've got multiples of a few. Most of our stock is used, so it changes out quite a bit. I can order anything you'd like, though."

"We'll go for the title that you have most of. That will make our decision easier. This is our narrowed down list, if you can believe it." Her rosy cheeks rounded as she snickered.

"Oh, I can. You should see my to-read pile. It's going to become sentient and devour me alive one of these days."

Her eyes crinkled at the corners and her cheeks turned ever-plumper at my joke. "Sounds too much like a horror novel for my taste. I'd much rather read something that'll make me smile. We weren't sure what to choose for our inaugural book club meeting, and these were all listed as Edgar Awards nominees, so we figured we'd find something we were interested in."

"Would you like a recommendation?" I curled my finger, inviting her to follow me through the narrow aisles. We stopped in front of a display Darla and I had made the summer before—stacks upon stacks of books that we'd acquired en masse, with a tidy little "Book Club Fiction" sign tacked to the shelf. "I was going to start a book club here, a little lending library of our most common titles. There are question sheets taped into the backs of each book, too, to kick-start the conversation."

"How wonderful. If we knew we'd have come to you first. How often do you meet?"

"Oh, no." I shook my head. "Charles, the owner, didn't want to do it. I didn't take the shelf down, but I never went forward with advertising the group or anything. I can give you a discount if you get more than five copies of any of these, though. The spirit of the club will be alive and well through your members."

She dragged a finger along the spines and a little squint appeared as she mouthed the titles. The passed-up titles each got a little headshake, but the more promising options were tugged from the shelf so she could skim the back copy. She sucked air through her teeth and tapped the cover of a recent romance novel. "This one. I know I want to read it, and they sent me out to make the purchase, so I'm making an executive decision. Besides," she nudged me with a shoulder, "the man on the cover is quite stunning."

I tugged copies from the shelf and giggled at the gleam in her eye. "How many do you need?"

She counted quickly on her fingers, paused, then counted again. "Seven. Oh, whoops, and me. So, eight. Eight books, please."

I brought the pile to the desk, tucked a branded bookmark in each, and rang up the total. She counted cash from her wallet, rubbing her fingers against a stack of crisp ones and fives to break them apart, then she jingled the change pocket to count out coins to make exact change.

"Sorry about the cash. I'm a bit old fashioned, I suppose."

"Cash is great, I love cash. It's worked for how many years, and it'll keep on working." I dropped the change into the register and slid her books into the canvas tote bag she offered. It had the logo for a book store in New York City plastered across the front of it. "Are you from New York?"

"My daughter worked at this store." She patted the logo. "That was while she was in college, but she's moved on. She always says she wishes she'd stayed in the city, kept her college job instead of becoming a marketing consultant."

"Being in marketing is probably exciting, though."

"I think she preferred the worlds she found in books to the reality of working a job she despises."

"I can absolutely understand that," I said. "I'm still here because there's something whimsical about it. I'm happy, so why change anything?"

Her cheeks raised again with another smile. "Indeed."

"Enjoy your book club, and if you need any more suggestions just let me know. I really can order anything you want, even if it looks like we only stock twenty-year-old books."

She looped the handles of her bag over her forearm and patted the straps. "Maybe someday we'll convince you to join us."

After she left, I glanced around the store, examining the cushy couch and armchairs, before shaking away the memories of all the things I had wanted to accomplish here. The poetry readings and book clubs, story times and writing group meet-ups. The activities that would have turned Dog-Eared into a gathering place rather than a convenient bathroom stop. All of the things Charles kept shooting down because a store was a place to make money, and offering free activities didn't make money. He never listened to my logic, but if my hauntings looked as real on camera as they did in person, if everyone could fall for the fibs just a little bit longer, my dreams for the place were going to have their chance.

When I made it back to the front of the store, James was leaning against the discount paperback table by the window, a worn paperback in his hand. "Long day?" he asked.

"The longest. What are you reading?"

He held up the copy of *Do Androids Dream of Electric Sheep?* I'd given him on an earlier visit and bit his lip. "Did you know they made a movie out of this?"

"You mean the cinematic masterpiece *Blade Runner*?" I crossed my arms.

"I'm thrilled."

"Please tell me you're joking. There's no way this is news."

He hopped off the table and smoothed his jacket. "I'm absolutely joking. We should watch it sometime. You know, if you ever need last-minute plans or an alibi or something. I'm your guy."

"And here I thought we'd moved beyond back-up plans and cover-ups."

He tapped the spine of his paperback against the flat of his palm. "Perhaps, but there's still something I desperately need you for." He raised his chin in my direction, smug and striking. "Books. I need another recommendation."

"I'm sorry, I saw your collection. You're going to have to leave some books for the rest of us."

"Maybe it's a test," he suggested.

"If there's one thing I've always been great at, it's acing quizzes."

I hooked my fingertips in his, and we wandered serpentine through the aisles, hitting all the best sections. I tugged books with bent edges and cracked spines from the shelves and stacked them in his waiting arms. A pile of eight books teetered in his grip, his hands sandwiching the finds in a not-quite-cutting-it hold.

"This should keep me busy for a while." He eyed the stack of Orwell, Bradbury, Huxley, and the handful of Vonnegut titles we had in stock. He slid the books onto the counter and retrieved his wallet from his back pocket. When his coat fell back into place, the outdoorsy scent of melting snow wafted my direction, and my mind went blank.

James slid a twenty across the desk, gathered his books, then walked toward the door. Steps before hitting the threshold, he veered to the left and settled into the worn armchair by the window. He placed his stack of books on the floor, retrieved the book from the top, and disappeared into the pages without a word.

"Really?" I asked.

"Shhh. You're impossible." He pressed a finger to his lips and narrowed his eyes at me, then made a show of jiggling stiff, outstretched arms, both hands gripping the book, as if shaking himself back into reading mode.

"Do you want a coffee?" I asked. He eyed me over the edge of his book, with one eyebrow hefted playfully. "Soy, no foam, right?"

"I bought a stack of books, and now you're shaking me down for coffee sales." He sighed exaggeratedly, then slid the book upward again, cutting off my view of his face.

"Suit yourself." I made myself a coffee instead, with plenty of knocks and crashes, and an extra spritz of the milk steamer just to get attention.

"So, my father has an extra lift pass for our visit. I told him I'm seeing someone, and he insisted you come along so he could meet you."

I'd have been stunned about his father knowing I existed, if it weren't for the spike of fear about skiing that shot down my spine. "Only if we're also riding the lift back down. I don't ski."

His eyebrows rose in surprise. "Not even a little?"

"No way. Last time I went, my sister and her boyfriend left me on some trail that was way too advanced. My parents had to have the search party head out looking for me. Not my scene. Not that I'm not thrilled at the invitation to meet your dad, of course."

He shook his head and waved away my apologies. "I'd prefer to avoid calling in the rescue squad. I'll tell him you're not available."

"I'd hate to disappoint him by not coming."

"Oh, I've been disappointing him since birth. Really, he's used to it. We have dinner reservations after, if you want to join?"

"Not if I want—if *you* want. I won't be offended if you don't want to complicate things by having me meet your dad. We've only been . . . we've only known each other . . . for a couple of weeks. I get it."

James placed a hand on top of mine where it rested on the arm of the chair. "I would love to have you there. Happier with you there, even. It's just that my dad is, umm, intense."

"As you've mentioned," I said.

"As I've mentioned." He nodded.

"I can handle it. I can sit back and ignore him. I can deflect. Whatever you need."

He bumped my foot with his booted toes. "I need you," he said. "Just you. However you are."

Meeting the family wasn't a minor event, especially considering the state of his relationship with his father. While we were hurtling toward something serious much more quickly than I'd expected when we met only a few weeks ago, I wasn't ready to put the brakes on. It felt okay—comforting, even—to have found this connection. "Dinner with your dad it is, then."

He tapped the brim of his dumb Yankees hat and went back to reading without another word.

CHAPTER EIGHTEEN

Natalie tapped at the rattly storm window of my kitchen door then let herself in. "I'm not waiting for you," she called as she shuffled her way inside. "I've already started eating. I'll be helping myself to yours when mine's gone, so get out here."

I rushed into the kitchen, tugging on the ugliest of ugly holiday sweaters as she set down the cardboard cup carrier and paper bag bursting with breakfast burritos.

"I'm here, gimme." I opened and closed my hands as if it would get me my breakfast faster.

"Good lord, what are you wearing? No, wait, I think I'm better off scrubbing this memory from my brain." She pressed a burrito into one of my hands, latte in the other, and gripped my face on either side before planting a kiss on my forehead. "Thanks a million for helping out today. This is why you're my dad's favorite daughter. Ready for treemageddon?"

"I was born ready. Just make sure your dad doesn't expect me to lift, cut, or tie anything."

"He learned his lesson the year you busted Mr. Tate's rear window. You're on booth duty this year."

I devoured my breakfast burrito while Natalie drove to the tree farm. I didn't have to do much talking because she filled every bit of quiet with her excited chatter. How well she and Julian worked together, the way he knew, instinctively, what angles were best or how to pause to build suspense. How often he complimented the crew and how everyone enjoyed working *with* him—she emphasized *with* over *for* multiple times.

She barely took a breath as she gave me a play-by-play of the evening they'd spent shooting additional footage around town.

"Sounds like the two of you make a great team."

Natalie gripped the wheel with both hands, looked at me, and grinned. "I like him."

"Me too, Nat. He's a nice guy."

"No, I mean. Lex, like, I'm *interested*."

"Ah." *Gee, I hadn't noticed.*

"I think he's interested, too. Maybe. I didn't ask because I wanted to talk to you first. Since, you know. You and his best friend are the hottest item in town these days. I didn't want to make anything weird."

Natalie didn't tend to prioritize dating. She'd had a handful of not-serious relationships after one long-term relationship directly out of high school, but she'd always been more focused on herself. I was excited for her, but my mind buzzed with the realization that if she moved forward with Julian, he'd likely break her heart when he left.

"So, is it cool if I—"

"I don't have dibs on the out-of-towners. Go for it if you're into it."

Natalie rolled to a stop at the red light and looked at me, brows furrowed. "I don't have to make a move if you're not feeling it. I'm sorry. Forget I said anything."

"Crap, no that's not it. Listen, it's fine. Just . . . remember that their situation here is temporary."

She wrung the steering wheel in her palms and focused on the light ahead of us. It flicked to green and she exhaled as she pulled away from the intersection. "I know. I just refuse to accept 'he might leave' as a valid reason to ignore what might be there."

The words weren't meant as an attack against me, but it stung anyway. I'd shaken it off by the time we got to the tree farm, where I hopped out to let myself into the semi-heated (but still freezing) cashier's booth.

* * *

I made it home, washed the pine needles from my hair and pitch from my fingertips, and slipped into my "impress the parents" dress—tasteful, semi-low-cut, in near black. I'd finished my make-up and settled in for a quick mug of tea while I waited for James to call to let me know he was on the way. My phone rang, and I answered instinctively.

"When do I get to meet the man you've been inviting to stay the night?" my mother asked, her tone either disapproval or surprise—but who could tell with her?

"Mother, I can make these choices without your opinion."

"Oh, I see. I'm not worthy enough to know when you've got a serious partner."

"I don't have to be in a serious relationship to have sex. I'm an adult, Jesus. How'd you know I had someone here, anyway?"

"I go way back with Steve Richards, the appraiser for your loan. You could have told us you were having money issues."

"I'm not having money issues, I'm paying for a house repair. Besides, I know your preference is for me to unload the place, not give it the attention it deserves. What does the appraiser have to do with my sex life?"

"He mentioned in passing that he saw someone leaving the driveway when he got there for your appointment. You must bring him along."

"What, who? When?"

"Your beau, for Christmas, of course. As if there's another time of year you choose to visit us willingly."

I'd visited every year at Christmas since they made their big move. Other holidays were hit or miss, but this was the one I was expected to attend, no excuses.

"I already told you, like three times. I can't come this year. I had to cancel because I couldn't afford the trip."

"That's nonsense, of course you're coming. Honestly, Alex, this is unacceptable, it's Christmas. Besides, we've already ordered the Cornish hens for everyone."

"Oh, well if you've already gotten the hens, we won't have enough for James, so maybe it's better if we sit this one out."

"James, is it? Wonderful name. We'll inform the butcher that we need another hen for James for Christmas Eve dinner."

James let himself into the kitchen as I sputtered excuses to my mother. She accepted none of them.

"Sorry I didn't call," he said. "I was running late so I skipped a step. Are you ready—"

I tried to shush him before he came into the room, but the damage had been done.

"Is that James? Put him on."

I groaned. "I will not put him on, Mother. I have to go. We've got dinner reservations and we can't be late."

"I don't mind saying hello," James said.

"See?" my mom said. I could practically see her tapping her long, painted fingernails against the tabletop in frustration. "I won't keep you long. Maybe he can explain why you can make reservations for your own meal, but heaven forbid I ask you to set up reservations to have a meal with your father and me."

"Your funeral," I said to James as I handed him the phone.

"Hello, Mrs. McCall, and how are you this evening?" He paused and his lips turned downward as she barked back. "Yes, I know it's not evening in your time zone, of course." He started a slow, determined pace back and forth through the living room, running a hand through the hair at the back of his head. "California, that's great. Yes, I've been many times. Of course. The Napa Valley wine tour was—" He gritted his teeth and inhaled as her snapping reply traveled across the space between us. "Oh. Yes, yes. I am aware there's more to the state than wine tours and Hollywood." He gritted his teeth and sent a deer in the headlights grimace in my direction.

I mouthed *I'm sorry.* "Mom, we need to leave. Say goodbye to your new friend," I said, rising on tip-toes as if it would help my voice carry.

"It was nice to meet you, Mrs. McCall. We're on our way out for dinner. My father is expecting us at the restaurant in half an hour." I made wild throat-slashing gestures, two seconds too late. "He's here for the weekend, so . . ." James paused, grimacing at his obvious error. I smacked a palm to my forehead. "Visit you? In California? That sounds . . ."

"Mom, we have to go!" I yanked the phone from his hand and hung up. "What have you done?" I laughed through my groan.

He whistled. "Wow. She's . . . she's scary. It's like, no matter what I said, it was wrong somehow. I'm terrified."

"Well, you're also afraid of haunted bridges and cemeteries, but you've still managed to film a soon-to-be-famous ghost hunting movie with your friend."

"First, I'm not afraid. I simply prefer to spend my time *not* freaking myself out. Second, does that mean we're going out to visit your family?"

"Oh, hell no. Even if I wanted to torture myself, I couldn't afford the trip. You're off the hook, no worries."

"It's only fair, you know. You're meeting my father—thank you in advance, I truly hope you come out unscathed. I don't mind returning the favor. She was, uh, very insistent. Something about Cornish hens dying for nothing. I see where you get your flair for the dramatic."

"The only thing I get from her is my chin shape. Anything else, personality or otherwise, was well-honed and intentionally opposite of her."

"I can move some things around, get a couple of days off. We can fly out for a few days. I even have a stash of parent-approved gifts for this exact circumstance."

"What, being forced into flying out to meet the parents of some woman you only just met?"

"Exactly."

"I can barely afford the gas, let alone a plane ticket."

"My treat?" James offered, but I swiped my hands through the air in a quick X motion before he got the words out.

"Not a chance. I hate taking money from people. I'll promise that we'll take a trip out for . . . Easter or something."

"Easter, huh?" He tucked his hands into his coat pockets and a flicker of cautious excitement appeared in his expression.

My blood froze. Easter was months away. His reaction wasn't particularly negative, but the presumption that he'd still be hanging out with me then was going to need some serious over-thinking later in the evening.

"Or whenever. Let's get this over with. If your dad's anything like my parents, he'll already be inside wondering why we haven't arrived for our 7 P.M. reservation at six-thirty."

"You're going to do just fine tonight," he said. He tugged a small package from the interior pocket of his wool coat. "Parent-approved gift for you to get on his good side. Bourbon, small batch, very pricey. If he asks any questions about it, just mention smooth oaky notes and a strong caramel finish, then change the subject."

* * *

The Burlington restaurant was quiet. Waiters scurried in and out of kitchen doors with tiny servings of food on plates big enough to warrant their own orbit. James's father had already arrived and was sipping something mahogany colored from a rocks glass. The straight-backed posture and tightly controlled movements gave off an air of superiority, while his dark, slightly wavy hair and well-defined jawline made his genetic connection to James evident. He stood when we approached the table, fastened the middle button on his blazer jacket, and offered a hand to James. After a single, firm pump of the hand, he turned to greet me. I'd already extended my hand.

"Hello, I'm Lex. It's nice to meet you."

He accepted my handshake. "Brooks," he said by way of introduction.

"Thank you for taking time out of your trip to have dinner with us. A little something for afterward?" I slipped him the package James had given me.

"Ah ha, I see you've picked a confident one this time, James. Well done, well done." He tapped the package. "This had better be bourbon; I simply can't abide inferior liquor."

He was making it so easy to instantly dislike him. "Absolutely. You'll have to let me know how you enjoy it."

"That I will, Lex, that I will." He swept a hand toward the table to invite us to sit.

James pulled my chair out for me, then pushed it in as I settled. James and his father both unbuttoned their jackets and sat one by one: James first, then his father. It was the performance my parents wished I'd offer.

"James isn't one for sharing details about his personal life. Color me surprised to learn that he's in a relationship. I'm glad I was able to convince him to invite you." James lifted his chin as if he wanted to break into the conversation, but his father plowed right through the attempted interjection, sharp eyes locked with James's. "My back-up plan was to have him sit out the dinner so I could get to know you without his interruptions. But, truly, Lex. Kidding aside, I am pleased you were able to join us tonight. Quaint little restaurant, isn't it?"

Quaint, like it was a roadside maple syrup stand instead of the hardest-to-get-into restaurant within an hour radius. So that was how he going to play it. Disguise his disapproval with niceties so he looked like the good guy.

James fiddled with his cloth napkin.

Brooks sipped, rattled the ice against the glass, then flagged down the next server to walk by. "Another, at your convenience. And of course, something for my dining companions here. Brandy? Martini? Wine? I think wine, don't you? A bottle for the table, sommelier's choice."

"Have you been to Vermont before?" I asked after the server left.

"Of course, we've often hosted business retreats in Killington and Manchester rather than Stowe. I'm no stranger to the state. Living here, though, that takes a special breed indeed."

"Can we get through appetizers before you start attacking me and my guest?" James muttered.

"Oh, come now. Nobody is being attacked. It's simply a matter of opinion."

"And one my parents share, actually," I said. I lowered my gaze in James's direction. I was here to be a buffer, so that's what I was going to do. "They've been trying to convince me to join them in California."

"California? What a waste. Nothing worthwhile there unless you're one of those tech start-ups looking to make a mark. No honest work in that. Conning people out of their hard-earned money for something so intangible as an idea. An *idea*, can you believe that?"

"Ah, we agree, then. I should absolutely not move to California."

"Absolutely not." He accepted a newly filled glass from the server, then gestured toward me when she waited for approval on the bottle. I nodded—I had no wine selection skills to back up my decision—then nudged my glass toward the server, who went through all the required pomp of pouring and waiting while I sniffed and sipped before she disappeared.

"Law, though. There's an honest career. James, here, would have made a brilliant lawyer, but he chose to forge his own path. Step out on his own. Go it alone. Brave soul." He leaned back in his seat and gestured with his glass. "Filmmaking. Now that's a vocation made for California. I don't know how one expects to pay the bills in a field based on the fickle whims of the population."

"May I remind you," James said, "that the documentary is a stepping stone, not a career. If everything goes in our favor, our current project could take care of the rest of the school loans Mom took out to cover my degree. We were invited to participate in a closed competition for documentarians, and if we win, the prize money will pay off her debt. She can stop paying for my *mistakes* with money we both know she doesn't have."

He spat the word, probably mimicking the same way it had been thrown at him. My head spun at the realization that the documentary wasn't just a fun way to pass the time—the prize money would help James clear debts, or perhaps his conscience. I knew exactly what that felt like—after leaving college, I took over my school loans, determined to not let my parents hold the debt over my head because I hadn't fulfilled their dreams for my future. And now with all my other financial obligations . . . I'd have already bought the bookstore and expanded in a heartbeat if I didn't have a stack of bills mocking me from the countertop.

Meddling in James's project didn't feel quite so harmless anymore. Not when his reputation and his mother's financial situation were at stake.

"Ah yes, that's right. I'd forgotten about your honorable quest. She chose to take on those loans when *you* chose to ignore the stipulations I'd set for your education. I'd tell you to leave her to her decisions, but we both know you'll never listen. Hell, if you'd taken my advice and studied something useful, at the school I'd determined as your best option, you'd have graduated without debt."

His father had gone from secret jerk to total asshole in the span of a few sentences. James swallowed a couple of times, then reached for his water glass and nearly drained it in two sips. I looked between James and his father, both of whom were gripping the table edge and leveling sharp stares across at each other.

"Some things are more important than status, Dad. Like joy. I seek joy. That's why I'm here, in this state, filming this documentary. I enjoy it *and* the life I've found, outside of your expectations."

"So, Lex, what is it that you do here in snowy, joyful Vermont?" His father turned his head in my direction, but his eyes remained fixed on James.

"I manage a local business," I said, then cleared my throat before continuing. "A bookstore. I've been doing my best to keep business chugging, but the owner is set on outdated business strategies. It's a labor of love, I suppose."

"Why on earth would one choose to go down with a ship that's not even theirs? You seem like a smart girl. Why not simply open a competing business and run the other owner into the ground? If you can afford the cost of starting a business, of course."

"Part of the draw is the physical location. It's a welcoming build-ing, perfectly positioned in the center of town." James's father sipped his bourbon and eyed me over the rim of the glass, his pinky finger pointed toward the ceiling and eyebrows aiming to follow suit. "However, I see your point. There may be value in the direct competition."

"A woman with a head on her shoulders, James, good for you. I'll be keeping an eye on her. And, Lex, any time you decide you're ready to go into business for yourself and need to bounce some ideas off someone, I'm your man. Free advice goes a long way."

The server slipped toward the table and clasped his hands in front of him, diffusing the situation just in time.

We savored our meals, James's dad making a point to send his "heartfelt thanks" to the chef for a dish that "exceeded expectations," but his tone hinted that the bar hadn't been high. We indulged in a sweet dessert and digestif before gathering our coats from the coat check and heading out the door.

We had parked in a nearby lot and walked the short distance to the restaurant, but that was too pedestrian for James's father. He instead presented a valet ticket and waited as the valet attendant searched for the appropriate key fob.

Somehow, the flashy designer leather and gold keychain was mundane against the sleek black and silver Mercedes key fob. He probably had a matching key chain to accompany his other keys—or at least one each for his vacation home and weekend convertible. The house probably had a bio-unlock feature that scanned his eyeball to allow admittance—no key necessary; can't mess with the minimalist aesthetic.

"She purrs like a kitten, but she runs like a cheetah. Give her a little extra gas around those corners if you want to see what she's got," he told the valet, who ducked into the parking garage to retrieve the car with a promise that he'd return shortly.

As we waited for the car to come around, James rocked heel-to-toe as if he was anchored in place. His father's posture mirrored James's: hands in pockets and grim expression. The difference was that Brooks managed it without the slight inward curve of the shoulders or constant fidgeting.

Headlights flashed through the garage opening, car tires squeaking slightly as the valet accelerated, then again when he tapped the brakes harder than was necessary. The corners of his mouth turned upward, farther than should have been physically possible, when he exited the car.

"Was I wrong?" James's father asked, nudging the valet with a fist.

"Not in the least," the valet said, holding the door open. James's father reached into his wallet and plucked a tip from inside. "For your attentive service this evening, thank you."

The valet accepted the bills and returned to the podium while we said our goodbyes.

"I suppose you'll expect the usual Christmas gift, then?" Brooks asked.

"It seems to be tradition at this point, why change anything?"

"If you insist."

"Have a wonderful trip home," James said. "Enjoy the holidays with Sheila. Or Pam? I've lost track. Best wishes for a healthy holiday season, either way."

His father adjusted his coat and climbed into the vehicle and James pressed the door shut, double-patted the hood, then offered a quick two-finger salute. After rolling down the window halfway, he hunched to peer upward at James through the opening.

"This one's not bad. I see potential in her. See if you can keep her around a bit." He winked. "See you around, Lex."

I sucked frigid air through my nose and into my lungs and fisted my hands in my pockets until my fingernails pressed little half-moons into my flesh.

"Don't get lost," James said, and his father glared through the driver's window, then sped away from the scene—nearly curbing the tires in the process.

James spun toward me, fire in his eyes, and twined his fingers with mine. Keeping a strong front was the priority right now; I couldn't let it show that I was freaking out inside about potentially ruining his shot at an important competition.

"Wow," I said. "He's . . . something."

James pressed his fingertips to his temples.

"He's so condescending," I continued. "All of that 'let me know if you want some free advice' junk. Who does he think he is?"

He shrugged. "Most people love him."

"What, they fall for that act? No way."

"Growing up, it was all 'you're so lucky he's your father, such a wonderful man.' Like, they don't know they're being insulted until they've gone home and mulled, and even then, they assume they're mis-remembering the tone. You held your own, though." James swooped in and pressed his icy lips to mine.

"I might have nightmares tonight. Him, standing over me, telling me how 'quaint' my store is."

"You know what might make it better? Dessert."

"We just had mille-feuille, are you honestly still hungry?"

The gleam in his eye proved that he was in fact still hungry. But two scoops of chocolate in a waffle cone wasn't going to sate his appetite.

He started walking along the salt-strewn sidewalk, and when the distance between us stretched far enough to tug my arm gently, I quick-stepped to catch up. We walked side by side, the chunks of rock salt crunching beneath our footwear that was very obviously not meant for icy sidewalks.

"Is that why you left New York?"

"Because of my father? No, I figured out how to deal with him a long time ago."

"So why did you leave, then?

James stopped, faced me, then grasped both of my hands in his. He closed his eyes and sighed, then looked me in the eye. "Have you ever felt like there's somewhere else you're meant to be? Like, where you are isn't where you're supposed to end up?"

"I'm one hundred percent sure I'm exactly where I need to be. This place is who I am."

"And you've always been sure?"

I pulled my hands away and waved them through the air, showing off the falling snowflakes and strings of colorful lights twined around the vintage-style street lamps. "Where else could you get this small-town charm? Though for some reason, I seem to be the only person who can be content here—nobody else, my family included, has had any trouble picking up and taking off."

"What about travel, then?"

I huffed a laugh. "The best part of traveling is knowing that I can go home when I'm done."

"Well, I've never had that. The feeling of coming home. I had a house; I had a job. I had a family that, for better or worse, loved me . . . I guess. But none of that felt like home. So, I keep looking for that feeling in my chest. The one that says, 'Hey, this is it. This is where you belong.' I figure if I try enough cities, one of them will speak to me."

I scuffed a toe through the grit and gravel that had built up on the sidewalk and locked my eyes on the trail my shoe left behind. "So, you're just going to keep on going until something feels right, then?"

James reached for my hand again, but I kept my fists tightly bunched. He was always going to be a moment away from taking off to some new, exciting location. Hunting that feeling of home. I got the draw—I hadn't even made it through college before crawling back home, back to where my heart pulled. I craved safe, while adventure called him at every turn.

"Can we just head back?" I asked. "Maybe, uh, watch a movie at your place?"

"Movie at my place it is." James brushed his gloved fingertips against the back of my hand, and this time I opened my palm to him so he could lace his fingers within mine again. We strolled toward the car at a carefree pace, shoulders bumping into each other as we walked.

"So, what's the usual Christmas gift?" I asked.

James chuckled and his jaw tightened as he smiled. "I make him donate to a literacy program for people who are incarcerated. It goes against everything he believes in—you know, basic decency, human rights, encouraging critical thinking and education. So, they get a ten thousand dollar check every year, and I've asked them to slap my father's name on the donor list instead of mine. Which means, he gets thank you notes from the people receiving the books. It's the gift that keeps on giving."

My heart warmed enough to melt through the wall of ice I'd been trying to build around it. Falling for this guy—hard—was inevitable.

CHAPTER NINETEEN

Natalie's truck rumbled into my driveway early the next morning, and she let herself in with her spare key. The rickety storm door crashed back into place behind her. I met her in the kitchen, my fuzzy pink bathrobe tied into place to chase away the chill that had settled through the night without the fireplace roaring.

"Oh, good, you're up," Nat said.

"Good morning to you, too, sunshine. Coffee?" I stifled a yawn with the crook of one elbow while shaking old coffee grounds from the filter with my free hand.

"Yes, please and thank you." She yanked her phone from her pocket and shoved it into my line of sight. "And while it's brewing, maybe explain this?" The screen displayed blocks of text, a paragraph for each message I'd sent her. Full-blown regret dripped from each one, explaining what I'd learned about James, the prize money, his mother . . . all of it.

I shoved the coffee carafe into place and pressed the brew button. "I know. Last night was a doozy."

"That's one word for it. Why have a conscience now, after the damage is done?"

"Better now than after it's too late to come clean, right?" I prompted.

"Coming clean means risking the bookstore, Lex. You'll never get another chance like this, and I can't watch you tank your dreams over some hypothetical. If anything, I think you've added to their story, not detracted. All of your teenage angst is stoking the fire that this documentary could be."

Nat pulled two plates from the cabinet and popped two bagels into the toaster oven before plunking into a seat at the table.

"He *has* to know *Haunted Happenings* was all fake. They're both adults who, I assume, have at least a sliver of common sense. You're telling me two adult men who direct documentaries for a living couldn't spot the inconsistencies or obviously cheap filming tricks?"

"Hey," Nat said, faking offense. "Those special effects were ahead of their time."

The timer on the toaster oven dinged, so I retrieved our breakfast, slathered cream cheese on my bagel, strawberry jelly on Nat's, and brought the plates to the table.

"There's a chance they thought it was real. I mean, people still believe the lunar landing was faked because of a few videos about shadow alignment and a wavy flag. If there's an audience that believes people would go to that much effort to pretend-explore a celestial object, then maybe there's a similar audience that believes every word Luna had to say. *Luna* does mean moon, you know . . ."

"Your confidence is astounding." I grabbed my phone and tapped into the YouTube app, nibbling my bagel and scrolling at the same time. "Look, I'll give you three examples of how unbelievable it all was in three seconds. One, two . . ." I prepared to show her the recent videos section of our long-abandoned channel.

A text popped up. *Reminder: Your United flight (UA7012) is coming up. Click here for flight information and check-in details. To opt out of text reminders, click here.*

I dropped my bagel onto my plate and opened my email with a crumby fingertip. There, staring back at me, was a confirmation email from the airline, thanking me for booking a flight. For two: Alex McCall and James Coen. The next email was a two sentence note from my mother. "Because money was apparently an issue, we have covered the cost of your tickets. Please consider it a gift. We look forward to meeting James."

"Guess who just got free tickets and a guilt trip after I told my parents I was staying home for Christmas."

"They didn't."

I showed Nat the phone. "They absolutely did. As if I needed more reasons to owe them, now they're flying me and James out to California, last minute."

Natalie's eyebrows raise. "That's one way to get the family together."

"Excuse me a moment, I have to make a call."

"Lex, think about this. You're only going to make them upset. It's—" She looked at her watch. "Damn, Lex, it's still the middle of the night there. Just hang up and give them a few hours to wake up. Think about what you're going to say before you—"

"I can't believe you'd be so incredibly fucking selfish, Mother," I said the moment the call connected.

"Alex?" My mother groaned into the phone. "Alex, please. Language."

"I will use whatever language I damn well please, Mother. I'm an adult. How dare you? How dare you book me plane tickets with asking first? But you win, because now I feel obligated to come."

"Is there an emergency, Alex?"

"An emergen . . . an emergency? Hell yes, Mother, there is an emergency. My parents are assholes who can't take 'no' for an answer. What if James and I had plans? We can't just drop everything. James has a dog. We both have jobs. Responsibilities. You can't force us into compliance, you know."

"If you're quite through, you can continue yelling at me over Christmas. I have obligations in the morning and simply must hang up since I only have . . . dear god, Alex it's four in the morning. Calling at such an hour, honestly I could just—"

"Well, it's seven here," I shouted into the receiver, but she'd already hung up.

Natalie approached slowly, peeled the phone from my grip, and set it just out of reach. She placed both hands on my shoulders and squeezed gently. "You good?"

I most certainly wasn't good. But at least I knew what to expect from my parents. I wished shock was an emotion the betrayal had drudged up, but I landed somewhere closer to "disappointed, but unsurprised."

"Totally good. I'm cool. They'll always find ways to piss me off."

"I'm not sure why a free flight is such a bad thing, and this is a friendly reminder that you might be overreacting. But rage if you must. I'm listening."

I dragged my fingers through my hair. "It's not the free ticket. It's that they think I'll fall into line if they throw their money at my problems. Like they can win me over that way, earn my forgiveness."

"So, use it to your advantage. Tell them all you want for Christmas is the money to buy the store and to stack your house repair fund."

"I don't need their help, Nat. I can *do* this. Besides, I'd rather sell the house to my worst enemy than ask them for money. Then I'll just . . . move into your bedroom. Your parents would love it. I can reclaim my role as their favorite daughter, and if you ever move out, I'll pack up and move with you. Or maybe I'll stick around since you'd be leaving your room vacant and all. It's a fantastic plan, and one that doesn't leave me asking anybody for help."

"Only by default, because you know there's an open invitation at my house." She flopped her head onto my shoulder.

I leaned in and rested my head against hers. "It's called a loophole, Nat. Honestly."

She nuzzled into my shoulder, laughing, then stood. "Okay so, the blizzard didn't hold back, and it's a nightmare out there. I'll be plowing all morning. I can throw you on speaker if you want to call and practice reaming out your parents more. Whatever you need."

* * *

Though still fuming when I got to work, the frustration ebbed when I heard a jingle coming down the street—and the swishing of James's wool coat to match. I unlocked the door, then double-kicked the bottom to encourage it to open just as the two arrived at the door. I stepped aside to let James in just as Lulu nosed her way past him and through the door. He followed her inside and took his usual spot in the most comfortable chair. Lulu climbed into the chair opposite James and wagged her tail, then yawned before resting her chin on her paws. I fired up the espresso machine, drizzled a bit of maple into the mug, then slid the drink across the counter toward him. "Soy, no foam, with a Vermont edge."

"For me?" He pressed his thumb into his chest and nodded, smug, as he came to get his drink. "The service here has improved tremendously since my first visit."

I flung a handful of wooden coffee stirrers at him, and they fell to the ground, except for a few that clung to his wool coat. His uniform was the same as ever—long coat, pressed pants, shoes not intended for icy weather, and that damned Yankees cap tilted just-so, but revealing his eyes just enough that I caught the playful gleam.

"Yes, well, it's been brought to my attention that I was a little unfriendly."

He cradled the oversize mug in both hands and inhaled the steam swirling off the top of it. After the first sip, he set the mug down, then leaned both elbows onto the counter and rested his chin on his closed fists. "What's up? You're chewing your lip, which means you're nervous about something."

"The fact that you know that is either sexy or terrifying. Not sure which." I sighed. "I have something to tell you. You might not like it."

He narrowed his eyes. "How much will I 'not like it'?"

"That depends on how much you enjoy being alone on Christmas Eve."

"You're canceling our *Die Hard* movie marathon? And I thought I knew you." His eyes crinkled at the edges, and he sipped his coffee.

"Okay, not intentionally. But I talked with my mom, and she's made it, uh, really truly crystal clear that I am expected at Christmas. She sent two tickets for us to fly out there."

"To . . ." He bit his lower lip, and his nose wrinkled. "To California. To see your parents."

I nodded. "Tomorrow morning. You are under no obligation to come. It's fine, you can stay here. I'll tell her you couldn't make it—"

"When do we leave?" James asked.

I pressed my fingertips to my forehead. "I could never ask you to put yourself through that kind of torture."

"Is it really so bad? I have some documentary business I can tackle while we're in the area. We can make it through one weekend with your parents. You've made it through relatively unscathed so far—*and* you've met my father."

"I just called my mother and yelled at her—the profanity-laced, name-calling, and no regard for propriety kind of yell. It's not going to be a snowflakes-and-eggnog sort of Christmas visit. I get to go make nice, pretend nothing happened. Visit with Jordan and her perfect husband and perfect children. Listen to my mother complain that she'll only ever have two grandbabies because I'm never reproducing. Suffer through my dad asking what my 401K sits at. Besides, if you come, who will look after Lulu?"

"Julian's a pro dog-sitter. I'll text him and make sure, but she's in great hands with him."

I wrinkled my nose while I searched for another excuse that would save him.

He took my hand in his. "It's one visit. Make nice, eat some Cornish hens, chat, exchange gifts. I can handle it."

"You obviously have never met my parents."

"You obviously want to keep that from happening."

"Trust me, it's for your own good. They're the worst."

"Then it's a good thing you've got a buffer." He offered a charming grin and his dimple appeared. "I think I owe you one."

"I'll be making this up to you for a very, very long time."

James combed his fingers through his hair and his eyes flashed with an emotion that hit somewhere between bemused and proud of himself. I'd just invited James to Christmas with the family. Christmas.

With *my* family. I couldn't think over the xylophone jam my heart was playing against my ribcage.

Maybe it wasn't a big deal to him.

But *oh* how I wanted it to be.

Having him meet the parents was a huge deal to me. Even the phrase "meet the parents" usually sent me listing off the ways it could all go horribly, terribly wrong—but with James, I didn't *want* to find excuses.

I'd put off introducing my partners to the family because I was convinced it would be the thing that ruined the relationship—rather than accepting that the relationships were already broken. And I'd always rationalized it: *She's only here temporarily; he has plans for a future elsewhere.* A merry-go-round of excuses that all revolved around the risk of being left behind when someone's future carried them forward.

What had Natalie said? The fact that he might leave wasn't a valid excuse to ignore what might be there.

It was incredibly fast to be meeting the parents—but maybe it was exactly the right pace based on the momentum of our relationship. Our forward motion would continue until an unbalanced force got in the way.

I couldn't be the unbalanced force. Not again; not this time.

The bell above the door jingled as a ski-jacket-clad trio slipped inside and sidled up to the coffee counter. "Latte. Oat milk, no foam." He held up three fingers and nodded to his companions, one at a time. They nodded back. "Make that three. Oat milk. No foam. You need to write down our names or something?"

"Nope, got it. Three oat milk lattes, hold the foam. Shredding the mountains today?"

They bobbed their heads. "Oh yeah. Yup, here to shred."

"Neat." I flipped on the milk steamer and scrunched my mouth to the side as I looked over my shoulder at James.

"Talk flight plans tonight?" James asked, grabbing his own out-of-town special latte from where he'd left it.

"I still maintain that this is above and beyond, and I will owe you so big."

"Passing this IOU back and forth might be the thing that makes this relationship work. I'm willing to keep trying if you are." He ambled backward toward the door, blew a kiss—ugh, adorable—and patted his hand against his thigh. Lulu slid out of the chair she'd claimed and trotted toward James, carrying her own leash in her mouth.

"James," I said. "I'm happy you're coming to Christmas."

A soft smile crossed his lips. "Me too." He hesitated a moment, a sincere twinkle in his eyes.

"Hey, on the table, right next to *Lord of the Rings*. *Catch-22*. That's your next assignment."

He scooped up the paperback on his way by. "I think I've heard about this one. I owe you"—he peeked at the label—"two-fifty."

The bell above the door hadn't stopped jingling before my phone buzzed with the bank's name flashing across the screen. I lunged to answer the call, caught between hope and terror. But the woman's voice on the other end had that "we're sorry to inform you" quality.

"We've had a chance to review your business loan application," she started—and I knew what was next. "Unfortunately, though your credit score is adequate and you've obviously got the chops for the book business, you just don't have the collateral necessary to back the loan. I'm sorry."

"Of course, thank you for letting me know," I said. "I appreciate it." I wasn't sure which was worse: wondering whether there was still a chance, or finally hearing that "no."

CHAPTER TWENTY

A 7 A.M. flight meant up at four, to the airport by five, and an hour of security and sitting around in the tiny Burlington airport, sipping drip coffee and wishing for breakfast. But flying and I had never gotten along. An empty stomach was the best option, especially if I was sharing a row with James, experienced traveler and all-around brave soul.

Except for where ghosts were concerned, obviously. I'd resolved to point out his fear of the paranormal if he so much as smirked at my green-tinted face.

We'd packed light: a carry-on each and no checked baggage. Buying gifts once we landed would save on baggage costs and meant less lugging in general. Lulu stayed with Julian, though I'd tried to convince James to bring her along. A long-haired, boisterous dog was exactly the kind of thing my parents would have hated to see bounding up their walkway. They'd hate it even more when she scrabbled across their hardwood floors and into the backyard—and, heaven forbid, into their in-ground pool. The hair in the filter, the hair on their furniture, the tracked-in dirt. It was their idea of hell.

I started the deep breathing exercises early so I'd have enough calm built up for waiting on the tarmac, and takeoff, and the flight.

Landing would never be easy, so there was no sense in trying to keep my cool that long. James's shirtsleeves were the only thing keeping my fingernails from digging into actual flesh.

The cost and the parents hadn't been the only things keeping me from visiting California: flying was also a nightmare. I hated the feeling of not being in control. At least I knew where I stood in my career, with my parents, with my friends. I could sit back and let someone else drive because I knew how a car worked. I knew the mechanisms, and I knew enough about car maintenance that I could jump in and change the oil or fix a flat if I had to. If the plane broke midair, that was that. See ya later, alligator.

Flying felt an awful lot like being in a new relationship. Launching myself into the great unknown and hoping aerodynamics—or at least shared interests—were enough to keep us afloat.

Once we reached cruising altitude, James's breathing slowed and a tiny snore took up residence in the space between us. I focused on the rhythm of his breaths so I could ground myself, regain my calm. I'd never had a bad flight, but when did fear ever make sense? Instead of dwelling on what could go wrong, I focused on the way the water rippled in the plastic cup resting on James's seat-back tray and counted seconds—up to ten, down to one . . . then up and back down again.

I stole a peek as James napped and wondered how he could be so relaxed. It was unfair that he was so laid-back about everything—including how quickly our relationship had progressed. He threw his whole self into everything—friendships, filmmaking, dog ownership, adventures, our relationship—no need for a toe-dip to test the waters. He was *all in*, no hesitation. Maybe our kindred nature was what made this comfortable instead of terrifying for me.

He was easy to be with, easy to trust, easy to . . . love?

No, not yet. I wasn't there yet, but I could be someday.

Unfortunately, not being ready to label it didn't mean the fear of losing him wasn't still hanging on.

The documentary was so close to being finished, and I wanted to ask what would come next—but what if the answer was that he was leaving? Then again, if he wasn't serious about us, he wouldn't have hopped into a cigar-shaped metal tube to hurtle across the country to meet my family.

James stirred in his sleep. When his eyes blinked open, and his dreamy, unfocused gaze landed on me, the stress melted away. He patted his shoulder, and I took the invitation, leaning in to rest my head in the crook of his neck. I resolved to bring up "the future" when we got back home. One big moment at a time was all I could handle.

The layover and second flight were uneventful, which is really all you can hope for when it comes to flying—especially on December 23. The flight arrived fifteen minutes ahead of schedule and by some miracle, James and I caught an Uber without much of a wait. The sixty-degree difference between Vermont and southern California was always a shock to my system. I couldn't have moved there; I'd never have survived the climate.

"So, here's the deal. If you want to survive my parents, the key is to not show weakness. Don't need anything. Don't ask for anything. One time, I asked to borrow a quarter for the meter when I was seventeen, and I swear I am still working off that debt. Pick your battles because you'll only win one—if you're lucky—and don't look them in the eye because there's a solid chance you'll turn to stone. Are you ready?"

"They sound as warm and caring as my parents. In essence, I was born ready."

"Glad one of us is confident."

We rolled through the cul de sac and into the driveway. The car stopped but I didn't budge.

The drapes in the huge front window shifted and my mother's face peeked through the crack. She dropped the drape back into place and her silhouette crossed the room to the front door. She pulled it open, then waved us inside.

"Can you fake the doors being stuck or something?" I asked the driver. James climbed out of the car, grabbing both of our bags, and offered a hand to help me out.

"Traitor," I whispered. I accepted James's hand while the driver eyed me in the mirror without a word.

With cement-heavy feet, I trudged up the walkway, past Jordan's car. I dragged a fingertip through the thin layer of dust that clung to the side of the vehicle, drawing a X_X face, then made the trek to the door where my mom waited.

"How do you get anything accomplished at a pace like that?" she said by way of greeting.

"Hello, Mother. My flight was as terrifying as ever, thanks for asking. Yes, it's wonderful to see you too."

She clicked her tongue. "Jordan and the children have been here for two days already—you just missed them, they walked to the library for cookie decorating and story time. They've claimed the guest house. Lucas will be here tomorrow. He took a few extra night shifts to give the other staff a break, isn't that wonderful?"

"ER doc," I whispered to James. "Mom, meet James. James, my mother."

"That was selfless," James said. "Nice to meet you, Mrs. McCall."

"Yeah, selfless. That, and he appreciates the shift differential he earns for his 'good deeds.'" I lifted an eyebrow.

"Life is different out here, Alex. You can't live on a shopkeeper's hourly wage. Which you'd understand if you'd come out of your bubble."

"I'm not having this argument again, Mother. I'll show James to our room."

"Rooms." She swished her index fingers away from each other, slashing an X through the air.

"You've got to be kidding me, Mom. I'm an adult."

"And both guest rooms have a single twin bed now because your nephews don't share a room anymore. I'd think that would be uncomfortable, but by all means, squeeze yourselves into a bed made for a child. I'm not the prude you wish to believe I am."

I pressed my lips together and the corners of my mouth pulled downward in disbelief. "Sorry, I thought I was being judged for my decision-making skills again. Guess I was wrong."

"Oh, honestly, Alex. The way you go on. We've given you nothing but freedom to make your own decisions."

"And this is where I excuse myself from the conversation so we don't fight the entire time I'm here. Thanks, Mom, we'll settle in. I'm taking James out for some last-minute shopping, so we'll find lunch while we're gone."

James grabbed both of our bags, slung his over his shoulder, and carried mine by the handles. "Thank you for your hospitality, Mrs. McCall."

"You're very welcome, James. Alex, see if you can learn some manners from your guest."

"Way to make me look bad," I whispered, squinting and wrinkling my nose.

"Don't worry, I'll make it up to you," James promised, one impish eyebrow hoisted high.

I swung the door open to the first guest room, the one I usually stayed in. I tossed my bag onto the tiny twin-sized bed and scanned the space. Nothing had changed, aside from the bed size. The queen must have been moved to the coveted guest house.

James was leaning in the doorway, his bag slung over his shoulder as he eyed the art on the walls. Most of it belonged to the kids. Stick figures and dinosaurs, cats and houses and sunshine. The only photo on the walls was one from their last visit to Vermont. I'd taken the kids to try sugar on snow, which was a hit. We sat at a long picnic table covered with a plastic red and white checkered tablecloth. The tray in front of us was mostly empty, with only remnants of the feast remaining: sticky syrup cups and balled up napkins. Jordan had called to the kids, "Thing One, Thing Two, say 'cheese!'" She snapped the photo just as I'd swiped a dab of maple onto each kid's nose, so we were giggling. Better than cheesing, any day.

"Looks like you're the fun aunt."

I was, and it was a point of pride. "They like coming to visit. They're all about the yard, and the farm next door, and the snow. I think they like the snow better than they like me."

"How often do they visit?"

"Once or twice a year. They get a hotel in Burlington, and we meet up a couple of times. I keep the kids for a night while my parents, Jordan, and Lucas go skiing. Mom won't let the kids learn to ski. She's more protective of them than she was of me. I spent my summers running feral through the streets, and they're in private school where only organic food is served. Your room is this way."

James stepped aside to let me pass, then fell into step behind me. He examined the art on the walls as we walked to the next room. A portrait of my sister, a giant wedding photo, a gallery wall dedicated to the kids, and my senior portrait—tiny in comparison. "They seem . . . proud of their family."

"Jordan can do no wrong. Her kids are the light of my parents' life. And then there's me." I gestured toward my senior portrait. "The last time they were proud of me was the day I graduated from high school with loads of small but prestigious merit-based scholarships. That was before I dropped out of college and ruined their opinion of me forever. I'm pretty sure I sealed my own fate there. I didn't think I needed them because my grandfather had left me that house. I figured I'd find some career that paid enough to show them that I could do just fine on my own." I waved the train of thought away. "Anyway, that's enough of the sob story. Shall we? I'm starving."

We grabbed lunch at my favorite sushi place. It was the only reason I looked forward to visiting my parents. Vermont had maple and cheese going for it, but when it came to good sushi, it was a barren wasteland. Every visit to my parents' required a long sit at the sushi bar where ordering omakase was a must.

As we plucked the chef's choice from the bar in front of us, I closed my eyes and savored each bite. James's grin grew. "You're worldlier than you've let on."

"What, just because I know how to order sushi in the city, I've lost my country girl label? Don't tell anyone, they'll take away my 'Local Super Hero' badge."

"I didn't say that." He sucked air through the tiny O of his lips and closed his eyes tightly. "Wasabi," he said, shaking his head as if to shake away the burn.

"One would have assumed that a well-traveled man such as your-self could handle a little wasabi."

"I'm not usually distracted by such fine company."

I rolled my eyes at him. "Spare me."

His lips curved into a cheery smile and the dimple appeared on his chin like a beacon. "It's the truth."

"Inadequacy has a habit of sneaking up on me. Something about being the second-born, disappointing child who didn't live up to her parents' expectations. My travel experience is limited—car trips down the East coast, flights out to Cali every now and then. Nothing like your travels."

"A few trips hardly count as traveling the world."

"I know, I know. Sorry. It's just that being here, with my fam-ily . . . It's rough."

He turned on his bar stool, pointing his knees toward me. "I get it. The desire to prove yourself, the . . . the whatever. But have you ever stopped to wonder if *you're* the one putting the pressure on yourself?"

I was surviving under the pressure, not creating it. I narrowed my eyes. "It's been there since birth, and my sister refused to take part in any sort of rebellion. That's why she's a doctor, and I'm too chicken to speak up when Charles shoots down my ideas."

"But when you buy the store, you won't need to go through Charles anymore. It'll be your ideas or bust."

"The bank called yesterday and said I didn't meet their eligibility requirements." I'd avoided telling him so I could hold onto the false hope just that much longer. The way his face fell made me want to take it back to spare him the bad news. "I'm just worried that since I didn't get the business loan, I'll end up in the same position all over again with a new owner. Sometimes it's difficult to separate everyone else's wants from my own."

"Then what do *you*—Lex, and only Lex—want?"

"For the people in my life to quit leaving." Shit. So much for saving that conversation for home. A sushi bar counter wasn't where I wanted to have this discussion, but now that it was out there . . . I rocked my tea cup back and forth on the bottom ridge of the glass, then ran my fingertip along the textured enamel finish. "Everyone either leaves or dies."

He took my hand in his and squeezed, just a bit. "Everyone?"

I nodded, not meeting his eyes for fear of what I'd see there. "Everyone."

"Natalie's parents aren't going anywhere. Natalie's sticking around. You're fixing up that house you love so much, a little at a time." He popped the last of his sushi in his mouth and reached for his wallet. "And, I'm fond of your weird little town's creaky used bookstores and creepy covered bridges. I can't go anywhere until I've seen everything."

I swallowed. Hard.

"I don't mean to assume, but I'm hoping that's a plus?" His voice was tipped with caution that replaced his usual confidence. He tucked a crisp bill beneath the check and set his tea cup on top of it.

He wants to stay. How long, I couldn't be sure. Months, years, he hadn't confirmed, but sticking around was on his mind—and that was just enough to replenish my hope. "Add a big check to the pro column, please." I swirled the last sip of tea, then tipped it into my mouth.

"Preference noted." He stood, tucked his corduroy jacket over one arm, and offered his opposite hand to me. "Now, if I remember correctly, I was promised a city tour."

"You've been here before, what do you need a tour for?"

"Because even though I've seen this city a dozen times, I've never seen it through your eyes. You have a habit of opening up entire worlds for me, Lex. I'm bound to discover at least four new reasons to love it here."

I rolled my eyes. "You give me too much credit."

James rested an elbow on the counter and leaned in to look me in the eye. "I think it's just enough."

A prickle of goosebumps raced across my arms and my chest warmed as he gazed at me. I lifted my chin, giving him plenty of room in case he went in for a kiss. Instead, he ran a fingertip along my jawline, then pressed himself away from the counter. "Where to first?"

"Bookstores, obviously."

"Stores, plural?"

"Absolutely. This isn't Stowe. We have options. A whole new world of books, a completely different demographic, and fresh possibilities for book inscriptions."

"Okay, but how many books can you fit in your carry on?"

I smirked. "Amateur. I'll ship a box home. Cheaper than checking a bag, and less to haul through the airport, too."

He shook his head, but the grin beat out the exasperation. "Lead the way."

CHAPTER TWENTY-ONE

Seven bookstores, three coffee orders, one vintage clothing store, and likely miles spent wandering serpentine through store aisles, and I had bags of gifts, an impressive stack of books, and a chunky knit sweater to show for it. We slipped through the front door of my parents' house to the sounds of kids chasing each other and dinner sizzling on the stove.

"Alex! We're sacrificing our health for your benefit. I'm making those crab cakes you love," Jordan called down the hallway to the front door, where we were unlacing our shoes. "Oh god, I should have asked if James eats crab. I hope he's not allergic or anything."

"I love crab, it smells delicious," James said. We walked into the kitchen, where Jordan stood flipping patty after butter-drenched patty.

She wore high-waisted, wide-legged trousers with a flowy subtly printed top—front-tucked but loose in the back, the long sleeves casually rolled to keep them out of the way of splattering oil. I'd thought my slouchy sweater and black jeans would be dressy enough for a family gathering, but I'd forgotten how Jordan could make the simplest outfit look glam without even trying. There was no question that we were sisters, though: I could see a reflection of myself in her, from the nose to the cheekbones to the blue-green eyes to the wavy blonde hair.

In another timeline, maybe we'd have spent more time together, maybe getting our hair done or going away for a weekend at some fancy hotel where we'd gossip over sparkling wine. I wondered idly if there'd be any chance to make up for lost time now. If I asked her to get away for a long weekend, would she accept? I shook the thought away before I could let it consume me.

"Jordan, this is James. James, Jordan." I gestured between the two.

"I am thrilled to meet you. So glad you could come!" Jordan went in for a handshake but paused midreach and held up her hands. "Forgive me, I'd shake but I'm a mess." She brushed her crab-and-butter-caked hands together over the sink before grabbing the spatula to flip, flip, flip some more patties off the griddle and into the warm oven.

"Look at you, a professional in action. Impressive."

"I'm hardly a professional but thank you for the confidence." She swatted at my hand with the spatula to chase me away from the pretty curled carrots she'd prepped. "You. Wash your hands and help me out here. Veggies in the fridge, you know where the good knives are. Chop, rinse, toss, and stop stealing the garnish." She swatted me again as I stole another thin ribbon of carrot. I leaned my head on her shoulder in a half-hug as I nibbled the contraband carrot, and she tipped her face downward enough to rest her cheek on the top of my head momentarily. "And I'm very glad you're here, even if you *are* ruining the presentation."

Jordan finished her flipping and turned back to the cutting board to slice cabbage paper-thin, which she added to the bowl with the carrots. She reached for a red onion next.

"I didn't realize you had so many talented chefs in the family, Lex," James said.

Jordan snorted.

"I can cook, Jordan. Just because my favorite meals aren't up to your standards . . ." I flicked water from my fingertips into her face and she shrieked.

"Honestly, Alex, *why*?"

I mouthed "sorry" to James, then gathered up the vegetables from the crisper drawer in the fridge.

"I'm more of a comfort food kind of guy. You know, chicken soup, mac and cheese. Good, hearty meals that stick with you."

"Well, there's enough butter in this to make it count as comfort food. We'll have salad, and my own special slaw recipe that you'll just adore. Everyone does." She was rambling, her words nearly tripping over themselves as they tumbled from her mouth. She alternated between chopping and gesturing wildly with the knife, occasionally reaching for her wine glass for a swig to break up the routine. Bubbly and outgoing, as always. Just because we had similar physical appearances didn't mean the genes aligned our personalities. She was like the Energizer Bunny, while my ambivert energy usually only kicked into high gear while I was putting on a show for fans of the vlog.

"Dad's outside grilling up some chicken thighs—imagine it, Alex. Dad. Grilling chicken thighs. On their last cruise, Mom and Dad attended a cooking workshop with that chef she loves. What's that guy's name? The one who she describes as Chef George Clooney? Anyway. They made fennel and orange chicken thighs. Dad's hooked. It's madness. He absolutely adores chicken thighs now. I know. It's just." She raised her hands, palms-up with the knife still gripped in one hand, and turned her eyes to the ceiling. "I never thought I'd see the day."

"My father has always said chicken thighs are not worthy of our dinner table," I explained to James. "Cheap meat is beneath him."

"To be fair, he special-ordered these from their butcher, so. Still on-brand-Dad. You should have seen Mom's face when he recommended we skip the Cornish hens this year. I was sure she'd pass out. But she talked him into adding to the menu for tonight's meal instead, and voila. Here we are. Dad's grilling, Alex. Grilling."

I shot James a bug-eyed look and blew air through my lips. "That's the strangest thing, wow. Mind, blown," I said with the barest hint of sarcasm.

"So how was the flight, Alex? Was it dreadful? Morning flights are the worst. Have you settled in? Mom said you were out shopping. I assume you've added a stack of books to the collection? Anything good this time?" She looked at James. "She and I have such different tastes in literature. What she lacks in general refinement, she makes up for in how well-read she is. I, on the other hand, haven't had that much time for reading since I graduated from med school and had the boys."

James grinned. "She's been giving me homework assignments since we met. Everything but the written essay portion."

"Ugh, you two are adorable. Alex, he's adorable. I can't handle how cute you are." She started pulling the crab cakes off the stove and layering them on a platter, on top of the slaw. She'd left my last four voicemail messages unanswered. The last time we texted, the dots bumped around for nearly two minutes before I received a two-word reply. I never heard from her unless I reached out first, but suddenly conversational Jordan had made an appearance. It wasn't unlike her to out-talk an auctioneer, but this was a whole new level of chattiness. Maybe she was trying to fill the air before quiet had a chance to settle in—she always preferred background noise or conversation to quiet contemplation, to my chagrin. "How's that salad coming? James, tell me all about how you met."

I finished tossing the mixed greens and veggies together and began to dig through the massive refrigerator for the salad dressing. "So, Italian dressing or . . .?" I asked, desperate to change the subject.

Jordan took a sip of her wine, then snapped her fingers. "The dressing, I forgot. Here, it's all set. Fresh and tangy—so much better than the store-bought stuff. James, care to give it a shake while we walk?" She pressed a canning jar into his hands. "I'm heading outside with the crab cakes, I'll let everyone know you're on your way."

She breezed out of the room, and the energy fell by at least half without her giant personality to fill the space.

"So, that's Jordan."

"She's . . . nice," James said.

"She got all the charm, all the energy, and all the talent. I had to work with whatever was left over."

"Don't sell yourself short, Lex. You charmed me from day one," he said, giving the jar an extra shake. "I'd never be able to keep up with all of that, anyway."

"Everyone else seems to think she's a breath of fresh air. Vivacious and effervescent, or something. I realized early on that no matter what I did, she'd outshine me simply by being in the room."

"And yet, you're the one who has my attention."

I smiled and leaned in to give him a kiss. "And you have mine." I put the salad bowl onto the wooden tray on the counter, alongside the plates and cloth napkin-wrapped flatware, and carried it to the sliding glass doors that led to the patio. The patio heaters were roaring, but my parents were both wearing double layers and knit caps.

My father waved his tongs at us, and my mother raised a wine glass in my direction. I introduced my dad to James, and the two shook hands briefly before Dad went back to poking at dinner, which had my stomach growling at the smell.

"Did you show the poor boy every bookstore in town? You've been gone hours."

"Just the used bookstores. How can I help?"

"You could track down your nephews to let them know we're ready to eat."

My eyes darted to James, whom I could *not* leave with my parents unattended.

"I'll keep him safe," Jordan promised. She plunked herself down in a patio chair, tucked both feet beneath her, and smoothed nonexistent wrinkles from her pristine trouser legs. She patted the seat next to her.

"He will be fine, Alex," my mother said, barely hiding the exasperation in her tone.

I slipped back into the house to round up the kids. Isaac and Levi were nowhere to be found, but the gentle rustle of my mother's floor-to-ceiling drapes gave them away.

"Hmm, where did they go?" I said, tiptoeing toward their hiding spot. "Maybe under the coffee table? Nope, not there." Snickers and more rustling cloth. "Oh, I know. Behind the throw pillows. Not there either! Who taught them to hide so well? I guess they must be upstairs somewhere . . . Dinner's going to be gone by the time I finally find them." More hushed giggles came from behind the drapes. I reached for the edge and peeled them back to reveal two wavy-haired kids, each with identical splashes of freckles and grins featuring newly sprouted adult teeth that didn't quite fit in their kid-sized mouths.

"Aunt Lex!" They leaped into my arms for a three-person hug that was more jumping and jiggling than actual embrace.

"Okay, first of all, you're both almost as tall as me and that's unacceptable. Secondly, I have a surprise for you for after dinner and you'll never guess what it is."

"Maple candy?" Isaac asked, then grinned. "You always say we'll never guess. And it's *always* maple candy."

"Hey, now, if you don't want it, I can eat it."

Levi's eyes went wide and he shook his head. "No way, we'll eat it."

"I thought so. Let's go eat." I ushered them out to the patio.

When we returned, James, my parents, and Jordan were all laughing. He had charmed them already, and it was only a matter of time before one of them asked me how I'd managed to find him.

"What are you talking about out here?" I asked, prepared for embarrassment.

"James is a delightful young man, Alex. Kudos." My mother, who had moved to sit beside him in the two minutes I was gone, patted James on the forearm.

"Well, I'll file that away for when I actually want your opinion on the person I'm dating, thanks."

"Oh, come on. Your mother is being nice. Why do you insist upon making her the enemy?" my father said.

"I have a few solid reasons—" I started, but James cleared his throat. Buffer mode activated.

"This looks fabulous. When do I get to dig in?" He rubbed his hands together greedily. "Our sushi lunch was ages ago and I'm ravenous."

"Oh, please tell me you did not force this dear boy to eat raw fish." My father's lips turned downward as he shook off a mock shiver. Isaac and Levi stuck out their tongues in solidarity.

"Thank goodness your daughter knows exactly what to order. Not a single bite I didn't love."

My eyes shifted from my father to James and back again as I waited for a reply. Dad merely grunted, carried the platter of chicken to the table, and set it down. Not a peep otherwise.

Every meal came with at least one instance of verbal sparring, usually between my mother and me. This evening was no different: Dad mentioned that he'd been reading a Bernard Cornwell book and I had the audacity to mention that I could send him the next in the series since I had a stack of them at the store.

"No wonder you don't have more responsibilities around there," my mother said. "Giving away books is not how you make money."

"I meant that I'd purchase it and send it as a gift, but yeah let's go with that." There was still time to pull back, to quit before I made dinner awkward. But I lacked the sense to stop. "Let's ignore that I've single-handedly improved the store's sales year over year and that there's an opportunity to expand the café menu now because customers have been asking. We can just gloss right over the fact that the place is running smoothly with one full time employee, one part time employee, and an owner who only calls to check in so he feels like he's fulfilling his boss duties rather than out of interest in the store. I haven't had a vacation since *last* Christmas, but—" I sent James a pleading look, begging for an escape from the impending argument.

"I've been impressed with the way Lex handles the store," James jumped in—the guy never missed a cue. He reached beneath the table and grasped my hand, giving it a gentle squeeze. "In fact, she's been working toward some marketing initiatives that I find very interesting. If the owner gets on board, I see great things for the place."

"Well, lovely. I do hope Charles realizes how much you do for him, then, and provides a suitable raise or bonus."

"You and me both," I mumbled. It would have been nice to be making it instead of just scraping by.

We cleared the table of every scrap of food. Chicken bones were picked clean and there wasn't a speck of crab or slaw left on the platter.

After the dishes were done, the kids disappeared to watch a movie and my mother and father began cleaning the kitchen. James, Jordan, and I were left alone with nothing but the propane hiss of the heaters to keep us company.

"More wine?" I asked, reaching across the table to fill Jordan's glass. She clapped her hand over the top of the glass. "Or not?"

"I have something better," she said. She slipped through the patio door and disappeared down the hall.

James lifted his eyebrows at me; I raised my shoulders and shook my head. Jordan shuffled back down the hall and onto the patio, a bottle of Bacardi in her grasp.

"Okay so I had to sneak this past Dad in my shirt—do not disappoint me, Alex Lenore McCall."

James's eyebrows arched and he mouthed "Lenore?" I gritted my teeth and rolled my eyes. Now was not the time to explain the long-held tradition of family names that had earned me that middle name.

"James, you're more than welcome, obviously. My husband's clocking hours upon hours tonight, so I'm sorry to leave you without company."

"I can leave you two to the fun . . ." he said, pressing his hands into the patio cushion to heft himself out of the seat.

"Oh, stay," I said, grasping for his wrist to keep him from abandoning me with my sister. "You're absolutely welcome, and it's far too early for you to head to bed. Stick around, do a couple shots. I'd . . ." I narrowed my eyes at him. "Appreciate it. Beyond words." I pressed my lips together and waited for a response.

"If you insist," he said.

Jordan squealed, clapped her hands, plunked onto the wrought iron bench, and tucked her legs beneath her. "Oh, shit, I forgot the glasses."

"It's alcohol, right? Kills the germs, we're totally cool." I grabbed the bottle and took a swig, then hissed as the booze burned on the way down my throat. "Smooth." I coughed.

Jordan reached for the bottle, opening and closing her fingers to urge me to hand it over faster. She took a swig, ran the back of her hand across her mouth to wipe away the nonexistent drips, then thrust the bottle in James's direction.

He accepted the bottle and tipped it to his lips just enough that the liquid brushed against them—but I could tell he didn't swallow.

"Yes, James, yes, fantastic! Get in on the party!" She reached for the bottle and took another sip.

After what would amount to four or five shots, her talkative nature went into overdrive. She flipped sideways, tucked a throw pillow between her and the arm of the bench, and rambled about everything. Her kids' grades, the lack of skilled baggers at the grocery store nearest her house, the sheer audacity that the dealership had charged her for the ding in the front fender of the lease she had just returned. Then the conversation turned toward my relationship.

"Where did you two meet? Don't tell me, he was . . . your life insurance salesman? No, no obviously I'm joking. But you do have that professional vibe, James. What are you, a lawyer?" He cringed visibly. "No, not lawyer, then. Architect? Something tactile? Doesn't matter. Tell me all about it, how did you find each other?"

"She harassed me one night when I stepped into her bookstore. Forced me to buy a book so I could use the bathroom."

"I did not," I said, my mouth hanging open. "It was a coffee, and I am offended that you'd forget such an important detail of our meet cute."

Jordan clasped her hands beneath her chin and sighed, her shoulders drew upward toward her ears. "Fabulous." She reached for the bottle and took another drag before shoving it into James's hand and flopping back into her reclined position. She didn't notice when he passed it directly to me. I imbibed.

"He's cheating on me, you know," she said out of nowhere, her voice flat, the cheer that usually soaked every word suddenly dried up.

Jordan picked at a cuticle while I sat in silence, absorbing the news. She didn't hesitate, there was no *maybe* in her accusation—no joking tone. I glanced at James and took a moment to blink away the surprise before asking Jordan, "Lucas?"

She clicked her tongue, winked, and pointed at me. "That's the guy."

I shook my head. That was impossible. "No, he's not."

She sat up, dropped her feet down over the edge of the bench, then leaned forward to place her elbows on her knees. She sucked air through her teeth. "He absolutely is. With a pharmacy intern. A freaking *intern*, Alex."

I wouldn't have gone out of my way to spend time with him, but I hadn't outright disliked him until this moment. Though, he'd spent his wedding reception flirting with the bartender and bridesmaids, so one could assume he had continued to nurture the audacity. The creep. "Does he know?"

"That he's cheating on me? Yeah, I'm fairly certain he is aware of this fact."

I held a breath, then blew the air through tight lips to calm myself before speaking. "Does he know that you know?"

"Of course I knew that's what you meant," she said, tipping sideways slightly as she swiped her hand through the air near where my knee was. She missed, then reached out again to try to pat it. I gripped her hand and squeezed, and she looked up, head wobbling slightly. "I don't think he knows I know, but now you know I know even if he doesn't know. Ha. That was a lot of 'knows.'"

James's eyes grew two sizes, and he gestured toward the door, as if asking permission to be excused. I gritted my teeth and nodded, and he slipped away without a sound. He wasn't ready for this amount of family drama. Saving himself was the best option.

"How do you know?" I asked.

She laughed, blowing a raspberry in the process. "I saw his phone, then I followed him, then I saw them. They weren't even being discreet. You'd think that the foremost trauma surgeon in the region would have a hint of discretion, but that's far too much to ask of someone so important. She was cute, at least. And younger than me, too. Score one for him. But honestly, traipsing around together like he didn't care if anyone saw. Disgraceful, truly."

"Do . . . Mom and Dad know?"

"Oh, god, Alex do not breathe a word of this to them, they'd honestly die of shame. They'd never let me hear the end of it. Do *not* tell them, I beg you." Her glassy eyes were wide and pleading.

"Okay, sheesh, I won't say anything." I guzzled another shot's worth of booze. I didn't have much practice keeping Jordan's secrets from our parents. She'd never confided in me growing up, and I'd always assumed it was because she could do no wrong. I did *not* have *perfect sister's perfect marriage blows up* on my holiday trip bingo card— and while I wanted to offer support, she'd locked me out of her life so often that I didn't know how. "What are you going to do?"

"I don't know." Her voice wavered, and I shoved the bottle back into her hand to fend off the waterworks. She raised it in a toast, then drank. "I can deal with there being another woman, I suppose. What choice do I have? Lose the house, lose my job probably, because he's on the board, and he wouldn't hesitate to fire me if he thought it would get him ahead. I should have known. How did I not see this coming?" She tucked the bottle between her knees and ground her palms into her temples.

"Hey," I said, patting her shoulder awkwardly, "even if your husband is trash, you're still Mom and Dad's favorite daughter."

Jordan laughed, and it morphed into a whine part way through. "If only that were true."

Well, it certainly wasn't *me* who was the favorite. "Uh, hi, hello? Earth to Jordan: they picked up and moved across an entire country when you left. You've always been their favorite. The perfect daughter, with the perfect grades and bright future. Mom starts every conversation about you with 'Jordan, you know, the doctor?' It's pretty obvious."

She flopped back onto the bench again and dangled the Bacardi bottle to the side, the neck slung between two fingers. "You should hear the way they talk about you, then."

"Oh, let me guess. The failure, the college drop-out, the ungrateful daughter who won't drop everything to move across an entire goddamned country to live near them even though they've offered money and a house to appease her. Something like that?"

"More like, 'Our daughter is going to own an independent bookstore someday, she's working on her business plan. If anyone has the know-how to pull it off in a dying industry, she does.'"

"Bookstores are *not* a dying industry." I snatched the bottle away and drank. Deeply. "Besides, no way they've ever said any of that."

"Their words, I swear it." She kissed her fingertips on her right hand, then flicked her fingers skyward, just like we used to do when we were kids making a promise to each other. "They know you won't fail, and that's why they admire you. They push you to keep you going, to challenge you. You've always, always thrived because you want to prove yourself."

"Well, that's a hell of a way to encourage someone. Pick up and leave them to wallow alone after they actually did fail and had to come home with their tail tucked between their legs. Great tactic, really. So encouraging."

"The timing wasn't ideal, no." Jordan grasped for the bottle, took the last sip, and let her head flop backwards onto the pillow. "Here's the thing, lovely. Mom and Dad only moved out here because I've been a failure since the moment I left the house."

"Oh, god, Jordan. Stop being so dramatic. Just because Lucas is a prick, it doesn't mean you're a failure."

"That's not it. I nearly failed Intro to Bio in high school. Way to break into the medical field, right? When they found that out they started keeping tabs on my homework, my AP courses, my extracurriculars. They left stacks of college applications for me to fill out and double-checked that I'd spelled my own name correctly. Then they sent me off to college—to my first, big, real-life experience—and I was wholly unprepared for a world in which I was required to make choices and perform without their oversight. I got hung up with this sorority that lacked decision-making skills, like, as a whole. I lost my virginity at my first college party, with some guy I didn't even really know—did you know that? I wasn't on birth control, so I cried until the guy went to get Plan B." She heaved a sniffling sigh.

The illusion of the do-no-wrong daughter was shattered in a single sixty second monologue. I'd never seen her so *human*, or so full of *hurt*. The real kicker was that if I had known any of this, I would have been in her corner without hesitation. Okay, sisterly bonding. I could do this.

"Jordan, plenty of people show up at college and get a little over-whelmed by the newness of it all. I straight-up *quit*, and I wasn't even studying anything so specialized as pre-med." I'd just had a chest-squeezing aversion to being left behind, but she wouldn't know about dealing with that.

"You didn't need Mommy and Daddy to jump on a plane and rescue you, either. You made your decision and stuck to it—damn the consequences. In fact, if they'd tried to change your mind or wanted to come help you, you would have sent them packing. *Get out of here, I've got this, because I'm Alex the Great. I'm tough and cool, and I have friends who support me.* Not like me, nope." She popped the "p" in nope, then shifted her body into a curled-up C, squishing the pillow around for extra comfort. "Mom and Dad moved out here to save me from myself, because I was about to destroy their entire plan for my future."

"This was ages ago, and you're a doctor now. You've made it, nothing was destroyed. It's in the past."

"Except now my marriage is failing."

"Listen, you're not to blame for your husband's bad choices."

"He never loved me enough, you know. He loved the *idea* of me. He loved that I was successful, and we could be a power team. Not like you and James. You don't compete. You complement each other."

I forced a smile while my conscience yelled, screamed, pounded at the walls of my skull, reminding me that I had spent the last month sabotaging his project just to ensure my own success. I'd been putting my own desires ahead of his needs. I'd thought it wouldn't matter, that his time in Vermont was an overlay between destinations. But after what he said at lunch today, I wasn't so sure of anything anymore.

"Lucas and I have always been vinegar and baking soda. Explosive and only to be mixed under parental supervision. You and James are, like, peanut butter and jelly. Apple and cinnamon." She chuckled. "Bacardi and our parents' house. You go together."

"For now." I chewed the inside of my cheek. "For now, we go together. Until he leaves."

"Now that's bullshit," Jordan said, pointing her perfectly manicured finger at me without lifting her head. "Why would he leave?"

I tucked my feet onto the seat of the chair—my mother hated it when I did that because it ruined the finish—and tugged my knees up to hug them to my chest. "You left."

"Well, yeah, but that was for med school—"

"Kyle left for music. Mom and Dad left because you were the better option."

"Jesus, you think they left because of *you*? They left because of *me*. I was failing at everything, Alex. And they stayed because things were only getting worse, and I needed help. I had two babies—one was in the NICU for months. I had postpartum depression and couldn't take care of myself, let alone two newborns and a husband who preferred the gym to coming home to help me out. You had your shit, and I wasn't going to stomp on it with my drama. But they did *not* leave because of you."

"Felt like it," I said. There was no way I was understanding her correctly. How could it be possible that my perfect, had-it-together sister had spent so long feeling the exact same way about me that I had about her?

"Mom and Dad knew you could handle yourself. You'd been handling yourself since the day you were born. You know what Mom's go-to anecdote was whenever anyone mentioned how strong the boys looked as babies? 'They get it from their Auntie Alex. She tried to crawl on her third day on this earth, and that's the truth.' She shared that story every time. You know what she never said? 'Oh, they get that from their strong mama.' They never equated their grandkids' strength with the woman who had actually birthed them. They knew you had things under control, one hundred percent of the time. You always have, and you always will."

My throat prickled and my eyelids burned as I held back the unexpected emotion. Even if she was only saying it because she was drunk, it was nice to feel strong and appreciated for once, rather than like a burden my parents had to endure.

Jordan flopped forward and groaned, and I startled out of my sudden moment of actual sisterly feelings toward her—just in time, too. "I am going to have a massive headache in the morning, and it's all your fault," she said.

"You're the one who snuck the rum out here in the first place, and somehow it's my fault? Come on." I looped one of Jordan's arms over my shoulder and helped her to her feet. "Let's go, beddy time, okay? I was supposed to be regaling my boyfriend with stories about my terrible childhood while we stared at the kids' glow-in-the-dark stars, you know. Romance."

"Well . . ." She swayed on her feet, but regained her balance by gripping my forearm. "You'll just have to stare at those stars with me, then."

"You're going to sleep in the kids' room with me? There's only one bed. And it's a twin."

"Their sleeping bags are in the closet. That carpet is incredible, almost as good as my memory foam mattress. No, I swear it."

"And the kids?"

"They're fine, Mom was going to set up a sleepover space in the den. They're not me, you know. They're in possession of independence. They're like you." She laughed. "You sure they're not your kids?"

"Absolutely sure, yes. 'Cool aunt' is the only kid-related title I ever need." She wobbled, I braced. I shuffled her weight slightly for better support, then we both snuck into the kitchen through the sliding glass doors and slunk down the hallway toward the bedroom. James poked his head out of his room when I unlatched my door, but saw the extra-drunk, nearly sleeping Jordan draped across my shoulders.

"So, that's your family?" he said quietly.

"That's my family."

"Interesting."

"What?" I eyed him.

He scratched the back of his head, plucked a piece of invisible lint from his sweater, then shrugged. "They seem pretty okay to me."

"Pretty okay?" I adjusted Jordan on my shoulder. "*Pretty okay?* Shall I recap the entire night? Can we start with the part where my father referred to his high school game-winning home run as his 'biggest and best accomplishment,' while his daughters and grandchildren were *right there*?"

"I'm just saying, overall, they're not the worst."

I thought about that for a moment. "No, I guess they're not the worst. Kind of close, some days. But occasionally, they can be alright," I agreed.

He rolled his eyes playfully. "See you in the morning?"

"Sorry, yeah. See you in the morning." I stretched my neck around Jordan's head and James leaned in for a tiny, sweet peck on the lips. "Wish me luck. I have a feeling we're about to get into some deep childhood trauma, and I may not be the same person when I come out on the other side."

"I've staked out the area. Donuts and coffee will be waiting bright and early."

"God, you're dreamy when you talk like that. Just not too early, please? That was, like, a lot of rum."

He leaned in and kissed me again and my limbs tingled. Damn this turn of events. We were supposed to be getting frisky in a twin bed tonight.

"No earlier than 6 A.M., got it." He winked, shuffled back into his room, and clicked the door shut behind him.

Haunted Happenings transcript

Date: December 23, 2006

Location: Smuggler's Notch Scenic Highway

> **Luna:** We're coming to you today from a snowy, icy Notch Road. It's closed to vehicles during winter, which means no interference from radios, electronics, engine sounds . . . Just us, nature, and—
>
> **Natalie:** Frostbite?
>
> **Luna:** Ghosts.
>
> **Natalie:** Oh yeah, those.
>
> **Luna:** Specifically, bootleggers who used this route during Prohibition. Smugglers transported supplies through here during the War of 1812, too, but I'm interested in the people who risked their lives to make and distribute booze in spite of Prohibition-era laws. Vermont was ready to keep the supply flowing because we had a sorta pre-Prohibition prohibition that started in the 1850s and ended in 1903.
>
> **Natalie:** What is it with the government always trying to tell people what they can and can't do with their own bodies?
>
> **Luna:** Right? Lay off, already. [Luna glares at the camera not at all subtly because she's had enough.] When booze was banned, thousands of men lost their jobs—at distilleries, breweries, and restaurants and bars that served alcohol, but elsewhere, too, like in factories that made the barrels and bottles. It basically ruined people's lives everywhere.

Natalie: And the people fought back!

Luna: Yeah, they did! Smugglers kept the booze biz running, including a *lot* of women. The laws actually unintentionally *protected* women from getting caught. Like, prohibition agents usually wouldn't pull over a vehicle with a woman in it, and they weren't allowed to search women—at all—so women would strap the alcohol to their bodies to hide the goods. And while Prohibition was an overall shitty idea, it *did* help obliterate some ridiculous gender roles. Women weren't allowed to drink in public, but, when Prohibition shut down bars, women started making alcohol at home and hosting parties to serve their homemade hooch. That led to speakeasies—many run by women—where women were welcome to drink and dance alongside men. So, like, speakeasies are more than just a party theme, got it? Women risked their lives and freedom to keep the booze flowing just to support their families—and some of them got filthy rich doing it.

Natalie: Hell yeah!

Luna: And, I mean, it was super dangerous, too. People *died*. But you didn't come here for a history lesson, you came here for ghosts. We have heard that a woman haunts this twisting roadway. It's said that while she was being pursued by Prohibition agents, her car was totaled—but nobody ever found her remains. So, the question is: is she haunting this area, mourning the fortune she lost . . . or did she get away on foot to enjoy the spoils of her efforts? Let's get our equipment set up and we'll see what we can spot.

CHAPTER TWENTY-TWO

The next morning, there were doughnuts and coffee, as promised, sitting on a tray outside the door. Two tiny foil packets of Advil and two roses accompanied them. I grabbed the breakfast offering and tore off pieces of fluffy, yeasty glazed donut, popping them into my mouth one by one. Jordan had cocooned herself inside the dinosaur print sleeping bag. Only her wavy blonde hair escaped the folds of rustley nylon.

I got dressed, then tugged the curtains open a bit to let some daylight into the room. The monster clock on the nightstand turned to 7 A.M., the latest I'd slept in ages, even without factoring in the time zone adjustment. A dull ache hung out at my temples, but it seemed that I'd mostly avoided a hangover. I hadn't been the one pounding shot after shot, though. That was all Jordan. Perfect, always proper Jordan.

"Hey," I said, quiet enough that maybe she wouldn't hear it and wake up. I wasn't ready for a recap of the night before.

"...time is it?" she mumbled into the crook of her arm. She peeked her head out of the sleeping bag. "Seven. Too early." She flipped the sleeping bag over her face again, then popped up again in seconds. "No, Alex, why didn't you wake me? Lucas will be here in half an hour.

I have to shower and get the kids up, Dad's going to need help getting brunch ready. Alex, honestly. I can't lounge in bed all day."

"Sisterly bonding time is over, then." I pressed my lips into a line, then handed Jordan her coffee.

Jordan sat up, pressed a palm to her left temple, and accepted the mug with her opposite hand. She blew her fringed bangs out of her face, then looked at me from behind her uncooperative hair. "Was there something else?"

"I don't know, things felt a little unfinished last night. Interrupted by dizzy spells and hiccups." That, and her slurred speech was more difficult to follow than her usual faster-than-fast chatter.

"We didn't drink that much." She sipped her coffee, then her mouth turned downward in a sour grimace. "Or maybe we did."

"What's the deal here? Do I pretend we never had this heart-to-heart?"

She gave me a look. "As opposed to what, exactly? Shouting at him about his affair over brunch? Just play it cool. Forget anything I said last night, okay?"

"Just answer me this—are you alright?" I asked.

"Alex, I am fine. It was the rum talking last night, nothing more. Relationships are simply meant to fail, that's the nature of the thing. It isn't sustainable to fight for something when both parties aren't invested. He's blowing off steam now. We will either work through it or be miserable forever."

"Cheery outlook." I ate the remaining bite of doughnut and dabbed the glaze from my fingertips.

"I'm a realist. We can't all have your carefree attitude."

Drunk Jordan considered me independent and strong, but sober Jordan went right back to the same argument my parents had for everything: I was too free-spirited to be trusted with my own decision making.

"Thanks for the confidence."

"Oh, I meant everything I said last night. Don't assume that I couldn't think clearly simply because I'd had a few shots. I just meant that—"

"Jordan?" Lucas's voice carried down the hall. "Mr. and Mrs. McCall?" The front door clicked shut and the rumbling of kids' feet sounded from somewhere in the opposite corner of the house. Cheers of "Dad!" and "We missed you!" mixed with laughter and the grunts that came with big, squeezing hugs.

My parents joined the welcoming committee, and James's voice joined as well. I gritted my teeth and raised my eyebrows at Jordan, who sprang to her feet and dragged her fingertips through her hair a few times.

"Do I look presentable?" she asked.

"As presentable as you'll ever be after half a bottle of rum."

"Shit, shit. Alex, shit. Mom and Dad are going to lose their minds. You look fabulous, as ever, not even a hair out of place and your clothes aren't wrinkled. They're already furious because Lucas took that shift last night, which is somehow my fault. And now I've got rum seeping from every pore."

I reached for Jordan's wrist and dragged her to the window. "I'll cover for you." I tugged the window open, popped the screen from its frame, and gestured for Jordan to make her big escape. "Sneak around back, take a shower in the guest house, and just pretend you were there all night."

She disappeared through the window, promising that she owed me one, and dashed around the side of the house to scale the fence into the patio area. I grabbed the sleeping bag from the floor, crammed it unceremoniously into the closet, then took a deep breath before opening the door to greet the newest arrival.

"Morning, Lucas," I said when I reached the entryway. Lucas was shaking the wrinkles from his jacket before hanging it. "I think Jordan's still in the guest house. Haven't heard a peep from her since last night."

James gave a slight nod of understanding. Finding a guy who would lie to my family for me hadn't been on my to-do list, but it was absolutely working out.

"Well, come in, come in!" my mother said. "Brunch isn't for another couple of hours, but we have doughnuts and coffee, courtesy of James. He happened upon a darling little bakery when he and Alex were out yesterday, and he surprised us all with delightful treats. A little more sugar than I'd usually have, but today, I'm indulging."

She shuffled him down the hallway toward the kitchen. James followed, but I loitered behind until they were out of sight. I wasn't sure what a cheating asshole would leave behind in terms of evidence, but I fished in his jacket pockets anyway. The snooping paid off: A balled-up baggage tag was crammed into the interior pocket. Destination: Maui. Returning flight landing date: Christmas Eve morning. So much for the selfless overnight shift.

I smoothed and folded the baggage tag and tucked it into my pocket. The kitchen island was piled high with doughnuts and croissants, two four-cup coffee trays stacked one on top of the other, and a giant bowl of strawberries.

I was halfway through my second croissant when Jordan slipped in through the back. "Morning," she said, her carefully done-up lips curling upward into the parent-pleasing smile she'd worked so hard to perfect as we were growing up. The same one plastered on her face in the billboard ads for the hospital where she worked: the face of the practice.

"I was about to give up on you and drink your coffee. Did you sleep in?" I asked, an eyebrow hitched in challenge. She couldn't talk back for once, and I was determined to take full advantage.

"Just catching up on the news, listening to a little NPR while it was quiet out there."

"Hmm." Lucas nodded as he sipped from his to-go cup. "I'm glad you were listening. I had it on in the car. They were talking about that poet I was telling you about. Did you hear? He read the piece about the freeway, the one I thought you'd like."

Jordan's eyes widened.

"Oh, I heard that," James cut in, to Jordan's visible relief. "I enjoyed how he connected the known world with the idea of possibility and newness, and how what's considered the most probable is not always a direct path."

"Exactly, exactly," Lucas said. He sipped his coffee, then gestured toward James with the cup. "I like him, Alex."

"Well, as long as you approve, I suppose that's all I need." I gritted my teeth as I sent an overly sweet smile in his direction. I'd never liked the guy, but knowing he was betraying my sister multiplied my distaste. "So how is Hawaii this time of year?"

Lucas flinched.

"I haven't been, but I assume you have? Seems romantic. Is it romantic?" I leaned on the counter, resting my chin in my palm.

"I'm sure it is," Lucas said.

"If you were going to suggest a location, would you say Maui is best?"

He shoved a large piece of pastry into his mouth and shrugged, his eyebrows standing in worried arches. He chewed slowly, his eyes aimed just over my head rather than making eye contact.

"Jordan and I have some last-minute shopping to take care of," I said, snagging her by the arm and tugging her toward my room. "Hope you don't mind. I'll have her back in a couple hours."

"You've got to be joking," she whispered. "It's Christmas Eve, I have obligations. I have to start the bread and help Mom with the hens."

"We have hours. Come on. We need to talk about . . ." I shook my head. "Just, we have to talk."

"Fine, I'm coming. I swear, Alex, you can be so dramatic." She slipped on her simple black ballet flats that turned her skinny jeans and slouchy sweater into a masterpiece of casual style and retrieved her bag from its place on the entryway side table.

"Need anything else for dinner, Mom?"

"I have everything we need; enjoy yourselves. And don't rush back, it's so rare that the two of you get along this well. A Christmas miracle."

I shuffled the jackets on the coat rack, and a familiar texture grazed my knuckles. I gripped James's Yankees cap and pulled it off the hook.

"I'll stay behind. There's a post-production supervisor who lives nearby and has agreed to meet with me so I can ask a million questions about wrapping on the film."

"Nerd," I said, ignoring the sinking feeling in my chest at the mention of filming ending.

"Go enjoy your sister time," James said, leaning against the wall.

If only it were that simple. "You sure?" I asked.

"I've got this under control. I'll just wow your mom with my knife skills any time she gets too personal."

I didn't have the energy to think about the ways my parents would pick at him, asking questions they had no business asking. But he didn't need me to protect him. He was an adult, and besides, he'd probably already figured them out based on what I knew of his father.

I ushered Jordan into the driveway, tugged on the passenger side door of her car, then gestured for her to unlock it when the door didn't budge.

"Why yes, Alex, I'd be delighted to be the chauffeur, of course." She fished in her purse for the keys, and I dove into the vehicle the moment the lock popped. "Had I known I was required to drive, I may have worn different shoes."

"Oh, shut up, you look fantastic. At least you got to shower." I ran my fingers through my unwashed hair and cringed at the greasy mess. I wasn't even wearing mascara, which wasn't abnormal—but I at least tried to look decent when I had to stand beside my tall, poised, perfect sister.

Their house was barely out of sight before I started in on her. "Please tell me you're going to divorce him."

"Divorce is not the answer. If I ever confront him about it—and that's a giant 'if,' because I can't call him out without evidence or *I'll* look like a moron—we'll figure it out. That might mean we try counseling. That might mean I agree to let him have his life on the side because it's better for the family."

"I'm not just saying this because I hate the guy," I said. "You need to end things with Lucas. Divorce that cheating asshole." I focused on her profile; the muscles twitched as she clenched her jaw and swallowed.

"A divorce affects more than just me, you know. Other people are involved."

"Yeah, your husband, who obviously doesn't deserve your love and patience."

"No, he doesn't. But do you seriously think that if we get divorced, he'll stick around for the kids? If I tell him to get out, do you think they'll see him again?" Her chin wobbled.

"He's *already* not around. What kind of argument is that? Did you know that Isaac told me last night Lucas missed his final soccer game? He promised he'd be there, but he didn't show. Zero explanation. Levi said he almost missed their birthday party—their *birthday party*, Jordan—and when he showed up, he barely glanced up from his phone. They're already feeling the separation, and you're still together."

Jordan's knuckles blanched as she wrung the steering wheel. "Leaving him won't fix anything. At least if we pretend, he has a chance to come to his senses."

"If you stay with him, how long until you have to explain to the kids why he works so late every night? And how long until they realize they've been lied to? Sometimes, sticking around is the bigger problem."

"Funny, I never pegged you as a quitter."

"Because I don't think you should let your husband run around behind your back while you keep it together at home?"

"I said we'd work it out."

"You work things out when he buys a stupid timeshare or gets a new car without discussing it with you. You talk about a gambling problem. Not cheating. Never cheating."

Jordan didn't respond. She held her hands at ten and two and kept her eyes on the traffic ahead of us. We'd gotten to the shopping mall and swung into the parking garage before she spoke again. "You're not always right, you know. Giving up on my relationship might seem easy for you because you can make it on your own. You know how to thrive. I've never had that chance. I don't want to hear another word about how difficult your life is. It doesn't have to be difficult. Part of me thinks that you like it when the world kicks you. It gives you another chance to brush yourself off and tell the world that you've got this, you're fine."

If she only knew. Though maybe she had more of a handle on how outward appearances could lie than I'd realized. "I've been fine so far, haven't I?"

"If you're so fine, then why haven't you bought that bookstore you love so much, huh? Or done *anything* with your life?"

I barked a laugh. As if it were so simple. "Success isn't always dollars or empires. Sometimes success looks like the quality of the people you have in your life—and that doesn't mean powering through a relationship that's not working. The wrong people are worse than no people."

She scoffed. "Oh, we're back to the 'woe is me' mantra, are we? Of course *my* marriage issues come back to how horribly *you've* been mistreated—"

"Whatever, do your thing. Stay with him. But don't be surprised when you realize that his tan isn't from your fancy rooftop pool or that the extra shifts he's been taking out of the goodness of his heart require a red-eye flight instead of a quick drive home." I pulled the luggage tag from my pocket and held it between my index and middle fingers. She squinted at the text, her face morphing from anger to confusion to disappointment—then back to anger.

"Out of my car." Jordan pointed into the dim parking garage. Her nostrils flared with each breath and her chest rose and fell at a quickened pace. "I do not need to sit here and have you explain exactly how much I'm ruining my life by making the decisions I have to make. If you can't support me, you can walk home."

I clenched my teeth and huffed, then grabbed the door handle and shoved the car door open. I half tumbled from the vehicle, tossed the baggage tag onto the passenger seat I'd vacated, then slammed the door behind me.

Jordan turned on the engine and squealed out of her parking spot.

So much for that bonding experience.

I scanned the lot, looking to see if anyone had witnessed her dramatics. But it was just me, standing all alone in the dim yellow glow of the flickering fluorescent overhead lighting.

I reached for my phone, but my back pocket was empty. Of course.

I plodded my way down the stairwell to the street, kicking bits of gravel along the way.

* * *

After two hours of walking at a brisk pace, I dragged my feet up the steps and through my parents' front door. I'd missed brunch, judging by the rattle of my mother's antique wooden rolling pin drifting down the hall. She was probably on the third pie crust by now. Guests had to have options, after all. That's common courtesy. Roll, press into the pan, and blind bake—it was like clockwork after so many years. The crust never tasted the same as my Gram's, never quite so flaky and light, but my mom churned them out every year anyway.

Lucas and Jordan were unaccounted for, though Jordan had left my phone on the entry table, so I had a connection to the world at large again. James was sprawled on the living room floor, a wicked grin on his face as he decimated my nephews at Life. Get used to it, kids, that's one game you'll never win—no matter how far ahead you think you are.

"Hey," James said when he caught my gaze lingering. "I'd get up for a proper hello, but I have a game to win."

Isaac bounced on his knees, like he was pleased to be deemed important by the cool, new adult.

"He knows the best rules," Levi said. "Like, when you don't have enough dollars for the stuff you land on, you can ask for the trivia round and if you answer right you get to skip the payment stuff. I got it right nine times, and James says it's because I'm brilliant."

"I'm brillianter, though," said Isaac.

"I think we can claim equal brilliance here, all parties are winners." I squeezed in to sit on the chair behind James. He grinned up at me, then took his turn spinning. I reached forward and dragged my fingertips through his hair, enjoying the way his body relaxed at the contact. As much as I had hated the idea of this trip, he was settling in better than I could have imagined.

"He's fun," Levi said. "He even lets us say 'dang it' when we lose a turn. Mom never lets us say 'dang it'."

I smiled. "He lets me say 'dang it', too. He's cool like that."

"Dang it," Isaac groaned, glaring at the spinner, which placed him on a "you're fired" space. "Can I spin again?"

"You get one spin, that's the rule," James said. "Anything else gives you an unfair advantage, and we can't have that. I've already told you the secret trivia rule."

The game continued without argument over take-two turns or special treatment. The man was a master at kid wrangling.

"What else have you talked about with fun James?"

"He says he has friends *all over* the whole country, like in a *lot* of cities. But it's been a long time since he saw some of them, and he misses them."

"Yeah?" I asked, raising a hand to squeeze James's shoulder.

"He said sometimes people have to leave because that's the way life goes. Like how sometimes the game doesn't work how we like but that doesn't mean we didn't try. And sometimes people try but can't win so they try something new."

"Big life lessons to be teaching nine-year-olds," I whispered.

"Seemed timely," James said.

My fingers halted against his scalp. Timely how? Like, he'd decided he wasn't going to be sticking around after all and he was gearing up for his next new adventure?

"Maybe family matters should remain within the family," I said, the hardness in my tone amplified to convey the exact gravity of the situation he'd created.

James leaned back to look at me, confusion behind his eyes.

"Never mind, I can't deal with this right now. I'm going to help my mother. Please stick to cartoons and fart jokes until further notice. No heart-to-hearts allowed until I've given express permission to engage. Enjoy the game."

I stormed into the kitchen and pulled my hair back into a ponytail tight enough to tug at the roots. "Where are we with the pie-baking? Jordan ditched me at the mall, and I need to roll some dough or chase after her with the rolling pin. And I'd rather not run, because I just walked six freaking miles home."

"She did what?" My father pulled his glasses down the bridge of his nose and peered at me over the top of the frames. "Well, you must have provoked her, in which case, I'm likely to side with her in the matter."

"Ugh!" I marched into my room and slammed the door. It didn't have the satisfying creak and smash that my bedroom door back in Vermont had, but it echoed sufficiently, given the situation.

Before I'd had the chance to sulk appropriately, a soft tap sounded at my door. I dragged myself from the bed and pulled the door open to reveal James. He scrubbed at the back of his neck, a frown on his face.

"I feel like . . . some wires got crossed?" He pressed his lips into a line.

"Jordan left me at the mall and made me walk home because I dared suggest she leave her cheating jerk of a husband. I have blisters. I want to go home to my cozy house to sleep in my own freaking bed. And I don't have a Christmas present for you because I didn't know what to get you so now you don't get to open anything tomorrow."

"Whew," James said. He slipped into the room and clicked the door closed. "Anything else?"

"And . . . and I'm mad about it." I flopped onto the bed and pulled the edge of the pillow over my face. "Oh." I let the pillow flop back open so I could glare at James. "And you're having a heart-to-heart with my nephews about people leaving and the timing is suspicious."

James sat beside me, slid up beside my feet, and squeezed my ankle. "Suspicious, how?"

"Like you're preparing them for something. Like their dad leaving. Or, like . . . you . . . leaving."

James muffled a tiny laugh. "Or maybe like their friend is moving to Colorado, and they won't be seeing him anymore. They wanted to know what it was like to move after they heard how many places I'd lived."

I slid my arm up to hug the pillow around my face again. "Oh."

"You're worried about me leaving?" His voice was soft.

"Why wouldn't I be? Traveling is what you do. You and Julian wander the country making films—how do I know Vermont is a long-term thing? If you were the 'stick around' type, you'd have registered your car in any of the dozen cities you lived in, or at least signed more than a month-to-month lease. What happens when it's time to move on, and I can't go with you? What then?"

"Listen," James said, sliding closer and moving the pillow from my face to make eye contact. "There's something I have to tell you. I'm not sure how you'll like it. I know how you feel about change, but—"

Levi and Isaac called for James then, their voices echoing down the hallway toward my room. His eyes shot to the door. If he was about to make some big confession about his plan to leave, or worse, beg me to leave with him, I wasn't in the mood to hear it. I'd probably get angry and kick him out or cry in front of him. Either way, it wasn't a conversation I wanted to have on Christmas Eve, at my parents' house.

"He's in here!" I called. The stampede of kid feet shook the floors and rattled the door, and they busted into the room and charged him.

"James, you have to come back. Isaac is cheating, and he took all of your dollars for his pile."

"No, I didn't, liar. Why are you always lying? I only wanted to straighten the pile up because it was falling over. James, you have a lot of money in your pile. At least, like, a million."

"A million, huh? Maybe enough to buy something extra nice, then. Shall we go see which piles of cash look different since I left?" He squeezed my ankle again, then stood. "Can we talk later?"

I smiled and nodded—then resolved to avoid the conversation at all costs for the rest of the trip.

CHAPTER TWENTY-THREE

The Cornish hens were a hit, as always. Isaac and Levi loved having a whole bird each, and not a scrap was left on any plate. As much as I mocked my parents for their annual Christmas Eve dinner choices, it wouldn't be the holidays without their perfectly portioned, neatly arranged dishes.

When I was a kid, they topped our plates with shiny metal covers that we got to pull away with a flourish. We were royalty, being presented with the finest meal. Lost in the magic of the moment, not worried about something as far away as the future. Adult Jordan spent dinner inching her chair away from her husband's while putting on an excited show for the kids who hadn't yet had the Christmas spirit sucked out of them by arguments and infidelity.

After dinner, James corralled the kids for a few rounds of hide and seek. Jordan and Lucas disappeared again. My father packaged up the leftovers and scraped plates clean while my mother and I scoured pans and cleaned up the post-Christmas-Eve-dinner mess.

"Has Jordan apologized to you?" my father asked.

I shook my head.

"I told her she should. She's being ridiculous. It's always something with that girl."

I narrowed my eyes at him. "She's figuring it out the best she can, Dad."

"I'm not sure what she and Lucas are arguing about this time, or how you got in the middle of it, but I'm willing to bet it's his fault. She's lucky I didn't send him back out that door to spend the holiday alone."

"The kids need him here. Honestly, Darren," my mother scolded him.

I sniffed back my opinions to avoid ripping into them about when *I* was a kid, and I needed them. It was done. I'd survived. There was no sense in punishing them for it, but I could make the effort to grow our relationship now that I'd made it through.

"So, James is lovely." My mother swished the sponge in the soapy dishwater, wrung it out, then set to work wiping the crumbs and stray seasonings away from the countertops.

I balled up the greasy tin foil that had topped the birds and tossed them into the trash. "He's pretty great, Mom. I'm enjoying spending time with him."

"He has some interesting things to say about you, you know," my dad said. He snapped the top on the last of the leftovers and stacked the containers into a teetering tower, too tall to carry in one go.

"Darren, goodness." My mom rushed to help him with the stack. It was nice to see them working together at something other than making me feel unaccomplished.

I took over wiping down the surfaces. "I'm sure he's got lots to say about me. We've been spending a lot of time together. I don't know how much longer it'll last, though. He's almost done with the show they're filming, and . . . well, you know how it is around there. People come and people go."

"He says that you've turned the store into something quite special."

It was the first time my mother had mentioned the bookstore without a shudder. It could have been the wine, or the fact that I'd already had one shouting match that day, but I wanted nothing more in that moment than to brag about myself. Let them know that I could do something for myself, even if everyone else thought I was wasting my time.

"You know, I have. Charles is a pain in the ass, as always. I mean, you knew him back when you were in high school, right? That guy just sticks to his guns no matter what. I didn't want to see the store fail so I took things into my own hands. He has ideas here and there, but I have turned them into things that work. He's almost on board with the 'If you liked, you'll love' blind-book-date table. I've worked with local crafters to sell little items, and I think it's done well enough that I can move to bigger book and café adjacent things. Mugs, carved bookends, that kind of thing. I've been managing the social media for the store, too. Interacting with local artists and writers, getting some buzz for the little things I can pull off without Charles's explicit approval."

"I didn't know the store was on the social medias," my dad said. "Probably a good idea, given the popularity of those websites."

"Exactly. And I've been looking into options for selling some of the more valuable books online. If we could tap into estate sales or even start an antique book consignment program, we could expand to online sales. Not that Charles would be interested, I guess. I can't even convince him to swap to online bill pay, so I'm sending out checks to pay the bills. Such a waste of paper."

"You're managing his accounts?" my mother asked.

"Yeah." I dried my hands and flipped the dish towel over my shoulder. "And payroll, and keeping track of sales numbers. I'm kind of his one-stop-shop for all things bookstore."

The corners of my dad's mouth turned downward, but it wasn't a frown. The way his eyebrows arched, he looked almost . . . impressed? My mother tipped her head, her eyebrows likewise raised. She slid a piece of pie onto the last plate and submerged the empty pie dish in the bubbly sink.

I grabbed the tray, walked to the living room, and called the crew in for our annual showing of *The Grinch*, complete with dessert. Christmas Eve was the only time we were ever allowed to eat somewhere other than the table—even as an adult, it felt like a special treat.

*   *   *

We exchanged gifts the next morning, the tree lights glimmering across the surface of a sea of discarded wrapping paper and packaging. My father despised glitter, so I chose the sparkliest packaging available simply to irk him. The glitter shedding was minimal compared to the carnage that came with two kids tearing into their gifts. Not a corner of gift packaging was spared.

My mother had wrapped a gift for James, a hunter green Henley. I hated the fact that it would probably become my favorite article of clothing he owned based on the way his eyes popped against the deep hue. Though she had her flaws, gift-buying was her best skill. Whether she made the purchases herself or tasked a professional to do it, I'd never know—but there was magic in opening a package with her handwriting on the tag.

Jordan and Lucas pretended—admirably well—to like the knife set I'd found during my last-minute shopping trip with James. The stomp rockets I got the kids were appreciated. By Levi and Isaac, at least. Plus, Jordan's glare was worth it.

My parents were impossible to buy for. My father had everything he could ever want. A membership at the country club meant he was well stocked on golf gear, he wasn't interested in hobbies otherwise, and he already owned every book written about modern aviation, so while it was a solid subject with plenty of giftable options, I wasn't confident enough to make that purchase.

My mother appreciated the finer things in life: subtle jewelry that only those with the highest taste could pick out as over-the-top expensive, and gin coveted enough to suit Jay Gatsby's soirées.

Because I'd never please them, I settled for slipping a Bouquet of the Month gift certificate into a cheesy reindeer card.

"Sorry, I don't have anything for you yet," I told James. Nothing was significant enough to offer, anyway.

"Swap when we get back?" he asked. "Yours isn't quite ready yet anyway."

The scene turned to chaos as gift wrap and tissue paper became projectiles, and we tossed them around the room while sipping coffee and picking at Jordan's homemade cinnamon rolls, our Christmas morning favorite since forever.

It felt like home, for the briefest moment. Like we didn't have thousands of miles and armloads of baggage between us. Uncomplicated, like the holidays are rumored to feel. The same warming in my chest that Christmas movies promised, the cheer and the merrymaking.

James caught my eye and hurled a chunk of wrapping paper at me, and I batted it away at the last moment.

My phone buzzed and I caught a glimpse of Natalie's face on the screen. I grabbed the phone and ducked into the kitchen to take the call.

"Merry Christmas, Nat!"

"Hey, how's the family? Any drama yet?"

"You mean before or after my sister abandoned me at the mall, and I had to walk home?"

"So, just a normal visit, then?"

"Basically, yeah. How's home? Did Derick yell at the carolers again?"

"Yup. He threw snowballs when one group insisted they finish the song before they moved to the next house," Natalie said.

"Oh, Derick. Someday he's going to figure out that you pay them to show up. I can't decide if I want to witness the day it happens, or if I'm better off hidden away."

We chatted about what I'd missed while on my trip, which was nothing because Stowe was a snow globe frozen in time; it was basically *Groundhog Day*, except more skiers and less Sonny & Cher.

Natalie laughed gently on the other end. "Yeah. Um, anyway. The theater is confirmed for the documentary screening, and I thought we'd turn it into a big party to celebrate how far the film has come. Can I get a hand decorating?"

"I'm in, text the details later." James tapped on the door and let himself in, so I nodded to let him know I was almost done. "Hey, Nat, I have to go. Give Mama and Papa Stiller hugs for me, okay?"

"Hey, Lex," Natalie said.

"Hmm?"

"Can we . . . do you want to have dinner when you get back?"

"Absolutely! I have presents for you, so come prepared to be wowed. We're flying back tomorrow. We'll catch up then. Good?"

"Good."

Natalie hung up and James and I slipped through the doors to rejoin my family in what was likely to be the happiest few hours of the year—when nobody argued or complained. Christmas morning was the only time we ever felt normal—whatever that was.

*　*　*

The distinct lack of familial drama had me hopeful. Like James was the magic that kept the chaos at bay. We'd even gathered for drinks—parents and all—when the kids were tucked away safely in bed after sugar crashes had turned their Christmas excitement into dull glazed stares. James had wound them up chasing the two of them around the house—and the sugar intake was likely also his fault. He had the same glassy look to his eyes as well, which meant he'd probably kept up when it came to sneaking candy canes off the tree branches.

But, like the season, the peace was only temporary.

"Have you started repairs on your house yet?" my mother asked, casually enough that I could tell she'd been waiting the entire visit to spring it on me.

"The home equity application was approved, and I have a contractor lined up for next week."

"Beats me why you won't just sell the place and move on." My father peeked at me over the tops of his rectangular eyeglasses, in the way that always made me feel like I was being scrutinized. The stare was always like a pop quiz for a subject I'd never even heard of.

"It's . . . my home . . ." I attempted, but the argument had never been sufficient for them. They'd picked up and moved away and didn't see why I couldn't do the same. They didn't know the way the heat from the fireplace felt like safety. They had no idea that I'd emptied the little alcove in the kitchen—where my grandparents had stored the broom, mop, and other supplies—to create my own little cave for those times when I needed a space that surrounded me like a hug. How I tucked myself into that nook and pressed myself into the corner for comfort. The personal thrill I got every time I spotted my grandfather's notes hidden in door frames and behind trim. They'd never know how much that building was family to me; that the uneven floorboards in the living room mapped my child-hood with scuffs and scrapes from dancing to the record player; how the creak of the screen door echoed in my mind, calling back to the way my grandfather always said "I love you, be safe" instead of "goodbye."

They didn't know that I'd hunkered down in the bedroom, brain-storming ideas for ghost stories, creating entire worlds and lives in my head and on film to fill the emptiness I felt. The now-empty house that used to burst at the seams with parents and grandparents and sib-lings and friends was inspiration while creating ghost stories featuring strong women who would never leave me. Inheriting my grandfather's house provided a connection to him and a place for the future, then was a safety net when I left college and needed a place to regroup when "the future" began to look scary and different.

I counted the corners and creaks and wobbly bits when I needed to come back to myself. They were my focus when I had none, when the grief of abandoning the future I thought I'd have came to shake me from my sleep. When the loneliness was deepest in my bones.

Besides, I knew what being left behind was like—and, while I knew it was just a house and it wouldn't know any better—I couldn't abandon it just because it wasn't perfect. It was safety, and it was steadiness. I wasn't giving up on it because it didn't live up to my too-lofty goals for it.

"I love that house," I said. "I was thinking I'd try to finish the basement so I can add a guest space for when you visit. You could spend less time at hotels, and maybe we could do Christmas in Vermont."

"It's a nice thought, but will it turn into another forgotten project? You're so smart, and you've got so much potential, but biding your time there means you're missing out on opportunities. You could have been this dedicated to school and a career, but instead, you fixate on these untenable ideas. Are an old house and a job at someone else's musty bookstore really worth the stress you're putting on yourself?"

I looked at James. His eyebrows pulled together in concern, but he didn't cut in. He knew I had to fight this battle myself. And, to do that, I had to give away a secret.

A big, terrifyingly damning, secret.

"Charles offered to let me buy the store. I had to choose between the house and the business loan, and I chose the house because it couldn't wait. But I haven't turned Charles down yet because I'm still hoping I can figure out how to fund the store. It's . . . a really good price." Leaving it there would have been easy enough. Even so, I looked James in the eye as I admitted the next part. "Charles is selling the store for next to nothing. Because it's haunted."

"Alex, for the love of . . . please tell me you didn't haunt his store," Jordan piped in, exasperated.

James's eyebrows arched, and he abandoned his quietly steadfast support to instead cock his head in Jordan's direction.

I kept my eyes fixed on James. "They were researching a ghost who was *already* documented."

"That's not an answer." Jordan crossed her arms. "Did you haunt the store? Like when Mom and Dad used to get calls about you running wild in the streets with your camcorder for that video diary? All of those fake ghosts and macabre stories painting the town like some sort of oddity." She turned to James. "You wouldn't believe how grim she was, all dressed up in her Hot Topic outfits, making up stories just to scare people on the internet. And they were pretty convincing, too. She should write books, not just sell them."

Nothing to do but to come clean. My kingdom for a sinkhole. "I may have . . ." I dragged my hands down my face, stalling. "Encouraged a few strategic, unexplained occurrences to fit the narrative. Just little things. Untraceable things, I hoped." Finally, I met James's eye. "Because I didn't want to risk your documentary. But yeah. We had people under Emily's Bridge for the scraping and rattling and a couple of hidden speakers for ambient sounds to amp up the spooky vibes. Umm, and Mary. I messed with the vents in the store to trip the temperature sensors." I swallowed. "And used a remote to trigger your equipment. The tech really hasn't changed, and it's easy to influence . . ." I took a shaky breath.

James's jaw clenched and he swallowed, his eyes seeming to focus beyond me for a split second before coming back.

"But I didn't make up *everything*," I insisted. "Some of the stories existed long before *Haunted Happenings*. Like Boots. And Emily. They're local legends, and I just built off their stories for the vlog. Then *Haunted Happenings* views picked up and people were messaging me asking for more investigations, and I got the hang of the storytelling aspect."

Jordan shook her head. "Honestly, Alex, what were you *thinking*? It's one thing documenting your little stories—one might call it entertainment—but faking ghosts because you benefit, personally and financially, is another thing altogether. Isn't that *fraud*? What if Charles found out?"

Exasperated, my parents both swilled their drinks, giving me a moment of quiet to regroup.

"Okay, to be fair," I reached for the bottle of wine on the table in front of us and refilled my glass, "he offered to sell to me *before* I'd staged anything. I didn't tell him it was haunted—the film crew did that, actually. He was going to end up selling to some chain company or shared office space manager anyway. Once he heard the word 'ghost,' it was all over for him in that location. And if it helps the documentary, I don't see anything wrong with that."

James hadn't released his casual grasp of my knee the entire evening—like an anchor in a storm—but his fingers began to loosen gradually the more I opened up about the added fiction I'd fed his fables. Regardless of not meaning harm, I could have ruined everything for him. For Julian. For the crew. Even after finding out that his mom's debt situation was his driving force, a situation I'd come to know well, I'd kept up the ruse—for my own gain. But we couldn't broach my misdeeds. Not yet. Not with my parents in attendance. Not that it mattered.

"I think I need a few minutes to sit with this information." He excused himself, squeezing my shoulder though his eyes were downcast.

To their credit, my parents waited until he'd left the room to continue the argument. "If you want that little store so badly, surely you could have made an offer."

"Sure, I'll just dig down into my deep pockets. I've been pouring everything I have into the roof over my head, but maybe if I reach a little farther." My father raised a finger as if he was about to cut in. I wasn't in the mood to be told how I could straighten up and do better. "You know what? No. I'm not having this conversation. It always ends with me feeling like I've done something wrong, and like you'll never appreciate the person I am. And I can't do it again. I'll fix the house and forget the store. Maybe whoever buys it will keep me on staff so I don't add 'unemployed' to the myriad of ways I've failed you both."

"Oh, Alex. You haven't *failed* us," my mother said, tutting.

"Are you sure? Because sometimes it's hard to tell. You assumed I left school because I was lazy or unambitious, or some combination, but I was *struggling*, Mom. I was barely making it, and you didn't ever ask."

"We talked to you on the phone constantly, Alex."

"You asked about classes. Grades. My major and my advisor meetings. Never once about how the isolation was tearing through my ribcage, or how I couldn't go to class because I felt entirely alone even with a lecture hall full of people. I couldn't stay behind in the dorm—couldn't skip class—because I didn't want to disappoint the professor or the guy who copied off of my notes or, whatever, the person in the mascot costume."

I closed my eyes a moment, willing away the tightness in my throat.

"I'd lie awake at night ruminating about whether I should ask for an extension on the paper due the next day because even though it was complete, I wasn't sure it was good enough. But what if I asked for an extension, and the professor thought it meant I wasn't ready for the coursework, and it tainted their opinion of me? So I'd vow to turn in the paper as written because at least it gave me a reason to *go* to class—a goal. After class, I'd skip lunch to rush back to the dorm immediately because I'd been up so late the night before, stressing, and my stomach was in so many knots from constantly, *constantly* trying to be mentally one step ahead.

"I'd hide out in the dorm and try to ignore the way my insides cramped, hoping the discomfort would go away, until something whispered in my head, 'Maybe it's appendicitis, wouldn't that suck.' I'd always had a high tolerance for pain so maybe it *was* appendicitis, and I had been ignoring it. And if it was appendicitis, would the surgeon tell me he was disappointed that I'd waited so long to go get it checked out?

"Then I'd wonder, who would even take me to the hospital? You probably can't drive with appendicitis. Bothering someone for a ride was totally off the table—I didn't want to be a burden. If I didn't show up to class because I was in the hospital undergoing surgery, would anyone notice? And what was the recovery time for an appendectomy, anyway? Catching up on coursework if I had my appendix out was going to be impossible.

"Groups would funnel from the building for whatever party or sporting event was going on, and I'd listen from beneath my comforter, in my bunny slippers—because even if I couldn't put on a happy face, at least my pajamas could. While the entire school was writing goofy 'getting to know you' notes on door-mounted whiteboards the first week in the dorm, nobody was writing on mine, since I'd missed all the icebreaker games. Meanwhile I'd wonder if I should skip class the next day just to give myself a break, maybe head back to Stowe to hang out with Natalie, because she was there for me, and I'd always have her, and that was all that mattered. But I couldn't skip class. What if there was a pop quiz, and the professor noticed I was gone?" I exhaled. "And begin again."

My mother's eyes widened and my father's *hemhem* reverberated through the room. Jordan scooted from her spot into the space James had vacated, and looped her index finger into my curled fingertips. The nearness, while unusual, warmed me from the inside-out.

"So I left, okay? I went home. Home was safe, I knew what to expect. Natalie and her parents gave me the care and comfort I'd always wanted from you but never got. So it's fine, really. Water under the bridge. But like, for *once*, could you please trust that I'm making the decision that's right for me and ask how it makes *me* feel instead of telling me all of the ways the decision doesn't work for *you*? Because this is what I want. I know it's a longshot but it's my shot to take."

The room was silent. My mother's eyes glittered with unspilled tears while my father clutched the knees of his pantlegs. Jordan's eyes trekked a triangle between me and our parents, staying quieter than I'd ever known her to. The person in my life who took up the most space was actively making space for me to share my feelings. I swallowed, my throat tight as I waited for someone—anyone—to say something.

"We had no idea. We assumed you had everything under control," my father admitted.

"You've always been so independent. We didn't know. We're sorry."

"Of course you didn't know. You didn't ask, and I didn't want to tell you that I couldn't manage the bare minimum of 'go to class' at college. It's fine."

"Is . . . there a way your mother and I can help?" my father asked hesitantly. "I don't mean financially, unless that's what you want."

"Now that you mention it, maybe pay for my therapy appointments? The out-of-pocket costs are cutting into my savings account."

My father patted his hip, like he was searching for a wallet.

"No, stop! I'm kidding! I might work in a tiny bookstore, but my health insurance is covering it. Honestly, you could come visit when it's not as a detour while on a business trip. Or, when you call me, start small by asking about my day before you hurl criticism in my direction. I'm doing better now, and even though my anxiety is going to keep me company for life, I still want my parents to check in. Or just ask how my day was."

My mother wiggled her bottom lip between her teeth. "How long have you felt this way?"

"I don't know. It's not like I can check it off on a calendar. I didn't write in my diary, 'Today I realized my parents like Jordan most.'"

"Hey," Jordan said, shoving me gently with her shoulder. We were going to be okay.

My father scratched at his hairline and brushed his fingertips together. "We assumed, with the ghost stories and all, that you were just expressing yourself. Normal teenager stuff."

My mother reached for the hand Jordan wasn't gripping. "You didn't seem to want our help with anything—and you still don't."

I let out a shaky breath and said maybe the hardest truth of all: "Going it alone has been my constant state for so long that now the idea of asking for help is terrifying."

We all sat with that for a moment. Then, my mother asked, "James didn't know about the ghosts?"

I pressed my lips together.

"Did we ruin it?"

A tremble shook my chin and my head began to throb from the stress of the evening. So much for a quiet night with the family.

"If anyone ruined it, it was me. I need to talk to him."

* * *

The door to James's room was open a crack, just enough for a sliver of light to creep onto the hardwood floor of the hallway that separated our doors. I'd planned to sneak across the hallway and slide into his bed that night, just to wrap up the holiday on a high note—but after the secret slipped about the documentary meddling, the chance was long gone.

A squeak of the bedframe filtered through the door. I raised a hand to knock, expecting that I'd find him reading or playing with his language learning app. A split second before my knuckles rapped the door, he spoke.

"If you think it's best, then I guess . . . cut the bookstore footage before word gets out? Maybe the bridge, too. We'll have to rework the flow, rerecord the voiceovers for some of the cutaways. There will be some tweaks to the credits." A zipper scratched. "I don't know. We'll talk about it. No, it's not important now." Another zipping sound, and the rustle of a jacket.

Was he packing? After everything, I probably deserved that he'd leave. All the more reason to never ask for the things I wanted: there was always a catch. Borrowing money came with interest, accepting help always made me feel beholden, and asking Charles to sell me the bookstore came with a side of fake ghosts. I'd never asked James to trust me, but I'd found the caveat there, too—he'd given his trust freely, but I couldn't handle it with enough care to keep it from blowing up in my face.

And listening by the door wasn't going to improve the situation any.

I knocked on the doorframe and nudged the door enough to peek inside.

He stood with his phone to his ear, a packed bag sitting on the bed.

"Can we talk?" I asked.

"Julian, I've gotta go. I'll let you know when I land," James said before hanging up and turning to me. "I got an earlier flight out. It's all hands on deck to fix this."

"What do you mean, 'fix' it?" I inhaled a shaky breath as owning the store slipped even further from my grasp.

"Any pieces where we weren't in control of the atmosphere need to be stripped and either refilmed or abandoned. The submission deadline is coming up fast, so it's looking like stripped is our only option."

"It *all* has to come out? Can't you at least leave the interview in? Take out the instrument tampering, but leave the story." Mary was more than a ghost story. Her existence, in my vlog and beyond, comforted me. Mary and all the rest of them, creating those stories had filled a space inside my ribcage where emptiness could have grabbed hold. But they were bigger than loneliness. Maybe they weren't *real*, but they were real to *me*.

"The documentary rules weren't specific about authenticity, but we need to make sure the project is saying what we mean for it to say. And, in this instance, it feels like we're saying it's okay to run small business owners out of town rather than help them."

"No, that's not what's happening here!" I gripped the edge of the footboard. "It doesn't have to be in the film! The idea alone is enough for him to keep up his end of the deal. We can make an excuse to Charles for why you cut the bookstore piece, but please don't tell him it was fake. Please," I begged. "He'd been thinking about selling anyway, he told me so. It just . . . moved the process along a little bit when your crew mentioned the ghosts."

"I suppose we should have done our research, then? We could have avoided the trouble if we knew what we were getting ourselves into." His eye contact was like flint striking steel—hard, and fiery, and charged.

"Oh yeah, real nice. Base your entire documentary on a vlog from fifteen years ago, then make me out to be the bad guy. Thanks a lot."

"You know there was more to this than your vlog. Don't be so self-centered."

Self-centered. Had he really just? He'd turned the argument into a tournament. "Sure, dropping everything to get you spectacular footage was self-centered of me. Welcoming you into this town, introducing you to my friends, my family. How selfish."

James sighed. "Lex, this could be a big opportunity for Julian. He's worked for years perfecting his craft, and he's sure this is the one that's going to break him into the industry. The prize money was important, too, for both of us, but this isn't about *winning*. It's about the future, and when we started this journey you weren't even in the picture. You could have been honest with us. We could have worked something out ahead of time, but instead you sabotaged our sets and manipulated the results—manipulated *us*. I know you have goals, too, but we need to do what's right for the project and crew. There's an entire world out there filled with stories to tell, and if we don't get this one right, there is no second chance."

I could have listened to his "broader horizons" speech, but I'd heard it too many times before. "California has the best medical schools, I just have to go," or "Your sister could really use our support right now, you understand," or "Honestly, babe, I think I need to explore this opportunity on my own." I didn't need to hear it again when it was practically a MadLibs exercise. Input reason here, sign off with half-assed apology there.

"I was perfectly happy working at my little store, until you strolled in and ruined everything." My chin wobbled to accompany the little break in my voice.

"Whoa, Lex. Wait." James's face fell.

"I didn't need you. I didn't need anyone. I had my job, and I had my house. Then, somehow you come around and show me that I could have more. Your perfect swagger and chilled-out attitude. No stress, just go with the flow. And your dog, too. Your perfect little dog with her perfect little face and impeccable manners. You come into my store, my town, and wave it all in my face. Just to take it all away. You could have gone anywhere. Why did you have to come fuck up *my* life?"

"That's what you think? I'm fucking up your life by being here?" His voice was thick with emotion. "Wow. That's . . . I thought we had something, but this is sounding a lot like you have already made up your mind, and I've been left out of the thought process." James crossed his arms.

"You're going to leave anyway!" I cried. "So what does it matter if Charles thinks the store is haunted?"

"You're right. I don't seem to have much to stick around for anyway because the ghosts aren't real and neither are your feelings for me. I thought we had a connection, but it turns out that I was just a pawn to get your precious store."

My jaw dropped.

"I—I didn't mean that." James reached a hand toward my shoulder, but pulled back last-minute as if he'd thought better of it. He took a breath. Centered himself. "Julian will absolutely murder me for telling you this, but . . . the hauntings aren't real."

I rolled my eyes. "Yeah, I know, we covered this. I messed up."

"Not those ghosts. *Our* ghosts. Before we filmed with you. We falsified our own results, long before you came along. Paranormal investigations are trending way up these days so we figured it wouldn't hurt to embellish a bit. That's why we were stunned by your results. We were counting on the power of suggestion and a few tricks we picked up along the way. The demand is there, and we wanted to get in early. Make our move before the popularity waned or the market was too full."

My teeth ground together as I digested the confession. "So, wait. It's only okay if *you* benefit from withholding the truth?" I'd lied, but he'd lied first. And I felt *guilty* about my involvement. Guilty for doing what I had to do to make my own dreams come true.

"I didn't expect to be around long enough for it to come back to haunt me, so I was less concerned with the repercussions," he admitted.

And just like that, it was happening again. I was going to be left behind to wallow while someone moved on without me. Off to some city somewhere, probably near a beach that's well-known for laid-back vibes and easy-going, all-day chill. Where people come and go, experience whatever they set out for before moving on. Meet some people, say goodbye, set off on the next adventure. Something decidedly not my style.

The cycle wouldn't end. I'd known better than to get involved with a guy from out of town. Whether he'd been there to ski or there to film a documentary, the reason didn't matter. It was leave or be left. And I'd already been on the losing side of that battle too many times.

"Listen, it's not like we were going to last anyway. Goodbye was always creeping up on us; a countdown clock tripped the day we met."

"I guess I really am a Sal, after all," James said, eyes downcast.

"Kerouac wouldn't be able to tell you apart," I said. An ache settled in my chest and my eyes blurred despite trying not to cry. "I think we're on different paths here, James. Which is a shame because I fell for you. Hard."

He hefted his bag over his shoulder and straightened the sleeve of his shirt beneath the strap. "I've been falling for you from the moment I met you, Lex. But if you can't let people in because you're too afraid of losing them, then I don't think you can ever fully love someone back."

My mouth gaped, goldfish-like, as his words hit like shrapnel. I'd have argued if I had any words, any declaration that could have salvaged us. Instead, he walked toward the bedroom door, and I let him, wordless.

"I'll find another way home. I need to clear my head and figure out where to go from here. Be safe." He lifted a hand, as if to reach for me, but awkwardly pointed at the door instead before opening it and walking away.

CHAPTER TWENTY-FOUR

The next day, I loaded a prepaid postal box with books, gifts, and souvenirs, slapped my address on it, and tucked it beside the door where my mother promised she'd remember to send it with the mail carrier. They were sorry to have missed saying goodbye to James before his flight, but were surprisingly apologetic for the moments leading up to his early exit.

Bags packed and the previous few nights' dinners and pies—and heartache—still weighing me down, another Christmas was finished. My parents hugged me in a two-parent sandwich and thanked me for the visit. It felt a little forced after our conversation the night before, but I wasn't complaining. I had hope. Isaac and Levi hugged me too, then disappeared into the kitchen to dig into the leftover pies while nobody was watching.

Lucas was scarce, but he offered a double-fingered wave from the doorway as I climbed into Jordan's car.

The car ride was quiet, aside from Jordan humming along to the music and drumming her fingertips on the steering wheel. At the airport, she pulled into the drop-off zone and put the car in park.

"Hey," Jordan said. "Thanks for coming. I think Mom and Dad were happy to see you."

"Oh, even if I am a failure who would rather chase dreams than find success?" I flashed a smug smile.

"You know they don't believe that. Stop. Listen. I think you were right. About Lucas, I mean."

"Which part? The him being an incredible tool?"

"No." She leveled an exasperated glare in my direction. "I confronted him. I told him I was leaving, and he agreed to call off the affair."

"And you believe him?"

She pressed her lips into a line and lifted her shoulders. "I said you told me he's not worth my time—"

"That's a loose interpretation of what I said."

"And that I trust you because you're the smartest, strongest person I know—"

"Wow, someone's been hitting the eggnog a little early, huh?" I smiled.

She rolled her eyes. "I'm being really nice to you right now, Alex, and I swear if you don't just smile and tell me you know it'll all work out, I'm going to throw you out of this vehicle."

I smiled. "I know it'll all work out."

She wiggled in her seat and pulled her shoulders back. "Thank you. He asked about couples therapy but wasn't willing to consider any counselors that I suggested. He kept steering me toward the guys he knew from his frat days, so we all know that wouldn't have worked in my favor. I told him I wasn't interested, since it seemed to be his goal to win rather than to heal, and that I hoped our divorce would remain civil. Anyway, I'll text you later if you're cool with that?"

She'd never texted me for anything beyond business. It was either a new leaf or those holiday feels that disappeared as soon as "Auld Lang Syne" ended and launched you into a new year. "Make sure you get the house in the divorce. I can't live without that backyard. Fight him for it, okay?"

"You're ghastly. Get out of my car, or you'll miss your flight and I'll be stuck with you until the next one."

As I climbed out, she tucked a card into my hand. "Oh, wait, I nearly forgot. This is from Mom and Dad. They said not to open it until you're on the plane, so you know what that means. It's probably going to piss you off, and they want you where you can't get to them easily."

She wiggled her fingers through the crack in the window and pulled away from the curb. I watched until her taillights were completely out of view.

The airport was packed with the usual post-holiday crowds, everyone scurrying back to their lives after promising to call more, text more, visit more. But, once they unpacked, they'd fall into the same too-busy routine.

As promised, James didn't show up at the gate for our flight home. I did get a text: Ghost Guy: *I'm home. Be safe.*

I began the long flight home watching movies, which distracted me from my location above the ground enough that my heart rate remained semi-normal. But still, I fisted the cuffs of my sweatshirt in my palms and squeezed. The fidgeting had nothing to do with turbulence or the little screen in the back of the seat ahead of me that proudly declared we'd be in the air for too many hours, at too many feet above sea level. This time, I was hoping the pressure would take my mind off the fact that I'd hurt James. Hurt him enough that he left. Not for dreams and not for opportunities, but because I'd pushed him away. I'd messed up. Big time.

I tugged my book from my bag and disappeared into the pages of *Neverwhere* by Neil Gaiman. I'd read it before, and I had a well-used paperback at home, but this copy had called to me from the shelves of the first store I'd dragged James into. I had flipped instinctively to examine the first pages—and was rewarded with an inscription: "Let these pages be a lantern held high as you set forth into the uncharted, exploring worlds where ordinary is left at the door and hushed whispers turn to a chorus of wonder." The worn-soft edges of the pages were perfect for mindless fiddling while I read, and if that couldn't keep me from worrying, nothing could.

I dragged my thumbnail across the pages, lost in the words as Richard faced the third trial: the monotony, the repetition. Day in and day out, everything the same.

James had lived in half a dozen states in fewer years. His life was adventure, whim, and excitement. When it came down to it, I knew James would also feel the draw of London Below—or just anywhere but Stowe. Especially now that I'd ruined everything and pushed him away.

When I hit the final page, I hugged the weathered paperback to my chest, then tucked it into my bag. It jammed up against the card from my parents. The envelope—a hefty paper with a subtle sheen, their return address embossed on the back flap—was from their personal stationery set. The good stuff that they used for sending party invitations and congratulatory messages. Not the plain envelope they usually mailed with lengthy missives. That didn't mean it would be good news, but perhaps it wasn't quite as rough as their usual notes.

I picked at the corner of the flap. Open it, or let it rest? Was it better to be frustrated now, in a tiny tin can hurtling through the air, or at home where I could destroy the peace of being surrounded by my belongings?

The tearing was big and noisy against the white noise of air vents and the hum of the plane, but nobody so much as glanced in my direction. I pulled a couple of pages of their fancy stationery from the envelope. Tri-folded, with perfectly crisp creases.

Alex,

We regret that our opinions regarding your choices have caused such harm in our relationship. We are impressed by your drive and dedication to your little store. You've taken the initiative in Charles's absence and seem to have found where you truly shine. It's not every day someone can build a career based on what they love—you are lucky to have found that. We do hope you can secure the loan to purchase Dogged Books.

I snickered at the botched name. Close enough.

We apologize, sincerely and deeply, for the rift we have caused. Had we known our actions would separate us to this degree, we would have made different choices. To prevent dredging up the past, and in an effort to move forward, we won't revisit the discussion in this format. But we do hope, with all our hearts, that this is an opportunity to move forward and heal, together. We're never more than a call or text away.

If you do renovate, we look forward to being your first guests in your newly updated guest room. And, while we'd prefer you hire a professional, if you choose to stretch your budget and DIY the construction, count us in to swing a hammer.

Please remember that we are here to support you and help you—just like we support and help your sister. It's not one or the other. It seems that each time you visit, a little more of your independence rubs off on your sister (for better or worse). Maybe, too, some of her willingness to ask for help can make its way into your personality. You don't have to do it alone. No judgment, no questions. We support you.

Please give our regards to James. We appreciate greatly that you felt comfortable enough to allow him to join you for the trip. Best wishes in the new year.

Mom & Dad

Not a breath escaped my lungs the first time I read the note. The second time through, my throat tightened and my eyes stung with the tears I held back.

The overhead speaker announced that we were coming in to land before I had a chance to start a third read-through, so I slipped the letter into my bag and prepared for descent back in Burlington, Vermont.

CHAPTER TWENTY-FIVE

A cycle of snow-then-melt-then-snow meant my driveway was a slushy mess. I had to climb out of bed early to shove the heavy, wet snow from my windshield before work. The driveway slush was bound to freeze up solid as the temperature dropped, but that was a problem for later-Lex. Now-Lex had other concerns.

The post-Christmas vibe at Dog-Eared was just as gloomy as the salt- and sand-darkened snowbanks that lined the streets. Though our Christmastime rush was never huge, the lack of patrons always left the space feeling a little less bright.

I was on autopilot for most of the morning. I plucked misplaced books from the coffee tables and windowsills and nestled them on shelves where they belonged. The consignment piles got sorted into "keep" and "we've already got a dozen," and I set aside any that included inscriptions worth adding to my collection.

The slushy snow kept most people off the sidewalks, aside from the dedicated few regulars who popped in for a coffee, chat, and paperback. And Natalie, who could never be more than five feet from a caffeinated drink at any given time.

The bell rang as she came through the front door. "Why did it have to snow just enough that people need a plow, but not enough that it's any fun?" She stomped the icy build-up from the tread of her boots. "I've got five houses to go, but most of them are still away for the holidays so I'm not rushing."

I examined the inside cover of a dusty old paperback, then dropped the book into the "book sale" pile when I found it blank. "Please tell me you have some new family stories to tell? I could use the boost."

"Uh oh," she said when she glimpsed my face.

I pressed my lips together to keep them from trembling. The urge to dump everything on her was strong—and her alarmingly on-point insight was especially needed at the moment. "Yeah."

"So, I hear you told James about the tampering?" Natalie said.

"I shared the general plot, but he didn't stick around for the end credits to roll."

"Oh, film reference. Very dark, very brooding."

I narrowed my eyes at her. "Could you not mock my pain, please?"

She rolled her eyes. "Okay, okay. I'm sorry. What happened then, after you told him?"

"We argued. I told him I fell for him. Then I let him walk away."

Natalie clasped a hand over her mouth. "Lex, you didn't."

"I can't hear the words again, Nat. I just can't. I'm so tired of being left behind. Do you think we ruined the film?"

"He and Julian were deep in discussion about their plan last night."

"Oh shit. Is Julian mad at you? How did everyone else take it?"

She moved into the café and started making herself a drink. "Julian's freaking out about post-production, so he's been holed up in the apartment splicing and superimposing or whatever. There was a lot of action happening. Everyone crowded around the monitors, and they crawled through the film, tallying each story we'd fed them."

"Oh. You were, uh, there for all of it, then?"

"Some of it, anyway. I mostly stayed out of the way, but I wasn't going to abandon them when they were cleaning up our mess. I mean, we did this to their project, you know? I was so caught up with a chance at reliving the old days that I didn't stop to think. Beyond the filming setup, I'm useless. It was literally the very least I could do."

"Do you know what they cut, then? Everything we helped with? Mary?"

"I don't have that kind of inside info, I'm sorry. They asked my opinion a few times, but I mostly played the role of silent observer. By the time I went home, they had a plan and were deep in the weeds, but they're probably still working on cleaning it up ahead of the deadline."

"Ugh, I know. I *know*, and I feel terrible. I guess my screwup means a clean break, since they're off for bigger and better things soon."

"It'll be a month or so before they pack up and move on. Julian says they can't submit to festivals until the results of the competition are announced. But even if it doesn't win the contest, this documentary is for sure going to get into a festival. They're ready to start pitching all kinds of events as soon as they're clear, though. You should see the organization; you'd be jealous. Spreadsheets and color-coded systems. It's amazing."

"Fab." I drummed my fingertips against the stack of books. Natalie was extra calm about the fact that they'd all be picking up and hitting the road in a few weeks—but she'd never said she and Julian were anything serious. Just a bit of fun with the tourist filmmaker, nothing more. Not like me, who—despite my best efforts—couldn't help but get attached even when I'd known all along that James was leaving.

"Looks like we'll both be flying solo again, so I guess we'll have to resume our weekly breakfast dates and laugh about my lack of sense."

"Sure, I'm all yours every weekend. For the next few weeks, anyway."

"Oh, you had a taste of hanging out with other people, and now you think breakfast with me is too boring to commit to more than a few weeks at a time?"

"Not exactly," Nat said, swallowing as she shifted her gaze. "I'm thinking of making a change. A big one. A life-altering one." When I didn't reply, she explained. "I accepted a job."

"A job? That's amazing! Doing what? Tell me all about it!" I'd never considered that she'd want to change careers—but she could do anything.

"The boss is someone you know. He's talented, and creative, and is a fantastic manager."

We lived in one of the most artsy towns on the planet so it could have described anyone.

"And the job involves quite a bit of travel." When I didn't reply, Natalie grasped my shoulders and looked me in the eye. "I'm joining Julian's crew. He mentioned needing to hire one more crewmember, and when I joked about wanting the position, he said he'd teach me what I needed to know. I was totally kidding. At first. But the more I thought about it, the more I *wanted* to. It's too good to pass up, you know?"

I blinked and willed my mouth to work, but producing sound was beyond me. There was no voice, even for argument.

She reached to grasp both of my hands in hers. "Please don't hate me. I think I've grown beyond this place, Lex. My parents have everything running like a machine, always have. They don't need me for anything."

"What about when they want to retire, then?"

"*My* parents, retire? Are you joking? My dad runs three businesses and thinks weekends are for learning new skills."

I fisted my long sleeves in each hand and tried to keep my tone even and accepting. I was losing. "You've never mentioned wanting to leave before. Why now?"

"I never wanted to stay here. Everyone else—you, included—assumed I'd stick around, work at the inn and tree farm, take over the business someday. Everyone thought I'd follow in my parents' footsteps, continue the life they built. But leaving was always so tempting."

I had been so focused on James that I hadn't considered the other ways this could have gone. James and Julian were a duo. Siskel and Ebert, except with ghosts. A pair, destined to stick together 'til death or a Hollywood-style feud tore them apart. Natalie leaving was never on my radar.

I crossed my arms to shield my heart. "You can't just leave!"

"And you can't just live life like you did when you were seventeen. Sometimes you've got to grow up and move on. I've been working at my parents' inn since I could walk. It's crushing me. I haven't had a chance to learn who I am because I'm stuck in their shadow. Everything I do, I do for them. That's the expectation. That's what I get if I stay here. I'm suffocating."

"If that's suffocation, bring it on. At least you have family who cares and wants you around."

Natalie's mouth fell open. "Open your eyes, Lex. Are you forgetting that you have family here, too? Sure, not by blood, but when have my parents ever turned you away for anything? You have me, whether we live in the same town or not. And you know what else you have? The town. The whole, entire town. An entire population that thinks you're some kind of royalty, because you're Thomas's granddaughter. If you want to shut out an entire support system, be my guest. That's your choice, but you can't hate me for wanting to find what I'm good at because it takes one person out of your bubble."

"You didn't even give me a heads up," I said. A shiver ran through my spine as every emotion bombarded me at once. Sadness, pride, fear, confusion, excitement.

"*I* barely had a heads up." Natalie tipped her head and let a guarded smile slip. "He offered while you were visiting your family, and it didn't seem like an appropriate time to mention, you know . . . everything. But, now that it's out there, how do you feel?"

"Which part, the film festival tour in the making, or the fact that my 'everyone always leaves' streak is still going strong?"

"It's not everybody leaving." She threw her head backward and rolled her eyes. "It's only me."

"And you're bigger than everyone to me." I inhaled, sucking back the sob threatening to escape, and dabbed the tears from beneath my eyes with the pads of my pinky fingers. "But *because* you mean so much to me, I accept that this is the right choice for you, and I hope it is everything you have ever dreamed. You're going to be okay, right? I mean, who is going to make you a coffee every morning?"

She smiled. "I will be fine, Lex. I promise. How about you?"

"I'll survive."

Natalie scurried around the edge of the desk and wrapped her arms around me to pull me into a giant, comforting hug. Her jacket's rough waterproof shell scratched against my cheek as she rocked me back and forth in the embrace.

Natalie's arms tightened around me for a second before she released, pushed me back by the shoulders, and squatted to look me in the eye.

"You could come too, you know. I doubt they'd limit the invitation."

"Yeah, if any of them are even talking to me still, I'm sure they'd let me hop on board. I'd rather take my chances here, with the house repair bills and bookstore that I'll never, ever own, than see the frustration on their faces or hear them say no."

"So you're just going to give up? Do any of those books you read have happy endings? Or do all the characters just give up and watch their potential futures burn in front of their eyes?"

I raised my eyebrows. "I read mostly classics and weird as hell fantasy, and you're talking to me about happily ever after?"

"I apologize, I forgot that you're never leaving that emo mindset behind. Listen. We're all leaving. Soon. And you're going to lose James if you don't *do* something. Get out of your comfort zone and make something happen. Call. Him. I can't fix everything for you if your default is to ignore the problem."

I hated it when she was right. I'd ruined everything. I lied and hurt him. And now I had to take the next step or pay the consequences.

I ripped my phone out of my pocket and swiped into my recent calls to select his number. My heart pounded as it dialed, then sunk as the call went straight to voice mail.

"And what if he doesn't answer?"

"Then try again," Natalie said, squeezing my arm gently. "And breathe. I'm on my way out but call, anytime, as always. I'm here."

"You got it, boss." I tossed a little box of maple candy to her, and she caught it in her coffee-free hand. "And Natalie? I'm incredibly proud of you. I know it didn't seem like it, but I am. When I have a chance to process everything, I want to hear all about your plans. I'll help you pack?"

"I'm looking forward to it." Nat pulled the door closed behind her, leaving the bell ringing.

* * *

I intended to sleep in my book nook that night. James had forgotten a sweater in my room, so I pulled it over my head like some lovesick girl who needed to assess her priorities.

Sleep wasn't easy, but neither was wakefulness.

Things I was set to lose: James.

Things I'd always have: a fear of loss.

How hard would it have been to uproot myself, offer to go along with him? I did like to travel. But no, I wasn't leaving my world behind for some guy whom I'd only just met. Life wasn't like that. You couldn't drop everything to follow love. Could you?

Even if I could scrape together the money to travel, I'd come home and the house would still need fixing. It would always need fixing. Each time I paid someone to come in, they found another issue.

I wasn't ready to give up on the bookstore, either. If I couldn't have Dog-Eared, maybe I could talk to someone about starting my own—if not here, now, then at least somewhere, sometime.

I spread my arms and legs wide, making a giant X on the floor, pulling breath from way down in my belly and letting my limbs relax. I couldn't force the sleep to come, but maybe I could trick my body into restfulness.

I peeked at my lock screen—ignoring the fact that the background featured me, James, and Lulu on one of our wintery walks. It was only three minutes after nine. No wonder I couldn't settle.

I unlocked my phone and scrolled mindlessly, looking for something—anything—to get my mind off James. I couldn't go with him, and clean break meant *a clean break*. A BuzzFeed article about books zipped past, so I scrolled back to it.

"Top Five Classics, Ranked," the article promised. J. D. Salinger and James Joyce tied for first, which was kind of a total cop-out on BuzzFeed's part. But, also, it was a complete bore of a list. *The Catcher in the Rye* always topped lists as an unmissable read. Yeah, it had merit—but where were the roundups that spotlighted James Baldwin, Salman Rushdie, and Zora Neale Hurston?

Maybe I could pick up a side gig writing listicles—at least I'd throw a few new titles into the fray. I dropped my phone and stared at the ceiling instead. It was far more interesting than the articles selling overrated books from online retailers, probably for affiliate payment too, lining their pockets while I scraped to make the smallest dream a reality.

CHAPTER TWENTY-SIX

The basement clean-up had been completed without the contractor finding new and different issues to drain my savings. A miracle, honestly. They did, however, find a little trinket tucked into the rafters near an overhead outlet: a dusty, patinaed keychain shaped like the Statue of Liberty, the torch bursting with a tiny heart-shaped flame in place of the usual fire. There was a note tied to the keyring. With shaking fingers, I gently unfolded the little love note left for my grandmother, and my grandfather's boxy letters hit like a hug.

Nearly finished now. Just loose ends, bits and bobs, the littlest pieces: Trim here, a loose door frame there. Soon, you'll be here, and maybe right away or maybe years from now the walls will ring with tiny voices; the halls will shake with tiny feet. If you prefer a farm to a gaggle of our own, I'll frame a barn the moment you insist. I've found my calling in lumber, a hammer, and some nails—and making your wildest dreams come true, of course. If you wanted to pack it in and fly to Paris next to try our hands at baking bread, or take a wander toward Florida to grow citrus, you only have but to ask.

I kept this keychain close while you couldn't be. A flame against the dark lonely nights. You're due to arrive next week—this time to stay—so it's time to retire her for you to find at a later date. No matter where we are in this journey, I hope it puts a smile on your face, darling.

With love (and a few remaining splinters),

Your Thomas

I'd known that my grandfather was a total romantic. I'd had no clue he'd had such a sense of adventure. Whether he'd really have dropped everything to chase my grandmother's whims was anyone's guess, but my heart sped up at the idea of it. Even my grandfather, who'd moved into this very house in his twenties and never left, hadn't discounted the idea of skipping town to see what else was out there. So what if the people had kept him here; even if he never left, the idea was in his head. Maybe he wouldn't have hesitated to take a leap, or maybe he was trying to convince himself he would.

Either way, he'd been braver than I was. When faced with losing someone important to him or stubbornly digging in his heels, he'd have taken a chance. Even if it scared him, and even if there were no guarantees.

James took chances and chased each opportunity. There was a corkboard map and a fridge covered in photos to prove it. Just a bunch of Bilbo Bagginses, the lot of them. Some of the stops may have been busts, but they always seemed to look ahead to the next—not behind. They had each other. A big, happy found family creating weird films and making it up as they went along. Instead of holding his father's choices against him, James had moved beyond their history to build a future of his own, on his terms.

I'd always thought that type of autonomy meant fighting tooth and nail to stay where I was, but maybe I was missing out by insisting I wouldn't—couldn't—change. My parents would just *love* to hear me admit that.

I tucked the trinket back into its space in the rafters, then pulled my phone from my pocket. I tapped into the last text from James, letting me know he'd gotten back to Vermont after our big argument over Christmas. I hit the call button and waited through the ringing, my foot jiggling enough to generate its own energy.

His voicemail greeting came through the line, and the familiar voice practically wrapped fingers around my heart and squeezed. "Knock knock," I said, after the greeting requested a message and joke. I hung up without providing a punchline.

Maybe he wasn't home. Maybe he was, and he was already packing to start his next adventure.

I scraped the holiday-hued nail polish from one thumbnail as I considered my options.

Wait for him to call.

Wait for him to text.

Wait for him . . .

No.

There was no more waiting. If I wanted this to work, it was on *me*. I had to make a move or lose him.

I climbed the stairs into my freezing little book nook. I scanned the shelves, eyeing the titles and considering what each communicated.

As I Lay Dying wasn't quite the message I wanted to get across. *Zen and the Art of Motorcycle Maintenance* was a solid no-way. I tapped the spine of *The Da Vinci Code*, remembering James's mocking grin as he discovered my secret hobby.

There, beside it, was *Iowa: A Travel Guide for Couples*. Not my idea of a romantic travel destination, but the title would do. I grabbed my archival ink pen from the shelf—the best option for taking notes in the margins because it wouldn't bleed or fade—and jotted a few words onto the title page. Then, I tucked the book into a cheesy Christmas gift bag and climbed into my car, taking off down the road without scraping away the snow that had built up on the windshield. After dark usually meant dodging the stragglers coming down Mountain Road or stopping at every crosswalk to let the dinner crowd through.

By some miracle, I made it from my house to James's apartment without hitting a single traffic jam, pedestrian or otherwise.

My knock was followed by a tiny jingle, then a snuffle and woof from inside.

"James?" I said, through the door. "Can we talk?"

Not a sound came in return, aside from the click of Lulu's excited claws against the tiled entryway floor—probably twirling in place waiting for someone to answer the door.

After a few seconds, the scuffling paw sounds quieted. The knots in my stomach pulled ever-tighter. If I counted backward from ten, and he didn't open the door, I'd give up. For the fairest chance, I tapped knuckles on the door once more. Lulu's shuffling was diminished compared to her first greeting. The longer a person was on the opposite side of a door, the bouncier she was, unless James was there to control the ruckus.

Ten. Nine. Eight.

Even if he did open the door, would my attempt at an apology be enough?

Seven. Six. Five.

Maybe the documentary was salvageable. If they'd saved that, even after my involvement, maybe we could save this.

Four. Three.

But only if he opened the door.

Two.

With gloved fingers splayed, I pressed my palm into the door and leaned my forehead on the cool fiberglass. It was too cold to cry outside. Instead, I curled my hand into a fist and completed the countdown in my head.

One.

With a metallic rattle, the world tilted as the door swung inward, and I stumbled into the entryway only to be caught by a surprised James. Lulu leapt and barked, snuffling at my knees and feet before wandering away as I worked to regain my balance.

"Would you like to come in?" His joking tone was a promising start.

Lulu sat at the end of a row of boxes, floppy ears perked up and tail swishing the floor. Her mouth cracked open and her tongue lolled in a doggy grin. The urge to ruffle the curly hair on the top of her head was strong, but I resisted. It was better to sever the attachment now—just in case my apology wasn't enough.

I tucked a curl behind my ear. "Here." I tugged the Christmas bag from my purse. He started to reply before opening the package, so I interrupted. "Sorry it's a little late. I've been . . . stupid. Just. Open it, okay?"

He pulled the corners of the bag open and ran his fingertip along the pages. "A book. Just Alex, who would have seen that gift coming?" His tone was mocking, but his eyes lit in that playful glimmer I'd grown to love.

He pulled the book free and knit his eyebrows, presumably at the book's title. "Iowa . . ." he said. Nimble fingers flipped to the title page, proving how well he knew me.

The original inscription said, "The birthplace of Captain Kirk, what could possibly go wrong?"

Beneath that, I'd scribbled my own note, so the title page read "*Iowa: ~~A Travel Guide for Couples~~* **you an apology. I'm sorry, I'm sorry, I'm sorry.**"

"I'll go with you," I said before he could speak. "Whenever you leave, I'll go, too. I'm ready to let go of my resentment and fears. I'm ready to take a leap. And it's not just because of you. It's partly you. I wouldn't even be considering it if not for you, but I've been protecting myself from being left behind for so long that maybe I'm pushing people away just in case rather than accepting that sometimes things work out."

The only movement was James's slow blink and the heaving rise and fall of my chest. Even Lulu was a statue.

"Why?" James asked.

Not a pop quiz; not a test. It was a challenge, and one I was fully prepared to accept after listening to his heckling over the last few weeks.

With locked gazes, I answered, "Because I wouldn't forgive myself for letting Lulu leave."

A quirk in the corner of his mouth. I'd gotten his attention.

"And I'd be distraught if she took you with her. I've been hoping that someone would decide to stay, but to my own detriment. I'm still terrified, but I'm not letting it stand in my way this time. I can do this. I can move on."

"But your house—"

"Is a building. Walls and windows and questionable wallpaper choices. It was home, but maybe it's time to see what's out there. It'll be okay. Home is not necessarily tied to a physical space, but the people you surround yourself with. You've helped me see that. I'll sell the house, or I can fix it up and keep it for when we come back to visit. It's still a mess. Just like me. I'm a mess. Constantly, without fail, I'll be a giant mess, and that's just something you'll have to accept if we do this. If you'll have me. I want to do this. Let's ride off into the sunset together, old plans be damned."

He knit his eyebrows and the muscles in his jawline worked over-time before he replied, "You might be getting the wrong idea here . . ."

"James." I reached for the sleeve of his shirt, hoping I hadn't com-pletely misread the situation. But then I stopped. If he was looking for an out, me offering to tag along was the exact opposite. I let go of his sleeve and straightened. "It's fine, I get it. We rushed into things, and I knew the risks."

He held up a finger, begging for patience, and dashed into his room. When he returned, a book was clasped in both hands. He thrust it toward me, pressed his lips together, and turned his eyes toward the ground.

There was no confidence in his stance. While his posture was usu-ally perfect, he stood before me with his shoulders hunched, hesitant. I accepted the book, and he pointed at the cover.

Ultimate Spooky Guide to United States Travel. A well-used atlas with worn edges, filled with bookmarks and sticky tabs. An abundance of reading sessions made the binding pliable; the book fanned open easily in my hand. Pages were marked, highlighted, and notated. Some more heavily than others: Each state had at least one comment in the margins, while others included notes detailed enough to draft a new travel guide.

"I found this in a library book sale in California a few years ago. We'd stopped over for a few months and rented a room at a really sketchy motel. We'd been wandering so long, trying to get away from the expectations of our parents, but we didn't have any real goals. Julian wanted to make films, and I wanted to find myself. Instead, I found this."

He tugged a bookmark from the center of the book, which was still firmly in my grasp, and passed it to me. A familiar logo stared me down—a stack of books and a steaming coffee mug I saw every day at work—the logo for Dog-Eared Books & More.

"Julian wanted to check out the top-ranked spots in the book. All of the places you hear about where spirits stalk and rattle and moan. But I wanted to check out this town. It seemed authentic. And the bookmark was a sign."

"A sign of what?"

James laughed. "I don't know, but I wanted to find out. Especially when I realized it was the very same Vermont town where Luna had stalked spirits. The comfort I got out of that vlog—the escape it gave me—felt timely when I was looking for a different kind of change. Something to make mine. I was all about living my life on the move, exploring new places and learning new things. Julian had his thing, but I didn't have mine. But wandering wears on a person, and seeking adventure turned into a desire to find *home*. And I thought . . . maybe I'd finally found it. Right here." I inhaled to cut in, but he didn't give me the chance. "Before you remind me, yes, I know you all have a strange dislike of outsiders and getting in is a longshot. I wanted to try, anyway."

Too much, too fast. My ears buzzed at the informational whiplash. After all of the absolute angst over the last few days, all I could manage to ask was, "What are you saying?"

The calculated strut was back as James breezed his way toward the kitchen. He dragged his tongue along his top teeth, slowly, while staring me in the eye. "Lulu," he called, without breaking eye contact. At her name, she bounded toward James, waiting for instructions at full attention. "Go get Lex."

She dashed back and forth between the two of us, then snuffed a spirited sneeze. Her bushy eyebrows shifted side to side before she gave up on my taking the hint. Gingerly, with as little tooth as possible, she nipped the knee of my pants to lead me toward the kitchen, and James. He took a step closer to me, and Lulu took a measured step to match. With one last puff of air, she released me.

A curl had slipped out from behind my ear again and James reached to tuck it back into place. "I'm sorry," he said. "I didn't think. I should have told you that I wanted to stay. But I didn't want to scare you away by seeming too eager."

James held out a business envelope, stuffed to bursting with paperwork, and I accepted it.

A line deepened between his brows while I pulled open the envelope flap and pulled its contents out. Tucked inside the tri-folded papers labeled "lease agreement" was a set of keys.

Specifically, two small Schlage keys. Shiny little house keys, shoved inside an envelope stamped with a rental agency's logo and phone number.

Home.

I pinched a key between my fingers and peered at it. "You are starting a nightclub and you're going to turn Stowe into a top-tier rave location?"

The corners of his eyes crinkled. "Cold," he said, and took a step backward.

"You're a secret cagophilist, and you thought this specific key was the perfect way to complete your collection?"

"Cold," he stepped back again.

"You're starting a library because you just couldn't stop purchasing duplicate books from the pretty bookseller in town?" I asked.

He tucked his hands into the pockets of his jacket, and his eyes glittered with laughter as he took a step forward. "We'll say warm, even though you're taking liberties with the storyline. The bookseller is a very persistent salesperson."

"You rented a place in Stowe because there was something about the town you just couldn't bear to leave?"

He took a step forward. "Warmer."

"The dog park, right? Lulu was too attached, and you—"

He leaned in, his lips a breath away from mine, putting the brakes on my mocking.

Still looking into his eyes, I took one final guess. "You decided to settle down in my weird little snow globe of a town because you fell desperately in love with the pretty bookseller who convinced you to stay using her uncanny ability to recommend the perfect books, and you couldn't imagine leaving her."

"Hot." James licked his lips, closed the inch of distance between us, and dipped me backward into a kiss. His mouth was warm and firm against my lips, and when he swept his tongue across my upper lip my body flushed with heat.

James was *staying*. For real. Not leaving, not moving on, but settling down. And I was finally letting myself believe it. I didn't even get a chance to overthink the words "desperately in love" before I blurted it out, and all for the better. We'd have time to explore what *this* was without a countdown clock—because he wanted it, and because I wanted it. Because maybe it was lust and maybe it was love, but mostly it was allowing ourselves contentedness. I dared to feel the excitement that came with setting out on a new journey, here, together—and he dared right back.

CHAPTER TWENTY-SEVEN

We didn't waste time heading to his new place to break it in, as it were. The apartment was perfect for James: cozy (small) and rustic (in need of a few touch-ups) with a sliding glass door that opened up into a fenced backyard, perfect for shaggy little dogs who liked to make their owner worry. Lulu had already made herself at home in the yard, made obvious by the dog-shaped snow angel that was no more than two feet out the back door. I got the grand tour after our acrobatic make-up session. A bedroom, an office that doubled as a guest room, combined kitchen and dining area, and a bathroom with a teeny tiny stall shower.

"A great start," James said. "Not splitting rent six ways really cuts into the budget, so no more ski chalet living for a while."

"So signing a lease must mean there's an income source?" I asked.

He raised a brow. "Are you looking for the temporary plan, or the long-term goals?"

"I think we've already made my stance on temporary quite clear." I crossed my arms.

James reached out, grasped my elbows in his hands, and squeezed. "I'm exploring my options, but have accepted a position as a cemetery

276

caretaker. I'll be able to take over the remaining school loan payments for my mom, but she doesn't want to accept money for back payments. She insists it's under control, but I want to see her thriving, not just managing. She's agreed to accept a small percentage if the film wins the competition, but only if it wins. The cemetery let me accept the position on a trial basis to start—and I think I might stick with it. Daytime hours only."

"Oh, good. If it was after dark, I'd be tempted to stage a few hauntings. You know, just to see how serious you really are about the job."

"Haunt your heart out," James said. "I'm not scared."

I beamed. "It's a bit ironic."

"How so?"

"If it wasn't for that cemetery, I wouldn't have fallen for you, and now it's what's keeping you here."

"This town is what's keeping me here," he said, deadpan.

"I stand corrected." I waved my hands sarcastically. "So, you've got your future figured out. Let's chat a bit about mine."

"The store?" James asked.

"I know we didn't really get a chance to finish this conversation the other day, but I found out last week I didn't get the loan. They think I'm a liability, which . . . fair. I was just hoping for a holiday miracle."

James cupped the back of my head with one hand and smoothed my disheveled hair with the other. "How about a fundraiser? The town would come together to raise the money. It's very feel-good, small-town holiday, happily ever after."

"How incredibly Hallmark. But no, I couldn't ask people to do that. They already do enough for me around here. Everyone bends over backward to make sure I'm safe and healthy and happy. Mrs. Norton offered to bring me a pot of stew yesterday because she thought my splotchy crying cheeks were from a cold."

"Lex." James swiped his thumbs beneath my eyes, wiping away tears that had already dried—and been made up for. "You can't live your entire life thinking you're an island. People are here for you, so let them be. Lean on someone else for once, please."

"I've spent too long striving for self-sufficiency, thank you. I'll figure it out. I'll ask Charles if I can have an extension or something."

"How long can you keep pushing it out?"

"I guess we'll find out. Besides, I feel guilty about the ghosts thing."

"Because of the documentary? Don't worry about it. We found an angle, and kept it in. Emily, too."

"You did?" My eyebrows pulled together as I considered what that meant, not only for the film's chances of being outed as faked but also for Charles. It was a hell of a time to find morals relating to fake hauntings. "I have to tell Charles the truth. If he only sells to me because we lied, that guilt will follow me. It's bad enough that I lured you here under false pretenses."

He rolled his eyes, then tugged me closer by the hem of my sweater. "For the last time, your vlog was a *perk*, not the basis."

"Maybe so . . ." I kissed him, a quick peck on the lips, then pulled back. My sweater popped back into place when he let go of his light grasp. "Why couldn't he have offered to sell before? I'd made my intentions more than clear for the last two years, at least. Then I'd at least be able to buy it with a clear conscience." And for far more than he was asking now, but at least the guilt wouldn't follow me. Though, my parents' guilt trips hadn't gotten me to follow them to California so maybe there was hope after all. If only I could turn their *we're sorry*s into cold, hard cash.

But that was wishful thinking.

Unless . . .

I tugged my phone out of my back pocket and gestured toward James's brand new guest bedroom slash office space. "Do you mind if I make a quick call?"

"All yours," he said.

I leaned a hip against the wall and closed my eyes, breathing deep to work up the courage to take the next step. Then I dialed my mother's number.

She picked up immediately and greeted me with an overly enthusiastic "Lex!" The way the nickname rolled off her tongue, only a tiny hesitation before using it, warmed my heart. Things were looking up, and all it had taken was thirty-three years and a giant holiday fight.

"Hey, Mom. Uh, how are you? Things good?"

"Things are fine. Is everything okay? What's going on?"

"Is, umm, Dad there too?"

After a whisper and a bit of crackling on the line, as if she was waving my father closer to the phone, she said, "Okay, he's here. Should I put you on speaker?"

"Unless you want to relay this to him, then yeah, that's probably a good idea."

I waited until she finished fiddling and confirmed that they could both hear me, then I prepared to make my request.

"As you know, I want to buy Dog-Eared from Charles. And, I may have made a few mistakes while trying to reach that goal. I have a favor to ask, a really huge one, and if you can let me finish my pitch before denying it, I would appreciate it."

"We're listening . . ." my father said, the skepticism almost comical.

"I want to buy the bookstore."

"We're aware—" my father tried to cut in, but I cleared my throat and he quieted.

"I want to make Charles another offer—a better one. I don't want to purchase it based on a lie or for less than its true value. So, I'm going to ask him to have it appraised and make a deal based on the store's worth as a business and real estate location. Because everyone knows that I'm a bad bet when it comes to financials, I'm on the market for a loan. Or an investor. Either way."

"We can give you the money, no problem," my father said. "Are you still banking at the same place?"

"No, Dad. I want to pay you back. With interest. It's a loan, because as much as I want to do this on my own, it will cost significantly more than the current offer. Every bank from here to the moon knows better than to do business with me so I think I need to ask for help. Not a gift, okay? A loan."

There was the briefest pause, and then Mom asked, "Is this your dream?"

"Absolutely," I answered without hesitation.

"We'll work up an agreement for repayment, then. With one important stipulation: You don't begin repaying us until the store is turning a profit."

"That could take forever, Mom. I can't accept those terms."

"Then no loan."

I laughed. "Seems a little backward to me."

"When have we ever made sense?" she retorted.

True. "Well when you put it like *that*. Okay. I agree to the terms."

Expecting the phone call to end after the business was complete, as usual, I prepared to say goodbye. But my father cleared his throat. "So, read any good books lately?" he asked.

A smile burst to life across my face. "A few, Dad. Are you looking for recommendations?"

* * *

After filling him in on the latest development in my bookstore saga, James let me pace through his kitchen for about five minutes before putting a stop to it. "You're going to wear a hole straight through the subfloor if you don't knock it off."

"Okay, okay. I'm doing it. I'm calling him." I dialed the number and hoped with everything I had that it would go to voicemail. Leaving a message meant I could go longer without my dreams being dashed.

Charles picked up on the second ring. "Everything okay?" he asked, as if the only reason I'd call him would be for an emergency.

"I can't give you forty thousand, Charles."

He didn't reply right away, and the little crackle on the line about pulled my soul from my body. When he did, his tone was full of concern. "If it's a matter of time, then I won't hold you to our original deadline."

"It's not time, Charles, it's the amount. You put everything into the store, and I feel like I'm taking advantage of the situation—of you—and it's not okay."

"I set the price, Lex. There's nobody being taken advantage of here." I squeezed my eyes closed. "There's no ghost. The whole thing was fake, and James and Julian had no idea. You're selling based on that lie, and if you let the store go for less than it's worth, I'll never forgive myself."

"What do you mean, there's no ghost?" The gravelly voice pricked goosebumps along my arms. Disappointing anyone was my worst nightmare, but especially Charles.

"I'm sorry, I really am. It all started with a few videos from years ago and—"

A chuckle came across the line, which grew from mild to merry, before Charles apologized. "You think I'd never seen *Haunted Happenings*? I'm old, Lex, but I know how to use the internet. I know about your vlog and particular talent for creating things that go bump in the night."

"You *knew*? And you were going to let the store go for that price?" It didn't make sense. He'd grown that store from a handful of shelves to an entire paperback kingdom.

"How else was I going to convince you that your time had come? You wouldn't have asked to buy it otherwise. You're the heart of that store, and I'm tired of trying to keep up with the times. Don't worry about the deadline—the store is yours, as soon as you've got funding in place. I won't let it go to anyone else."

"Charles." I wasn't speechless. The opposite, actually. I had too many things I wanted to say, and none of them felt *enough*. "I want to pay a fair price for it. I've got a loan lined up, and I don't want to rip you off."

His laughter returned, this time a full-blown guffaw. "I will take the agreed-upon price, not a penny more, and you'll hang a photo of me on the wall beside the desk so I can keep an eye on the place."

My heart warmed. I slapped a hand over my chest with my free hand and squeezed the phone with my other. "Thank you, Charles."

He tutted. "Thank you, for always making sure my dream could grow bigger than I imagined."

CHAPTER TWENTY-EIGHT

It took three hours, but we turned the movie theater's lobby into a venue to rival even the flashiest red carpet. I picked my way along icy sidewalks with arms full of cheesy decorations and bruised my bicep with the number of times I had to bump open the glass doors at the theater entrance. Ronnie insisted it remained closed while we were trekking back and forth because he refused to heat the neighborhood on the theater's dime.

But by the time we were finished, the shoulder pain was the last thing on my mind. The building had been transformed. Halloween-themed decorations were strung up throughout the theater. Ghostly cut-outs plastered across the walls; fake spiderwebs and black and orange streamers twisted down the hallway. We'd even propped up mirrors painted to display ghostly apparitions and eerie eyes, turning the entire post-Christmas event into something decidedly All Hallows' Eve in nature.

Julian invited the crew, Natalie and her brothers, and any locals who wanted a sneak peek. Fancy "Reserved" cards were propped on the front row seats, one with my name in orange glitter—something else that was likely to put Ronnie over the edge.

I arrived early, in a long, white dress that turned me into something ghostly. Though the over-the-top aspect of it all was eye-rollingly ridiculous, I was happy to support James and Julian on their big night. We set up the snack buffet—theater foods like popcorn and boxes of candy, and spooky favorites like candy apples and hot cider. With the remaining winter holiday decorations still hung in the lobby paired with our Halloween-inspired feast, it was difficult to tell where on the calendar we landed.

I'd finished unwrapping the trays of white-chocolate-covered strawberries made to look like ghosts, when Julian rushed up behind me—wearing an Ebenezer Scrooge costume, further confusing my grasp of the season.

"Lex, hi! Thank you for coming."

"I wouldn't miss it for the world. How are you doing? Ready for your big premiere?"

"I'd be more ready if I didn't have to worry about you heckling me from the audience."

I met his playful smile with a genuine grin. "As long as you worked Boots in, like I asked—"

"Demanded," he corrected.

"Like I *demanded*, then I have no complaints. Is there anything else I can do to help?"

"Just sit back and enjoy. We're all celebrating! It wasn't just us out there. You and Nat were knee-deep in snowbanks and up to your elbows in gobo lights, too. Revel."

Ronnie and his staff ushered the waiting attendees down the length of the rope-light-illuminated ramp—significantly more than the small group we'd expected. James sat on a three-legged stool, in front of a giant movie screen. The usual Henley had been swapped for a fitted suit, but that stupid Yankees cap was still perched on top of his head, calling to me like a beacon.

He noticed me slip in and wiggled his hand down beside his leg, a quick little greeting. I ghosted down the aisle and settled into my reserved seat beside Natalie's brother.

They introduced themselves to cheers, and a wave of excitement washed over me. Not for the vlog stories I'd invented, which had become so much more—though the ghost story longevity was both surprising and vindicating. But for the next few months, years, decades I'd get to spend with James.

". . . and when James said, 'How about Stowe, Vermont? That place sounds cool,' I laughed," Julian joked from his spot on stage.

"He did." James nodded. "He laughed, then he agreed, because he knew I was right. This place has so much history. And passion. And some really spooky locations. So, we packed up and hit the road."

"James drives like a granny, so I've learned my lesson. If you want to arrive somewhere in time to shoot during nice, warm weather, take the wheel before he does. We showed up just as the first snowstorm blew in. We might have missed the good weather, but we got the maple coffee and starlit sleigh rides. You Vermonters sure know how to embrace cozy. I've gotta admit, though, we were worried that we'd completely dropped the ball by missing Halloween—prime paranormal season. That's when we figured out an important detail: you've got a really spooky wintertime scene. There's that ghost who haunts the Christmas shop in the plaza—he's a real jerk, you know. He knocked over a whole display of glitter pine cones."

James clenched his jaw, wrinkled his nose, and raised his hand. "That was me."

"That was you?" Julian repeated, faux surprise earning a collective chuckle from the crowd. "Okay, but there was that incident with the broken lampshade. It was in perfect shape before we went into the inn, then it was shattered."

James's mouth scrunched to one side. "Me again, I'm afraid."

Laughter rippled through the room again as Julian pressed his fists to his hips and gave James a bug-eyed look. "You mean to tell me I convinced Mr. Smithe that he had a poltergeist, all for nothing?"

James lifted his hands, palms-up. "Afraid so."

"Right. So next you're going to tell me that you accidentally knocked my hat off my head while we were filming at Emily's bridge, or that you dropped a bowling ball down the stairs at the Green Mountain Inn, and it wasn't actually a ghost tap-dancing on the roof?"

The crowd leaned in, all as one, listening for James's answer.

"Oh, well. No. Those weren't me at all."

Julian slapped his hands against his cheeks, slapstick comedy at its finest. There was a reason crowds flocked to him. Charisma. The guy had more of it than was fair.

"I guess you've found yourself a couple of real, true spirits, Julian." James flashed a mischievous smile and leaned forward to rest an elbow on his knee.

"Really, folks," Julian said, his hands raised to quiet the laughter. "It's been a pleasure to get to know you all. I know James especially enjoys the doughnuts from the bakery."

"Don't rat me out—everyone will know I've been getting my pasty fix at places other than Dog-Eared." James nudged Julian, who grinned.

"I'm getting the all clear from Natalie in the projection booth, so that means our film is ready to go." He pointed at the audience. "Thank you. Thank each and every one of you for welcoming us into your town, letting us get to know you, film in your inns and restaurants and stores and homes. James was right. Stowe was the place to go. You showed us community and love, and we will forever be grateful. The next step is to take this show on the road." Julian paused, looked at James, and they exchanged tight-lipped smiles—the band was breaking up, but they'd only be a call away.

"And now . . . as the crew prepares to wander from coast to coast, small towns to metropolises, mountaintop chalets to greasy diners—" Frank let out a whoop that earned a round of applause from the crowd. "Now, we show you your eerie town from an outsider's perspective. You've let us poke and prod and explore. And this is our gift to you. As we prepare to submit our competition entry—and hopefully win, or at least get into a couple of indie film festivals along the way—we're excited to show you the finished product."

"*Mostly* finished product," James interrupted. "You still have to edit out that part where I sneeze, and it looks like I jumped."

"You absolutely jumped," Julian said.

"It was a sneeze," James said, to the delight of the audience. "I never jump. Nerves of steel."

Julian raised his hands above his head. "Boo!"

James jumped. The crowd broke into laughter that morphed into applause as the lights dimmed. Then the documentary began as James slipped into the reserved seat beside me.

The movie screen flashed an eerie scene from Emily's Bridge, the night before they filmed our haunted tour. Curling, twisting fog and exaggerated shadows stretching across the dirt road and scraping at the opposite snow bank. Julian's voiceover narrated, explaining the evolution of Emily's story, detailing the events that led to her untimely death, after her lover abandoned her. Throughout the film, collective gasps came from the crowd as the on-screen ghost hunters pointed at eerie apparitions beyond and recounted spooky tales.

The narrative brought our tiny town to life through stories (and rumors) about real residents and fictional phantoms—highlighting the way the local lore made everything feel just a bit more magical, and made everyone feel a little more connected. The film took the position that ghost stories were more than a simple answer of "yes, ghosts" or "no, ghosts." Not knowing what was real and what was imagined, but accepting the possibility anyway, infused the town with a special, infinitely shareable kind of magic. A few *Haunted Happenings* shout-outs—and inset clips of teenage me, setting the scene for some of the less-believable tales—brought my ghost stories full-circle. What I'd started had grown beyond me, giving my spirits life.

The standing ovation at the end of the film was unexpected, but wonderful. Julian and James beamed, thanked the crowd, then encouraged everyone to eat and drink to their hearts' content. While James and I dipped into the punch bowl and snacked on the brownies, Natalie and Julian worked the room like they were interconnected— like they'd been partners for ages.

I spied as Natalie and Julian chatted with Mama and Papa Stiller in the far corner—the big conversation about her leaving. The discussion appeared civil, but Natalie wore her concern in the pull between her eyebrows. When Papa Stiller gave Natalie a playful knock in the shoulder, I let out a sigh. That was basically code for "go get 'em, tiger," the same encouragement he used before we'd rushed onto the soccer field before every game. Mama Stiller hugged Julian, then Natalie's dad offered a hand for Julian to shake. New Year's Eve was a time for forward motion and new experiences. Everything good happened on the thirty-first of December.

I congratulated Natalie and Julian on the successful sharing of news, and on the crowd that blew our original estimated head count out of the water. "I'm glad you've been able to celebrate," I told them.

"We're just getting started. We were going to take some champagne to Emily." Natalie smiled, then rose onto her tippy toes to peek over my shoulder. "Hey, James! Want to see if we can get any ghosts to come out and play?"

James swept up beside me. "The answer is an emphatic no, but thanks. Unless Lex is going too, to protect me."

"I think I'll pass this time," I said. "I've got a date with some guy who just moved to town."

"I hope he's got good taste in books," James said.

"He's got at least two copies of all of the best ones." I grabbed him by the collar of his coat and pulled him to me for a kiss. "And now, if the witty banter portion of the evening is over, can we go home now? Ronnie must have the heat set on fifty. This room is freezing."

James slipped out of his wool coat and draped it over my shoulders. "Someday you'll figure out how to dress for the winter weather," he said.

I wrinkled my nose. "Make me."

* * *

There was a late-winter blizzard rolling in, and with Natalie and Julian heading out in two weeks, I had to get used to shoveling. Snowflakes were falling by the time I got outside to head to work. The giant, cold kind, with wet-sounding smacks on the pavement when they landed. My favorite.

James was leaning against his car in the driveway, waiting to drive me in to the bookstore. "Oh, I see, now that you're going to own the place, you think you can saunter in late whenever you want?"

I shook my head and sucked air through my teeth, then leaned sideways to scoop up a handful of snow. It was packed into a snowball before I was upright again. I chucked it across the driveway.

The snowball exploded into a million ice crystals when James blocked it effortlessly before bending to pack his own snowball. I was less fortunate: His snowball grazed my chin and I shrieked—both in surprise and amusement.

"Oh, crap!" James rushed over to where I stood, shocked, then leaned in to brush a thumb along where the snowball had struck. "The one time my aim is spot-on. Sorry." I laughed as he examined my face, reveling in the care he was taking, then swallowed the giggles when he leaned in to press kisses along my jawbone.

"Okay, okay, but I really am late. Even if Charles isn't calling at opening anymore, I have a list of things I have to do to get this purchase moving." We drove down the long hill toward the bookstore, hands clasped atop the center console.

I performed my morning ritual of unlocking and double-kicking the bottom edge of the door to release it. "Works every time."

Lulu nosed her way through the crack in the door, then catapulted herself into her favorite chair.

"First order of business as the incoming owner," James said. "You have to do something about this coffee club. It's a privacy data nightmare. I have it on good authority that one of the employees was using the phone numbers gathered to solicit dates."

"Oh, well obviously that won't do," I said. "Suggestions?"

"I hear that punch cards are a much safer option. Fewer customer details to keep track of, too."

"Very wise choice." I contorted my face into a mock-serious glare. "I'd also like to propose a new rule." I pointed to the chair where Lulu had flopped onto her back, all four feet splayed in the air. "Someone has got to put a sign on that chair because I think she's claimed it fair and square."

"Completely reasonable." James leaned in and kissed me, looping both arms behind my back and clasping his hands to pull me tighter. The kiss was comfort and safety and togetherness all in one.

His embrace was better than home.

EPILOGUE

One Year Later

A Christmas wedding in California not only appeased my parents but meant that our wish for a small ceremony was granted: their backyard only accommodated so many people. After retiring over the summer, my dad had picked up a garden shovel and never looked back. He'd turned the open area into a sprawl of flowering bushes so the wedding was standing room only with a guest list I could count on my fingers. Being a country away from Stowe meant we wouldn't have wedding crashers popping in on us uninvited.

But a wedding in California didn't mean we'd get out of a Stowe reception. My parents, Jordan, Isaac, and Levi joined us on the flight back to Vermont. James's mom and her husband made the trip out for the reception and booked a weeklong stay at the Stillers' inn, so we got plenty of time to get to know each other. His father sent an expensive marble canister set and congratulatory note in lieu of attending. Julian, Natalie, and the entire crew detoured back to town for our New Year's Eve shindig, with a few new accolades to brag about. The film hadn't won the contest, but it was running circles around the competition in the independent film festival networks.

"Your ride awaits," James said, sweeping a hand toward the sleigh waiting in our backyard—he'd moved into my beloved house and every inch of the place had morphed from "mine" to "ours." Holly and Jolly shuffled and snorted contentedly while the lanterns turned the backyard to a field of crystals.

I dashed to the sleigh, holding the hem of my skirt high. After climbing aboard and getting Lulu settled on the sleigh's bench, we set off. Holly and Jolly snorted and pulled, the sleigh gliding through the snow back toward the Stillers' inn.

Even the inn's overflow parking lot was filled with cars. Rounded dress shoe footprints and tiny pinprick heel marks dotted the gravel where guests had worn a path through the lingering snow to the inn's front doors. We slipped inside and ducked behind the reception desk to swap out my boots for event-worthy heels.

Lulu danced beside us, prancing on little canine tiptoes, yipping all the while.

"Lulu, sit," I said. She plunked into a furry pile, more of a "down" than a "sit," directly in front of me, waiting politely for me to finish getting ready.

We entered the party together, arm in arm, with Lulu leading the little parade.

Lights, champagne, servers passing delicious food, and cheer. So much cheer. James knew how to waltz, but was also a master at the "Cha-Cha Slide"—and he knew every move to "Thriller," which pleased the crowd beyond imagination. Lulu had given up after two rounds of "Let's see how many people will pet me," and she curled up on the rug beside the fireplace.

"I've been thinking," James said as we took a break from the festivities to eat an extra slice of cake each. After all, we deserved all the wedding cake we wanted. "Lulu's been an only dog for her whole life, but maybe it's time to expand the family."

I leaned over and scrunched her ears with my hands, smooshed her little furry doggy cheeks, and smoothed my hands down the back of her head and neck in gentle pets. She wiggled.

"Expand the family, huh?" I asked. "I could be persuaded."

"Really? I was worried you'd think it was too soon." James grinned. "I've been thinking about this for a while and was nervous about bringing it up."

"I am nothing if not open to change," I joked. James narrowed his eyes in challenge.

"So, here's the thing. I already talked to the animal shelter. There's a shaggy terrier who's been there for almost a year, and I think you'll love him. They said we can stop in tomorrow to meet him. If you're open to it, that is."

"On one condition." I held up a finger. "We *have* to name him Hold Me Closer Tiny Dancer."

James howled, a deep, impressive belly laugh. "Tony Danza for short?"

"What?" I shook my head.

"Like the misheard song lyrics," he explained.

"Perfect." I gripped his lapels and tugged him in for a kiss as midnight struck—and everything *was* perfect.

ACKNOWLEDGMENTS

I wrote the first draft of *Haunt Your Heart Out* in 2020 when everything was chaos and each day felt impossible. I was lonely and tired and needed something more than faces in little Zoom squares. I escaped into this story, hoping to remind myself that there's good in the world—even when it's hard to see. Through each draft, I got to know my characters—but I was also learning about myself. Lex and James helped remind me of the importance of connection—to people, to places, to imagination—when I needed it most.

I am incredibly fortunate to have my agent, Eva Scalzo. Thank you for welcoming me to #TeamEva with such enthusiasm. Your guidance and expertise are beyond compare and I'm grateful to have you on my side. Saint Gibson, thank you for helping this story find its publishing home.

I couldn't imagine a more perfect editor for *Haunt Your Heart Out* than Jess Verdi. Thank you for understanding and loving this story and characters and helping them become everything they are. Working with you has been an absolute highlight of this whole author gig.

Thanks so much to the team at Alcove Press—Mikaela Bender, Dulce Botello, Mia Bertrand, Stephanie Manova, Megan Matti,

Acknowledgments

Rebecca Nelson, Thaisheemarie Fantauzzi Pérez, Doug White, and Matthew Martz—for all the hard work behind the scenes. Ana Hard, *wow*, thank you for the dreamiest graveyard romance cover. It's more beautiful than I ever could have imagined.

I'm so grateful for my critique partners, Sarah Adler and Regine Darius, who always cheer me on, make me laugh, and inspire me. Regine, thanks to you my books are always a little more dramatic—because you dare me to go there. Sarah, you're amazing at helping me consider the big picture when I'm too laser-focused on the little things. Thank you both.

Audrey Goldberg Ruoff, gosh. You're everything. I'm exceedingly lucky that *Star Wars* memes and writing brought us together—and luckier still that we now chat all day, every day. Thank you for being my person. I owe you all the maple everything.

Writing is weird in that it's both a solitary thing but *also* requires all hands on deck. I'm so glad to have found support in the writing community, including SF2.0, RomanceFriends, through other Alcove authors, and after busting into DMs totally unannounced. Courtney Kae, you're an absolute treasure—thank you for everything you do for romance authors and readers everywhere. Lindsay Lovise, I'm so glad to have had the opportunity to get to know you through this wild process—thanks for everything! And to Nikki, Dani, Mallory, Maria, Julie, Dallas, and Claudia: thanks for always being just a message away. Katie McCoach, thank you for believing in me, even when I forget how.

Without Christie Anna Ertel demanding that I make Lulu's book happen, this project may have stayed unfinished. I think I need to grovel, though? I am exceedingly, super-duper, wildly sorry that James wears a Yankees cap—and even sorrier that I kept that fact from you until the very last minute. I promise that I will include a Red Sox fan in every book from now through eternity to make up for it. To the thanks: the cheering, writing memes, gifs, and historic artifacts in the form of conversation screenshots are what keep me going and I couldn't do it without you. ★

Acknowledgments

While lots of romance authors cringe at the thought of their family reading their book, my parents and sisters get the play-by-play as I write. Thank you, Mom, Dad, Jean, and Camden, for tolerating the constant writing commentary in the family chat, for telling *literally* everyone (I mean, literally, *everyone*) about my books, and for always grabbing the front-row seats at every event.

None of this would be possible without my husband, Eric. We met at a Vermont bookstore, too! While there were fewer ghosts involved (but maybe more than zero ghosts...), the setting inspired me a smidge. Whether he's enduring my mumbling while I'm revising or reminding me to eat while I'm in my writing cave, he's the real MVP. I'm beyond grateful. Thank you, I love you.

I'm indebted to my kiddos, Brian and Elias, for being so insistent that I meet my self-imposed writing goals—even if they're only encouraging me to write extra because it means they get bonus Xbox time.

My Waldenbooks and EB Games crews helped me find myself when I was lost and showed me worlds beyond my wildest dreams. To the mall pals who introduced me to Emily's Bridge and stood in knee-deep snow while I watched for apparitions: those winter nights laid the foundation for this premise. Thank you for spending the mid-00s being weird with me. Thanks also to Waldenbooks Mary, the best bookstore ghost a gal could have shared a workspace with.

I'm particularly grateful for Steph Mehl, whose love of creating entire worlds—even when characters don't seem to listen to reason—inspires me every day. Thanks for letting this awkward bookseller befriend you all those years ago.

This book is a love letter to bookstores everywhere, but especially to Bear Pond Books in Montpelier, Vermont. Thank you for always being the place where I could escape. Though your floors are less creaky now, the vibes are still impeccable.

Special shout-out to Cults: *You Know What I Mean* was on repeat while I wrote and revised this book, and it fueled me.

If I forgot to list you here, I apologize! These last few months have been a roller coaster, and I can't even remember what I had for

Acknowledgments

breakfast this morning. But please know that you have my endless thanks, as well.

And you, readers: you've allowed me to fulfill my wildest author dreams. However you found this book, thank you for spending time with my characters. I hope you were able to take what you need.